The Dragon's Mystic

Book Two of
The King's Mystic

Randi-Anne Dey

Spoilers

Before you go any further,
Have you read book one, The King's Mystic?

If not, Please do as this book is ALL spoilers.

The Dragon's Mystic takes place right after King Zane is dethroned by the King's seer.

This book also spans the course of 350 years because of the way I wrote the first book. Therefore, there will be time jumps between some of the chapters in order to give the King's Mystic closure.

Thank you for understanding and
I hope you enjoy the past and the present.

Dedication

This book is dedicated to those that have entered into my life, be they still in my life, passed through my life, or have crossed over to the other side. Thank you for enriching my world and making me who I am today.

It is also dedicated to all those that requested a continuation of The King's Mystic.

Thanks

Thanks to my parents, Dia and Rob,
for supporting me in all my crazy endeavors!
Thanks to my pups, Azlyn and Sandor,
for putting up with hours at the computer writing.
Thanks to my neighbor Roger, for all the help
he has given me while I am distracted with writing.
Thanks to all those that added to the process and creation of this book.
Thanks to everyone that purchased my first book
and supported me in that endeavor.

Contents

Ferfolk Ocean
Ragevin
Shery
Fezra
Slario
Hontby
Kakra
Oxfrost
The White Heights
Oblait
Sroni
Westshore
Thetis
Teshem
Nantou
Pleta
Vline
Terrenwood Heights
Malahat
The Heartless Sea
Grim Tundra
Vidip
Rumtia
Roburg
Bay
Lamadow
Terreview
Ewhela
Rixlen
Khotin
Zido

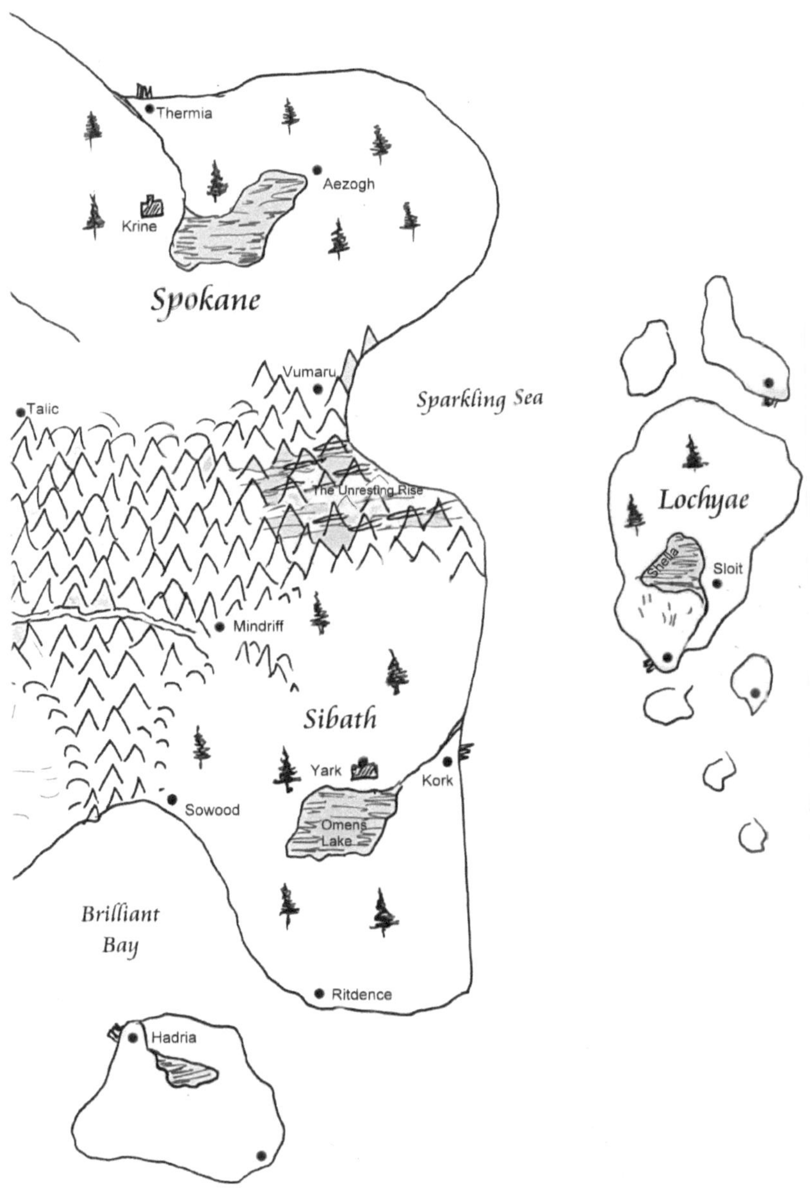

Thermia
Aezogh
Krine
Spokane
Vumaru
Sparkling Sea
Talic
The Unresting Rise
Lochyae
Shella
Sloit
Mindriff
Sibath
Yark
Kork
Sowood
Omens Lake
Brilliant Bay
Ritdence
Hadria

One

Echos of the Past

A letter to the King

King Zane.

I know at this point, you will have watched me being taken away and seen Martha in the gardens below, arriving moments too late to stop me. You will have stormed to my rooms, finding and confronting her on the stairs. Deryn will mention that I sent a satchel to her, thus dragging her to the kitchens where you are standing now. As you are reading this, you will discover some of the power I have concealed from you, for the letter Martha read has faded, and this one is writing itself. You were right in that I was holding back my powers, but you never did discover to what extent, and you never truly will. I have bound within its writing, magic that has forbidden Martha from speaking of what she has read. So do not waste your time trying to retrieve that information.

Flickers of purple lights appear as the letter splits apart in his hand, swirls around, and creates an illusion of the seer standing before him. She is nine years old again, looking up into his eyes, the wonder portrayed there fades to a hardness that should not be seen in a child. The child speaks, not with the childlike innocence she had upon arrival but the cold cunning seer she has become.

"I knew at nine years old when my parents sold me to you that you were evil, Zane, and I made the decision at that moment you would not see all I had to offer." The image reaches towards Martha, stopping short of touching her, retracting her hand back slowly. *"Martha is right. I am a Mystic. She even warned you my powers would grow as my eyes shifted from lavender to violet, and they*

did. But I gave you just enough to ensure you didn't question it. One might even say I played you, Zane, keeping my cards close at hand, encouraging you to play yours. All the while growing up faster than a nine-year-old should."

The image smiles, shifting to when she is twelve years old. *"I set things in motion six years ago to escape the evil this castle has and the abuse I knew was coming. Abuse I had hoped to avoid, but I couldn't find the threads to weave it out completely. I just needed to keep you happy and delay it for as long as I could, and I did, unlike your past seer who died at your hands. I saw the darkness within you growing. I saw what you did in secret, hoping it was beyond the scope of my sight. It was not."*

The illusion ages four years; the night of the ball, diamonds glittering all around her as a small dog appears momentarily in her hands. *"But I did make a mistake on the night of my sixteenth birthday by giving you a hint of a power I've had since I was nine years old. And that is granting my sight to others. With, but an uncontrolled touch, you received a glimpse of your death in the breath of a gold dragon."* The diamonds fade as she stands there, images of the vision appearing behind her, showing Zane what he has tortured and beat her to see again. A gold dragon drawing in and breathing out a wave of flame upon him and his throne. The heat of the vision fills the room as everyone flinches before fading away in golden motes of light.

The seer's eyes grow frosty as she narrows them on Zane. *"I suffered in silence at your hands, Zane, knowing I could have lessened the punishment if I just given what you wanted. But I was not willing to grant you access to that power, and so I didn't. I knew it was never going to be enough, so I drew boundaries and kept them no matter what I had to endure to make it happen. The sad thing is, you never did figure out what caused my slip-up. It wasn't control; it wasn't fear; it certainly wasn't the torture you bestowed upon me often, but happiness, Zane. I was truly happy at the ball that day, and that was what caused my mistake. Had you recognized that, you could have had so much more of the power I wield, and I would have given it to you. We all have a point at which we convert, where the sides become blurred, and one can be beckoned to walk the other path."*

The image takes his face gently in her hands, rising on her tiptoes, and kisses his lips softly. *"I would have helped you rule the realm and move your troops into the right places to make that happen. If you had just seen... For that was my turning point."* She returns to standing, her fingers running lightly over his lips as her eyes meet his. *"It would have taken but a kiss on that dance floor to own me completely. I would have changed everything for you and made the gold dragon disappear... Everything... It was, in fact, my point of trusting and following you blindly, without the hand of force, until it was too late for me to turn back. You played your game well, my King, and you almost had me... but not well enough because you didn't see."* She pulls her hand back as sadness crosses her features. *"But I did see my mistake in your anger. I did see the demon arise and realize what I had done. So I shut it down, for the threads changed even as we stood there. It was an emotion I never dared to feel again, until today, that is, as I flew away from your demon...One that even I could not tame."*

She shifts to become another illusion, dressed in a dark cloak, hiding her features. Soft laughter echoes in the kitchen, causing the maids to shiver slightly. *"The thing with a mystic Zane, is unlike a seer, we can rewrite storylines. Or twist them to our desires as we see many endings to get the one we want. We have the power to create and destroy, to conjure and dismiss. To see, feel, and speak into people's thoughts and minds, among many other talents I won't get into. Whereas a seer only sees what is and cannot change what they see. It was the day before the ball that I first sensed the power, but in my distraction, I did not recognize it for what it was. It was not until a year later, while I was on my balcony, that I truly felt the power of the dragon within the city in his mortal form. One that was to be my way out of this castle. I tried to reach out telepathically but received nothing but silence back. I suspect he was curious, though, for he returned to the city several times after that. I knew, as I was sneaking out to meet him, that you would catch me. But it was a thread that I required to be woven to ensure you played a card I knew you had and one I needed... poison."*

She pushes the hood off, her gaze landing on Martha a moment before it shifts to the pantry behind her. The doors open, and from deep within its darkness, small vials float forward into the seer's hand. She turns the vials over, watching the liquid move within them. *"I knew when each meal was poisoned by your guard's hands, for I could see the darkness in it, even though you kept that particular guard out of my sight. It was a dangerous game I played, but I ate it anyway because I did not want you to know that I had the power to see things as they truly are. Although I did give that away the day I arrived when I commented* on the magical flames within the castle and how they were different in the secret room. It was something that was overlooked, and for that, I was grateful." She smiles his way, a cunning look entering her eyes as the vial lids slowly twist off by themselves. The poison lifts from the vials, floating in the air above the hand that held them. "Just as I knew which meals I needed to eat to get the antidote, but what happens when you can magically lift the antidote from the food."

A soft gasp escapes Martha at her words, her eyes narrow on the King, understanding immediately why some days the guards collected her food from the kitchen. "YOU were the one that poisoned her?"

"Now you ask, why would I lift the antidote out of the food? Why would I even eat the poisoned food when I could have removed it as well. The reason is fear. I wanted you to feel fear before I left, Zane. Fear that you might actually lose something you value. Something that is worth more than all the gold in this castle to you. I wanted you to feel it so that you would recognize it within you as you stand before this image. And as much as I have had the power to leave you for many years, there is a reason for everything, and it's all tied together to the threads I have woven." Her gaze moves to the liquid, watching it flow through her fingers before it splatters on the floor. The vials follow shortly, glass shattering and spreading at their feet.

Zane glares at the image, picks up a chair, and throws it through her. He watches as the motes of light scatter only to reform before him. She offers him a bow, a knowing smile crossing her lips as the image shifts to that of this morning. "I can feel your rage, Zane, even from where I am, free from your clutches. I did warn you next time you would not catch me, and you didn't. I am aware you will search for me, but do you have the power to find me? I know what cards you hold and can bring to the war room table. For I have played them all, but you have only had a glimpse of mine. Right now, you are looking to pick a fight, Zane, and I am willing to grant it, but not in the way you want. It is not my destiny to end you. It is another's. I will just set the playing board up with all the pieces to counter yours, to ensure that happens."

The image reaches out again to caress Zane's cheek lightly. "Did you ever wonder why there was never a gold dragon brought to you? That's because they had advance warning any time someone hunted them, even from within the confines of the castle. I saved them all, Zane, just for you. But there is one thing that surprises even me; I cannot see which of the six gold dragons currently *in existence will kill you, but one will. And so now, I will become the Red Phantom's seer. It will be most interesting being a seer for a legend, the strongest and most feared dragon in all the lands.* "The image fades, the soft laughter of the seer echoing throughout the castle. *"Oh, one last thing. You have approximately two years, Zane, before the vision comes true, and I have that time to keep the gold dragons safe. The war has been called, and may the best player win."*

Two years later

The King's seer looks at her hands, watching her fingers elongate into claws as gold and purple light surround her. She returns her gaze to Zane, her violet eyes burning with righteous fury, unveiling her true power as she shape-shifts into a formidable dragon, her tail swishing around behind her. The symbol of Raya clearly etched upon her golden scales amid the myriad of colors glinting off her from the stained-glass windows in the hall.

"King's seer, let's talk about this!" Zane feels his reign crumbling down around him as he stares in shock at his seer, struggling against the magic that holds him in place.

"There is nothing to talk about Zane. You were warned. You should have listened."

The room trembles with her power, golden scales shimmering as the inferno grows around her. Her dragon eyes flash with power as she unleashes her fiery breath upon the King and his throne, engulfing them in flame. She catches the fleeting flash of green within as the room fills with the crackling of burning wood and the scent of singed fabric.

"Is it done, King's seer?"

"It is... For now."

In another realm, time, and place, a witch and a king lie in pain on the edge of a beach, the waves crashing over them. The water extinguishes the fires feeding upon them while the remaining two lashes strike the king as he slips into darkness, cursing the seer.

Two

A Dragon's Rule

The King's seer stands on the balcony with Rendgren, overlooking the city, seeing the bound guards being guided into the castle by Honors Light and the other dragons that assisted in the takeover. She turns to Rendgren, knowing he had planned to retire before she dragged him back out into the world. "Are you up for this, Gren? We can appoint another to stand in our place."

"No, it needs to be done, Seer."

"There will be a lot to do. We need to go through the castle staff and find out who is for or against the King. For the people the King killed, we need to inform their families of their loss, find where the King buried them, and place markers on their graves so their families can mourn them properly. Send out missives to the other Kingdoms, welcoming them to meet the new rulers of Oblait. Also, reset the failing economy that's due to all the taxes the King placed upon the people to fund his dragon hunts; perhaps we could use one of the dragon treasures to assist with that. To add to all that, some of the people may not accept dragons as their rulers, so it will be a challenge."

Rendgren chuckles. "And here I thought retirement was going to be peaceful."

She places a hand on his cheek, rising on her tiptoes to kiss his lips. "I love you, Gren."

"And I love you, Seer. I never thought it would be possible."

She smiles, turning to face the people that are gathering below, taking Rendgren's hands in hers as she moves a step forward.

Rendgren pulls her back a moment, his eyes searching hers. "If I am to rule with you, *King's* seer, I should at least know your true name as you seem to know mine."

"I knew yours when I was twelve, my darling Gren, when I picked up four necklaces in the market, each one bearing one of your names. Zalgren, Rendgren, The Red Phantom, all within your True name..." She reaches out to touch his cheek lightly, her thoughts mingling with his. *'Zalgrenzarendaguran.'*

"Twelve, huh? And is that how the goddess knew it?"

"I wouldn't know, my love."

He arches a brow, not entirely believing her. "Now stop dodging, love. True name, now."

She rises to her toes, whispering softly in his ear. "It's Pandora, Gren. Pandora Concordia Boxxe."

He chuckles, pulling her in and kissing her deeply, forgetting all about the people that stand watching their new rulers on the balcony. Rendgren caresses her gently, catching the cheers of the people before begrudgingly letting her go to face them. He steps behind her, resting his hands on her shoulder as she addresses the populace. "People of Oblait. As decreed by all the other Kingdoms in this realm, King Zane has been removed from the throne with his Kingship and title stripped from him. Rendgren and I, being Pandora, will be stepping into place as King and Queen." She pauses to survey the mixed reactions of the crowd, realizing that not everyone was familiar with the true nature of King Zane.

"First, I want you to know that we will be resetting the Kingdom, and that includes the economy. Dragon hunts end today. There will be NO more gold offered for dragons, and due to the fact that we ourselves are dragons, we will frown upon any that hunt them actively. The dragons that have assisted here today have agreed that mortal races are off-limits so that we might live in harmony. Now, with magic gates and portals, dragons from other realms may appear, and we do give you permission to defend your lands and your people. Should this occur, we will happily intervene between the two and put a stop to the dragon's killing spree. They will get a choice to adapt, return to the realm they came from, or suffer the wrath of us."

"Second, taxes are going to be lowered." She pauses at the round of cheers from the people. "I know the King raised them to fund his hunts, most especially for Rendgren and myself. I can't specify what they will be as we need to go through the books and registries, but we will do our best to sort out what will work for the Kingdom. As it stands, this month only, everyone is tax free until we figure it out. I can guarantee it will be reasonable and it will be done to benefit the failing economy."

"Third, if any of you have or know of someone who has missing friends or family that worked in this castle, I would like to see them one week from today."

"And lastly, for now, Rendgren and I ARE dragons. Rendgren being the Red Phantom himself and the one that stole me from the garden two years ago. Our son takes after his father in the color of his scales. I will not hold it against any of you if you want to leave the Kingdom. All the other Kingdoms have open doors for those wishing to relocate, as that was part of the deal I made with them in order to secure a safe takeover here. You are more than welcome to stay, as I understand we will need to prove ourselves as rulers. But know this: we aim to do that and bring peace to the realm."

Rendgren arches his brow. "Wait, really?"

Pandora turns to him and nods. "Yes, I want people to know that wherever they choose to go, they will have a home."

Rendgren smiles, kissing her cheek. "I wondered what your pearl of power said to them."

"Each one was different, but in all, I secured places for those wishing to relocate and gave up the spies, among other things."

"I will learn those later?"

She smiles, her voice teasing him quietly. "Perhaps. Now, if you truly controlled me, you would already know, wouldn't you?"

He wraps an arm around her waist, whispering in her ear. "One day, my love."

"We will see." She smiles at him before turning back to the crowd.

"Now, to those dragons that are here, I thank you for your assistance. There is a large matter of those killed and on display around this city." She lifts her hands as purple motes of light spread from her, bringing forth twenty-two dragon heads floating in the air in front of them. "I apologize if any of these dragons were your family, friends, or comrades. These were the ones I granted the King in order to survive. They were also the ones razing towns and killing mortals for fun. I cannot take back what I have done, but I will grant you their heads if you wish to give them a partial funeral." Her eyes scan the dragons on the allures, seeing none of them requesting one.

Sadness fills her gaze as she calls for the remaining eighty-seven that are around the city. "These I did NOT grant the King. His gold bought their kills, and while I tried to keep them safe, there was only one of me and many hunters. I did what I could while trying to keep my magic hidden from the evil within the King." She closes her eyes, showing images of the King whipping her as she struggles against the guards that pin her to the bed. "I am sorry, I could not save them all. Even with the torture he put me through weekly to grant him his monthly dragon." The townsfolk and dragons gasp, unaware of what her life was truly like within the castle.

Ten dragons step forward to claim their kin. Pandora separates them and floats them gently down to their feet, wishing she could have saved more than she did. "For those remaining, I will lift them into the sky, and you dragons can give them a funeral of fire above the town."

The dragons shift and take to the skies, circling around the town as the populace watch with mixed emotions of fear and awe. She draws further on her powers and lifts the heads high into the sky as fifty dragons breathe fire upon them, turning them to ash and dust to float freely with the wind. "And so it is done. Dragons and mortals shall now live as one." Purple light surrounds her as images appear to all the other Kingdom rulers of the funeral held in the skies above Teshem. Her voice filters softly through the illusion. "Dragons are once again safe and welcome within the realm of mortals. I thank you all for being a part of this, and may we have many years of peace and harmony across the lands."

Three

The Staff Within

S he turns her gaze back to the people below her. "Now, I need to return to those within the castle and sort through what the King has done. Court will resume within the month. I ask that you please give us that time to adjust and figure out how to repair this country." Pandora smiles at the cheers of their people as she gives them a bow, knowing their work is just beginning.

Pandora heads back to the throne room, where she left the guards pinned to the walls. She opens the doors, allowing Honors Light to herd the ones captured by the dragons inside. She gives Gwynevere a nod before reaching out with her thoughts to those in the castle. *'I would like everyone in the castle to come to the grand hall immediately.'*

Turning toward the bound guards, she magically removes the swords from their hands, placing them behind Rendgren. "Engage in combat against me, and your life is forfeit. Do you understand?" Once they agree, she removes her magic and unbinds them. They cautiously eye the pair while the remaining guards are ushered to stand beside them. Perplexed castle staff trickle in and are directed to line up against the wall with the guards. Pandora extends her draconic senses, detecting the rest moving toward them, and within ten minutes, all the staff stand before her and Rendgren.

"Now, as you may or may not be aware, we have removed King Zane from the throne. Rendgren and I will assume his position as the ruling monarch." She pauses at the expressions of shock among the staff who hadn't been present in the main hall. "There will be changes within the castle, but first, I need to determine who among you shall retain your positions and who will not." She examines the ones standing before her, recognizing many from her upbringing, along with a few fresh faces. "Most of you know me as the King's seer. My given name is Pandora, and henceforth, that is how you will address me. Queen Pandora. This, for those who are unfamiliar, is my husband, King Rendgren, the Red Phantom himself. Our son, Junior, also a red dragon, will be joining us in the castle."

Pandora moves deliberately along the line of staff, studying them as she speaks, delving into their thoughts and sensing their reactions to the news. Stopping at the end of the line, she retraces her steps, directing half of them to the other side of the room. She stops in front of Kenworth and singles him out to standalone with Honors Light. She guides ten from the first line to stand near the thrones. Tension fills the air as the staff members in each group exchange uncertain glances, perplexed by Pandora's actions. Once she organizes them, she wanders around, giving them a final once-over to ensure the accuracy of her decisions. Finally, she turns to address the original group. "You still have your positions and may resume your duties." They bow happily to their new Queen before exiting the hall, a lightness to their step.

She turns her gaze toward the group opposite them, her eyes flashing slightly. "It seems this group holds more allegiance to Zane than to me. You have a choice. Walk out of this castle right now, leave Oblait behind, and never look back. Seek another Kingdom; understanding that if I catch sight of you back in Oblait, you'll find yourself in the dungeon. The alternative is adaptation. Work with us to forge peace in this land. But know this, if you choose to stay, I will be watching you closely." Moving through them one by one, she extracts their thoughts, revealing to each what she has seen. The majority pale at the display of her powers, but lower their head in reverence and remain where they stand. Twelve nod to Pandora and swiftly exit the castle. To those who remain, she offers a slight smile. "So be it. You may return to your duties."

She shifts over to the ten standing near the throne, studying them carefully, noting the nervousness evident in their stances. "This group harbors no particular allegiance to Zane or myself, but the fear of dragons runs deep within you, overpowering any rational judgment. I recognize that overcoming such fear is no easy task. Considering our draconic nature, this would inevitably strain your work here. You may collect your belongings and depart from this castle. Each of you will be granted twenty gold to help settle in a new place. If, at a later date, you manage to overcome your fear and understand who we truly are, you are welcome to return and inquire about your position." Pandora observes as all but one leaves, her attention now focused on the solitary individual who remains. "Wilma?"

Her voice shakes as she addresses her Queen. "Please, Miss Queen. I cannot leave until I find my brother. He worked here, and none of us have heard from him."

Sadness fills Pandora, knowing the feeling of fear versus determination and that her brother was likely not in the land of the living anymore. "And who is your brother?"

"William, Miss Queen. He was one of the guards here."

"So be it. You are permitted to stay until we find him."

"Thank you, Miss Queen."

"You may return to your bunk for now; I will not put you to work. Tomorrow, we will go through the dungeons. If we find your brother down there, he is yours to take home. If not, then I am afraid the news is grave, and he never left this castle alive."

"Can you not see it, Miss Queen?"

"No, his threads are not immediately tied to yours. If he is not downstairs, then we will sit down, and I will find him."

"Yes, Miss Queen, Thank you."

Pandora approaches the last remaining figure, halting before Kenworth. She observes his pale features and the noticeable tremor in his stance. Her eyes reflect a cold intensity, matching the sternness in her voice. "Captain Kenworth, I could end you where you stand, but that would place me no better than King Zane, or even you for that matter. You are free to leave. I do not want to see you return to this land... ever. If I see even a single toe crossing the borders into Oblait, I will destroy you, and it won't be pretty. Do you understand?"

Kenworth nods.

"Good. My suggestion is the town of Hadria. It is best suited for one of your ilk. You have three days to be gone from my territory."

"That's not enough ti...." He grows silent at her look, understanding in that second not to test her.

Her eyes grow frosty as they narrow dangerously. "Then I suggest you start riding."

Kenworth turns and runs from the castle.

Pandora watches him go, sensing him mounting up on his stallion. She follows his path towards the city gates before turning to her husband. "Well, my love; it looks like we might have to hire some staff."

Rendgren draws her into his arms, chuckling. "Well, if you didn't drive them all away, my dear, then we wouldn't have to. I mean, you even threatened to kill one. What happened to my sweet loving understanding wife?"

Pandora laughs. "I will try to do better from this day forward."

Rendgren tightens his hold on her, whispering softly in her ear. "You did far better than I could have. Facing Zane and those who stood by and let you get tortured. I would have razed this castle with everything and everyone in it."

"Thanks, Gren." She turns to Gwynevere and Honors Light. "Thank you for assisting this day. I cannot begin to repay you for all that you have done."

Gwynevere moves forward, taking Pandora's hand. "You owe us nothing, for our goals are aligned. You have already united the dragons with mortals, a feat in itself and something I never thought I would see." She smiles up at Rendgren. "If you ever need us, just let us know, but perhaps with some warning next time."

Rendgren chuckles. "So no more stealing the priestess. I got it."

Ridgestalker mutters. "That's right, Dragon."

Cecil grumbles under his breath. "I was this close to finding you, Dragon, and then Sol would have ripped you to shreds."

"I am sure you were. You do realize my lair is magically shielded from the likes of you."

"I would have found a way."

"You keep telling yourself that, Mage."

Pandora sighs an exaggerated sigh. "Alright you guys! Enough."

Gwynevere laughs. "Men will be men, my dear; you best get used to it."

Pandora scowls. "Gren will be sleeping in his own room if he doesn't stop."

Rendgren growls under his breath. "Hey, they started it!"

Gwynevere smiles at Rendgren. "You both started it. You do tend to bait my group, Rendgren, and stealing me that day did not help matters."

"It was an emergency; I didn't have time to deal with them."

"I understand. I am just pointing out facts. Now, on that note, I will take my group and retire at the inn for the night. It's been a long day for everyone, more so for others." Her gaze lands on Pandora. "And some of us could use the rest because they have a long month ahead of them."

"Thank you, Gwyn." Pandora nods, looking up at Rendgren, taking his hand in hers.

"You're welcome." She turns, leading her group back out of the castle.

Pandora watches her go before turning to Rendgren. "Let's find that room now."

"Deal!" Rendgren smiles, lifts her into his arms, and carries her through the castle, up some stairs, and stops in front of a door. "Do you think this one is vacant?"

"I guess we are going to find out." She laughs as she reaches out to open the door, pushing it open. Her eyes scan the room, seeing the emptiness and a slight layer of dust over the dressers. "Looks like it's ours for tonight."

Rendgren steps in, kicking the door closed behind him, and moves to the bed, placing her down upon it gently before crawling in next to her. "My Love. My Queen. My Seer."

Pandora lifts a hand to caress his face before cupping it and pulling him close, kissing him gently. "Yes, all yours."

He groans, an arm snaking around her waist and drawing her in as he deepens the kiss, each of them becoming swiftly lost to the other as the night passes.

The next morning, Pandora wakes, her skin prickling in dread at what she is going to see downstairs. She rolls over and buries her face in Rendgren's neck, pulling the covers over her and not wanting to face the world just yet.

Rendgren wraps an arm around her and hugs her tight, breathing in her scent as she curls up into him. "What's up love? I can feel your stress."

"I just don't want to face the dungeons yet."

"We will face it together, and if you need to lean on me, do it."

She nods, staying in the comfort of his arms, feeling his calm wash over her and steady her nerves. She squeezes him gently and sits up, scanning for her gown that was tossed to the side last night, muttering under her breath. "I really need to get sleepers again."

Rendgren watches her move around the room collecting her garments. "Sleepers?"

"You know, soft clothing for sleeping in."

Rendgren growls slightly. "What? No. I much prefer you with no clothes."

Pandora laughs. "And when we pick up Junior this afternoon and he wants to sleep with us because it's a new place? I slept in dresses in the cave, but sleepers are far nicer."

"Right, we will look into sleepers this afternoon." He slips from the bed and pulls his robes and hanfu on.

Pandora smiles as she slips her gown on and fumbles with the ties at the back. "That's what I thought. You will like them; they are soft, very soft."

Rendgren chuckles. "Hmm, and how easy are they to remove, my love?"

"For you? Easy."

He moves over to his wife, taking her hands in his for a moment before moving to the lacings and fastening them up. "Then I might enjoy them. I would say we should look at getting a maid for you, but I like dressing and undressing you. And they would be in our space, and I don't want that."

Pandora smiles, closing her eyes at her husband's touch. "I don't need one, love. Most of the dresses I can get into myself. I just like your hands on me."

Rendgren leans in and kisses her neck, his hands moving to rest on her hips. "And I like my hands on you too. But if we keep this up, we are never leaving the room and we have things to do. I recognize your dodging tactics, love."

"You're right." Pandora sighs and looks down, dreading today worse than yesterday. "Let's go."

They head down to the main floor, causing a few of the maids to gasp when they enter the kitchen. "Your Majesties, you should not be getting your own food. We will bring it to the dining hall for you."

Pandora smiles, recognizing the one reprimanding them. "It's quite alright, Elo; these first few weeks are going to be off schedule as we sort things out. After that, I promise, I will let you serve us."

"Yes, my Queen."

Pandora carries her plate to the dining hall and sits down, eating in relative silence. She ponders what she will see downstairs, mentally bracing herself for the pain she knows she is going to face, especially from the King's special room.

Rendgren watches his wife pick at her food, recalling the night she broke down in his lair, lying on his bed crying silently. Showing him visions of the torture the King bestowed upon his people. Having her explain that emotions were not allowed at the castle despite her feeling the agony of all those the King inflicted his wrath upon. He reaches out to take her hand, causing her gaze to snap up. "Perhaps we should eat after. It seems all you are doing is pushing the food around."

Pandora looks down at her plate before giving a nod. "I am not really hungry."

Rendgren rises. "Right then, let's get this over with."

Pandora takes the lead, guiding the way to the stairs leading beneath the castle. She moves down slowly, stopping at the wall with key rings. She collects them all, looping them around her fingers as she approaches the main door to the dungeon. Trying a few keys, she finds the one that unlocks it and pulls it open with a slight creak. The stench of death fills her nostrils and causes her to stagger back in disgust.

Rendgren places his hands on her hips, steadying her and offering her support. "You can do this, love. Think of it as people you are saving."

Pandora nods and steps into the dungeon, allowing her eyes to adjust to the darkness. A frown crosses her face as she looks around, realizing they are not granted any form of illumination. She lifts her hands, conjuring purple lights that filter up to the ceiling and weave their way down the hallway, dispersing the shadows and revealing the grim conditions surrounding them. She proceeds cautiously down the aisle, pausing at each cage to study the listless figures inside. With each passing enclosure, a torrent of anguish washes over her as she feels the torture they have undergone before being returned to the cells. Through the pain in her mind and body, she struggles with the decision of determining whether the prisoners are innocent or rightfully confined. Tears slip from her eyes while she shakily leaves a key in the door of those that are innocent. The remaining keys jangle in her hands as she works her way to the end. She stops to stare at the last door in terror, suddenly overwhelmed with images of what happened behind the door.

"Let me take this one, love." Rendgren slips the remaining keys from her hands and tries them in the door until he successfully unlocks it. He pulls it open just enough to slip inside, taking in the four men in various states of torture. Pandora collapses to the floor, her cries wracked with agony, flinching at the pain in her body, clutching her head in desperation, attempting to halt the onslaught of the visions she is witnessing from the room.

Rendgren returns to her quickly. He kneels before her and pulls her into his arms, holding her tight. "Pandora, you need to tell me if these men can go free."

She sobs against him, and her body shakes uncontrollably as she struggles to even speak. "Innocent... All four. So much pain... Wilmas' brother William... It hurts so much, Gren. I can't make it stop... Please make it stop..."

Rendgren rises and carries her out of the dungeon at a swift pace, back to the room they stayed in for the night. He places her on the bed and sits with her, caressing her hair lightly as soft red magic encompasses her. "Shhh, love, I will deal with this. Think of other things. Allow the magic in and sleep now." Rendgren brushes the tears off her cheeks as she hugs the pillow tightly. He watches her body relax to his spell as slumber takes her. Once her breathing stabilizes, he rises from the bed and leaves the room. He senses outward, finding the closest staff, and stops them. "You there...?"

The maid bows. "Kelsey, your Majesty."

"Right, Kelsey. Unlike my wife, who knows them all already, I will learn your names eventually."

"I wouldn't expect you to learn my name, your Majesty."

Rendgren frowns at her words. "I will learn them all, but that's not what I am here for. I need healers fetched immediately and Wilma, wherever she is staying. There is also a priestess, Gwyn, at the local inn. Hopefully, they haven't left yet. Her group is called Honors Light. Fetch her too. Tell her we need a lot of healing and have them brought to the dungeons."

"Right away, Sire." Kelsey curtsies and races off, heading to the kitchens to find out if anyone knows where the healers are in town. Elo nods. "The guards Iyan and Benson should know." The castle staff scrambles, a few of them heading to the guards, while another races to the servants' quarters to fetch Wilma and bring her to the King. Once Iyan and Benson are found, they run into town, one heading to the inn and the other arriving at the healer's district.

Wilma enters the room where Rendgren paces, moving to the corner to watch him nervously as they wait. Her voice shakes as she bows and addresses him quietly. "Is the Queen not joining us, Sire?"

"She's already been down here. It was too much for her to handle, so she is in a room resting."

"I don't understand, Sire."

Rendgren turns to look over the timid maid, all but practically cowering in the corner. He sighs. "You know she is a seer, yes, and a mystic?"

"Yes, Sire. I know she sees visions."

"It's a bit more complex than that. With a mystic, not only do they see the visions, they feel them, as if they have undergone what the person has. They cannot block it out. My wife has amazing strength and learned to deal with a lot, but downstairs…" He shakes his head at the horrors down there. "She felt the torture the people went through as if it was her own. In all honesty, we should have split it up over the course of a few weeks. But there are people in dire conditions down there, and the dungeons are a disaster. So she struggled through until the last room, the torture chamber, where she collapsed."

Wilma pales drastically. "Will she be alright?"

"I am uncertain. Right now, she is in a magical sleep in hopes that the images will fade from her mind. I think many do not understand the drain visions have on seers, let alone mystics. She has shown me what she goes through and what she feels. I know for a fact I could not do it. I would be a raging mess, and yet, she is not. She is the most amazing person I know. Sweet and loving, gentle but strong, and most of the time, solid, but things like this, they can break her."

"I'm sorry, Sire."

"Thank you. That means a lot since I know you do not like dragons."

"It's not that I don't like them, ah you… Sire. It's just that you scare me. They scare me."

Rendgren chuckles. "Well, I suspect that's natural for most people, Wilma. One day, you might realize not all dragons are bad, although I earned the reputation I had until Pandora tamed me. Now I have to be good because my wife can take me out if she wants to. Let alone the Goddess Raya that I practically pledged my soul to for Pandora."

"Wait, you follow Raya?"

Rendgren nods, sliding his hanfu down and showing her Raya's mark burned upon his chest. "All three of us are marked by Raya herself."

Wilma studies the mark. "So you have to be good if you follow her."

"That is pretty much the way of it. It means I can't just eat mortals like you for breakfast." He smiles, teasing the maid gently. "Not anymore, anyhow. If my wife doesn't turn me over her knee for doing so, I am pretty damn certain Raya would."

Wilma laughs at his comment, relaxing a touch at his joking. "That would be funny to see, Sire."

"Perhaps for you. Certainly not for me."

The guards return at that moment, each of them leading in the healers they found. Iyan bows. "These are the two best healers in town, Sire, Healer Irma, and Master Roger."

"Thank you. Welcome." Rendgren nods, looking at them carefully. He immediately notices the gentle brown eyes of the woman, the soft brown hair that frames her face perfectly, and the healer's kit in her hands. He can feel the magic within her, knowing she is in touch with the divine arts. Shifting his gaze to the man beside her, he sees the same look in his eyes, the graying hair kept short, but not sensing the same magic within, suspecting he is a mender and herbalist. He lifts his gaze as Gwynevere steps into the room, Solilque and Myrlani at her side. "And here you thought you could get away from this castle."

Gwynevere laughs. "Yes, your man caught us as we were packing up to leave. I left the instigators back at the inn with the horses."

"Much obliged. Thank you." He turns to address them all. "What you are going to see downstairs is not of our doing, but of King Zane's hand. There are many that will need healing, so conserve your spells. The doors with keys already set in them are the innocents. The ones without are actual criminals, and I *will* be in those cages with you. We prioritize the innocents first so that we can move them from the cells. I gather this castle has an infirmary somewhere?"

Iyan and Benson nod. "Yes, Sire."

"Right, they get moved there when the healers give the say-so. They will stay until they are well enough to decide where they want to go." Rendgren looks at Iyan. "I would hazard a guess that the guard posted down here is one we let go?"

Iyan nods. "Yes, your Majesty. All three were actually."

"Right, find me new ones. I don't care who it is; just find someone to cover this until we hire more. The cells also need to be cleaned. They might be criminals, but downstairs is a disgrace. I want a team to do that. Again, DO NOT step into their cages without backup. My wife left them there for a reason, and what that reason is, I do not know. She's not in any shape to answer right now."

"I will see it done, your Majesty." Iyan bows and runs off.

Rendgren leads the group down into the dungeon, heading straight to the end where the four are lashed to tables or racks. He catches Wilma's cry of pain as she moves to her brother's side, tears spilling from her eyes. "He's alive, Wilma, barely, as all four are. I suspect each one will get minimal healing to start, enough to ease their pain and suffering, but they will need rest before they can leave.

Once they are upstairs, we can decide who will get more healing. If you wish to be useful, find some staff to help carry the mended ones to the infirmary." Rendgren works on unlashing those restrained as the healers spread out, seeing to their wounds.

Irma looks over at Wilma, her voice softening to soothe her. "Yes, we will need to conserve our powers, depending on how many are down here, to ensure everyone gets some healing."

"Yes, Sire... Miss." Wilma nods, giving a glance to her brother, before running from the room to find more guards.

Solilque mutters under her breath. "I knew I should have shredded him after seeing what he did to the Seer."

Benson lifts the first one off the table and drapes the lucid man's arm over his shoulders. While supporting his body around the waist, he staggers out of the room with him. Rendgren moves to the second one, untying the leather bindings. "It's done. Now, we need to make amends for it."

"But these people suffered, just like her. How he got away with this for so long."

Rendgren lifts the unconscious man into his arms. "It's over Sol. Pandora ended it. We are fixing it. That's all we can do." He places the man in Solilque's arms, knowing she can handle him, before moving to the third. "Take him upstairs."

"Right... Sorry."

Hours later, all the cellmates are healed to some degree, with the innocents moved to the infirmary to rest. A group of twenty guards and maids set about cleaning the empty cells, grimacing at the condition of the dungeon. New cots are brought in, and the remaining prisoners are placed in clean cells. A locksmith is called in to secure the torture room and all its devices. Rendgren collects the keys tied to the door and magically shifts them to his lair, so the door will never open again. Wilma remains next to her brother in the infirmary, his hand in hers as she waits for him to wake up. Rendgren remains back and watches the healers do their thing, feeling his son and Vynloren enter the castle. "It seems my son has arrived. I will return later this afternoon. Thank you for all your work." He turns and heads out to the grand hall, picking up Junior after he scampers over to him. "Did you have fun, Junior?" He smiles at Junior's nod as the little one yawns and curls up in his arms. Rendgren turns to Vynloren. "I hope he wasn't too much trouble."

"Nah, the scamp is a joy. How did it go over here?"

"As well as to be expected. We removed Zane from the throne, and my wife fired a third of the staff yesterday. We walked through the dungeons today and are mending the innocents, which was most of who was down there. It's gonna take time and work to correct this place."

"That's rough, man. If you need help, let me know."

"I will. I believe the remainder is stuff for my wife and I. Finding actual quarters to stay in rather than the dusty room we picked last night. Hiring new staff, setting schedules, going over the payroll and what the castle has to fund it."

"Understood. The offer still stands."

"Thank you and thanks for looking after the pup for us. He looks exhausted, which is probably perfect for today."

"Yes, he spent most of yesterday and this morning wrestling with the council. He really has no fear for a young pup."

"I'm sure that's entirely his mother's doing."

Vynloren chuckles. "Good thing she can't hear you say that."

"Oh, when she wakes up, I will probably get an earful."

"She's still sleeping?"

"Yes, I put her to sleep magically, something else I am certain I will catch hell for."

"Oh boy, will you ever. Why would you do something foolish like that?"

"We went to the dungeons this morning, and the pain of the visions overwhelmed her. It was the best option."

"Ouch, that's a hard spot to be in, but I understand. If you need a place to hide for a while, you know where to find us."

Rendgren chuckles. "I might have to take you up on that offer."

"Right, I am getting out of here before she wakes up. Nice knowing you, Red!"

Rendgren rolls his eyes and watches Vynloren teleport out. He looks down at his child dozing in his arms, having missed him for the past twenty-four hours. Heading upstairs to his wife, he opens the door quietly, seeing her still asleep where he left her. Placing Junior down on the bed, he watches as he snuggles into his mother, her arm instinctively wrapping around him. Knowing there is one still missing, he creates a ring of fire and steps through the portal into his lair. Rendgren strides to the bedroom, finding Spider curled up on the bed, smiling as his lips twitch, flashing white teeth at him. "One day Mutt, you and I will go at it, but not today. It's time to return home." Picking Spider up despite his growling, he portals him back to the castle and places him on the bed with his wife and son. He watches them sleep, his family together once more, finding it more and more difficult to recall his days without them. Moving around to the other side, he crawls in behind his wife and pulls her into his arms, breathing in her scent, allowing himself time to doze with her.

After an hour, he drags himself from the bed, knowing he needs to check on things around the castle. He pauses as he leaves the room, looking back at his wife, seeing the peace in her expression, knowing he made the right decision in forcing her to sleep. Closing the door quietly behind him, he heads down to the infirmary to check in. The healers look up as he enters, each one giving a report on the people they are tending. He wanders down through the room, grateful they are going to survive, suspecting that while most will recover body-wise, the emotional scarring will take years to deal with. Anger fills him at what they endured under the demon's hand as he stalks from the room. He strides from the castle and shifts shape, lifting himself into the air and takes to the skies, feeling the need to de-stress.

Sometime later, Pandora opens her eyes, her head pounding from the onslaught of visions, feeling a weight on her shoulder and a warmth against her. She reaches up to pet Spider as her other arm tightens on Junior, earning a quiet snarl from him. Her thoughts drift to what Rendgren has done, sensing outward but finding the castle empty of his presence. She reaches for him mentally.
'Gren?'

'My love.'

'Where are you?'

'Flying. I needed to get out of the castle. Is it safe to come home?'

'Yes, Gren, it is. I understand why you did what you did.'

'It was the only way I knew how to ease your mind.'

'Thank you, Gren.'

'You welcome, love. I should be home soon.'

'Alright.'

After a few minutes, Pandora pushes herself up and slips from the bed, feeling a hunger gnawing at her stomach. She places Spider down on the ground and collects Junior into her arms. She wanders through the castle, finding herself in the kitchen, pondering the food in the ovens.

Ray shakes his head as Fil guides her away to the table. "No, my Queen. It's our job to cook. Elo will bring you food."

"Thank you." She sits and places Junior on the table, catching a few of them eyeing him warily while others with adoration. "Junior, these are the castle staff. You are not to chase or bite them. Mom already fired a bunch yesterday; I don't need the rest quitting."

A few of the calmer ones laugh at her comment. "We would not quit, your Majesty. The Prince is adorable and welcome in the kitchen anytime."

"I would watch what you say, for I will hold you to that. He has his moments."

"Well, if he has his moments in here, we will just send him back to you. How does that sound?"

"That sounds fair to me."

Elo moves forward, placing a plate of bacon and eggs before her and meat down for Spider. "What does the Prince like?"

"Oh, he eats pretty much anything, Elo, mostly meat like Spider."

Elo nods and returns a few moments later with a plate full of meat.

Junior gobbles it up quickly before jumping from the table trying to steal Spiders.

"Junior, if you are still hungry, you ask for more food. Do not steal Spider's."

"Rawr."

"Right, another plate of meat please, Elo."

"Yes, your Majesty."

Junior jumps back onto the table, pacing around until another plate arrives, scarfing it up just as quickly.

"Did you not get fed Junior?"

"Rawwrr."

"Right, perhaps you shouldn't wrestle so much."

"RarrwrrR!"

"Well, I am certain there are training dummies in the barracks you can practice with, but I think the council is pretty experienced. It might be awhile before you can beat them."

"RaAAawr."

"Alright then, good luck." She watches him jump off the table and race away, only to see Spider hot on his heels.

Elo turns to Pandora. "Is that Dragon language?"

Pandora laughs. "No, that's the child language of one who hasn't learned the common tongue yet."

"But you understood him."

She shakes her head. "I didn't, but I can see and feel his thoughts, so I know where they went. One day soon, he will talk, and everyone will understand him."

"That's impressive, King's seer... Sorry, your Majesty."

"It's fine, Elo. It will take some getting used to. Thank you for the late lunch. I think I am going to wander for a bit."

"Yes, your Majesty. Thank you. For everything you have done."

Pandora turns, studying Elo for a moment. "You're welcome, Elo."

Four

Facing the Past

P andora wanders the halls of the castle aimlessly, searching for a set of rooms they could call their own, feeling Gren arrive back at the castle. Her mind is numb, still filled with the pain of the dungeons and the atrocities that the King bestowed upon those imprisoned there. Not that she wasn't aware of his violence or his inclination to create pain, for she had suffered herself for two years at his hands. But even then, she was unprepared for what she had felt and seen down there. She pauses when she finds herself in front of a familiar door, staring at the padlock that remains. She reaches up to touch it, hearing its chink in her mind as it opened and closed each time she left the room. Stepping back, her eyes remain on the locks that kept her in, working on steadying her nerves as images of her past join with those she saw this morning.

Rendgren returns to the castle from his flight and shifts shape, noticing one guard back away in fear. He stops to talk to him, attempting to calm him down. "Sorry, I needed to go for a fly after going through the dungeons this morning. It was far worse than I thought it would be."

"Understood, Sire. I mean, I know you are a dragon and that she is too. But you are much larger than I expected, and well... You are human, so it's just strange seeing your other form. It's somewhat surreal that you really are a dragon."

Rendgren chuckles. "Well, I am the Red Phantom. Not many can challenge me and win."

"You mean, there are some that can?"

"Only one, my dear man, and that would be my wife." He looks up, feeling his wife's stress blending with a numbness along their bond. "Speaking of which, I believe I need to check in on her." He gives the guard a nod and strides into the castle. He reaches out with his senses and surprisingly finds her standing in a corridor on the second floor. Rendgren travels through the halls, seeing her leaning on a wall, her eyes fixed on the door with a padlock. "Love?"

She shifts her gaze from the lock to him, her voice quiet. "Gren. I thought you were downstairs."

"I was, but I could feel you along our bond." He turns his gaze to the door. "It's your room, isn't it? You don't need to go in there."

"Yes, I do."

"It does not have to be today, not after everything you have been through. There are other rooms we can make our own."

"I know, Gren, but I need to do this."

He nods, understanding she is punishing herself for not being able to stop what happened downstairs, but remains silent on that matter. He places a hand gently on her shoulder, squeezing it lightly. "Then I will be right here with you."

She looks into his eyes for a moment before returning her gaze to the lock. Purple motes of lights surround it, and she watches as it falls to the ground, flinching slightly at the clang on impact. She takes a deep breath and moves to the door, pushing it open. She steps into her old room as memories of her life flood back, causing her to sway slightly.

Rendgren reaches out and places his hands on her hips, moving in behind her to offer support.

She steps back, leaning on him as she notices the condition of the room. Her table and chairs are in pieces. Her dresser toppled, the drawers lying broken around the room. The wardrobe doors hanging ajar, a few of her dresses still hanging within. Her desk, overturned and broken, with papers lying scattered around the room, and ink stains on the carpets. Her gaze drifts to the bed, a slight smile crossing her lips as she notices her sword and banner exactly as she left them. All of which is covered in a thick layer of dust. She steps away from Rendgren and drifts to the bed, lifting the sword carefully and turning it over in her hands.

Rendgren arches a brow, taking in the violet wraps. "Yours, I presume?"

She spins it around gracefully. "Yes, the one I trained with until the King locked me in the room."

"So, does that mean I finally get to see you sword fight?"

Pandora smiles mischievously at him. "Call a sword forth, Gren, and I will show you just how good I am."

Rendgren chuckles. "Perhaps the barracks would be a better place to fight, my dear."

She teases him softly. "Are you scared, Gren?"

He growls slightly under his breath and calls forth his sword. Long, thin, a red handle, with streams of fire licking the blade.

Pandora studies the blade, noticing it is a touch longer than hers, wondering momentarily if she made the right choice. She draws on her powers, clearing the surrounding floor before charging Rendgren. He jumps back in shock, his blade barely deflecting hers. The two of them duel and parry for an hour before Rendgren forces Pandora to forfeit with his blade at her throat. "I win, love. Hand your blade over and submit."

"Damn." Pandora sighs and hands her blade over to his free hand, muttering under her breath as she collapses to the bed behind her in defeat.

Rendgren grins and dismisses his blade, placing hers off to the side. He turns to her on the bed before crawling on top of her. His eyes darken with desire as his hands wander over her body, pinning one of her hands above her head. "My dear Pandora. I will admit, I do love dueling with you."

She closes her eyes with a soft sigh, feeling his weight upon her as she magically closes the door. "Well, you are definitely a touch better than my guards."

He kisses the side of her neck and along to her ear. "I better be. I have been dueling longer than them. Now, I do believe I will claim that which is mine and won in a fair battle."

"Hmmm, I wouldn't call it fair; your sword was longer than mine, and I am out of practice."

He nibbles on her ear as his free hand trails along her side, down to her waist. "War was called, my love, and I have my spoils. I shall inspect them thoroughly."

She inhales sharply at his touch, feeling the passion that only he creates filling her. Her voice is light as her body arches to his commands. "I suppose they are..."

"Indeed they are." He chuckles, his eyes roaming over her as his hands shift to her ties, spending time exploring her body, lightly teasing and tormenting her before succumbing to his own passion. Several hours later, they lie together, content and at peace. Pandora murmurs against him before drifting off to sleep.

"This will be our room."

"So be it." Rendgren caresses her cheek lightly, allowing himself to doze with her.

Later that afternoon, he rises from the bed, hearing her murmur of complaint. He leans in to kiss her cheek softly and slides a pillow into her arms. Rendgren pulls the banner over her and smiles at the picture before him, seeing the peace in her expression. He dresses quickly and glances around the room, knowing they need to replace the furniture in here. Slipping quietly out of the room, he picks up the lock and carries it down to the infirmary, checking in on the innocents and the healers. Once he determines they have food and their needs are met, he finds Kivu at the main door, knowing he is the money man from his visit here before. He calls forth a small satchel of gold and places it down at his table. "We need new furniture for the Queen's old room. She has chosen that as our room."

Kivu's eyes widen in surprise before he nods. "Yes, Sire."

"I assume she also had a tailor of some sort here?"

"Yes, Sire, Master Habo, though I believe his son Alex has been assisting him with a lot of the tailoring now."

"Right, she will need dresses, robes and sleepers. The sooner, the better."

"I will see it done, Sire."

"Also, knowing where her room is, which room would you recommend for our son?"

"I would suggest the one her maid stayed in. It has a large bed and its own bathing chamber. Essentially a mirror to the Seers', but no private gardens."

"Done; does it need furniture as well?"

"Not that I know of, Sire. The King's rage was at you and the Seer... or rather the Queen."

"It's alright, Kivu. I know she's been the King's seer to you for many years. It's going to take time to adjust."

"Thank you, Sire."

"Now, I need to go find my son; he's been unattended far too long."

"I believe he's in the training area, wrestling with the guards."

Rendgren rolls his eyes. "Like he didn't get enough fighting yesterday and this morning. Thank you."

"You're welcome, Sire. I will track down furniture and have Habo arrive this evening after dinner."

"Good, the Queen is currently resting. It's been a trying day for her. We will change the furniture tomorrow, but she will need sleepers for tonight."

"As you wish, Sire."

Rendgren heads to the barracks, seeing Junior and Spider madly attacking a training dummy as the guards stand and watch. He sighs softly. "Junior, have you not had enough fighting in the past few days?"

"Him and the dog have been at it all afternoon, Sire. They have already destroyed two of them." They chuckle and point to the two very dead training dummies.

Rendgren glances in that direction. "I knew you were going to cost me gold, Junior. Alright, whelp, let's wake your mom up and get dinner. Perhaps we can go for a fly after dinner to wear out some of that energy."

Junior growls, biting the dummy one last time before bounding over to Rendgren and jumping into his arms. "I will have new dummies brought in with the furniture tomorrow."

"It's quite alright, Sire; we have a surplus at the moment. We will set them up."

Rendgren nods and carries Junior back to the bedroom with Spider at his heels. He opens the door next to theirs and steps in, looking around, watching Spider race into the room. "This will be your room, Pup, but if you get scared, your mom and I are right next door. Now, I need to wake and dress your mom, so you might as well explore your new room for a few minutes. Try not to burn it down."

"Rawr."

Rendgren chuckles as he places his son down on the bed, patting his head gently, earning a swipe of the claw. He turns and heads back to their room, opening the door quietly and closing it behind him. He moves to the side of the bed, smiling at the pillow still tucked in her arms, and sits down next to her. "Love, it's time for dinner."

She mumbles under her breath and rolls over, pulling the pillow over her head.

Rendgren gently lifts the pillow. "We need to get you dressed, love. You haven't eaten all day."

She rolls back over and scowls at him as she snatches the pillow back. "I had lunch while you were out."

"And now it's dinnertime. Get up."

She smacks him with the pillow. "Yes, sir."

Rendgren's eyes darken with desire as the pillow strikes him. "We already know I can win at swords, my dear. Do you really want to go there?"

She sighs softly, muttering under her breath. "Fine."

"I thought perhaps after Master Habo arrives, we could go for a fly."

"Wait? Habo is coming?" Pandora sits up abruptly, shock and excitement in her eyes at seeing her old dressmaker.

"Yes. I talked to Kivu, and *he's the one*, he said. I figured you might want sleepers for tonight."

"Thank you, Gren." She leans in to hug him and slides off the bed to pull her robe and gown on. She skips to the bathing chamber to freshen up before returning to her room.

Rendgren watches her excitement, wondering if there was something going on between the pair when she was here.

Pandora smiles, moving over to kiss his cheek lightly. "No, there was not, but he makes the best dresses and sleepers. Him and Martha though, they had a thing after Master Habo's wife died."

Rendgren growls softly. "Are you reading my thoughts again?"

Pandora laughs. "It's written all over your expression, Gren. Come, let's fetch Junior and get food. If Kivu summoned Master Habo, then he will arrive shortly." She senses Junior in Pippa's old room and bounces over to collect him before running to the dining hall, Spider hot on her heels.

Rendgren grumbles under his breath at the children in the family before following at a more respectable pace. By the time he arrives at the dining hall, his family is sitting, and the maids are placing the dinner trays on the table.

Pandora looks up and smiles. "About time you got here, Gren."

"I don't run, my dear; I am too old for that."

Pandora smiles slyly, her violet eyes flickering with hints of a glow. "I bet you do if given the right incentive."

"Rawwrrrr."

Pandora laughs, "Sorry, Junior, and you're right; he did run once."

"I did not."

"Really Gren? Would you like to change that answer?"

"No, I would not."

She lifts a hand, drawing forth an image of the cave and Rendgren standing in front of the kitchen, with Junior bouncing off the invisible wall before him. "Shall I continue to play it, Gren?"

He sighs as he sits down, pulling a plate forward. "Bloody Mystics."

Pandora laughs and rises from her chair, kissing his cheek lightly. "You do know I love you with all my heart, no matter how old you are."

"I know, love. I feel the same for you, no matter how young you are." Rendgren snakes an arm around her and pulls her into a tight hug before releasing her. "We should eat if Habo is as prompt as you say. I would still like to go for a flight tonight. I think we need it."

"That sounds lovely. It feels like it's been months, but I know it hasn't." She moves to sit in her chair, eating the food the maids bring in, catching them silently clearing the plates and refilling as needed.

"Less than a week, but I understand what you are saying. It's been a long twenty-four hours."

"It really has."

It isn't long before they hear a knock on the door, and Kivu steps in, bowing slightly. "Master Habo has arrived."

"Thank you, Kivu. Please bring him to my chambers."

"Yes, my Queen."

Rendgren scowls. "Wait, he comes to your chambers."

Pandora laughs as she rises. "He just needs to re-measure me, love. Once that is done, you can kick him out, but I think you will like him."

Rendgren grumbles slightly. "Oh, if he has any designs on you, I will do more than kick him out."

Pandora smiles and gives him a slight bow. She turns and runs from the room, her laughter filling the air. She arrives at her room and pushes the door open, realizing as she surveys the destruction that perhaps she should have chosen another room. Kivu arrives shortly after her, leading Habo into the room, catching his expression at the condition of it.

"Master Habo! Don't mind the room; we haven't had a chance to fix it yet. Apparently, the King threw a wee bit of a temper tantrum when I left here." She glides over and hugs the old man tightly, stepping back to look him over while holding his hand. She notices a few more gray in his ponytail and some in the brows above his gentle brown eyes. "You haven't changed at all."

Habo smiles, squeezing her hand gently. "Neither have you King's seer, or rather Queen now. In fact, I would say you look more vibrant than before."

"Yes. Queen I suppose, and thank you. I have missed your jingles. I trust they are still selling well?"

"Indeed. You definitely predicted that one back when we first met."

"They are my favorite Master Habo."

"Just Habo, child... my Queen."

"Oh Habo, you may still call me whatever you like."

Rendgren walks in, seeing her holding the hand of the tailor, narrowing his eyes slightly. "Love?"

"Gren! About time you got here. Habo, this is my husband, Rendgren; Gren, this is Habo, the best tailor in all the realms."

Habo turns and bows to Rendgren. "Sire. It is a pleasure to meet you."

Rendgren looks the older man over, seeing very much a grandfather figure standing before him, understanding immediately why his wife loves this man. He smiles, shaking the man's hand. "Habo. I do hope you brought some sleepers. My wife has been complaining about having to sleep in dresses for the past two years."

Habo chuckles. "Indeed I have." He turns to look over Pandora and pulls out two sleepers, one in a pale gray and the other in lavender. He hands them over to her, then reaches in and pulls out his measuring tape.

Pandora pulls them up to her face, reveling in the softness, hugging them close. "Oh Habo, you make the best clothes."

"Thank you, child. I, of course, do not have much purple on hand since I haven't been making dresses for the castle seer, but I will remedy that now that I know you are back. It does not look like you have changed much, but I would still like to take a few measurements."

She nods, moving to hand the sleepers over to Rendgren before stepping back to stand with her arms out.

Habo chuckles. "Still remember the position I see."

"Of course."

Rendgren gently caresses the sleepers, feeling the exquisite fabric, knowing it would only accent the softness of his wife's body. He lifts his gaze to her, understanding now why she prefers them to sleeping in dresses.

Pandora's eyes drift to Rendgren as Habo measures her. *I can feel those thoughts, Gren. Would you like a pair?'*

Rendgren chuckles, answering back in his thoughts. *'I have you to cuddle with, love; why would I need a pair?'*

'Junior?'

'Right.' Rendgren watches Habo measure his wife, seeing the seriousness in his expression as he steps back. "I was right. You haven't changed. I will have some dresses and more sleepers by the end of the week. How does that sound?"

Pandora smiles. "That sounds wonderful, Habo. Also, Gren would like a pair of sleepers, but he prefers red or black if you have some."

Habo nods. "Right, please come stand here so I can take measurements. I did not bring any for you, for I was not expecting to be dressing you as well, nor did I have any idea of your size. The child I have been dressing since she was nine, so I took a guess."

Rendgren arches a brow at his calling his wife a child, a slight grin crossing his lips, before handing the sleepers back to her. He moves to stand where she was, holding his arms out, watching as Habo measures him. After ten minutes and a few hmms and nods, he steps back. "Alright, I think I got it. It looks like you are wearing a hanfu. Is that your preferred style?"

Rendgren nods. "Yes, though I do have a wardrobe of clothing, both in my lair and at my mansion. I just need to retrieve them. My lovely wife only has eight dresses, one I bought here in Teshem two days after I stole her and seven I bought in Yark when she stole my robes."

Pandora laughs. "They were not stolen, Gren; we had this discussion."

Rendgren rolls his eyes. "I did not grant you permission to wear them; thus, they were stolen."

Habo glances between the pair. "How did you move around in them, child? He's a good foot taller than you, let alone the rest of him."

"Oh, I tied them tight, Habo, and hiked them up when I walked, but I wasn't in them longer than a night. Gren left as soon as he saw me in his robes and came back hours later with dresses."

Habo looks over the slightly wrinkled dress in black and purple, fitting her perfectly. "I gather that is one of them. I am impressed at how well they do fit you. Not many can eye a person's shape that accurately."

Pandora looks over the dress and smooths the skirts, her eyes lifting to Rendgren's. "Yes, this is one of them. Actually, all seven of them fit this well.

I never really thought about how he managed it. Clearly, he was paying more attention than I suspected."

Rendgren coughs slightly. "You were dressed in my robes that clung to your body. It was not that hard."

Habo chuckles. "I see how this went."

Pandora shakes her head. "It didn't, Habo. I even told him he was welcome to take the robes off me if he wanted them back."

Rendgren chokes. "My Dear!!!"

Habo bursts out laughing, patting his back slightly. "Your Majesty, there is nothing either of you can say that will phase me. I am old. Now, clearly, you are both in love, so it ended well. Yes?"

Pandora laughs. "I think some days he wants to strangle me, but yes, it ended well. I love him, and he loves me most of the time."

Habo moves to gather his things before rising to face her. "I think that's typical of any man that loves a woman. Thank you for hiring me again. I missed seeing you these past two years."

Pandora steps forward and hugs him. "I missed you too, Habo."

"Alright, now I need to return to my home. I will be in touch this week. Welcome back, child... Your Majesty."

"Thank you, Habo."

Pandora watches Habo leave the room and moves over to Rendgren's side. She wraps an arm around his waist, the other still clutching the sleepers as she rests her head on his shoulder. "I see you didn't kick him out, Gren."

Rendgren chuckles and kisses her forehead gently. "I like him; he seems like a grandfather type. Even if he calls you, *child*."

"He has always called me child, Gren, and to him, I always will be."

"I suspect you will. Now, shall we go for a flight now?"

Pandora nods and places the sleepers on the bed before returning to take Rendgren's hand. They stop at Junior's door and collect him, leaving Spider to sleep on the bed as they head out of the castle to the main courtyard. Pandora looks around in confusion at the staff lingering about as she places Junior down. "What's going on?"

Rendgren shakes his head. "I am not certain, love."

Pandora's eyes land on Wilma, hiding in the back, as Elo approaches them. "Sorry, my Queen, word spread fast that you were going for a flight. Some of us have never seen a dragon, only the heads on the stakes, and well... they.... I mean, we know you are dragons 'cause you said so, and it's kind of hard to believe you really are when you look just like us. So, if it's alright with you, may we stay and watch you?"

Pandora smiles. "I am certain you will get used to it in the upcoming years, but yes Elo, the staff may stay. Now, you will need to back up as we take up most of this courtyard. Also, if someone can please let Spider out later this evening, I would appreciate it. He's in Pippa's old room."

"I will, your Majesty."

She waits until they back up before giving a nod to Rendgren, watching as he grows and shifts to his dragon form. He flaps his wings, stretching them out as a few of the staff gasp and back up further in amazement. His red scales glint in the evening's sun, the mark of Raya upon his chest all but glowing within it. Rendgren lifts a foot and gently plants it around Junior, enclosing him in his claws.

Junior shifts around inside to enable his wings to flap and pokes his head through. "Raaarrrr!"

Rendgren chuckles and lifts himself into the air to give Pandora room to shift, hovering as he waits for her.

Motes of purple light surround Pandora as she shifts herself, taking up nearly as much space as her husband, but her scales are golden. Raya's mark shimmers with purple as she takes to the air after her husband, leaving the staff standing in awe as their Royals fly off into the setting sun.

Hours later, the family returns, feeling refreshed from being at peace in the skies. The wind over their scales soothes them, and the beating of their wings exhausts them. They each land in the courtyard and shift back, giving a nod to the guards who remain waiting for them. They drop Junior off at his room, confirming he will be alright, earning a growl as he launches onto the bed and curls up with Spider. Pandora smiles and closes the door behind him. She takes Rendgren's hand and leads him back to their room, grabbing a pair of sleepers and heading to the bathing chamber. "Let's have a bath."

Rendgren pauses. "We will need to find staff to bring water in."

"No, we won't." She places the sleeper on the table with the towels and moves to the tub.

Rendgren follows her in and glances around the bathing chamber. "This is impressive, my dear."

"It gets better. It's like your plates and washing bowl." She runs her hands over the silver circle, watching it glow. She touches the blue, filling the tub with water before placing her fingers over the red as she dips her other hand in to test the temperature. "How's that for no buckets?"

Rendgren moves to the tub, arching a brow her way as he tests the water. "You had this all along and didn't see what my plates did?"

Pandora laughs as she sheds her clothes and steps into the tub, sinking into the water. "They just looked like plates. Martha showed me how this tub worked when I was nine, though I wasn't allowed to do it myself till I was older. Pippa always drew it for me." She shifts forward as Rendgren steps in behind her. She leans against him with a soft sigh and pulls his arms around her, feeling the warmth of the water and his love surrounding her. "Thank you, Gren, for helping me today."

Rendgren caresses her arms lightly, kissing the top of her head. "You're welcome, my love."

Once the water cools, Pandora rises and dries herself off. Happiness dances in her eyes as she pulls her sleepers on. "How I have missed these. To sleep in sleepers, soft sleepers!"

Rendgren smiles at the delight in her expression, grateful to see the emotional onslaught she faced this morning seems to have faded from her. He dries himself off and moves over to her side, caressing her cheek gently. "Should I be jealous of sleepers, love?"

Pandora laughs. "Oh yes, Gren, you really should."

He chuckles and draws her into his arms, feeling the soft fabric that hugs her body, groaning softly. "Ok, you are right. I am jealous. I want a pair of my own."

Pandora giggles. "I am certain Habo will have some for you tomorrow. Come, let's get some sleep."

Rendgren lifts her up and carries her back to the bed, pulling the covers back as he places her in it. He crawls in beside her, pulling her in tight as his hands wander the fabric that encases her. "My wife, my delight, and my life. I cannot begin to say how much you have changed it, but you have in so many ways. I love you, Pandora."

"I love you, Gren, I always have." Pandora snuggles close to Rendgren, feeling his emotions envelop her, her voice soft as she feels sleep calling to her, with him following shortly after.

The next two weeks pass in a blur. New furniture arrives for their bedchamber, making it livable again, along with a variety of clothing from Habo. The victims in the dungeons mend, thanks to the healer's diligence, with most of them opting to part ways with the castle. A few decide to stay on and keep the duties they had before being imprisoned, including Wilma and her brother William.

Pandora and Rendgren sit with Kivu and go over the finances of the castle. They determine rather quickly just how dire it is, as Kivu explains the expense reports. Rendgren dips into one of the treasures Pandora granted him, bringing back two large sacks of coins to help get the castle back on its feet. They sort through the taxes, going back through the reports on who has paid what, and settle on a reasonable rate that would encompass all aspects of the Kingdom. They work diligently, trying to determine the quickest and smoothest way to reset the broken economy, knowing many are struggling financially but also not wanting to drain a dragon's treasure.

Every day, the pair summons all the staff in the grand hall. Rendgren works toward learning all their names as they listen to the staff's requests and ideas on how to better the castle. They also go over who does what in the castle presently and what needs to be filled. Notices are posted to all the boards around the kingdom, stating the castle is hiring guards, maids, and general staff. Pandora interviews the applicants while Rendgren tests and sorts through the skill of those defending the castle.

After some debate, they opt to shorten the public court hours. Monday to Friday, nine in the morning till noon, retaining the daily staff visit before court. On Saturdays, much to Rendgren's dismay, Pandora decides she will resume her walk through the city with a small entourage of guards, helping people with her visions and building a community. Sundays remain a day of rest to spend the time as they desire, with each staff member receiving time off throughout the week. At the end of two weeks, court opens early, as announcements spread throughout the town via town criers.

Five

The Past Returns

Pandora glides gracefully through the halls to where court is, her fingers playing with the jingles at her waist, loving the fact that they are back there. She looks up at Rendgren, smiling at him. "Are you ready for this love?"

Rendgren looks down at his wife, reaching out to place an arm around her waist. "As ready as I am ever going to be."

She laughs. "I know it can be boring, but there is also so much to see."

"Perhaps for you with your visions. For me, it's just sitting there."

"Oh, Gren, you don't have to; I can hold court alone if you like."

His arm tightens around her. "NOT a chance. Some merchant might arrive, sweep you off your feet, and steal you from the gardens a week later."

Pandora teases him gently. "It has been known to happen."

Rendgren growls. "It's not happening again."

"No, Gren. I don't foresee it, as I am very happy with the merchant that stole me away."

He pulls her in and kisses her, earning a snarl from Junior at his feet, causing him to chuckle. "Right, sorry, Junior. We will get to court." Taking Pandora's hand, he leads her into the grand hall, guiding her to the trio of thrones that sit there. He waits until she settles before lifting Junior and Spider onto the smaller chair between them and sitting on the throne next to them. He motions to Kivu that they are ready and to let the others in.

Junior curls up with Spider and drifts off to sleep as they meet with the staff first, before opening the doors to the public.

After an hour, Kivu steps into the hall and bows. "There is someone here to see her Majesty, the Queen." Behind him enters a familiar face, an older woman with light brown hair, graying with age, and gentle pale blue-gray eyes.

"Miss Martha!" Pandora rises abruptly and runs across the hall. She envelopes Martha in her arms and hugs her tight, tears slipping from her eyes.

"King's seer... Or is it Pandora now?"

She steps back and studies her, noticing the differences in their two years apart. "It was always Pandora, just no one ever asked. What are you doing back?"

"Well, I heard there are new rulers of Oblait who are in dire need of a head housekeeper."

Pandora laughs. "I will admit, the castle can use your touch."

Rendgren rises and moves over to stand next to them. "Love?"

She turns her gaze to his. "Gren, this is Miss Martha. She's the one that cared for me when I was here. Miss Martha, this is Rendgren, the Red Phantom that stole me from this castle two years ago."

Martha smiles and steps in to hug Rendgren, who stands there in shock at another woman wrapping her arms around him. "Thank you for saving her."

Pandora laughs at his expression. "Oh, Miss Martha, I think you might be in his space. He doesn't just let anyone in, you know. I had to work for it!"

"That's right, my dear." He wraps his arms around Martha to the surprise of Pandora. "But I am willing to make an exception for her."

Pandora shakes her head, muttering under her breath. "Dragons!"

Rendgren chuckles. "You are one of us now, love."

Martha backs up to study the pair. "I heard that rumor. One day, you will tell me that story as you didn't state you were a dragon in your letter to me on the day of your escape."

"I wasn't. Gren went behind my back when I died and called in the Goddess Raya. She brought me back to life and made me a gold dragon."

Rendgren reaches out to touch her cheek lightly. "And I would do it again, love."

"Gold huh? One that was seen in my kitchen the day you left?"

"The very one, Miss Martha, and I know you would, Gren."

"I am glad. I understand you have a child as well?"

"Yes, Junior, though he is a handful." She turns to face the tiny red dragon, lazily draped over the chair on top of Spider.

"He is adorable, may I?"

"I would wait for him to wake up first. He takes after his father. A hellion bent on destruction."

Rendgren arches a brow. "I think he's more like his mother, a royal pain in the ass."

Martha laughs. "Much like the seer that moved into this castle eleven years ago."

Pandora smiles. "Perhaps, but I will never admit to that."

Rendgren kisses her cheek lightly and wraps his arm around her. "That's my line, love."

She sighs, resting her head on his shoulder. "Yes... yes, it is."

Martha smiles at the pair. "Well, alright, I will meet Junior later. So, do I get the job?"

"Miss Martha, you don't need to work for us."

"King's seer... Queen Pandora. It's all I have ever known, and it will please me greatly to return home with rulers who are clearly in love, honest... well, mostly honest, as it seems some darling seer kept secrets better than expected." She gives her a wink. "And fair. Also, one of whom I love like a daughter."

"Oh, Miss Martha, I love you too. You are the mother I never had, and it's just Pandora and Rendgren to you. No sire, majesty, queen, or king, understood? And I would be honored to have you back."

"I do, though I will admit, it will be a hard habit to break."

Rendgren shakes his head. "Don't I get a vote in this?"

"No, Gren, you don't."

He mutters good-naturedly. "Woman!"

She mutters back and nudges him playfully. "Men!"

Martha laughs at the pair. "Well, my dear. You show me where I can park my belongings, and I will have this place back in shape within the month."

"Your room is still there, Miss Martha. You may return to it."

"Thank you."

"You're welcome, Miss Martha. I will see you in the kitchen later?"

"That's correct. Assuming my table is still there."

"It is."

Pandora watches her head out of the hall toward the kitchen and her room and turns to Kivu. "Kivu, add Miss Martha to the payroll once more and double what the old King paid her."

"Yes, my Queen. I will see it done."

Rendgren leads her back to her throne. "Double? Are you digging into another one of *my* dragon treasures you promised me?"

"Yes, she's worth it. If not for her, I probably would have died when the assassins struck me. It was her quick reaction and knowledge of herbs that kept me alive."

Rendgren arches his brow and lifts his gaze. "Kivu, triple that amount for the head housekeeper."

"Yes, Sire."

Pandora wraps her arms around him, kissing him softly. "Thank you, Gren." After court, Pandora grabs Junior and Spider and runs towards the kitchen, hearing the chuckle of her husband behind her.

"So, do I have to compete with Martha for your attention now?"

Pandora stops and turns, offering him a slight bow. "Yes, for at least an hour a day, but you are welcome to join us in the kitchen."

Rendgren moves forward to kiss her cheek lightly. "Me, in the kitchen? I think not. That's why my cave has magical plates. I will leave you to your lady time. I, on the other hand, will go and challenge the skill of the guards that protect this castle."

Pandora laughs. "One day, Gren, you will learn to cook."

"I doubt it!"

She winks knowingly at him before turning and continuing on her path. Happiness fills her as she sees Martha, a stack of parchments scattered on her table. She places Spider on the ground and settles in the chair beside her. "Miss Martha."

"Just Martha dear, you are Queen now."

Pandora smiles at her. "You will always be Miss Martha to me."

Martha studies the child she helped raise and define. "Just like you will always be King's seer to me."

Pandora nods, laughter dancing in her eyes. "Well played, Miss Martha. It will be just Martha from now on."

"Good. Now that we have that settled, let's see your little one."

She hands him over. "Junior, this is Martha, Miss Martha to you. You are NOT to breathe fire or chew on her."

Martha arches a brow as she takes the little wyrmling into her hands, lifting him up to look him over. Noticing the violet eyes staring back at her, the tiny teeth and claws, suspecting they could damage if he set his mind to it. She places him in her lap and pats him lightly. "He is adorable, Pandora."

Junior growls slightly, his violet eyes narrow before shifting around and curling up against her warmth.

"Just you wait until he fully wakes up! You will change your mind about how adorable he is. He's been terrorizing the staff around here. I am surprised they stay."

"So he takes after his mother, then?"

Pandora's eyes widen in shock. "Martha!"

Martha chuckles at her expression. "I seem to recall a certain young seer that shut this castle down more than once and threw it into upheaval."

Pandora shakes her head. "Yes, I suppose you are right."

Martha reaches out to take her hand, squeezing it gently. "You did good Pandora, really. You survived and endured everything with grace, honor, and strength when you were here. Even if it was a shock at just how well you were keeping secrets. Better than any expected, I think, and you will not find me faulting you for that. On top of that, you tamed the Red Phantom! I never thought anyone would be capable of taming him."

"I wasn't entirely certain I could Martha. He resisted all my attempts at first."

"Well, you do have a way of winning people over." She glances around the kitchen at the servants that stay despite the dragons in the castle, her eyes traveling down to the pup in her lap. "And now we have another child in the castle creating havoc."

Pandora's eyes move to Junior, content in Martha's lap. "Yes, that we do."

Martha watches the pup sleep on her lap before turning to Pandora. "So, you are a dragon now. I am guessing this little one caused this?"

"Yes and no. As you suspect, a mortal cannot survive the birth of a dragon, and I did not. But Gren stole the Priestess Gwyn, who in turn prayed for help from her Goddess Raya. The goddess brought me back, but not before Gren swore an oath to her and offered up his immortality for me."

"But how was the goddess even watching at that moment? They just don't answer summons or calls like that."

"I might have had something to do with it."

"WHAT?"

Pandora sighs softly, reaching out to pull on the chain around Martha's neck, exposing one of the four necklaces she bought when she was twelve.

Martha reaches up to the necklace, looking at her questioningly.

"When I saw these in the market, I saw my future, as well as Rendgren's. Each necklace represents an aspect of him, Rendgren, Zalgren, the Red Phantom, and his true name. You wear his true name, which was why I could imbue it with twenty-four hours and the others only six. I saw him destined to walk the path of good despite his past and that the Goddess Raya would place her mark upon his chest. But the path on how to get him there was uncertain while I was buying them in the market. When I returned to my room in the afternoons after court, I spent months playing with the threads tied to him, trying to determine how it was to happen. I might have touched the Raya's threads in the process, drawing her attention to what I was searching for. She adjusted mine to where I needed to take them. Part of that involved putting him with the Priestess Gwyn. In order to do that, I actually needed to eat the poison Zane was feeding me. I knew I wouldn't die in the castle because Zane ensured I took the antidote as soon as I dropped, but I needed to plan when it would happen. It had to draw Rendgren's interest. I also required enough time to mend that he risked giving me more so that I would fall under Rendgren's care. I will admit, it was nerve-wracking, placing trust in the fact the Red Phantom would even want to heal me, and so I lowered my wards. Ones that stopped me from transferring visions without my express intent and, in doing so, transferred a vision to him of Zane's abuse upon me. It was enough that he followed the threads I directed him to, and retrieve Gwyn. The downside was Gwyn and Sol suffered a vision as well."

Martha takes her hand in hers. "Pandora, I had no idea. That is a lot for a twelve-year-old to sort through, on top of dealing with Zane."

Pandora squeezes her hand. "Yes, especially as I knew on that particular path, the whippings would start. I tried to avoid them, for I felt their pain in my sights, and the whip hadn't even struck me yet. But in doing so, I almost sided with him on the night of my ball."

"That would have been wrong, Pandora. While I do not agree with what Zane did, I am glad he drove you away."

"It would have, yes...the world would have ended had I stepped onto his path." She shakes her head, recalling the night as if it were yesterday, her voice growing quiet. "But the sparkling lights, the ball, the magic of the night all made me feel so happy. The wine blended with his thoughts and desires... He was gentle, warm, and inviting as we danced, and he was the one that granted it all to me. I just pushed aside who he was for the night, wanting that feeling to last forever. And then suddenly, he was mad at me, and I didn't know why. It was later in my room that I realized I had passed over a vision as the threads changed to those I had been trying to avoid. I knew at that moment the game had changed, and I could no longer appease him."

"I am sorry you had to go through that, Pandora. I wish I could have stopped it, but magic prevented me from going against Zane at that level."

"I know Martha. I saw that the day I arrived here, along with a lot more than I let on. I begged my parents to take me home, but as soon as I saw the King, I knew I was staying. I even debated not giving him a vision, but then the beatings would have started at home, for they just wanted the gold. At least here I could delay them and perhaps find a way to rewrite them."

"You kept so much from us, child. I had no idea."

"I had to Martha. Zane would have exploited my gifts far more than he did, and the world would have ended in destruction. I did not want him to succeed at what he was planning."

"It's still a lot for a nine-year-old. You grew up too fast, Pandora."

Pandora smiles sadly at her. "The visions force you to grow up, Martha. I didn't have a choice."

"And how are they now?"

"I still see them. Every day on everyone, but I have learned to tune a lot of them out, much like background noise."

"And did you see that I was going to come back?"

"No, I did not, Martha, but to be honest, I wasn't checking your threads. I actually tried not to sort through yours and Pippa's. But now that you are back, I can see you stayed with the elves of Lamadow for two years under their protection. That you fled as soon as Zane left the kitchen, hitching a ride in a carriage with a family out of the city. Then you walked through the Grim Tundra until an elf found you and brought you before Queen Diadradey. She will miss you running her castle."

Martha chuckles. "Yes, likely she will, but my heart is here with you. Although she is the one that sent me back."

"I know, Martha; I saw that when you stepped into our court today."

She laughs. "Does anything make it past you?"

"Spider did until you came in with the basket. And Gren taking me to the realm of the faeries to dance with them."

"He did what? The faeries let a red dragon into their realm."

"Yes, apparently. When we arrived at their clearing, there was a white flag fluttering in the breeze, so he clearly bartered a deal."

"And do you know what that deal is?"

"No, I didn't look to be honest. I danced with the faeries. We ate their food, drank their wine, I danced some more, then Gren came down to dance with me." A slight blush crosses her cheeks as she recalls the day.

Martha catches the blush, arching a brow. "I am assuming more happened than just the dance?"

Pandora's blush deepens. "Let's just say, after our first kiss on the dance floor, Rendgren portaled us to his lair, and Junior was conceived somewhere in the next three days."

Martha coughs slightly. "Three days?"

Pandora nods, her eyes straying to her pup sleeping in Martha's lap. "It was pretty damn magical, well it still is, but I will never forget what he did for me in taking me to see faeries."

"I am not surprised, child. You can clearly see the love he has for you, and you have for him. It radiates off the pair of you. I am extremely pleased to know that you have finally found happiness and peace."

"Thank you, Martha. Gren is…" She pauses, uncertain as to exactly what he is to her other than her everything.

Martha smiles. "I know, child, I can see it."

Pandora returns her smile, drifting in her thoughts, feeling Rendgren entering them as she sits there.

'I can feel those thoughts, love. If they continue on that path, I might just steal you from the kitchen.'

Pandora looks down to her lap, pulling at the ribbons on her dress as another blush crosses her cheeks, answering Rendgren softly. *'Martha was asking about us…'*

'And your thoughts went there? What exactly are you discussing with the woman?'

Martha watches the blush cross her cheeks. "Pandora?"

She mumbles under her breath. "Sorry, Gren felt where my thoughts went. He's asking about it."

"Right, I seem to recall something in the letter to Zane, to see, feel, and speak into people's thoughts and minds. When did that start?"

"I always have had it before I even arrived at the castle. There were several people in court that got extra messages behind Zane's back."

'Love? You haven't answered me. Should I be there supervising instead of here?'

'No Gren... You...' She sighs, trying to figure a way out of his questions, shifting in her seat. *'It's fine; just the faeries came up and Junior and the three days afterward.'*

'I see. You must be close if you are discussing that with her.'

Martha watches her shift, reaching out to pat her hand gently. "Go to him, child. I will watch Junior and see you tomorrow."

Pandora shifts her eyes to Martha in surprise. "Are you certain?"

"My dear, I can see where your thoughts are. I am older and wiser than you, remember?"

Pandora laughs and rises, giving Martha a hug, and runs from the kitchens. *'Gren, I will race you to the bedroom.'*

Rendgren pauses in the training exercises, feeling the guard's sword strike him, hearing the immediate apologies, but chooses to ignore them at the moment. *'You're not serious.'*

Pandora laughs as she hikes her skirts, running through the hallway. *'I am. Martha is watching Junior.'*

Rendgren turns to the guard, seeing his pale countenance, and reaches out to pat his shoulder. "It's fine. I was talking with my wife, and this is training. I dropped my focus; you took advantage of it. Well done. Now, my wife has requested my presence. Keep up the good work." He creates a portal straight to the bedroom and steps into it, closing it behind him just as the door opens, and she races in.

"That's cheating, Gren." She pouts at the closing portal before backing up and closing the door behind her, her eyes roaming over him as desire darkens her eyes.

He steps forward and pulls her into his arms, his hand lifting to caress her cheek lightly. "My wife invited me to the bedroom. How could I not cheat and get here first? After all, I know where your thoughts were in the kitchen, love."

Pandora closes her eyes at his touch, a sigh escaping her lips as she feels his closeness wrap around her. She sways slightly at his intoxicating scent. "If only I could portal..."

Rendgren leans in and kisses her softly, pinning her against the door, his hands slipping down her body to the ties at her waist. "I have to say, if socializing with Martha gets me this, then do so anytime."

Pandora feels her body pinned to the door, craving more from her husband. Her hands wander over his chest, latching onto his hanfu and pulling him closer. Her voice was light against his skin. "She asked if anything made it past my sight, and I said the faeries did."

Rendgren chuckles, kissing her neck, moving down to her shoulder as he slips her dress off. "I see how this went where it went."

She sinks against him. "Mmm, I did not intend for it to go there."

"I am not complaining, love." He feels her body responding to his touch and lifts her gently into his arms, carrying her back to the bed. He places her within its softness, loving that she gives herself so freely to him. He strips his own hanfu and lies down beside her, pulling her close as his fingers lightly caress her, the two of them spending the afternoon in exploration and bliss. Hours later, Rendgren watches his wife sleep in peace beside him; her body flushed from their afternoon together. He kisses her forehead lightly, drawing her tightly in his arms as he ponders the amazing woman that is his wife before drifting into sleep with her.

The next morning, Pandora wakes, stretching lazily as she rolls over, resting her head on Rendgren's shoulder, her fingers lightly roaming over his chest. She can hear his soft groan as his arm wraps around her, pulling her close, his eyes opening to hers.

"Do we have to get up for court this morning?"

"Afraid so."

"Let's just go back to the lair for three days."

Pandora props up on an elbow, meeting his gaze. "You're the one that agreed to running the Kingdom, Gren."

"What was I thinking? I do recall making a promise to each other to retire to the cave forever."

"Yes, and one day we will, but not today."

"Damn, tomorrow then?"

She laughs, playfully swatting at him. "Not tomorrow either. At least here, Martha will look after Junior."

Rendgren pulls her in, kissing her gently. "Good point. We will stay here. On that note, I will get us breakfast in bed so we can stay here longer."

"Sounds lovely; thank you." Pandora nods and curls back up in the covers, pulling the pillows around her.

Rendgren rises, dresses quickly, and heads down to the kitchens to fetch breakfast. He catches a few of the cooks and maids blushing at his presence. He turns to Martha with a questioning look, seeing her shrug her shoulders but catching the knowing look in her eyes. Rendgren frowns slightly as he leaves with a tray of food, wondering if Martha has spoken to the other maids, knowing she sent his wife to the room. He makes a mental note to speak with her later in private, especially as it is clear how much his wife loves her.

Six

The Morning After

T he pair eat breakfast together, enjoying the quiet time in the room before getting formally dressed. They head out and find their son, ensuring that he stops by the kitchens to eat food before court. A short time later, they are in court with the staff for their daily report before opening the doors to the public. The hours pass as people come and go, some just wanting to meet their new royals, some seeking a vision, and yet others with comments on the changes that are instilled.

After court, Pandora rises and kisses Rendgren softly. "I will be in the kitchen, Gren."

He chuckles. "I gather this is going to be a daily occurrence?"

She laughs. "It is! Have fun training."

His eyes darken slightly as recollections of the afternoon cross his mind. "Well, if the talk ends up like yesterday, I won't mind at all."

Pandora blushes softly. "I am sure it won't."

He reaches out, pulling her into his lap, his hands cupping her face as he studied her. "I wouldn't complain if it does."

She sinks into his lap with a soft sigh, feeling herself responding to his touch, her eyes meeting his, before hearing the soft growl of Junior next to them. She kisses him gently, resting her head on his shoulder as she curls up in his arms, enjoying the security that he brings her. "I love you, Gren. You mean more to me than I can even say."

"I love you, Pandora." Rendgren tightens his hold on her, kissing her forehead gently, holding her for a few minutes before lifting her out of his arms and placing her on the ground before him. "Now, go talk to Martha because otherwise, you won't make it to the kitchen."

"Right. Thank you, Gren." She laughs as she grabs Junior and Spider and skips to the kitchen, settling into her chair as she watches Martha sort through her papers.

Martha lifts her gaze to Pandora, seeing the happiness in her expression, before glancing around to those in the kitchen. "Come child, we need to talk."

Pandora frowns slightly in confusion. "We can talk here."

"No, we should go somewhere a touch more private."

"You're worrying me, Martha."

"It's fine, child, but this is something that should be between you and me. You can decide after whether you will let the other staff know."

"Alright, Martha, we could go back to my room."

"That works." She rises, waiting on Pandora.

Pandora feels a slight nervousness as she leads her back to their chamber, opening the door and letting Martha in.

Martha turns, looking at the pup in her arms. "They should probably run and play."

"Go find Daddy, Junior." Pandora places Junior down and watches him race off with Spider, turning to face Martha as she closes the door.

Martha gestures to the table. "Sit, please."

"Martha, you're scaring me. You are not leaving, are you?"

"No child, I love you, and you are stuck with me. But we should discuss something."

Pandora moves to the table and sits, watching Martha sit across from her.

"Alright. Now, tell me how your powers work. You said that you can share visions, as well as see, feel, and speak into people's thoughts and minds. In your letter to Zane, you showed you can display visions clearly, for I saw the gold dragon and felt the heat in the kitchen. You also mentioned you took some sort of wards down in order to assist your husband in running to get a priestess."

Pandora nods. "Why do you want to know Martha?"

"I will get to that."

"Well, there are many things I can do but yes, I can share visions with a touch or an illusion. I can also feel people's emotions and often see the reason behind them, on top of seeing their past, present or future." She shifts to her telepathy.

'I can speak in their mind if I need to so no others can hear me and read your thoughts back to me.'

Martha ponders it, answering in her thoughts. *'So you can read these then?'*

'Yes, and I can reach across the castle, or town for that matter, and touch anyone I have met or seen in a vision.'

Martha nods. "Ok, back to normal talking, as that's a touch unnerving. So these wards you have, can you put them back?"

"Yes, but I don't need to. I trust Gren with my powers. They were only up because I didn't want the King knowing what gifts I had. I didn't want to make the mistake that I made on the night of the ball while I slept or was unconscious."

Martha reaches out to take her hand. "I think you need to put some of those wards back up, child."

Pandora frowns, shaking her head. "No. Gren and I have an open relationship. I won't do that to him."

Martha smiles patiently. "It's not him I am worried about Pandora."

"What do you mean?"

"Well, you recall what we were discussing yesterday."

A light blush crosses Pandora's cheeks. "Yes, and you sent me to my room."

"Correct. Let's just say everyone in the castle felt what you felt yesterday afternoon. I do not think most have put two and two together to figure out why they were feeling happy and flush, but I did."

Pandora shakes her head as her blush deepens. "No, they didn't... I didn't..."

"Ooh we did! You did and you are truly blessed to be feeling that with him, but it is something that should be kept between you and Rendgren. Seeing and not feeling your love is enough."

"Oh my!" Pandora stands up, feeling mortified and embarrassed at what she has done. She recalls the bounce in their steps, the smiles on their faces, some even having a slight flush to their cheeks as they looked her way.

Martha chuckles at her expression. "It happened, Pandora, you can't take it back. But if it keeps happening, the staff WILL figure it out if they haven't already."

"Oh NO, Martha, I didn't mean to. I'm so sorry. We've always been in a cave, and well, a few times here..." She pales as a sinking feeling strikes her in the pit of her stomach. "Oh wait, Junior too?"

Martha rises, drawing Pandora into a hug. "Don't be sorry, child. You made everyone extremely happy yesterday, myself included. As for Junior, some sort of purple lights surrounded him momentarily, and he continued to sleep. I suspect he protected himself, but others cannot do so. This is why I brought you here to talk about it. So my suggestion is that you talk to Rendgren and get some wards up, either around this room or around the pair of you."

Pandora nods, her thoughts racing as to what she has done. "I will, Martha. Thank you."

"Good. Now, this old lady needs to return to the kitchen and back to her duties. It seems no one worked yesterday because of being distracted." She reaches out to touch Pandora's cheek gently. "You are truly blessed, my child. Hang on to him. Many only dream of having a love such as yours."

"I intend to Martha."

"That warms my heart to hear that." Martha turns and leaves the room, heading back to the kitchens.

Pandora watches her leave and paces the room for a few minutes. She ponders the situation and how often she and Rendgren had done what they had done, which only furthers her embarrassment. Twisting her hands in front of her and knowing she needs to get away from the castle to think about what's happened, she leaves her bedroom. She blushes softly as she runs into a maid, giving her a nod, and picks up her pace. Within a few minutes, she passes the two guards at the door and pushes the barn door open. She steps into the warm stables, knowing if she shifts to her dragon, Rendgren will sense it, and she needs time to think alone.

The stable hand runs forward at her entrance. "My Queen, what are you doing here?"

"Sandor, right?"

"Yes, your Majesty."

"I would like to go for a ride."

"Which horse would you like?"

"I am not sure yet."

Sandor nods, gesturing to the ones on the left. "Might I suggest these, my Queen? They are more for casual riding. The ones on the right are high-spirited and more of a warrior's horse."

Pandora smiles. "Thank you, Sandor. I will look through them." She wanders down the stalls, eyeing each of the horses, pausing at an empty one. She runs her hands over the nameplate marked. 'Sundancer.'

Sandor shakes his head. "You don't want that one, my Queen."

Pandora turns to Sandor. "What do you mean? It's just an empty stall."

"Yes, my Queen. She's in the end stall. We had to move her because she's wild and is lunging at guards."

Pandora spins and runs to the end of the barn, stopping at her appaloosa standing at the back of the stall snorting, a wrap over her eyes, hobbled legs, and bound to the back wall. "Oh Sundancer, what have they done with you?" She unlatches the gate, hearing the horrified gasp of the stable hand.

"No, my Queen, she's dangerous."

"Find me a saddle. There may be a purple leather one around that will fit her."

"Yes, but I don't think..." He pauses at her look before bowing. "Yes, my Queen."

Pandora approaches her horse, her fingers lightly caressing her face, watching as she snaps her head back. "Oh my girl, you have suffered so, just like I did. I'm sorry; if I could have taken you with me, I would have." She reaches out to pull the wrap off her face gently, running her fingers over her muzzle softly, hearing the soft wicker in response. She caresses down her neck, sliding her way down to the hobbles, and unfastens them. "We are going to go for a ride, like old times, alright girl?" She turns as Sandor places the saddle over the bar and backs away. "Thank you, Sandor." She moves to it and lifts it onto her horse's back, working the straps and tightening them before slipping the bridle on. Once satisfied, she takes the reins and leads her mare out of the barn.

"My Queen, I would highly advise against taking her."

"She will be fine, but thank you." She pulls herself up into the saddle, feeling the energy of the horse beneath her guiding her to the back gates.

Sandor follows for a moment. "Your guards, my Queen? They have not saddled horses."

"They can catch up." She knees her horse gently, feeling her bolt beneath her, as they gallop out of the courtyard and onto the back country roads.

Sandor stares in horror before turning and running into the castle, asking the closest servant where the King is. He finds him in the barracks with his son. "My King, the Queen just took off on an unpredictable horse without guards."

Rendgren turns to the panicked stable hand. "What do you mean by that exactly?"

"She's a wild mare, your Majesty. Ever since I arrived here a year ago, we have had to hobble and blind her to keep her calm. But the Queen just walked into her stall, saddled her, and rode off on her."

Rendgren reaches out with his senses, feeling the stress in his wife and the speed at which she rides. "Is there another horse saddled?"

"I suspect so, Sire. The guards were saddling their horses, but she didn't wait."

"Right then. Stay here, Junior. Behave." Rendgren turns and runs to the stables. He grabs the reign of one of the guard's horses. "I will follow her alone." He pulls himself into the saddle and urges the horse into a gallop, reaching out to find his wife and where she is heading. *'Love, what's going on?'*

Pandora continues to ride, tucking low and giving Sundancer free rein, the wind blowing on her face, her hair and skirts streaming behind her, enjoying the freedom of just riding. She feels Rendgren's thoughts in her mind and frowns at how quick the stable hand is. *'I need to get away from the castle.'*

'Exactly my point, love. This morning we were talking about staying, and now you are riding a wild mare at top speeds out of town.'

'She's not, she's just misunderstood.'

'Pandora, you are dodging my question.'

Pandora pulls Sundancer to a stop, spinning her around to look back down the road, sighing softly in her thoughts. *'I don't know that I am ready to talk about it yet.'* She feels Sundancer prance beneath her, knowing she still wants to run. She reaches out to pat her gently. "We will as soon as Gren gets here girl." It doesn't take long before she spots him riding up the road towards her.

"Pandora?" He eyes the horse prancing nervously beneath her.

"We should move, Gren; Sundancer still has energy to burn." She turns and urges her into a gallop, knowing he will follow. Ten minutes later, she slows her down, walking her past the farms as Rendgren pulls up beside her, riding in silence as he studies his wife's pensive expression. She turns her mare onto a narrow path, winding her way along it until she comes out of the forest onto the shores of the lake. She slides off her horse, leading her over to the grass to graze before turning to face her husband, her hands moving to smooth her skirts nervously.

Rendgren dismounts, and moves to his wife's side, placing a hand beneath her chin to meet her gaze. "What's wrong, love? Because clearly, something is."

"We have to talk."

He frowns slightly but gives a nod. "I gathered that."

She sighs softly, gesturing for him to sit on the grass.

"That good, huh?" He moves to where she indicates.

The corners of her lips lift a bit as she settles down facing him, taking his hands in hers. "How to start... Two years ago, when you kidnapped me, I might have played with your threads a bit."

"I already figured that out, love."

"Yes, but there are things you don't know. When I was at the castle, I placed protection wards around me to keep myself safe and to stop myself from passing or sharing my powers while I slept. The day you kidnapped me, I removed them because I knew you needed to get a vision from me to encourage you to go to Gwyn."

Rendgren studies her carefully. "I will admit, I wondered about that and also whether the King received one as he carried you away from the grand hall."

"The only one he got unintentionally was the night of my ball. But back to the wards. I never put them back. I trusted you with my powers and never felt the need to."

"Are you saying you don't trust me anymore, love?"

Pandora blushes, shaking her head. "It's not that."

"Then what is it, my dear?"

Her blush deepens as her fingers play with his hands nervously. "Well, you know those feelings I share with you in the bedroom?"

"Yes, they are pretty damn exquisite."

"Let's just say the entire castle staff felt what we did yesterday afternoon because I didn't have wards up."

Rendgren shakes his head in astonishment. "Oh no, they didn't!"

She nods, not daring to meet his gaze. "They did. Martha spoke to me about it after court. I don't even know how many times it's happened or that I could share beyond you to the entire castle. I mean, I can share if I focus on one, but everyone..."

Rendgren chuckles, feeling his wife's distress at the situation, and pulls her tightly into his arms. "That would explain a lot. I thought perhaps Martha gossiped with the way the staff were blushing around me this morning when I fetched breakfast."

"Martha would never gossip, but there were others in the kitchen when I was talking to her. She knew because of where she sent me, but it wouldn't be hard to figure out the reason behind where those feelings were coming from."

Rendgren kisses the top of her head. "My love. You do know I love you immensely, and apparently, so does the rest of the staff now. If you need to place wards back, then do so. It's not changing how I feel about you."

She groans softly, burying her face in his chest. "I know, Gren; I just like the open connection we have without them."

"So ward us both. Is that possible? That way, you can keep our connection open."

"I have never tried it, so I am uncertain."

"Then let's try it. What do you need to do?"

"I need to meditate and work my magic."

"Well, we are here and alone. I will watch over you as you do."

Pandora nods, tightening her hold on him a moment before shifting in his arms, positioning her back to his chest as she straightens. She places his hands on her legs and rests hers on top of them, twining her fingers with his. She closes her eyes and focuses inward, seeking the protections that she once had in place. Small purple motes flicker and dance around them, each increasing in size until a dome surrounds them. She reaches for their connection, their mate bond, their open link, as runes appear along the edges of the dome, spinning around vertically, each with tiny tails of light.

Rendgren watches the magic in awe, seeing the purple shield surrounding them, feeling her tug within and allowing her access.

She remains still, her mind seeking, searching for the powers that will bind them and block out the others. Writing appears within the tails of the runes, as some of them change their pattern, now moving horizontally but blending with the vertical as they pass each other. The surrounding shield solidifies, resembling a stained glass window crafted entirely from purple glass. The ethereal barrier encases them, casting a soft, otherworldly glow as it maintains its protective presence.

Rendgren closes his eyes, feeling her power creep into him and the intoxication that it creates within. His hands shake beneath hers, knowing he has his own, but hers is a league well above his.

Time stands still for the pair beneath the dome as each of them connects with who they are and how they tie together. Whispers surround and wrap around them, each accompanied by a delicate tail of light that caresses them gently. *'Be this our ward, our shelter, our sacred space that does not pass to others outside our binding. A place where we may connect and be as one, and so it is done.'* Purple threads weave around their bodies, creating intricate patterns that tie them together. As the shield collapses inward, it covers and fills them, joining them in a web of shared strength and safeguarding. She closes her eyes and slumps against him, feeling her energy ebb from the power she expended to put her wards back.

Rendgren catches her as she sinks into his arms, his hand caressing her hair lightly, his eyes roaming over the woman that is his, bound more tightly than even he imagined. He notes her breathing stabilize, feeling her slip into a light sleep. He whispers quietly as he watches over her. "My dear Pandora, you are truly amazing. You bring me more joy and love that even I could hope for."

An hour passes before she stirs, feeling Rendgren's arms around her. She opens her eyes to look up at him. "I'm sorry. Wards are a bit draining."

"There is nothing to be sorry about, love. I felt the power. It just confirms I never want to get on your bad side."

She smiles, her voice lightly teasing him. "What bad side, Gren?"

He chuckles, running his fingers lightly over her cheek. "The one I know you have in there. I have seen it."

She laughs and pushes his hand away playfully. "I do not!"

"Hmmm, let me see. Yes, you do."

She sighs, rolling her eyes slightly despite the smile on her lips. "I don't know what you are talking about. You love me!"

"I do, heart and soul, but that doesn't mean you don't have a bad side. It's just a touch more methodical than my bad side... Well, perhaps a lot more. I just razed towns I was angry with. You very decisively plotted to destroy Zane."

She takes his hand in hers as she plays gently with his fingers. "That I can agree to."

"You better, because I was there, love. I know the truth."

"Indeed you do, Gren. I love you. I couldn't explain to Martha what you meant to me, but you and Junior are everything to me. And it doesn't even seem like that's enough to describe what I feel."

Rendgren pulls her tight against him, breathing in deep of her scent. "I know, my love... I know."

She nods and closes her eyes, wrapping her arms tight around him as she just holds him, safe in his arms, feeling their connection. The light breeze flows over them while the soft chirp of birds surrounds them, each enjoying the peace of the moment. Twenty minutes later, she sighs, not wanting to leave the clearing. "I suppose we should head back. The poor stable boy probably thinks the horse has thrown me and broken my neck."

"He was a touch panicked when he said you rode off on a wild mare." His eyes drift to the mare grazing nearby.

"She's not wild. She is mine. I received her for my fourteenth birthday from the King. She's never let anyone near her but me."

"The King let you go riding?"

"With him and an entourage of guards, of course."

"Did you never try to give the guards the slip?"

Pandora shakes her head. "Not until the day I snuck out to meet you. I made it to the inn district before Zane caught and picked me up as he rode by, dropping me across his lap. That ended up with me being beaten and locked in my room from that point forward."

He caresses her gently. "You risked a lot in the hope that I would come looking for you. What if I hadn't?"

"Then it was very possible I would have died at his hands weeks after you took me."

"It was that close?"

"Yes, Gren, it was. I had power, but not enough to escape as fully as I did with you, and I searched many timelines for a way out. You were my only solid hope. But I will say this; I wasn't going down without a fight if you didn't come get me."

He tightens his grip on her. "Then I am glad I stole you from the gardens."

She teases him gently. "So you were not glad before?"

He chuckles. "That is not what I meant, and you know it."

She laughs. "Really? I seem to recall some of your thoughts in the cave. Let's see; the many ways to strangle me, to end me. How infuriating I was and to kick me out as soon as this quest was done."

Rendgren kisses her lightly. "Damn Mystics are a pain in the ass. You were not to be reading my thoughts."

She sighs under his kiss, her voice soft. "We were connected even back then,

Gren; how could I not?"

"Well, I wasn't willing to admit it yet. Space, my dear, and I valued mine."

"I know you did. That's why I never went down to the treasure room when you were there."

"No, you had my soft bed. Why would you?"

She reaches up to caress his cheek lightly. "Because you were there, and I had been waiting since I was twelve."

He reaches up to cup her hand. "I wasn't ready to accept a mortal for a mate."

"I know, Gren."

They stay at the water's edge for another half hour before rising and moving back to their horses. They mount up and ride back to the castle at a leisurely pace, talking and bantering. As they walk through the gates, the relief on the guards is palpable. Pandora laughs quietly. "I think they were nervous."

Rendgren chuckles. "Do you think so? All of their expressions relaxed at the same time. I am certain I can see the pace marks in the dirt." He leads the horse to the guards and passes the reins over as he dismounts.

"You cannot!" She pulls Sundancer up next to him and slides from the saddle, watching as the men all back away, knowing their fear of her horse. Smiling, she reaches up to pat her mare's neck and leads her into the barn herself. She opens the gate of her original stall and guides her in, ignoring the objections of the stable hand.

"She will be fine, Sandor." She gently pulls the saddle off and drapes it over the rail before removing the bridle as well. Once that is done, she places fresh hay and water in her stall and sets about doing a quick brush down, lifting each of her feet to check for stones.

Rendgren sits on the railing nearby and watches his wife handle the horse, surprised that she even knows how to care for the mare afterwards. "I think you are spoiling your mare, my dear."

"She needs it, Gren; they locked her in the end with hobbles and a blinder. I bet she's been that way since I left, and who knows what the King did to her. I am half surprised he didn't actually kill her like he did with everything else tied to me."

"That's because he couldn't, your Majesty."

Both Pandora and Rendgren snap their gaze to Sandor. "What do you mean?"

"I wasn't here, but I heard the stories. Every time the King tried, or he sent someone in, some sort of magic protected her and flung them across the barn."

Pandora frowns and turns back to her horse. She places both her hands on the side of her face, reaching into her horse's thoughts. She drifts back in time, searching through the life threads as images flicker faintly above her.

Sandor backs up and whispers. "What's happening?"

Rendgren watches the images closely. "She is searching through the horse's life to learn her past."

"She can do that?"

"Yes, it's within a mystic's power."

After a few minutes, a smile crosses Pandora's face as she hugs her horse close. She caresses her hand down her neck and along her back to the hindquarters, stopping at one of her dots. She moves her hand over it as it shifts, forming the shape of a sun. Laughing softly, she shakes her head as a few tears slip from her eyes.

"Love?"

"She is a gift from Raya and protected by the goddess herself. She bears the mark of the sun on her."

Rendgren nearly falls off the railing in shock, landing on his feet. "WHAT? I thought the King bought her for you."

"He did, but I saw when I was ten that I was going to get a polka-dotted horse for my fourteenth birthday. She was watching even before I knew she was."

"Damn."

She steps into Rendgren's arms, hugging him tight, catching Sandor's pale expression. "Sundancer will be fine now. She knows it is safe once more."

Sandor nods, turning his gaze to the horse. "Raya's horse..."

Rendgren caresses her cheek gently. "Let me guess, you named her."

"I did."

"So somewhere, you already knew."

"Perhaps, but subconsciously. It was not something I saw back then."

Rendgren chuckles. "I suspect, and it's just a hunch, that back then, the goddess would not let you know she was hers, hence the covered mark."

"Perhaps you are right. Come, we should go back inside. I should let Martha know the wards are back and the castle is safe."

Rendgren kisses her cheek. "Safe? What are you implying, love, that we are dangerous?"

Pandora laughs. "Yes, in more ways than one. Apparently, no one worked yesterday because of us."

Rendgren pulls her close, running the back of his hand over her cheek. "Because of you, my dear, I had nothing to do with it."

"Oh, Gren, you had everything to do with it."

He kisses her softly before deepening the kiss, feeling her body responding to his. "Ok, perhaps you might be right. I will accept twenty percent of the blame."

Pandora rests her head on his chest. "Fifty percent love... In fact, I am certain it's closer to seventy. I have NO willpower when it comes to you."

Rendgren rests his chin on the top of her head as his fingers trail along her body. "And I love you for that. You give yourself freely. It is... refreshing, delightful, and somewhat exhilarating."

Pandora laughs, poking his chest lightly. "You just like that you have control over me."

"Perhaps you are right. Come, love, let's get out of the stables." Rendgren grabs her hand, laughing with her as he gives a final glance back to the mare before leading her into the castle.

Once inside the castle, Pandora heads to the kitchen while Rendgren returns to the barracks, seeking to return to training the guards. The days pass through the week, with the pair of them settling into a routine during the day before retiring to their chamber to sleep, Junior and Spider joining them more often than not.

Seven

Children's Delight

Pandora rises, knowing it is her first Saturday in the market as their Queen. She gingerly slips out of the bed, feeling the excitement fill her as it had back when she was twelve. Tiptoeing across the room, she pulls a set of clothing out of the wardrobe. She stops, hearing movement in the bed, and turns, pausing at Rendgren in his red sleepers, curled up with Spider and Junior. Smiling at the sight, she moves to the bathing chamber to freshen herself up. She pulls a dark purple robe on, slipping a dark green and purple hanfu over it. Fastening the black belt on, her fingers linger over the jangles there, before placing matching ones across her chest and fastening them to the shoulders of her cloak. Pandora smiles, thinking Habo has certainly improved on the gowns in the past two years. Running a brush quickly through her hair and de-tangling it, she gathers sections and braids them, before twisting it up into a bun. She drives matching hair pins through either side, strings of dangling beads and gems hanging from the end. Pandora slips out of the room and heads down to breakfast, grabbing a quick bite before heading into town.

Kivu stops her as she steps out the front doors. "My Queen, not without guards."

She rolls her eyes slightly and stops to face him. "Damn, I thought I could get away with it."

Kivu chuckles. "In a castle full of staff? As well as a husband that predicted you would sneak out early? Not possible. Now, your guards will be but a minute. You are earlier than I anticipated."

Pandora sighs, muttering under her breath. "Fine. You do know I can just command the guards to stay, right?"

Rendgren steps out of the shadows. "But you won't, will you, my dear?"

"Gren! You were sleeping! How did you get down here so fast?"

"You don't think I didn't notice you leave the bed, love? I just waited until you left the room and sensed you moving through the castle."

She scowls at him. "Dragons!"

Rendgren chuckles and moves to her side, taking her hand in his. "Wives. Now come, if you wish to walk the market, I will be at your side, along with the guards. We are still new to ruling, and not everyone out there may accept you just yet. Perhaps in a year, you can venture out there alone."

"You do recall I am a mystic. If I don't want them near me, they won't get close."

Rendgren kisses her cheek softly. "I know. It's more about image and unity right now."

She rolls her eyes slightly. "So be it; I will wait."

Within a few minutes, four guards step out, surrounding the pair on the corners as they head into town. Pandora wanders the market, sensing and feeling the people's nervousness at the guards. She stops and studies the men with her. "Right, this isn't working. How about you four follow? Gren will keep me safe, and perhaps this way, the people will be less timid. Especially since last time I walked the market, nine guards surrounded me." She waits as they shift position to trail the couple, noticing an immediate change in the populace as they travel deeper into town.

One child bravely moves forward. "Are you really a dragon?"

Pandora crouches down to his level. "Yes, little one, I am."

"Can we see? Mama says you are, but I have never seen a real one."

The other kids around him cheer as well. "Please!"

Pandora glances at Rendgren, who shrugs his shoulders. "Alright then, let's go to the center of town where there is more room."

"Yah! We get to see the Queen's dragon." The kids jump around and follow Pandora, gathering a crowd as they move. Pandora keeps the same pace despite them trying to usher her faster.

Once she arrives, she looks around to judge the size as Rendgren and the guards help to clear the square. "Here you go, little ones." She seeks within and shifts, her golden scales shimmering in the sunlight as she towers above the houses nearby. Understanding she is intimidating in size, she lies down, resting her head on the cobblestone at their level. Some of them back away immediately while the braver ones move forward to touch her scales, catching the gasp of the parents as they do. "I will not harm the children."

Rendgren moves to her side as the four guards shift around Pandora to protect her.

After about ten minutes, the children relax in the presence of her dragon. Some crawl into her claws, pretending to be captured, so she lifts one foot to make a cage with spaces wide enough they can slip in and out. They play their games around her; rescuing those she captures; trying to stop her tail from swishing as ten of them pounce on it, giggling as they slide around. One even crawls up her back and sits between her wings, placing his hands in the air. "Look, Mom! I am a dragon rider."

"Kyle!!! Get down off the Queen right now!"

"But Mom!"

"I am sorry, your Majesty. He is just a child; he means no disrespect."

Pandora lifts her head and looks towards his mother, feeling her mortification at her son's behavior. "It's perfectly fine. The children are having fun, and that's what matters. In fact, if they want to go for rides at a later date, I am certain we can accommodate that, but my husband would need to be with them."

"I can do... Wait." Rendgren turns, sensing other dragons in the nearby vicinity, adjusting his casual stance to a protective one. His eyes focus on two elves approaching, relaxing as he recognizes them as ones he recruited to their cause.

They both bow to the couple. "King Rendgren, Queen Pandora."

Rendgren nods. "Myrsky, Violetarion. What brings you to Teshem?"

"We are here to request your acceptance in allowing us to live in Teshem under your rule."

Pandora studies them for a moment; Myrsky's deep azure eyes and light blonde hair, with highlights of blue in it, enhanced by his navy robes. She shifts her gaze over to his lady, Violetarion, shorter than he is, with the same azure eyes but dark brown hair and violet robes. "Welcome to Teshem, Sky and Violet. I believe there are several empty houses around. You may claim one as your own."

Both smile and bow. "Thank you, your Majesty. Would the children like more dragons to play with?"

"I am quite certain they would. But if you do, you could end up getting pounced on regularly."

"True, but it will be worth it." Myrsky shifts into his form, about half the size of Pandora's, with pale blue scales, matching the sky above them, and curls up nearby. The children squeal in delight as a second dragon appears, some of them moving over to him. Violetarion smiles, shifting herself, her scales a deep purple along the outer edges with a pale lavender in the center. She is slightly smaller than her husband as she moves to lie beside him.

Rendgren mutters under his breath. "Thanks a lot, you two."

They shift their gaze to his. "What did we do?"

"Make me feel guilty about staying in human form." He moves to stand behind his wife and shifts into his dragon, remaining sitting though, towering over his wife as she lies curled up at his feet. A few of the adults back up at his size, sitting taller than the castle at two stories high and half the height of its towers.

"You didn't have to switch; you were guarding perfectly fine in human form." They tease him gently as each of them eye him up, realizing just how large he truly is.

"Clearly, I did."

Most of the children seem to avoid Rendgren and remain playing with the other three. Only one or two are brave enough to approach the Red Phantom. Each one daring the other to touch his claws and running away, before creeping out and doing it again. An hour later, the group of dragons shift back to their mortal forms, much to the dismay of the children, which had multiplied exponentially by that time. "I will be in the market every Saturday, little ones. I have to check things out within the city, but after, we can have playtime. The town crier will announce it so your parents can escort you here."

Children's cheers fill the market as they all race back to their family, who stand nearby watching the encounter. Pandora gives them all a bow before approaching Myrsky and Violetarion. "Thank you for joining us today. The children love it, and I think it helps the morale of the people to show we are not always a destructive force."

"You're welcome, my Queen. Thank you for allowing us to be a part of it and for letting us make a home in your city."

Pandora hugs each of them. "Any time. Do stop in at court and say hi."

"We will...King Rendgren." They bow to the pair, turn, and head into the crowds, looking for a place to make their home.

Pandora takes Rendgren's hand and wanders back as the guards step in to follow. "I appreciate that you shifted and let the kids clamber over you, Gren. I know that goes against who you are with your space."

Rendgren chuckles. "Not many were brave enough to in all honesty, though a few dared their friends to touch my claws. It is different. It is not something that would have happened before I met you, love. But if it makes the city happy, then I will tolerate the rascals climbing over me. No adults, though. I will draw the line there."

Pandora stops, turning to look up into his eyes, reaching up to caress his cheek gently before cupping his face to kiss him. "I understand. Thank you... I will always love you, Gren."

Rendgren pulls her close, returning the kiss, before holding her tight in the middle of the market, resting his chin on the top of her head. "You are the world to me, love. I will always love you as well." He notices some of the populace stop to watch, caring less that they saw the affection displayed. After a few minutes, he steps back and takes her hand again, leading her back to the castle.

Eight

Council's Demands

A month passes as the Kingdom and the castle adapts to the new rulers, with Pandora and Rendgren adjusting to life in the public eye rather than a quiet lair. They sit in the thrones, talking quietly, knowing court was over for the day when Kivu enters with two trailing behind him. "My Queen, My King. Apparently, you have one last piece of business for the day. The diplomats Jeodina and Vynloren from the council of Lochyae. It seems they are here to place a complaint."

Pandora rises, confusion in her gaze as she looks over at the pair standing before her. "A complaint?"

Rendgren mutters under his breath. "My complaint is there are dragons in my court."

"Gren, play nice."

"I am playing nice, my dear."

Vynloren steps forward, bowing to the pair. "Yes, your Majesty. We have a complaint. We feel that as rulers, you have been neglectful in your duties."

Pandora frowns slightly. "We have?"

"Yes, you have."

Jeodina moves to stand up beside Vynloren, nudging him gently. "Stop teasing her. What he's trying to say is we haven't seen the scamp in over four weeks, and we miss the little whelp."

Pandora laughs, moving forward to hug the pair. "You two! You had me worried."

"So, when do we get the scamp back? Perhaps weekly even?"

Rendgren growls slightly as he rises and moves to stand beside his wife. "Never. He's our pup."

"Oh Gren! I am certain he would love it. When were you thinking?"

"How about today?"

Pandora laughs, turning to look at Junior sleeping with Spider. "Sure, if you want to wake him up."

Vynloren backs up, shaking his head. "That's on you Jeo! Good luck!"

Jeodina laughs at his response, also knowing better than to wake a sleeping dragon, no matter how old he is. "How about tomorrow then, or perhaps Saturday or Sunday?"

"Actually. Saturday sounds perfect. I think he gets bored with the market days. Might be best not to have him chase the townsfolk."

"Deal! We will return Saturday for the scamp."

Rendgren mutters under his breath good-naturedly. "Love, are we really going to send Junior to be influenced by them once a week?"

Pandora smiles. "Of course we are. You are, after all, the one that picked them as Junior's watchers."

"What was I thinking?"

Vynloren laughs. "I don't think you were, Red!"

Rendgren growls at him. "I can still take you out, whelp."

"But you won't because apparently you need us!"

"Actually, we don't; we have Martha now."

Pandora places her hands on her hips, scowling at the pair. "Rendgren and Vynloren. Behave, or I will use your true names on you."

Jeodina bursts out laughing. "Ooh, the mother tone, and the true name threat. Ouch!"

Vynloren scowls at Jeodina. "One day, Jeo, she will use that tone on you." He turns to Pandora. "And you don't know mine to use it, *Mother*."

Jeodina smiles at him. "I doubt it, Vyn. I don't provoke like you do."

"Yes, she does, Vyn. She knows them all." Rendgren scowls at his wife. "Fine, Saturday it is."

Vynloren turns his gaze to Pandora, shaking his head. "No, she doesn't?"

Pandora levels a look at him, matching his stare. "Would you like to test it out?"

"No, I don't think that I do, actually."

Pandora smiles. "Great, then we can do market day, and Junior gets a play date with Aunty Jeo and Uncle Vyn."

Rendgren's eyes snap to Pandora. "Wait, I did NOT agree to call them aunt or uncle."

"You didn't have to, Gren; I did."

Rendgren rolls his eyes. "Had I known just how much of a royal pain in the ass mystics were, I would have left you in the gardens, my love."

Pandora wraps her arm around him. "No, you wouldn't have. I have power, and you wanted it."

Rendgren pulls her tight against him, kissing her forehead lightly. "Yes, I believe you are right. And now I have it."

Pandora rests her head on his shoulder. "I suppose you do."

Jeodina smiles at the pair. "Then it's settled. We will arrive Saturday morning and take the scamp off your hands to give you a day of rest."

Rendgren smiles down at his wife a moment before turning his attention back to the pair. "Yes, it seems so. Thank you. Now, are you staying for lunch? The cooks Fil and Ray are pretty darn good actually."

"That would be fantastic."

Pandora laughs and moves to collect Junior into her arms as Spider jumps down and follows along. "Right then, let's head to the dining hall, where you can provoke each other further while we eat."

Rendgren and Vynloren glance at each other, chuckling at her comments before Vynloren dares to comment. "Of course, my Queen, if that is what you wish?"

Rendgren groans slightly. "You should have remained quiet, Whelp."

Pandora turns to look at Vynloren, seeing the mischievous glint in his eyes. She returns it as she reaches out to him telepathically. *"Vyndrakoloreth, are you really testing me? Because I wouldn't suggest it. You will lose, just like my husband does."*

Rendgren chuckles, seeing Vynloren stagger back slightly at her power within his thoughts. "Oh Damn, she just reprimanded you. Didn't she?"

Vynloren scowls at Rendgren. "She did not; she just proved a point is all."

"Oh, she does that well when she wants to. It's like a brick slamming you upside the head."

Pandora turns her gaze to her husband. "Gren! I can do the same to you."

"Sorry, love. Shall we get lunch?"

Jeodina bursts out laughing at this point. "Oh Pandora. They are not changing. It started the first time they met, and it's been ongoing. Might have something to do with them being both males and dragons."

"Yes, well, they can learn to get along. At least in the presence of Junior. I don't need him learning those bad habits."

"Rawwr."

The three of them chuckle at Junior's response as he wakes up in Pandora's arms.

Rendgren pulls his wife back in his arms and kisses her cheek. "He's a red, love, he's born with them."

"NOT my child."

Rendgren smiles, leading his wife and the others into the dining hall, gesturing for them to find a place to sit. Pandora places Junior in the chair beside her as she sits down next to Rendgren. Jeodina and Vynloren sit opposite the pair, with Rendgren at the head of the table. The maids filter in with plates of food shortly, placing them down, along with jugs of mead, juice, and water. The group enjoys their meal together, bantering easily among themselves. After lunch, they give them a tour of the castle before Jeodina and Vynloren part ways with the promise to return Saturday morning, first thing, to collect Junior.

Nine

Family Made Right

Months later, Pandora makes her way to the kitchen for her daily visit with Martha. She eases into a chair, observing as she organizes her papers in her usual spot. A smile plays on Pandora's lips, impressed by how swiftly she transformed both the castle and its staff, taking a moment to survey the busy kitchen.

Martha places the paper down and looks over at Pandora, studying her for a moment. She reaches out and takes her hand in hers. "So, Daughter. When are you and Rendgren going to do right by each other?"

"What do you mean, Martha?"

"I am talking about him putting a ring on your finger."

Pandora shakes her head. "We haven't really had time to discuss it."

"But you had time to make a child."

Pandora blushes. "Well, yes, that just kinda happened after the faeries, Martha. You know that."

"So you can make time."

"I suppose we can look into it."

"Good. Let's go back to your chambers."

"Right now?"

"Yes, right now." Martha guides her back to her room and enters. Upon the bed is a gown in shades of red and violet, adorned with intricate gold and red dragon-themed embroidery along the sleeves and hem. Diamonds embellish the neckline and rubies and amethysts glitter within the eyes of the dragons.

"Oh, Martha, it's beautiful." Pandora moves over to her bed and fingers the dress gently.

"Put it on."

"Me?"

"Yes, it's your wedding dress. Now strip!"

"Yes, Ma'am." She arches a brow at Martha, moving to shed her gown and pull the other one on. She stands still as Martha works the lacing and fastens the ribbons, recalling her time here when Pippa and Martha both tended to her.

Martha guides her over to a chair to sit and brushes out her hair. She pulls a few sections out and braids them, looping them around and pinning them in place. She weaves some ribbons down the back before pinning strands of rubies over the top of them. "There, now call the King here." Martha moves over to the bed and lifts the covers, exposing a matching hanfu lying beneath it.

"Yes, Martha." … *'Gren, could you please come to the bedroom?'*

'I am in the middle of training guards, love.'

'I get the impression Martha is not giving you much of a choice.'

'Right, I am on my way.'

"He's on his way, Martha." Pandora watches Martha tap her foot as she waits, following her husband through the castle until he arrives at the bedroom door.

Rendgren's eyes roam over his wife, sitting in a chair, dressed in an elegant purple and red gown, before turning his gaze to Martha, who stands tapping her foot with her hands on her hips. "Martha, how can I help you?"

She points to the robe on the bed. "That's yours. Now get changed."

He studies it carefully, noting it matches the dress his wife is wearing. "I don't wear purple."

"You do today."

Rendgren turns to his wife, noticing she is now actively avoiding his gaze. "What's going on, my dear?"

Martha's foot taps louder, pointing to the bathing chamber. "In there... Now! Or I will do it for you like I did with Pandora."

Rendgren nods and picks up the hanfu, marching to the bathing chamber. He strips out of the one he is wearing and pulls the new one on, muttering under his breath at the choice of colors and a maid overstepping boundaries. He strides out of the bathing chamber, scowling slightly at Martha. "Are you happy now?"

"Not yet." She studies him in the hanfu, giving a nod of approval. "Good; now you will portal us to your lair."

"Wait, what?" His gaze shifts to his wife. "Pandora?"

"I wouldn't argue with her, Gren. Remember, she raised me."

"And what of Junior?"

"Oh, I believe he's coming with us."

'You will tell me what's going on, love.'

'Ah no, I am not crossing Martha when she has set her mind to something.'

Martha shakes her head. "None of that telepathy! Let's find Junior and go."

"He's in his room."

"Good." She ushers them out of the room, heading to Juniors, and knocks on the door. "Junior, are you ready?"

The door opens, and a tiny red dragon grumbles slightly, a purple bow tie around his neck. "Perfect. Now portal us."

Rendgren growls, creating a portal to his lair, watching as Martha steps through and looks around. He scowls darkly at Pandora as she steps in after her, Junior on her heels. He closes the portal after him, shifting his scowl to Martha. "Do you mind telling me why we are here?"

"I just want to see where Pandora stayed with you. And since you won't likely portal me again, I am making use of it now." Martha walks around, exploring the compound, the rest following her. She frowns at the sparse kitchen and main room, knowing it could do with a bit more decoration than a simple table and chairs in each. She pauses at the bedroom, lush in decoration versus the past two rooms, from the bed that dominated the room to the dragon-carved dressers. Smiling in approval before making her way down the passage, she stops at the lake with the light mist hovering over it. Martha continues down to the piles of treasure, her eyes widening at the sight of it all, moving in despite Rendgren's snarl of warning. She wanders around, lost in thought as she surveys the size of the cave and all the gold within it. "Right then, I have seen what I need. Let's go to Lochyae and find Pippa."

"Martha, Pippa hasn't seen me since I left the castle."

"Exactly. It's been over two years; it's about time you saw her."

Pandora glances at Rendgren. "I don't know where she is on the Isle, Martha."

"The Council does, though." Martha turns her gaze to Rendgren for confirmation.

Rendgren nods. "Yes, they know where she is."

"Good. Take us to see the Council then."

Rendgren frowns at Martha before opening a portal onto the Isle of Lochyae.

It isn't long before Jeodina and Vynloren arrive. "Junior! Red, Pandora. And...?"

Martha steps forward to offer her hand to both in greeting. "Martha. Head housekeeper. I wish to know where Pippa is."

"And who is Pippa?"

"She came here two years ago with a couple of others. Your Council knows who they are."

"Right." Vynloren arches a brow at Rendgren and Pandora, dressed in matching outfits. He hides a smirk as he leads them into the woods while Junior races off ahead.

Within ten minutes, they stand in front of a group of five bears. Treefeared attempting to pin Junior down as he tackles him.

Martha steps forward and bows. "I wish for you to bring the one known as Pippa to us, or us to her. It seems the two behind me have been delinquent in taking their marriage vows seriously. As in, they haven't..."

The Council members snap their gazes at the pair. "You are not married?"

Pandora blushes and looks down at the ground as Rendgren scowls at Martha. "We have been busy dethroning a king and trying to return some semblance of prosperity to a kingdom."

"Exactly my point. Neglectful. And since she's my daughter of choice and Pippa is her sister of choice, we will be witnesses and see it done. Today."

"WHAT? You can't just marry us like that, Martha."

Martha turns to face Rendgren. "I can, and I will! And it will be done today. Besides, the Council will be the ones marrying you. I saw the shock on their faces when they realized you are not married yet."

Rendgren turns to Pandora, growling under his breath. "Tell her to stop meddling, my dear."

Pandora shakes her head, keeping her gaze pinned on the dress that she is wearing. "I can't do that, love. It's Martha."

Rendgren turns to scowl at Vynloren, who is chuckling behind Jeodina. "Are you two married?"

"Of course. The Council made us when we got here." Vynloren turns to the others. "We'll hold Red here while you go get this Pippa."

Martha turns to Vynloren, placing her hands on her hips. "Oh, he's not going anywhere, cause I WILL turn him over my knee if he runs."

Pandora starts to cough, feeling Kittymoo approach and pat her back gently.

Rendgren shifts his gaze to Pandora, his voice slightly edged. "Pan.. Dor... A... Dear... Did you have something to do with this?"

Martha matches his tone, having raised enough children in her time to recognize it. "No... She did not. I am just tired of seeing her in my kitchen every day without a commitment from you. It's about time you did right by her, so I am making it happen."

Rendgren grits his teeth and turns to glare at the woman; fire's dance at his fingertips at the audacity she has. "You do know I love her with everything I have. Hell, I even sold my soul to a goddess for her. I don't need a ring or paper to tell me she's my wife."

"Then what we are doing here today shouldn't matter."

Rendgren starts to say something but shuts his mouth and glowers at her, understanding completely where his wife got some of her traits from.

"Perfect." She turns to the council. "Please go get Pippa now."

The Council members nod as Jeodina creates a portal. Jeodina, Keandre, and Yuui fade from the clearing.

Silence passes, with Rendgren glaring at Martha, who matches his stare-down. Pandora remains silent by Kittymoo not daring to meet anyone's gazes, while Junior wrestles with Treefeared and Auggie. Vynloren stands back and watches with an amused smirk on his face, grateful that he didn't have this woman breathing down his neck. Ten minutes later, a portal opens in the clearing, and four humans walk through, followed by Keandre, Yuui and Jeodina.

"Miss!"

Pandora's eyes snap up at seeing Pippa, tears creeping from them as she runs across the clearing and hugs her maid. "Pippa! I have missed you!" Pandora gives a nod to Dunivan. "Dunivan, Xyl, and you must be Xyl's wife, Melissa; nice to meet you."

"How is this possible? You said we were not seeing each other again."

"We were not supposed to, Pippa. I am only standing here because Rendgren made a deal with the Goddess Raya and brought me back to life."

Pippa turns her gaze to the man having a stare down with Martha. "You're not going to win, Rendgren. Miss Martha always gets her way."

Rendgren shifts his attention to the newcomer, noting the sparkling green eyes, the bright red curls, and the pregnant belly. "*The Pippa,* I am assuming."

"I am, and you are the dragon that stole her."

"Indeed."

"Did you destroy King Zane?"

"Pandora dealt with him."

"Good, now I understand you wish to marry her?"

"Martha wishes us to be married, yes."

"But do *you* wish to be married to her?"

Rendgren's gaze moves to Pandora, his eyes darkening on her. "We are already married in my mind."

"Perfect, so let's get you legally married, and then we can talk."

The Council gathers around and gestures for the pair to step forward. "Alright then, let's get started."

Pandora braves a glance at Rendgren and takes his hand to stand before them. Martha and Pippa shift to stand on either side as witnesses while the others back away to watch the ceremony. Junior moves to sit in front of his mom, his bow tie now slightly crooked. The Council looks over the pair, smiling at them, before going through the rites of matrimony. Martha pulls out two gold bands, each with three gems inlaid in them, two rubies, and a yellow sapphire, representing the colors of the dragons in the family. Within the half-hour, both of them are signing the wedding papers, followed by Martha and Pippa. At the end of it, the council gestures to the pair, "We now pronounce you husband and wife...Officially. You may kiss your bride."

Rendgren turns to his wife and places a hand under her chin, lifting her gaze to his. He reaches out to caress her cheek softly before pulling her close and kissing her gently. "I love you, Pandora."

"I love you too, Gren."

Pippa claps her hands. "Great! Now that Martha is happy, we can relax and talk back at our house. I have two wee daughters that you will want to meet, Pandora."

Pandora looks over at her in shock. "Really? Already? And a wee boy, if I recall correctly."

Pippa pats her belly. "In a few months, yes."

Rendgren moves to the parchment and picks it up; a smile crosses his lips as he looks it over.

Vynloren moves over to him. "Congratulations, Red, it's official."

"Yes, it is." His eyes stray to Martha talking with his wife and Pippa, knowing his wife would have foreseen it and said nothing. "Now she is officially mine."

"Well, I am not sure you own her, but yes, in a roundabout way, she is yours."

"Indeed I do. She was mine the second I stole her from the King; now I just have a paper with her signature stating it."

Vynloren chuckles. "If you say so. Come, let's go socialize now."

The group talks for a bit in the clearing before they return to Pippa and Dunivan's house. The ladies move to the daughter's bedroom as the men sit outside and chat. Rendgren studies the two men that Pandora rescued, wondering if there was anything between them while they were at the castle.

Dunivan chuckles, catching the looks and recognizing them for what they are. "Not I, dear Dragon. I just taught her to fight. I suspect I was entirely a side effect of her ensuring Pippa was happy, for Pippa and I were already together at that point. Now Xyl on the other hand, he had a crush on your lady."

Xyl coughs and sends a dark look Dunivan's way. "I did not!"

"Really? I could have sworn you did. Isn't that why she saved you?"

"I wouldn't know. I am just grateful she did."

Rendgren chuckles. "I can always ask her."

"I would rather you didn't."

"That is enough of an answer."

"Fine; she was hard not to have a crush on. I mean look at her, she is the strongest, sweetest person I know. My responsibility was to keep her safe, which I failed at."

"Oh, I don't know about that; you did take a beating for her, so you tried. You cannot fault yourself for the King being stronger than you or having eight other guards siding with him."

"It was still hard to watch, knowing it was happening."

Dunivan nods. "Yes, it was. Something happened at the ball that turned the King against her."

Rendgren nods, feeling hints of anger at what his wife had endured at the hands of another. "Yes, something did."

Dunivan and Xyl snap their attention to him. "So you know what happened then?"

"Yes. A vision got passed over to the King of his death at the hands of a gold dragon while they were on the dance floor. The King felt it was her, but in fact, it was the Goddess Raya."

"Why would she do that?"

"Because she saw my wife crossing over to the dark side and didn't want that, so forced her to play the threads she avoided in order to keep her on the path she was meant to be on."

"That's harsh."

"It is, and I have never told her, though I am certain my wife knows."

Pandora's voice is soft as she answers Rendgren. "Your wife does know Gren. She knew the second she returned to her room the night of the ball, although I didn't see what he saw until I searched through the threads. Remember, I had wards up to stop that exact thing from happening."

He jumps up in shock, spinning to look over his wife standing there with the others behind her. "My love."

She smiles gently at him and moves to his arms, feeling them tighten around her as she rests her head on his shoulder. "It was a magical night, but it had to end. I just wasn't ready for it, and so the goddess did what I could not."

Pippa gasps in shock. "That's why you cried back in your room."

"Yes, Pippa, I knew what was coming. It was something I did my best to avoid, but could not find the threads to do so. If the King succeeded in crossing me over, we would not be standing here as the world would have ended about two months ago by my hand."

Rendgren kisses the top of her head. "Well, I was not happy when the goddess said she was responsible, but I have no regrets about the way everything turned out, especially with us."

Pandora lifts a hand and places it on his chest. "Neither am I, Gren. I am sorry I got distracted along the way."

"You did not get distracted. Anyone in their right mind would try to avoid the abuse you went through. It was the way it was meant to be; you have to know that. If the King had not done what he had, I would not have gotten the vision and run for the priestess to save you. You put us together so that she was the one I went to when you died. The goddess said as much. That you had woven the threads better than some gods she knew for a mortal of such a young age."

The Stolen Soul

She nods against him, not willing to leave his arms. "I didn't weave them all right. Which is something I need to talk to Pippa and Dunivan about."

Pippa moves to sit with Dunivan. "What do you mean, Miss?"

Pandora's eyes find Martha's, knowing that besides Rendgren, she is the only other one that knows.

"It doesn't have to happen now, love."

"Yes, Gren, it does." Pandora steps out of his arms and moves to kneel in front of Pippa and Dunivan as Martha steps up to stand next to Rendgren.

"I don't think I like this, Miss."

"Pippa, my maid, my best friend, my sister. I am going to step us back to when I was twelve. It was my first day out in the market." An illusion appears above her head, hearing the collective gasp from Pippa, Dunivan, Xyl, and Melissa at what she is doing. It moves through the market, Pandora within her entourage of guards, stepping back into Xyl, who steadies her. It changes the point of view to a lady standing in the distance. Long dark hair, black eyes, a long jagged scar on her face, staring malevolently at the group.

Xyl gasps. "Wait! I remember that day. You said you saw nothing on her, but I didn't see her."

"I didn't, Xyl. She had something upon her that blocked my sight. But I am a mystic and I can play with life threads, so I searched for her in the afternoons. It took time, almost a year actually, but I found a way past her block and discovered that she is a witch. Her name is Lavinia."

"Is?... So she's still alive?"

"Yes, she is. She is no longer in this realm, but I will get to that. She was in love with King Wallace, Zane's father. Wallace knew Lavinia loved him, but he loved Rimorhia and thus, rejected her. Because of this, Lavinia swore revenge and stole the soul of the baby in Rimorhia's womb. Zane's true soul and replaced it with a demonic one." Pandora pauses, seeing the surprised expression across each of them. "I was not strong enough at thirteen to defeat the witch, and the demon who was not willing to relinquish the body. I tried, but I failed." Pandora reaches out to take Pippa's hands in hers. "And so I stole Zane's true soul; a good, kind soul, and I placed it within you, Pippa. This was the reason the assassins attacked me. She sent them to get her soul back, but by then, it was already gone."

Dunivan rises to his feet in shock as Pippa pales suddenly. "You did what!?"

Xyl shakes his head. "We never did figure out why the assassins attacked, but I do recall you taking the blame. We just assumed it was because you hadn't seen them fast enough."

Pandora bows her head, her shoulders slump, understanding why they are panicking. "I didn't, Xyl. She still had magic blocking me, but yes, I was the reason. Only me. It was the first time I tried to play with life threads; however, I did not look at them all. Because of that, four men lost their lives. It is something I have had to live with, but I learned from it and helped their families as best as I could." She lifts her gaze, scanning them before returning it to Pippa. "I know you are in shock and thinking I placed evil within you. Do not think of this soul as the Zane we know because it is not him. That Zane is still very much alive with his demonic soul. This soul is pure and innocent and the rightful ruler of Oblait. Rendgren and I have talked about it. We will rule Oblait until Zane's soul returns, and then we will train him or her to take over the throne. It will be one of your lineage, Pippa, but where along your line, I cannot say. I won't know until I see the child." Pandora kneels in silence as the group digests the information.

Pippa studies her friend before asking quietly. "Why me?"

Pandora squeezes her hand. "Because you were destined to have children, Pippa, whereas Martha was not. You are also one of the kindest people I know, so I knew you would raise your children right after I died."

"But if you died, how would we know they are to rule?"

"They would know, for it is their destiny."

"Is it in my girls?"

"No, it is not."

"And you are certain this soul is good?"

"Yes, I held it in my hands before I placed it within you."

Pippa looks over at Dunivan, reaching a free hand over to him to take in hers. "Then I am good with it."

Dunivan sits back down, drawing Pippa into his arms. "I agree. It's a bit of a shock, but I have a question. Will this witch be coming after the soul, and should we be worried?"

"No. She has no way of knowing where it is. I am guessing she assumed I replaced the one in Zane as she sent assassins for him as well. I could have put it in any of the castle servants or the townsfolk. Even if she could, two weeks later, when the mages were sweeping the castle, I mind-blocked her to forget about me and the soul. When we returned for the King, we crossed paths again, and her memory came back, but too much time passed. Besides, she has her soul. She rescued him and took him to another realm before my breath killed him. When she returns to this realm, she will bring Zane with her, and they will come straight for me."

Dunivan pales slightly at the thought. "Will you win?"

"Honestly, I don't know. It depends on how effectively she instructs Zane about his true power."

Rendgren growls softly. "Pandora will win; I will make sure of it."

Pandora smiles his way. "I can say I will do my best to end Zane and Lavinia's evil."

Pippa sighs. "Good. Now, enough serious talk. I can't believe you almost beat me to having a child!"

Pandora laughs, her eyes moving to Junior romping around the yard. "Only because a dragon's gestation is four months. It wasn't a race or anything, and you did have a head start, Pippa. You already had Dunivan. I had to spend a year convincing Gren he liked me."

Rendgren coughs slightly. "It was not a year!"

Pandora rises and moves to his side, wrapping an arm around his waist. "I stand corrected; it was a year before he admitted it to himself."

Rendgren shakes his head. "That doesn't sound much better, my dear."

"What would you call it then, Gren?"

He mutters under his breath. "A rough start."

Martha pats his back gently, laughing softly. "It's quite alright, Rendgren. You have done right by my daughter, and you clearly love her and the pup. That's all that matters. Even if everyone in the realm assumed the Red Phantom was un-tamable."

"I was not tamed!"

Dunivan and Xyl laugh out loud. "You were tamed! Just like we are. It's best to just admit it and move on."

Xyl shakes his head, sliding a glance his wife's way. "Women have these powers, you see; there is no way around it."

Melissa nudges him gently. "That is not true."

Xyl turns to her. "Can you, or can you not, shapeshift into animals?"

"Besides the point. I didn't use them on you, Xyl."

Pandora laughs, lifting her gaze to Rendgren's. "I did, one hundred percent, but he ignored them."

Rendgren growls slightly. "I don't just let anyone in, my dear Seer."

"I know; It took me a year to work my way in."

Pippa shakes her head. "I would say less than that. More like a week because he DID come back and steal you."

"Good point! But if we are getting technical, I first sensed Gren the night before my sixteenth ball, but I ignored him."

"Wait, you ignored me?"

"Yes, Gren, I did. I had never had a ball before, and I was excited. I could feel your call, but the ball had more power over me."

Rendgren mumbles under his breath. "Do I need to throw you a ball?"

The group laughs at Rendgren's mutterings.

"No, love, you already have me."

Pippa smiles. "But she was beautiful in her dress that Habo made."

Xyl smiles, recalling the night. "Yes, she was."

Pandora looks down, a blush crossing her cheek. "It was a magical night."

"I want to see it, love."

"The dress? It still hangs in Zane's closet. It was the one thing he took from my room to keep."

"Really?"

"Yes. I reckon he might have regretted not kissing me on the dance floor when I was offering it to him."

Rendgren's eyes flare with jealousy, his arm tightening around her waist. "I am glad he didn't. You belong to me."

"I suspect that would be why the goddess did what she did. He chose anger, and I retreated."

He kisses her lips gently. "Now, let's see it."

Pandora smiles up at Gren and lifts a hand in the air. Purple motes of light form in the center of the group as an image appears. Sixteen and standing in a violet gown with white inlays and diamonds that adorned her skirts and sleeves. Her hair is woven in a myriad of braids and pinned up in an intricate design, embellished with matching strands of diamonds. Soft music surrounds them as she moves with grace through the dance hall, the diamonds glittering like stars around her in the ballroom lights.

"Wow, I would have stolen you sooner had I been at the ball."

"You were not meant to be there, despite being in town."

Xyl chuckles, watching the image. "I think all her guards wanted to steal her away that night."

"Not all of them, Xyl, only a few of them."

Xyl nods. "I was one of them."

"I know you were."

"Is that why you saved me?"

"I saved you because you were a strong enough person to stand against Zane, even at the risk to your own life. You deserved to be saved; the others did not. They sided with him and did not question or fight his actions. I made my choice and do not regret it."

Xyl nods. "Thank you. I wish I could have done more."

"It was enough Xyl. You needed to be here with Melissa, and so I made it happen."

"What's that supposed to mean?"

Rendgren bursts out laughing hard enough that he starts coughing. "Oh damn! Are you ever in trouble."

Pandora scowls at her husband. "Rendgren, that's enough."

"Oh no dear. Do not use that tone and look on me. I recall when you said those exact words to me." He turns to Xyl. "She will not give you the answer, but it will hit you like a brick when it happens."

Xyl looks between the pair, muttering under his breath. "That does not bring me comfort."

Pandora returns her gaze to Xyl. "You will not be hit by a brick. He's exaggerating because he refused to see what was in front of him. You will be fine. That's all I can tell you."

Rendgren mimics running away behind Pandora, stilling as she turns to look at him. "I saw that, Gren."

"Saw what, my dear?"

"You're telling him to run."

Xyl chuckles at Rendgren's antics. "I did run, all the way across the realm. Are you telling me to run further?"

Pandora growls slightly at her husband before turning back to Xyl. "No, you are to stay here on Lochyae."

Rendgren burst out laughing again. "See! You know it's bad. She growled at me!"

Xyl rolls his eyes, a sarcastic edge to his tone. "I look forward to it."

The group laughs, switching to lighter topics as they spend the afternoon together. As evening draws upon them, the groups bid their farewells, promising to return for visits.

Rendgren portals the group back to the castle, arriving in the grand hall. He watches Junior race off before turning to Martha as he wraps his arm around his wife's waist. "Thank you, Martha, for stepping up when I didn't."

Martha turns to Rendgren, studying him carefully. "Rendgren. You already stepped up when you saved my girl. You made an oath with a goddess to keep her alive. I am not faulting you for not marrying her, but I know Pandora. She would never have pressed or asked for it, and well, you are a male, so that would not cross your mind. After all that you have been through together, you should be legally married, and I knew the only way that was going to happen was if I stepped in."

Rendgren chuckles. "A male dragon, but you are right. In my eyes, we were already married. I did not think about the other aspects of it."

Martha hugs them both before giving them a slight bow. "That's why you hired me to be the head housekeeper. Now go enjoy your wedding night." With that, she turns and heads towards the kitchens, a bounce to her step and a smile on her lips.

Rendgren turns to Pandora, his eyes darkening in desire. "Our wedding night?"

Pandora blushes under his gaze. "It would seem that way, Gren."

He scoops her up gently, cradling her in his arms as he carries her back to the bedchamber. As she reaches out to open the door, she gasps in surprise at the sight that greets them. A myriad of flower petals are strewn delicately across the floor, atop the dressers, and even on the bed where the sheets are turned down. Warming stones nestled at the foot of the bed, radiating a comforting heat. The air filled with a sweet and subtle fragrance of vanilla and lavender emanating from the candles adorning the dressers. "Oh my."

Rendgren steps into the room and kicks the door closed behind him. He chuckles softly as he strides to the bed and places her down upon it. "Martha certainly is a miracle worker."

Pandora looks up at Rendgren standing in their colors, matching for the day, love within her eyes. "Yes, she really is. Now enough talk; I seem to be in this bed alone."

Rendgren growls slightly and crawls into bed beside her, pulling her close and kissing her deeply. He pulls back and caresses her cheek lightly. "Tell me you knew?"

She reaches up to his hand and twines her fingers with his. "I had an idea, yes, but not when. Not until she marched me into the bedroom."

"Why didn't you warn me?"

She pulls her hand back and looks at the ring on her finger. "Because Martha put a lot of thought and work into the dresses, as well as the rings. I was not taking the surprise from her."

"Wait, are you saying she made these outfits? I thought Habo did."

"Well, Habo provided some assistance, but she designed them and did most of the sewing herself. She worked on them in her room during her free time and with him in the evenings. She hired artisans to craft our rings and personally selected the gems to match our dragons; All at the cost of her wage."

"Damn, and here I objected to putting it on."

"She has already forgiven you, Gren. Besides, I think you look dashing in purple."

He chuckles. "Dashing huh. Perhaps the same way I feel about you in red and black."

"That's about right." Pandora laughs, cupping his face gently in her hands.

"Thank you, Gren."

Rendgren's eyes darken at her touch, his hands traveling over her to her ties. "You're welcome, love. Now, enough talk. I think I desire to explore my wife on a more personal level."

"She's yours to explore." Pandora sighs softly, succumbing to his touch as the two spend their wedding night together.

Eleven

Royal Hue

Six months later, on a Saturday morning, the pair wander through the market, noticing a lot of the populace no longer pay attention to the guards. The city folk bustle around, most taking the moment to smile and bow at their Royals before continuing on with their shopping. Some parents stop to talk as their children wait impatiently for the dragon playtime. They make it about halfway through the market when Pandora pauses, a frown crossing her features as she glances around.

Rendgren stops and looks her over carefully. "What is it, love?"

Her eyes glow softly as she turns suddenly and pushes Rendgren back just as a small cloaked gnome races up to them with a crystal bull outstretched.

"Could you please appra..."

Pandora's magic surges forth, ethereal threads snapping the bull out of the gnome's hand and flinging it to the ground. "You will NOT give that to the King."

The gnome drops to his knees and hastily picks up the bull, his voice filled with desperation. "Please, I need it appraised, and who better to do it than the King?"

Pandora shakes her head, keeping herself between her husband and the gnome. "No, it's cursed to drain the wealth of whoever touches or holds the item."

"But I have no more wealth, and if I don't get rid of it, I will die."

"Can you not give it to anyone?"

"No, it tells you who it wants."

"The statue told you to go for the King?"

"Yes, he has the most wealth in the realm. It can feel it."

Her eyes move to the statue. "So it is living then. What does it do with it?"

"It makes you give it away until you have none." Tears of despair slip from the gnome's eyes as he shakes before her.

Rendgren places a hand on her shoulder. "Do not get too close, love."

"It's fine, Gren. The person who gave it to you. What happened to him?"

"I don't know. I just thought it was something he wanted to sell. That's what it does."

Pandora ponders the pair for a moment, holding her hand out. "Give it to me."

The gnome shakes his head. "It won't let me. It wants him and will only go to him."

Rendgren's hand tightens on her. "Love, don't you dare touch that statue."

She keeps her focus on the gnome. "Can you put it down?"

The gnome shakes his head. "Never. It always has to be on you."

"Pandora, don't you go there!"

Pandora rises and faces her husband. "I have no wealth, Gren, you do. It's not going to like it when I touch it."

"We do. I am pretty certain that counts."

"No, if it was a we, it would jump to me. It's the person's wealth. What gold do I have?"

"A castle full."

"The gold in the castle is yours, donated to pay for staff and to reset the economy. I have some wealth in dresses that are mine, but that is not what the statue wants."

"I don't like it, Pandora."

"Gren, please. It's cursed; it needs to be stopped, and I am the only one that can. I will need the children though."

"Children?"

Pandora smiles, her eyes glow softly as threads filter in her mind. "Yes, they have no gold. We will need as many as you can round up, and we will meet them in the city square."

Rendgren recognizes the look in his wife's expression and turns to the surrounding people. "Right, you heard your Queen; spread the word."

Pandora turns to the gnome, offering a hand. "Come, Somassen. Let's go and see what we can do to help you."

"Wait, how did you know my name?"

She smiles. "I know a lot of things."

Somassen takes her hand and follows her, occasionally glancing back at Rendgren.

Once they reach the city center, Pandora tells Somassen to stay in the middle as she clears the people out of it.

Rendgren remains back at a distance, not liking the risk his wife is placing herself in, but also knowing she is powerful enough to deal with it. His gaze shifts down to the statue, thinking it looks innocent enough when he hears the soft whispers in his mind. He narrows his eyes and backs up further, forcing it out as he reaches for the bond with his wife. *'Whatever you are going to do, love, you better make it quick. It's locked onto my mind and calling to me.'*

Pandora spins, her gaze narrows, and shifts downward on the bull. "Oh, you think so, my darling bull? He's mine, and you will not be playing with him." She draws a small rune in the air and sends it into Rendgren, staggering him back a step as a purple shield of shimmering light encompasses him and holds him in place.

"Pandora, let me out!"

"No, Gren, the statue has power and will seek to control you now that he's latched on. You are safer there." She turns to the castle guards. "Stay and protect him. Do not let anyone near him." They nod and surround him, keeping the people away from him. Pandora eyes the gnome, watching him twitch nervously where she left him, staying between him and Rendgren. As the kids filter in, she adjusts her position to set the kids up in a circle, smiling as they understand what she wants and start forming the rest of the ring. She growls quietly as Somassen bolts suddenly. Pandora spins quickly and sends threads of purple his way, latching onto the wrist with the bull and pulling back sharply.

He pivots around suddenly as he comes to a stop with her magic; the bull flying from his grasp and sliding back towards her.

Pandora quickly shifts her strings to the bull and jerks it towards her, knowing it is but seconds before the gnome retrieves it. She reaches down to grasp it, just before his hands do, and lifts it up out of his grasp as both Somassen and the statue wail in agony. Pandora weaves her magic around the gnome and locks him down as she has Rendgren. She can feel the anger within the bull as she moves to sit in the circle, knowing it is only going to grow as she works to destroy it. She smiles at the excitement of the little ones, now sitting in a curved oval, before addressing those that are there. "Alright, kids, here's the deal. First, we need to break the bull; then, we can play. In order to do that, we are going to play pass the potato. It can only touch each of you once, and must be held for a count of thirty. So when each one of you gets it, we will start counting, then move on. It's going to scream at each pass, but whatever you do, don't drop it. If you do, do NOT pick it up again. The next child in line must pick it up. We got that?"

A resounding yes fills the square as the children cheer.

Pandora looks at the bull in her hands and weaves purple lights around it, placing a few runes along its crystal edges. She can feel it vibrating in anger as each hieroglyph clings to it. Happy with her scripture, she passes it over to the child on her right. The bull screams, causing all the children to jump, but he clings tightly to it as they count down from thirty. The child passes the statue off, earning another scream, but this time, they are prepared and scream back at it. It works its way around the oval as cracks appear on its exterior. Pandora keeps her senses on the statue, feeling it crumble under the aura of the children's innocence and their lack of gold.

Once she is certain it's getting close to breaking, she rises and moves to the other side where the statue is. "Keep going kids; we are close to defeating it." The children cheer and keep counting, passing it over before a high keening wail fills the air from both Somassen and the statue. Pandora weaves a few protection spells. She sends one into the gnome and another into her husband before turning her attention back to the child holding the statue. She watches the statue glow red, causing the child that is holding it to throw it to the ground. "Alright, kids, scatter now!" The kids rise and bolt from the clearing as Pandora draws a shield up over herself and the crystal. She weaves her magic into the glyphs along its edges, sending waves of power through them, watching the crystal shatter, bouncing off the magical walls surrounding them.

A purple heart beats on the ground as a demon rises from it, hissing in anger. "What have you done?"

"Ended your curse and your destruction of lives on Cantara."

"You have no right!"

Pandora narrows her eyes as anger enters her voice. "I have every right. You targeted my husband."

The demon's eyes move to Rendgren, still bound by Pandora's magic. "Gold corrupts, and he is mine."

"Gold does not corrupt everyone, and he's already bound to me, so you can't have him. You failed, and thus, your curse has ended."

The demon's rage boils over as he turns to attack Pandora. She weaves her hands and sends him flying back, slamming him into the shield that pens them in. "I would not challenge a mystic, Demon. You WILL lose. On top of that, your time here is ending, for you no longer have the body to sustain you."

"You will pay for this!"

"Actually, I won't. You will never make it back to this realm." She watches his body fade, breathing a sigh of relief when he disappears. She lowers her shields before dropping them on Rendgren and then Somassen.

Rendgren runs over and draws Pandora tightly into his arms. "Never do that again. You hear me?"

Pandora sinks against him, resting her head on his shoulders. "I don't intend to, Gren."

"Good. And I am not talking about the binding. I am talking about facing a demon alone."

Pandora laughs softly. "I didn't face it alone, Gren; I had many children helping me." Her gaze drifts to all the children, watching from a distance. "Children that I owe a dragon to now."

Rendgren caresses her cheek lightly. "Right, well, I will leave you to play. Thank you for saving my treasure."

Pandora looks up at her husband, rising to her tiptoes to kiss his lips gently. "It was not his to take, just like it is not mine, even though we are married. I swore an oath to you. Spider for dragon treasure, so I can never claim it. It will always be yours, Gren. That is how I knew the statue could not take from me."

"Gawd, I love you, Pandora. You are truly amazing." Rendgren tightens his hold on her, burying his face into her neck and hair.

Pandora wraps her arms around him. "I love you too, Gren. I would never have risked it if it was questionable. You know that right?"

"I wasn't concerned about the gold, my love."

She smiles. "I am a mystic, Gren; I see almost everything."

He steps back and studies her. "I know. Now I think I will go talk to our gnome that's crying over there. Perhaps give him some gold to survive until he can make more."

Pandora smiles, her eyes drifting to Somassen a moment before returning to her husband. "Thank you, Gren. Now, I get playtime, so shoo, get out of the center."

He chuckles and strides away, moving to pick up the gnome off the ground. "Come, little one. Let's go talk."

Pandora shifts and settles into the center. The kids cheer and race to her, climbing all over her. "Thank you, children. You all did amazing in defeating the monster." She places her head down, catching children in her claws and spending a few hours soaking in the happiness of the children that surround her.

Twelve

Kingdom at Peace

The years pass as the kingdom settles into a reign of peace with the other kingdoms, each doing their part to maintain it. Rendgren and Pandora continue to hold court in the morning, Monday through Friday. After court, they have lunch together before parting ways for a few hours. Pandora goes to the kitchen to visit Martha daily and enjoy their mother-daughter time. Rendgren takes Junior to the training barracks and teaches him the proper way to attack the dummies. Three times a week, Pandora joins them in the barracks as they battle it out with their guards.

Pandora ventures into the market with four guards on Saturdays to do the rounds and play with the kids in the city square. Myrsky and Violetarion often join her in the market, having a love of children but unable to have any of their own because of being different colored dragons. Rendgren leaves her to that, knowing she is more of a people dragon than he is. He returns to the map in his lair during this time, collecting the treasures Pandora promised him when they first met. Junior learns to speak and continues to visit Lochyae once a week on Saturdays. He trains under their guidance, as well as his parents and the castle staff. Sundays, being a day of relaxation, vary from lounging around reading, riding horseback through the countryside, taking to the skies and visiting other friends in other kingdoms. Over all, just enjoying the peacefulness of it all.

A few dragons cross the borders into their realm, but they are quickly put into place by the quartet, Pandora, Runestone, Jeodina, and Kittymoo. Those that do not adapt are sent back to where they came from. Rendgren and Junior are placed on monster patrol and swiftly put a stop to rampaging creatures attacking their people. Honors Light retires to the Isle of Lochyae and attends the visits that Rendgren, Pandora, and Junior make to the Isle. The realm prospers with the people themselves, creating a yearly holiday on the day the dragons brought peace to the realm, as celebrations fill the streets.

All is well and at peace for ten years.

Thirteen

Loss and Chaos

Pandora races down to the kitchen on Saturday morning before her trip to the market, frowning at the empty table. "Where is Martha?"

"She said she was tired this morning, your Majesty; she went back to her room."

Pandora pales as an image filters into her mind. "NO!" She pivots and runs out of the kitchen to Martha's room, pushing the door open and sees her lying on the bed. Immediately noticing her pale skin, her closed eyes, and labored breathing. "NO, Martha!" She drops and kneels at the side of her bed and clutches her hand.

Martha opens her eyes to her. "My child."

"Please, Martha! I will find a healer."

"Child, it is my time."

Tears escape Pandora's eyes as she pulls her into a hug. "I can't lose you, Martha."

"You can, child. You have a wonderful family; you should be proud. I am."

"Martha, you are my family too."

"Pandora, daughter of my heart, you and your family are the best thing to happen to me, and my only regret is that I don't have more time with you."

"You could; we could figure it out."

"No child, you can't." Martha reaches up to caress Pandora's cheek lightly. "I love you. I have from the day I first saw you in this castle, at nine years old, when you hugged me and asked me to be your maid. How I wanted to say yes that day and take you away, but I was bound to this castle. But you... you granted me a gift I never thought I would see, and that was my freedom. And with that, love from a daughter I never expected to have and her family. You..." She draws in a staggered breath. "You are the one that gave me peace, child, and I cannot express how you touched my life. But your life, it's just beginning. Live, love, and be free, Keep your family close... My child." Her fingers linger on her cheek before her hand lowers to her side, and she draws in her last breath.

"NO!" Pandora feels her drop from her senses as her heart stops. "Noooo Martha." She grabs her shoulders and shakes. "Martha PLEASE! Don't leave me!" Grief and anguish fill her, deep from within the core of who she is, feeling it grow, magnifying with every second that passes. A keening wail escapes as she kneels beside Martha's still form while the pain of her emotions fights for a way out.

The maids that followed back up and gasp as their Queen's body shifts, not into a dragon, but into bright purple cosmic energy, outlining her mortal form, which is no longer there.

Rendgren stands with Vynloren and Junior in the grand hall as he turns around, narrowing his eyes slightly. "Do you feel that?"

Junior ducks his head and places his claws over his face, his voice barely a whisper. "It's Mom."

"What do you mean?"

Just then, power billows out from Pandora, spreading through the castle at a great rate, waves of purple energy knocking people off their feet, shaking the very foundation of the castle. Rendgren and Vynloren find themselves flat on their backs, groaning in pain. Black curtains roll down over the windows of the castle as the green banners recolor to match, lowering to half-mast. The flames within the castle dim as the bells of mourning ring throughout the city. Rendgren rises, searching the castle with his senses and finding his wife in Martha's room, realizing exactly what's happened. "Oh Bloody Hell."

Vynloren stands unsteadily to his feet, rubbing his head. "What does that mean, Red?"

"It means my wife is in trouble."

"Did you need a hand?"

"No, this is between her and I."

Rendgren sprints to Martha's room, seeing two maids crawling away from the room in pain. He finds his wife at Martha's side, slumped over her dead body and sobbing hysterically, a purple glow still illuminating her. "My love?"

Pandora turns her glowing eyes onto Rendgren, feeling the rage within at what he has done. She stands up slowly to face him, her voice shaking with anger. "This is your fault!"

Rendgren nods, reaching out a hand to her. "I will accept that."

She backs away, narrowing her eyes, her body filling with another surge of power, fueled by the rage inside, arcing it his way. "She's dead! And I can't wake her up!"

Rendgren feels the power and draws up a shield, staggering back under the hit. His gaze darkens as he presses forward against her power with his own, seeing her stumble back at his attack. He strikes quickly and grabs her wrist, pulling her into his arms before she can react further. "I know love."

"No. You can't know or even understand! I was never supposed to see her die! I WAS supposed to die! Martha was going to live forever and *never* die on me!" She struggles in his arms before pounding on his chest with her fists. "You did this to me!"

Rendgren tightens his hold on her, taking the beating, one hand stroking her hair gently. "Martha was never going to live forever, love. She is mortal."

"But she was..." She sinks against him and sobs, her body shaking in misery. "She was, and you ended that."

"Shhhh, I know, love."

"But you don't...."

He holds her close until her sobs gradually quiet down. Gently, he scoops her up into his arms, feeling her head rest on his shoulder as exhaustion takes hold. Carrying her back to their bedchamber, he lies her down on the bed and watches sleep claim her. He remains beside her for a moment before turning and leaving the room, arriving back in the main hall where Vynloren stands with their chamberlain. "Kivu."

"Yes, your Majesty."

"Prepare for a funeral; Martha has passed on. She is to be buried in the Royal crypt."

Kivu bows his head. "Understood Sire."

Vynloren shakes his head. "Damn. Your head housekeeper?"

"Essentially her mother. Martha is the one that raised her here at the castle when her true parents sold her to the King. I don't believe she even shed tears when Zane killed them, but I cannot be certain."

"Double Damn. I didn't realize they were that close. I will return home and leave you to mourn. If you need to send Junior to us, let us know."

"I will, thank you."

Vynloren teleports out and returns to the Isle, hearing the bells of mourning ringing. "Triple damn." He heads straight to the council, who sit on a bluff overlooking the city below, staring at the church, each trying to determine why the bells were ringing. Vynloren sighs as he approaches them. "Pandora just lost her mother."

Treefeared answers as the others nod. "Then they will ring for an hour. That is the protocol for a Royal's death."

"The fact that she is ringing them here, though."

"I suspect they are ringing across the land. She's a mystic."

"Yes, I was in the castle when her power exploded. I was flat on my back before I could even react."

"Mystics' powers are tied to their emotions, and she is going to be fragile if she lost her mother."

"Oh, I wouldn't say that was a fragile hit, but I understand what you are saying."

"Moo and I should go to the castle. They will need healers for the mortals injured in her break."

"Assuming they survived, Treefeared."

"Her power is chaos magic, but she follows Raya. Even in her grief, she will not willingly kill someone. The knock backs will be the only injury, nothing more."

Vynloren rubs the back of his head. "Right, let's head back then and see if they need a hand."

Rendgren moves around the castle, checking on the staff, rounding up all the injured, and assisting them to the infirmary. He moves to the balcony and stands there, overlooking the city, noticing the castle shrouded in black on either side, along with the banners around the city. He knows his wife has power, a lot of which she keeps to herself, but to close a city down as she has in her grief is un-compared to anything he has seen in his life as a dragon. Lifting his hands, he rings the bells to call the populace forth, knowing not many will hear it because of the mourning bells ringing. To those that appear, he speaks clearly and concisely, loud enough to be heard over the mourning bells. "People of Oblait. I apologize on behalf of my wife for any injuries today. I will cover any and ALL expenses of healers that are required because of it. My wife lost someone she considers her mother, so the castle will be in mourning for a month. A funeral is being scheduled, but we ask that you respect our desires for solitude as we deal with the loss of someone very important to both of us. Please pass this throughout the city and let your neighbors know. Thank you for understanding."

Meanwhile, on the isle of Hontby, the mourning bells ring, startling everyone in the city. King Ludy moves to the balcony and looks out as Runestone moves up beside him. "It is not us ringing those, my love."

King Ludy shakes his head. "No, there is an aura of purple around it. Chaos magic, mystic magic. Take Myke, find out what's happening."

Runestone nods and fades away, finding Myke in another part of the castle. "We need to investigate Teshem."

"Is that why the bells are ringing?"

Runestone smiles. "That's what we are going to find out."

"Right, let's go."

The two teleport into town and immediately notice the bells ringing here as well. Runestone's gaze moves to the castle, seeing it draped in black with the banners matching at half-mast. She frowns as people stagger around them, looking slightly disoriented. "Oh damn, That's not a good sign."

"No, not at all."

"Ludy is right; it's mystic magic surrounding the city, strong, stronger than even me."

Myke shakes his head. "It's stronger than both of us, Rune; I wonder what happened."

They work their way towards the castle, seeing the gates are closed, with purple magic surrounding them. A group consisting of two elves and a human they recognize stand in front of it talking.

Runestone approaches them. "Greetings."

Vynloren turns, giving a once over of the mages. "Rune, what brings you here?"

"King Ludy sent us to investigate as the bells are ringing with chaos magic in Slario."

"Pandora lost her mother, and there is backlash to it. We suspect they will need healers, for it sounds like the castle staff took the brunt of the effect."

"We have a healer, one she has met. Myke can fetch him."

"Then I would suggest you get him because I bet the town healers will be busy."

Myke nods and teleports away, returning a few minutes later with Gronkus.

Fifteen minutes after the effect, Kivu returns to his post and spots the group at the gate. "The castle is in mourning, Vyn. You know this. You just left."

"Kivu, I brought Council's healers, Moo and Tree. King Ludy sent his healer as well. You're going to need them for the ones injured in that backlash of power."

Kivu sighs softly. "Right, yes, there are quite a few staggering around." He moves to open the gates but finds they remain locked. "Hmmm."

"She's locked them with magic; allow me." Runestone creates a portal just inside the gate, watching as the others step through it, only to buckle slightly at the power emanating from within before stepping through herself. "Wow, she's burning hot."

"She's sleeping." Kivu leads them into the castle towards the main hall.

"What!? She's burning like this while sleeping."

"Yes, and no one can get in the room."

Runestone looks Kivu over. "What do you mean no one can get in?"

"It means she's a glowing ball of energy, the same as she was before she hit the castle the first time."

Treefeared looks at the other two healers. "We need to find out who needs healing and heal them fast."

Concern fills Runestone's eyes. "Agreed, and we need to stop the next wave, or it could shred the very fabric of reality."

Kivu nods. "Yes, the first one hit hard enough. Vyn, take the others and find the King. I will take the healers to the infirmary."

Vynloren shakes his head. "He's coming to us as we speak. Go heal the castle staff."

Kivu nods and leads the three away.

It isn't long before Rendgren shows up, a scowl on his face and looking more than a little beat up. He studies the people there. "What are you doing back, Vyn, and why are the others here?"

"We are here to help, Red. The world is feeling the breakdown."

"It's gonna be another breakdown because I can't even get in to help her."

Runestone steps forward. "Where is she, Zal?"

"In our room." Rendgren studies Runestone for a moment before nodding and leading them to their bedchamber.

Runestone gasps at Pandora, hovering above the bed, her body translucent with a myriad of purple lights dancing within her.

Rendgren gestures at the doorway. "Good luck."

Vynloren stares at Pandora. "Damn, you were not kidding when you said she has power."

Rendgren shakes his head. "No, I was not. She is the only one able to defeat me and defeat me she has. I can't get past her barrier."

Runestone weaves a spell and steps in. Seconds later, she is flung back and slammed against the wall, slumping to the ground in pain. "Ouch! Good thing we brought Gro."

Myke reaches down to help Runestone up. "This castle, and beating casters up. At least this time it was you Rune. When did this start, Rendgren?"

"When Martha died in her arms earlier. The first wave hit us, knocking us off our feet, darkening the castle, and ringing the bells. Two of the maids saw her like this just before they were flung backwards. I found her at Martha's side, glowing purple but not translucent. We had a discussion in Martha's room, and I carried her back to ours and placed her down to sleep. After dealing with the staff and the populace, I came back to this. When she shifted to translucent again, I am uncertain, as her power has been radiating since the first one and hasn't calmed down. She has thrown me out of the room numerous times, feeling the bite of her power, just like you did."

Myke glances back at Pandora. "But death is natural; what would cause this reaction?"

"She's angry with me. She was supposed to die and not watch her loved ones die. But I saved her and made her immortal, so now she has mortal feelings and attachments with an immortal body. This is the first person she has watched die of old age, and she's placing the blame on me. I suspect Pippa will be the same when her time comes."

Runestone brushes her skirts off as she faces Rendgren. "Oh hell. That would explain it. Mortal grief with mystic and dragon power. You need to be the one to reach her, Zal. It can't be us. Myke and I can put a dampening shield up if she peaks, but it needs to be you in there."

"I can't even step into that room. Her rage at me is justifiable."

"So show her your love. Show her what an immortal is and what it means. She's struggling right now. She needs you."

"She's blocked me out; how do you propose I reach her?"

"How did you reach her before?"

"I didn't. It was all her. She broke through my resistance. Never the other way around."

Vynloren places a hand on Rendgren's shoulder. "Red, you love her. That much is clear. Find that bond; find your connection. That's your way in. Recall what she did to win you over and return the favor."

Rendgren stares at Vynloren before turning his attention back to his love. He steps to the edge of the barrier and reaches out to her, feeling the sting of her rage and taking it. He closes his eyes and focuses his thoughts, knowing she can feel them, read them, and share them. Rendgren draws on their past, returning to the realm of the fey. Listening to the music around them as petals dance in the air with faeries, the scent of flowers engulfing them. To their first kiss and feeling the intoxication and power within it. The longing and desire it creates when their lips touch, catching the soft sigh coming from her. He feels the squeeze on his shoulder. "That's it, man, keep reaching for her."

He travels through his thoughts to the bedroom and places her carefully on the bed. The scent of her overwhelms him as he asks for permission before taking what she offers. He feels her fighting his thoughts and pulls them back a moment before reaching back gently, moving through the three days they had together, the tender touches, the exploration, the love that they have. He envisions her violet eyes, the way they light up and the way they darken when she looks up at him. The innocence and knowing within, sending the love he felt each time she turns her gaze his way, back to her. His thoughts continue to draw up memories as time passes before he is finally rewarded with what he seeks. Her walls dropping and the connection returning. He holds back his sigh of relief. *'My love, please, let me in.'*

'Why Gren?'

'Because I love you.'

'No, why does it have to happen?'

'*Because it is the way of life.*'

Her thoughts pull away. '*I loved her.*'

'*I know you did, and she loved you. I am here for you. If I could save you from this pain, I would, but I can't.*'

'*I killed her.*'

'*No. You did NOT kill her, and don't you ever think that you did.*'

Her thoughts remain silent but connected.

'*My love, she died of old age, of time moving forward. Not you.*' He steps into the room, feeling a weakening in her shield, his thoughts drifting to holding her tight in his arms, trying to offer her the love and security she needs right now. '*My dear, you know I would do anything within my power for you.*'

Her thoughts are faint when they return, a tiredness laced within. '*I don't know if I can do it, Gren.*'

'*You can, Pandora. Because you are strong. This is just another step.*' He moves slowly, creeping his way to the bed.

'*There is always another step...so many... I don't want any more.*'

'*I know, and I would love to say that it will get easier, but it will not.*'

The rest watch with their fingers crossed, knowing by the body language they are communicating, each silently praying that Rendgren makes it all the way to her.

Rendgren feels her thoughts processing, edging closer to the bed. '*I love you, Seer; I want you by my side. Please, love, Let me help you. Let me be the husband you need or want. Lean on me if you have to.*'

The body flashes slightly, pushing Rendgren back with its power. Her eyes open, glowing purple orbs landing directly on Rendgren, standing fifteen feet from the side of the bed.

He stills and meets her gaze, not backing down from the emotions that flood him, feeling her pain, her anguish, her rage. He takes what she sends him, staggering slightly under its power. '*I will take it all, my love, if it makes you feel better.*' Rendgren forces himself forward as she watches him, taking the assault she is placing within his mind. He reaches the side of the bed and grabs her wrist, seeing her eyes snap down to it at the touch. He releases his own emotions back at her now that her attention has shifted. All the love, the joy, the delight, the happiness he feels. How she has changed him for the better, overwhelming her pain as her power falters, dropping her to the bed in mortal form. He immediately pulls her into his arms, kissing her forehead lightly. "Oh, my love, we will get through this."

She curls up in his embrace as her powers dissipate, sobbing against him, missing the sighs of relief from the others in the hall.

Vynloren whispers softly. "I knew you could reach her, Red. Take care of her; we will deal with those in your castle until you are ready to leave this room."

Rendgren looks up, tightening his hold on his wife. "Thank you, Vyn."

Vynloren nods and closes the door. "Right, let's see how the healers are doing and find where the child is hiding."

Rendgren shifts her over and lies down next to her, drawing her into his arms, kissing her cheek softly. "I will never let you suffer alone. I want you to know this. You never have to. I WILL always be here for you."

Her voice is light as she turns closer into his embrace. "I love you, Gren."

"I love you too, Pandora, more than words can say."

"Don't ever leave me."

"I won't, love, I promise." He closes his eyes and just listens to her heartbeat calm as her scent envelopes him. He remains there, holding her in his arms as she sleeps, feeling her nightmares, her anguish, and her fears that enter his thoughts. He sends his love to soothe them each time they creep through. A few hours later, he hears the quiet click of the door latch, opening his eyes as Junior and Spider creep into bed and curl up against them. He reaches out to pat his son gently before closing his eyes, returning his focus to his wife, keeping her grounded throughout afternoon and the night while three of the four of them slept.

Dawn breaks and Pandora opens her eyes, feeling a drain in her being, the heat of her husband's arms wrapped around her, her son pressed against her back. She lifts her gaze to Rendgren's, meeting his red ones watching her intently, her voice barely a whisper. "I'm sorry."

"There is nothing to be sorry about love. You lost someone very important to you."

She nods, closing her eyes again, as silent tears slide from them, not wanting to get out of the bed and face the world.

Rendgren caresses her face gently, feeling where her thoughts drift. "You don't have to, love. You put the castle in mourning. Its banners are flying black for a month. If you want to stay locked in here for that month, then do it."

She tightens her hold on him and cries herself back to sleep in his arms. Several hours later he rises, hearing her murmur as he leaves, caressing her cheek lightly. "I will return within the hour, love. I have things to check on."

Junior crawls around and snuggles into his mom's arms as she tightens them around him, drifting back into slumber.

"Thank you, Junior." Rendgren slips out of the bedroom and closes the door quietly behind him. He heads down to the main hall, sensing outward to determine where people are. He finds Kivu at his post, staring at the paper before him, knowing everyone in the castle is going to feel the loss of Martha. "Kivu, how are you doing?"

He looks up with a start. "Your Majesty. Sorry, I was lost in thought."

"It's fine, Kivu; you do not need to be at your post."

"I couldn't stay in my room, Sire."

"I understand. Have the arrangements been made?"

"Yes, Sire, they have. It will be tomorrow at three. How is the Queen doing?"

"She is struggling with it, but I am certain she will work through this."

"That's good; I am worried about her."

"Thank you. I sense the others are still here?"

"Yes, Sire, they are in the kitchen doing what they can to delegate, but no one feels like doing anything."

"Then we don't. Things will wait. People still need to be fed, but they can eat in the kitchens. The only thing that really needs to be maintained are the horses in the stables."

"Thank you, Sire."

"You're welcome. Now, I will head to the kitchens and take everyone to the infirmary where the rest are. Please bring the guards that are in the barracks there."

"Yes, your Majesty." Kivu rises and runs off to the barracks.

Rendgren heads to the kitchens. A smile crosses his lips, seeing his friends staring in confusion at Martha's parchments spread out on the table. "Thank you for staying and helping this evening."

A few of them jump at his voice. "Shouldn't you be with your wife?"

"Junior and Spider are with her, and she is sleeping. I will return within the hour, but I have things to say. I wish everyone to come down to the infirmary where the others are." Rendgren catches the staff's look of confusion at his words. "Everyone, including the castle staff." He leads them to the infirmary, watching as they file in, seeing the guards sliding along the outside of the walls. His eyes move to the Council members and King Ludy's people, giving them each a nod. Once they are all positioned, he addresses them quietly. "As you all know by now, head housekeeper Martha, a woman that my wife considered her mother, has passed away. Her funeral is tomorrow at three, and you all are welcome. We are going to feel this loss for some time. I know many would expect a castle to carry on as normal as she was simply a servant, but that is not the way this castle runs. This castle has staff, yes, but all the staff here are part of our family. It's going to be hard. We are going to cry. We are going to break down. We are going to want to take our anger out on something at the unfairness of it all. I implore that you use the training dummies in the barracks for that. My wife has already taken her anger out on me and some of you. For that, I apologize. I am the one that made her immortal, and she had never expected to watch Martha die. In her mind, Martha was going to live forever. Some of you have been here since we took over, others are newer as staff has retired. If you wish to leave because of my wife's action, I will give you a glowing recommendation and enough gold to travel where you wish."

He watches as they all shake their heads. "Thank you. I really appreciate your understanding of that. Now, this castle is shut down for a month, and judging by the confusion I saw in my friend's expressions, Martha's papers and scheduling are going to take time to sort out. I know she was training someone?" He looks around, watching as a petite woman raises her hands. "Joelene, right. That's a start. Now, I am not demanding any of you to work over the next month, but I ask that you assist. Dusting, cleaning, that can wait. Hell, if it was up to me, I wouldn't even dust half this castle like you all do." A few of them giggle at that. "Even protecting the castle can wait, as my wife placed a barrier up over it. Cooking for those in this castle and cleaning the dishes? Yes, that still needs to happen. The horses need to be fed and the stalls cleaned, though most can be let out into pasture to graze for the month. You will get paid your wage as if you are working normally, and if you step up this week in particular, you will get a bonus. Most of the week I will be with my wife, as she is extremely fragile right now, and we don't need another wave to strike us. But after that, I will be out helping as much as I can. If you see my wife wandering aimlessly around, tell her this is NOT her fault and send her my way."

Treefeared turns to Rendgren. "Wait? Is she feeling this is her fault?"

"Yes. Her exact words were, *I killed her.*"

"There is more going on then, if she feels that?"

"I suspect so, but I wasn't pressing it while I was pushing through her barrier. I didn't need a repeat of her explosion."

"Wise plan."

Rendgren turns to the six that stayed. "Thank you for staying and watching over the castle as we slept. I cannot repay your kindness for what you have done."

Vynloren moves over and grasps his shoulder. "It's alright, Red. You owe me once more, and Jeo won't be able to negate it this time."

Rendgren chuckles at his friend. "Deal, but I have a feeling when the women find out, it's gone."

Vynloren laughs. "I have no intention of telling them."

"You forget my wife is a seer, Vyn."

"Damn, that's right. I will just keep her away from Jeo."

"Well, you are safe for at least a month, so savor it."

"Oh, I will!"

Runestone moves forward, placing a stone in his hand. "Anytime Zal. If you need us, call us with that stone, and we will be right here."

"Thank you, Rune, and please thank Ludy as well."

"I will. We will take our leave now." She draws a portal forth and follows Gronkus and Myke through, closing it after her.

Treefeared and Kittymoo move forward. "We have healed all that we can; now they just need rest. Take care, Red. Keep us informed and do let the scamp visit. I am sure he doesn't understand what's happening, and you need alone time with your wife."

"After the funeral, I will send him to the Isle for a few days."

"Sounds good. Let's go Vyn, Moo."

Vynloren nods, creating a portal for them as they walk through. Vynloren follows, giving one last look before closing it behind him.

Rendgren returns his attention to the castle staff. "Right then, let's make this work, however that might be. Organized chaos, I suppose. Now, I need to return to my wife." He gives them all a bow and leaves the room, pausing at the doorway. "I do have one favor to ask. That everyone brings a flower tomorrow, either for my wife or for Martha. Talk to Lisette who tends the gardens, perhaps a wildflower from the fields, or take them from vases around the castle. I don't care where you get it; bring a flower." Rendgren turns and makes his way back to the bedchamber, feeling the staff scatter around the castle. He opens the door and slips in, seeing his wife where he left her. Moving to the bed, he crawls in behind her and wraps his arms around both his wife and child, hearing her soft sigh of happiness at his touch. He kisses her cheek softly before letting sleep take him.

The next day, Rendgren rises and moves to the bathing chamber, filling the tub full of hot water, placing a few drops of scented oil in the water for his wife. He returns to the bedroom, watching her stare at the bed canopy before moving to her side and sitting on the bed. "Love, you need to get up."

"I don't want to Gren."

"I'm afraid you don't have a choice in the matter."

"If I go, it will make it real."

"It is real, Pandora. Martha would want you there."

"I don't want it to be real."

"I know, my love. I know."

Her eyes focus on Rendgren's a moment before nodding slightly and moving to get out of the bed. Rendgren assists her and leads her to the bathing chamber. He undresses her as she stands there, staring at the wall, before guiding her into the warm water, watching as she sinks into the tub. He moves to the table nearby and places a bar of soap on the edge. "I will leave you."

She reaches out to grasp his hand in desperation, not wanting to be alone. "No, stay."

He nods and moves over to the chair, pulling it up beside the tub, reaching out to caress her cheek gently, pushing the desire away at her nakedness in the tub, knowing it is not the right time.

"Thank you, Gren." She looks down at the water. "Join me?"

Rendgren shakes his head. "I am not certain that's such a wise idea, love."

"Please."

Rendgren closes his eyes and groans, fighting the war within. He rises and moves to the door, closing it and latching it. Turning back to the tub, he sees his wife watching him, the loneliness, the emptiness, the sadness radiating from her. He approaches the back of the tub and strips his robes off. "Alright, move forward." He waits until she does, then steps in behind her, drawing her into his arms as she leans back against his chest. The soft scent of strawberries, mixed with his wife's scent floods him as his arm tightens around her, kissing the soft skin on her shoulder.

She sighs softly, one of her hands roaming over his arm as the other drifts down along his legs.

Rendgren growls softly at her touch. "Love, you are not ready for this right now."

She turns around in his arms, her eyes finding his, her voice a gentle whisper. "Yes, I am…"

"No, my love. I want to. Believe me; it's taking all my willpower to do this, but I will not take advantage of your emotionally fragile state."

Pandora studies his eyes, seeing the desire and the resistances within. She sinks against him and lays her cheek upon the sun tattoo on his chest. Slipping her arms around him, she closes her eyes, hearing the quiet beat of his heart, the rise and fall of his chest beneath her, and succumbs to the peace he is bringing her.

Rendgren closes his eyes, exhaling slowly. He brings a hand up to run his fingers through her hair as they soak, playing with it gently. As the water cools, he picks up the soap and slowly works it over her body and hair before rinsing her off. He lifts her carefully out of the tub and places her on her feet where he dries her off, lingering on her matching tattoo, and wraps a towel around her. He quickly dries himself and pulls a black robe on, leading her out to the bedroom. "Come, love, we should get you ready." He throws a cover over Junior. "Stay Pup. I'm dressing your mom."

Junior growls and buries his face in the pillows.

Rendgren smiles, turns to the wardrobe, and pulls out a black under-gown. He dresses his wife in it silently as she stands there. He moves around the back and fastens the ties gently before returning to the wardrobe. His fingers hesitate at the black and red gown before continuing to the black and violet gown. He turns to her, seeing her eyes drop to the gown, the barely perceptible shake of her head. "Are you certain, love?"

"Yes."

Rendgren nods and places it away, returning to the black and red and pulling it out, dressing her in his colors for the funeral. He slips the hanfu over her, fastening it where it needs to, before tying a wide red waistband around her waist, draping the ribbons to dangle into the skirts. "Alright, Junior, it's safe." Rendgren catches Junior peek out from the pillows before moving to lie on the end of the bed and watch. He guides Pandora to the chair, where he sits her down, running a brush gently through her hair. Braiding a few strands and weaving black and red ribbons through them, he pins them with rubies at the crown of her head. He watches her carefully, feeling the numbness in her mind and wishing there is more he can do. "Alright, my love, I need to get dressed, then we can head down."

She reaches out to take his hand, squeezing it gently.

He squeezes it back. "I know, love." Rendgren moves to his wardrobe and pulls out a black hanfu with hints of red embroidery in it, studded with red rubies. He pulls it on quickly and draws a matching wide red waistband on. He pulls the ribbons through in the same position as his wife's before moving to the mirror to pull his hair up. Once he is done, he returns to her and takes her hand, guiding her to her feet. "Come Pup. We have a funeral to go to; then, you can stay with Uncle Vyn and Aunty Jeo for a few days. How does that sound?"

"Rawr."

Rendgren leads her out of the room, guiding her through the hallways and out towards the back of the castle where the crypts are. He can see people already gathering and feels her hand tighten on his. "You can do this, Pandora. They are looking up to you."

"But I hurt them."

"Yes, and they forgive you."

Her violet eyes fill with tears as she looks up at her husband. "I wouldn't."

Rendgren draws her into his arms. "Shhh, yes you would. Now, take a deep breath and turn and face your people."

She looks up at him and nods, straightening her shoulders as her eyes move to the staff.

Rendgren offers his hand, leading her over to where the casket sits open. He notices her gaze avoiding it, knowing the only way she is going to face this is for her to face Martha. He half listens to the priestess as she speaks her words about life and death and the Sun Goddesses plans, his eyes intently watching his wife, keeping his thoughts strong and fixated on her.

Pandora stands beside Rendgren, aware the priestess is speaking, yet not fully comprehending the words. She remains stoically beside her husband, her gaze pinned to the ground beneath the casket. As the service concludes, she steps forward towards the casket. Tears flow from her eyes as she reaches in to touch

Martha's cheek lightly. Her caress follows it down to the chain around her neck, tucking her fingers under it to lift the dragon necklace out from beneath her clothing. She stares at the necklace, her eyes narrow ever so slightly, before whispering softly. "I'm sooo sorry, Martha." She steps back as purple lights surround and close the casket magically, the dragon around her neck etched into the top, along with the scrolling script. *'Forever loved.'*

Rendgren watches his wife move forward, catching the narrowing of her eyes on the necklace. He knows it is one of the four mentioned and wonders why she is apologizing for it yet engraving it on her casket. He opts to remain silent, making a mental note to ask her about it later.

As the guards carry the casket into the royal crypts, some of the staff approach Pandora with flowers, while others place them on the coffin. Pandora nods in thanks to each of them, her shaking hands taking as many of the flowers as she can before she hands some to Rendgren.

Vynloren approaches with Jeodina, each one giving her a white lily and offering condolences before stepping away to talk with Rendgren about taking Junior away.

Pandora watches the three of them talk and slips off quietly, her steps taking her first to the kitchen before following through to Martha's room. She curls up on her bed, drawing her pillow into her arms, and cries against it.

Rendgren follows his wife's footsteps, knowing the second she slipped away, feeling Jeodina's shake on his shoulder. "Sorry Jeo; just following my wife."

"Well, she's right... oh no wait, she's not here anymore."

"No, she's heading to the kitchens where Martha used to sit."

"Understandable. I got the pup. You go find her."

"Thanks, Jeo. I will see you in a few days. Junior, have fun and behave."

Junior offers a toothy grin. "Rawrrrr."

Rendgren chuckles, rubbing his head and earning a growl. "I know you better than that. Jeo, you have permission to discipline if needed."

"Daaad!"

"I love you, Junior."

"Love you too, Dad. Tell Mom I love her."

"I will Son."

Rendgren enters the castle, following his wife's path to Martha's room, seeing her curled up on her bed among a variety of flowers, clutching a pillow, and crying silently into it. He steps into the room quietly. "Love."

"Go away, Gren. You don't like tears, remember?"

He sits on the bed and draws her into his arms. "I don't, but you are my wife, and I will not let you suffer alone. I love you, and I am here for you."

"How do you do it? How do you watch them age and die and not be able to stop it?"

"You don't, my dear. It is the curse of being immortal. That's why I never got close to anyone until you. And when I lost the one person important to me, I kidnapped a priestess who called upon her goddess to help. One I was willing to give up my immortality for so that we would age together. You are the only one in all my life that I got attached to, and remember, I am old, much older than you."

"I don't know how to survive without her."

"You will. You will take it one day at a time and remember her for the wonderful woman that she was."

"If I had just left her... she would still be alive. It's my fault she's dead."

"No, Pandora, she died because she was mortal."

"No! She died because I removed the curse that was on her with that necklace. She was bound to Zane and his lifespan in hopes she could tame him. I took that away and caused this. I'm the one that did this!"

"Did you wrap that necklace around her neck and force her to wear it?"

"No but..."

He places a finger to her lips, shaking his head. "Love. There are no buts at all. You gave Martha the choice, and she chose to put that necklace around her neck. She chose the freedom you gave her, and that's what it was. Freedom from being bound to evil. Freedom to choose her own life. Freedom to come back and be with you and live happily for the remainder of her life. She chose you. She loved you, and you need to remember that. This is not your fault; it's simply time passing."

She looks up at him, misery in her eyes. "How can you be so certain?"

"Because, my dear, she put the necklace on, and she loved you as a daughter."

She nods and curls up in his arms, crying herself to sleep. He shifts to sit against the wall, his fingers caressing her lightly as he remains holding her. Feeling her settle into a deep sleep, he lifts her into his arms and carries her back to their room, passing by staff who stop to check in on the pair.

A few days later, Pandora rises from the bed and roams through the castle, eventually finding herself standing in front of Martha's room. She opens the door and slips inside, closing it quietly behind her. Moving to the bed, she picks up her pillow, holding it close as the familiar scent comforts her, noticing as she scans the room that Martha has very little decor.

She sets the pillow aside and approaches the dresser, opening the top drawer and expecting to find clothing. To her surprise, she discovers satchels instead. Pulling one open, she reveals a bag filled with gold coins. She digs quickly through the drawer and finds the same in each, pouring them out onto the floor. Her eyes fill with tears as she moves through the other two drawers to the same effect, staring in confusion at all the gold piled together. Her eyes shift to the trunk at the foot of the bed. She opens it and finds a letter addressed to her on the top of more gold. Her hands shake as she picks the letter up and turns it over in her hands before unfolding it.

Pandora, daughter of my heart.

If you are reading this, then I know I have moved on. Time has finally caught up to me. I do not want you to place any blame on your shoulders for what has happened, as I know you will. You gave me a life free of binding, something I never expected to have, and I made that choice willingly. With that choice, you granted me freedom. And in that freedom, I loved again, with a family I am proud to call my own. You are my family, Pandora. You, Rendgren, and Junior. You have brought this old lady so much joy and have from the minute you arrived in this castle at nine years old. I never imagined what you could have granted me or that I would even have a chance to love again, but you gave me that without asking for anything in return.

You are such a special soul, Pandora. You have enough power to rule everyone, and most would let that power corrupt them or use it to better themselves. But you have not. You have only used it to better people's lives, mine included. You have the ability to destroy, and yet you suffered until you could free us all. Now, I know you meant well when you increased my pay, but I had everything I needed here with you. Happiness, love, family, and a home I do not regret coming back to. I also realize for dragons, treasure is important, and the fact that you were willing to part ways with it to pay me means the world to me.

Now, you may be a dragon now, but you are still a human at heart. You don't care about the treasure the way dragons do because your heart seeks only love, and you have it in your family. This I know because I have seen it. I have seen the bear and the book I gave you, protected in Rendgren's lair. It has meaning to you, more than any gold value, and that is why you took them when you left. Even the lair is evidence as to who you are. Going from a castle where wealth surrounded you to the simple life of a cave, and you made it work, Pandora. Most wouldn't.

Now your husband and Junior are dragons through and through. Rendgren, the Red Phantom, has his hoard, and a large one at that. Junior does not. And while your family is close, he is still a dragon, and so I donate all my earnings to my grandson, Junior. This will be the start of his hoard. Please keep it safe for him when he does find a lair away from home because all kids grow up and leave home. Some younger than they should, my darling daughter, but I am truly grateful that you came into our lives. You brought happiness this castle has not seen in a long time. You brought love and the world into an era of peace. My child, I am so proud of you. A mother could not ask for more. Do not spend too much time mourning me. Remember the happiness we had, the times together, and go forward with your life, Pandora. Live, Love, and be Free, something you granted me and I took full advantage of.

Martha.

Pandora picks up some of the gold and throws it at the walls in frustration, grief, and rage. Pain grows deep in her heart at her loss as she sinks to the floor on top of it. She clutches the letter to her chest as tears slide from her face, desperately missing the woman that was her anchor here at the castle.

Rendgren staggers in pain through their bond. He travels through the castle and finds her curled up on the gold, her eyes red and puffy and her breathing ragged as she stares vacantly at the wall. Rendgren gently pulls the letter out of her grasp and reads it, understanding the pain his wife is going through and wishing there is something he can do to help her. He lifts her up into his arms, hearing the soft whisper in his thoughts.

'Gren, it hurts so much.'

'I know, love. Only time will heal that.'

'I hate time.'

'No, you don't, Pandora. Sleep now.' He weaves a soft red magic over her, feeling her body relax to his spell. He creates a portal into his lair and places her down on the bed, tucking her teddy into her arms. Once he is certain she is at peace, he moves about the lair, deciding on where to place a den for Junior. He magically creates a new room and steps into it, inspecting its size. Once he is happy, he creates a portal back to Martha's room and transfers all of Junior's treasure into it, placing the letter on top of the pile once he is done. An hour later, he checks in on his wife, knowing his spell should keep her out for some time. He heads back to the main room, where the map with the amethyst sits, watching as it still spins all these years later. Rendgren makes the decision that he might as well collect more treasure while his wife sleeps. He gathers his bags and heads off to the next lair, suspecting he must be nearing the end of them with all the ones he has cleared out in the past ten years. Several hours later, and another two dens empty, he drops one bag in Junior's room, adding to the stack that

Martha left for him. He glances at the map, seeing the gem in a new location. A grin crosses his lips at the thought of another treasure out there waiting for him. He lifts his gaze, feeling his wife rising from the bed, and turns as she pads out of the bedroom.

Her eyes land on him standing next to the map. "Gren, we are at the lair?"

"Yes, love. You needed rest, and I moved Junior's treasure here."

"Wait, into your room?"

Rendgren chuckles and moves to her side. "No, it's his; I created a room for him. Come, I will show you." He leads her down the winding passage to a new passage on the right.

She steps into the smaller room, contemplating the large stack of gold. "There is more here than just Martha's."

"Indeed, I emptied another two lairs as you slept and added some to his."

Pandora smiles, leaning her head against his chest. "Thank you, Gren; I am sorry I am such a mess right now. It's so hard to…"

"Shhh." He places a finger to her lips. "My love, you lost someone very important to you. I do not expect you to walk around as if it didn't happen. In time, you will heal, and while you will always feel the loss of Martha, it will not hurt as much, for the happiness of your time together will override the sadness you feel right now. I promise."

She tightens her arms around him, giving a nod as she stares at Junior's horde. She murmurs quietly. "Junior will love that he has his own treasure room."

"Yes, he will. I will bring him here when he returns from Lochyae."

"Thank you, Gren, for everything that you do for me and Junior."

"Pandora, you are my everything. If it's in my power to do it, I will. If it's not, then I am certain you will."

Pandora laughs softly. "Perhaps."

"Come, we should probably return to the castle. It's been nearly half the day."

"I slept that long?"

"Yes, you did."

She lifts her violet gaze up to him, studying him for a moment, feeling him shift under her scrutiny. "You used magic to make me sleep."

He reaches out to caress her cheek lightly. "I did."

She nods.

He tightens his arm around her. "I love you. You know I would not have used my magic on you if I didn't feel you needed it."

"I know, Gren, I am not mad. I trust you completely; I am just tired."

He kisses her forehead before turning, creating a portal to their bedroom at the castle. He leads her through and over to the bed. "Then rest more. The castle will survive without you. I will cover things."

She crawls into the bed and curls up, drawing a pillow into her arms as she hugs it close.

Rendgren sits on the bed beside her, caressing her hair gently, catching the tears creeping into her eyes as she drifts back to sleep. He sits with her for an hour before rising, knowing he needs to check in with the castle.

Fourteen

The Golden Surge

Two weeks later, somewhere in Spokane, a gold dragon arrives, having jumped through gates across the realms. He shifts to his human form and heads towards the city he can see. Wandering through Krine and hitting the public notice boards, he looks over the wanted posters, searching for something in particular. He pulls down a tattered poster for the Red Phantom, turning as the town crier works his way through town with daily announcements. The dragon looks over the price on the Phantom's head, realizing rather suddenly, if he was worth this much gold, the town crier would have mentioned it. He scans the nearby market and moves to the closest lady. He bows, noticing her clothing indicating she has some measure of wealth behind her. "Excuse me, m'lady. Might I have a moment of your time?"

The woman turns, looking over at the well-dressed man bowing to her, taller than her, which isn't hard, wavy blonde hair, and blue eyes with a decent build and frame. She smiles in delight at what she sees before her. "Well, that depends on what you intend to do with that moment of time, good sir."

He chuckles, giving her a wink. "I suppose we could discuss that, but all I am seeking are some answers to questions I have."

"Darn, and here I thought you would ask for more."

"I would never dare to ask for more of a lady such as you."

She flutters her fan slightly. "Oh my, well, ask away, good sir."

He pulls out the poster. "I am new to this realm and was wandering by the notice board. Who is this Red Phantom? These posters seem weathered and old."

"That's because they are. He's the current ruler of Oblait, and the fines against him were dropped."

"Wait, you're letting a wanted felon rule the land there?"

"Indeed. He and his wife brought peace to the land. The Royals of each Kingdom pardoned him."

"So he's still the strongest dragon in all the lands?"

"Well, I suppose, but his wife is no pushover either, and she's the one that tamed him, so it's all perspective, I believe. All you need to do is look at her, and you can understand how she did. She is stunning and powerful."

"Fascinating. I believe I need to meet them."

"Well, it will be a few weeks before they reopen the court. The Queen lost her mother, and the castle's in mourning, so they have shut Teshem down for the month."

"Interesting. Her mother, you say?"

"Yes, everyone felt the loss. The bells rang all over the realm for an hour the day she died."

"Thank you for your information."

"You are most welcome. Do come again when you want more than questions."

He reaches out to take her hand gently, kissing the back of it. "Thank you m'lady. I might just take you up on that offer."

The man departs from the town and transforms into his dragon form. He soars through the skies, heading for Oblait. Arriving the next day, he surveys the city, noting the black banners at half mast, the absence of guards, and the castle draped in black. Hovering over the city, he senses other dragons; two swiftly approaching the castle and three within its confines. He touches down on the houses adjacent to the castle, some of the bricks crumbling beneath his weight. His eyes lock onto the two elves before him. People scatter but he ignores them, knowing they are not who he seeks. "I am here to challenge the Red Phantom for his rights to the throne. Step aside."

The two elves shift into their Draconic form, both half the size of the gold perched before them. "Sorry, we can't do that. Leave the city now."

"Priceless. A blue and purple protecting a red."

"We protect our Royals, no matter the color of the scales in this realm."

Pandora hears the demand and places her book aside. She rises and leaves her chamber to the main balcony, feeling a rage bubbling within. Within a few minutes, she steps out to face the dragon that sits outside on the top of her people's houses. She narrows her eyes dangerously as she studies him carefully. Her voice is eerily cold as she addresses rogue dragon. "The castle is in mourning for another two weeks. Go away."

"Ah there is the Queen. They said you were a beauty, and they were not wrong. You will make a fine consolation prize. I will enjoy bedding you."

Myrsky and Violetarion cough. "Consolation prize? Our Queen? Clearly, you didn't ask the right questions or do any sort of research when you arrived in this realm."

Rendgren pauses in his training as he feels the sudden well of rage from his wife, finding her out on the main balcony. He reaches outward from her and senses Myr and Violet, along with an unknown dragon, suspecting whatever is happening can't be good. "Something's wrong with my wife." Rendgren hands him the sword and leaves the barracks quickly.

Pandora's eyes glow softly, an edge of annoyance entering her voice. "This realm is under a banner of peace, Dragon; *Back down* NOW!"

"Well, you are feisty. I will enjoy that when you are mine. Where is your King, my Queen?"

Pandora's voice becomes chill as her anger grows at this dragon, breaking rules she had set in place ten years ago. She hisses in anger. "Not your Queen. If I was, you would respect the rules of this realm and that the castle is in mourning!"

"Rules of any realm are as follows. You can challenge the ruler whenever you like, and if you win, you take the throne and all it entails, which would include you."

Rendgren steps onto the balcony, placing his hands on his wife's shoulder. "Shhh love, deep breaths, stay calm."

"There he is. The legendary Red Phantom." The gold dragon looks over the red with disdain that such a legend is now living a life of luxury.

"Retired, thank you very much."

Pandora clenches her fists. "I AM calm, Gren, but getting furious fast."

"Retired or not. I WANT your throne and your wife."

Rendgren's shoulders sink. "Oh Bloody hell. Of all the places, you had to go there?"

"What's the matter Red? Are you scared of a gold?"

"Hell yes, but not you. Of my wife, and since she's the one that *took* this throne, she's the one you will face." He kisses Pandora on the cheek and steps back. "Have at it, love, teach the whelp a lesson, but be careful, judging by his size; he's getting up there in age and power."

Pandora's eyes narrow on Rendgren momentarily, returning them to the gold dragon challenging her. She clambers up the balcony railing and steps off. Purple lights surround her as she shifts into her dragon while descending before lifting up above the one that challenged her.

"Wait, you're a gold, bedding a red?"

"Colors don't matter here, Dragon and the castles in mourning! RESPECT has been requested, which you ignored. Now, I am going to teach you what respect actually means in our realm."

Myrsky and Violetarion cheer beneath her. "Yes, smack down incoming by our Queen."

Pandora roars, allowing the rage of her emotions to overtake her as the city shakes below her. The cheers of her people echo in the city beyond as her gold scales fade, her body becoming purple cosmic energy, with the sun glowing deep in the center of her core.

"What the hell?"

Rendgren chuckles. "Welcome to our world, where a mystic is the force to be reckoned with. She's the gold I am afraid of, and now she's pissed."

Pandora tucks her wings and dives at the dragon's head, who ducks it easily with a laugh. "Stupid dragon, you missed."

Pandora glides along his body and latches onto his tail, her claws sinking in deep as she draws on her power, lifting herself up and bursting forward, catching his yelp as he is suddenly dragged with her.

Rendgren laughs at the shock in his expression. "She didn't miss; you just misread her target of attack. She won't risk her people in town." He jumps over the edge as well, shifts, and follows his wife and her prize across the lake. Violetarion and Myrsky take to the air and trail behind, not wanting to miss this.

The gold beats his wings, trying to pull against the one with a death grip on his tail, but finds the power pulling him too strong. He feels her barrel roll with his tail clutched in her grasp, spinning him wildly, and feels a faint hint of doubt creeping in at what he has done.

Pandora ascends high above the lake, her wings beating forcefully against the air, the strength of her rage lifting him as if he were nothing more than a mere mortal. She scans the forest edge along the opposite shore before diving. Just moments before striking the ground, she releases her cargo. It slams into the earth, bouncing along and tearing down trees in its path upon impact. Swiftly spinning around, she breathes fire on the targeted dragon, his scales melting beneath her mystic fires before lifting up once more into the sky.

Rendgren settles on the shore with Myrsky and Violetarion.

The gold dragon rises to his feet, experiencing the sting of her breath upon his body, an entirely unfamiliar sensation for him. Narrowing his eyes on the Queen, he inhales deeply and breathes fire in her direction as she makes another charge. The flames flow through her cosmic body, seeming to have no effect on her as she continues her relentless assault.

She strikes his neck, her teeth sinking into it as her claws dig into his shoulder. Her momentum slams his head into the ground, taking him off his feet and forcing his body to roll over. She swiftly bounces away, taking to the air once more.

He growls in rage and snaps at her but finds her already out of range, leaving him nothing to latch onto. He spins around to face her as he grapples with the realization that this Queen is unnaturally quick and outmaneuvering him.

Rendgren watches the battle intently. "I have to say, after two weeks of having her mood swings directed at me, it is refreshing to see it focused elsewhere."

Myrsky shakes his head. "I feel for ya man; a woman angry at you is one thing, but a mystic... This dragon is about to find out why the realm is at peace. None of us want to face her."

Violetarion chuckles. "None of us are crazy enough to you mean. No offense there, my King."

"None taken Violet. I wouldn't face her either if I had the choice."

Pandora's rage grows as she rises and hovers, watching the gold dragon right himself, reading his thoughts of retreat. "Oh no, I am not done with you." She plummets towards him, streams of purple trailing behind her as she aims once again for his head before twisting and barrel-rolling along his side. Her claws tear through his right wing before she grasps his tail once more as she passes it, yanking him off the ground.

Rendgren cringes slightly. "Oooh, this is gonna hurt. I would have thought he would have caught on to the same move used twice on him."

Myrsky shakes his head and looks away while Violetarion watches in awe. "Well, to be fair, it was slightly different. Either way, you are correct. I would not want to be him right now."

Pandora pulls the gold high into the air as he struggles to free himself, attempting to spin around and bite the claws that hold him. However, she shifts her position skillfully, preventing him from making a connection. Hovering in place, a thousand feet in the sky, she glares down at the gold in her claws, power billowing from her. Suddenly, she turns around, making a beeline straight for the ground.

The gold dragon intensifies his struggle, beating his one good wing as their speed increases. Fear and panic grip him as he realizes the ground is closing in at a rapid rate, knowing there is a genuine possibility he is not surviving this fight. At the fifty-foot mark, he closes his eyes and braces for the impact of death, only to have his breath knocked out of him as he is snapped sideways suddenly, feeling just how close the earth got to him.

Pandora pivots around, her wings beating hard to keep her in place as his body slams into trees and uproots them. She lifts him back into the air and hovers one hundred feet above the ground. There, she releases him, watching him plummet to the land below. Following suit, she descends and sees him struggling to crawl away in pain, binding him to the ground with strands of purple light. Pandora lands beside him, cosmic purple energy fading back to gold scales as she glares at him. "Forfeit."

The gold narrows his eyes and draws in a jagged breath, breathing dragon fire over Pandora. "No!"

Pandora's eyes glow with rage as the flames encompass her, further angering her.

Myrsky shakes his head. "Damn, he's stubborn."

Rendgren chuckles. "He'll figure it out. I did."

"We all did, my King."

"Two can play that way, Dragon, but my breath's gonna hurt." Pandora breathes on him, hearing his scream of agony as his scales melt beneath her breath, mystic power blessed with the power of the sun. She stands up tall, places her front foot on his head, and presses it down. "Show respect and BOW." The purple bands surrounding him tighten, forcing him to bow before her. "That's better. Now, you have two weeks to think about what you have done. You either convert and accept the rules of the land, or I send you back to the realm you came from Askookattorhenrensurge, otherwise known as the Golden Surge or Henri. And if you return after I send you back, you will die. If you harm or kill ANY of my people while you lie here and think about what respect actually is, my bindings will cut through you like you are butter. I hope that's clear enough for you." She watches him narrow his eyes as he lifts his head defiantly to glare at her. "Also on a more personal level." She slaps him across the face, watching his head snap at the force of it. "The only one bedding me will be my husband. I will end you before I let you touch me." She takes to the sky and leaves the dragon bound there, returning to the castle.

Rendgren approaches the confined dragon with Myrsky and Violetarion following. "Well now Surge. I guess my wife gets to keep her throne after pretty much destroying you, pup. And she used the mother tone with your true name. Even I haven't gotten that yet, although I believe our wyrmling has come close a few times. You know the only reason you're alive is because she willed it. I am pretty certain that the thousand-foot plummet would have killed you."

The Golden Surge sinks to the ground beneath the bands that hold him. "What the hell is she?"

"She is a mystic and a gold dragon. The most powerful creature in the realm, and if she wants to mourn in peace, she gets it."

"What the hell is a mystic?"

Myrsky starts laughing. "You have no mystics where you come from? That would explain your mistake."

"No, we don't."

"Do you at least know what a seer is?"

"Yes, one with the ability to foresee the future."

"Well, a mystic is that, but with the power to rewrite the future. Add a bit of magic; perhaps some pure chaos; the ability to read thoughts, and then some, and you have yourself, our Queen. You were never touching her. No one does."

Rendgren chuckles. "That is not true! Before her mother died, I got to touch her all the time. I just know better than to pick a fight with her."

Violetarion chokes. "My King!"

"Just stating the facts, my dear purple."

His eyes darken on Rendgren. "How does a gold willingly lie with a red?"

"Because in this world, colors are simply the color of our scales. It's what's in the heart that matters. My wife, child, and I all follow the Sun Goddess Raya. Bringer of peace and light. You would have done wise to learn that before attacking the champions of one of the favored goddesses in the realm."

"Yes, they even have it burned on their scales, man. Any city across the continent would have told you that she brought peace to these lands ten years ago. The world loves her, and you just challenged her. Good luck surviving here on Cantara. You're better off going home as no one will want you here once they find out what you have done."

Rendgren turns to the pair. "More like... We brought peace."

"Sorry, my King, we know it was her; you were just the messenger."

Rendgren mutters under his breath. "Yes, you're right. On that note, I need to return to my wife to make sure she's calmed down."

Myrsky and Violetarion nod. "We'll return with you."

"Wait! You can't leave me here bound like this! What about dragon hunters?"

"Sorry, Surge, you are bound for two weeks. I don't have the power to defy my wife's magic. I guess you better hope they don't find you. Something you should have thought about before you picked a fight." Rendgren takes to the air and flies back across the lake, hearing the cheers of the people as he lands in the courtyard, sensing immediately for his wife and finding her in their room. The others land with him as he turns to face them. "Thank you for standing and defending the castle."

"Anytime, my King. Never thought we would ever see the day, but we love your rule and will always defend you and the people of this city. And seeing your woman fight; that is a sight to behold."

"Yes, that it is." He shakes both their hands and heads into the castle, straight to his wife. He pushes the door open, seeing Junior and Spider curled up next to her as she sits and calmly reads a book as if nothing has happened. "My love?"

"Gren."

"Everything alright?"

"Yes, it's fine."

Rendgren moves to the bed and sits down. He places a hand beneath her chin and lifts her gaze to his, immediately noticing the rage simmering below the surface. "Are you sure?"

She closes her eyes with a sigh and tosses the book to the end of the bed before crawling into his arms. "No. Why would someone challenge a castle in mourning?"

"He wasn't challenging the castle, dear; he was challenging me. Some dragons don't believe in following protocol. I was like that once till I met you."

"No, Gren, you still had standards, even when you were the Red Phantom. This dragon does not."

"I will never admit that, my dear."

"You don't have to. I can see it."

He kisses the top of her head gently, tightening his hold on her. "I've missed you."

"I know, Gren, I'm sorry. It's just hard to envision this place without her."

"I understand, my love. Only time will heal that."

She shifts herself to look up at him before reaching to caress his cheek lightly, her hands cupping his face as she rises to kiss his lips, feeling the rush of emotions at his touch.

Junior growls in disgust and jumps off the bed. He races from the room, followed closely by Spider.

Rendgren groans softly, magically closing the door after them. "My love, are you certain?"

She nods, pulling him down into the bed with her. "I am."

"Oh gawd Pandora." He follows her down, deftly undoing her ties as his hands wander. Pushing her robes off her while, he feels her touch seeking along his robes. He pulls his ties loose, shivering in delight as her fingers find his skin, finding her lips once more. Each of them rapidly become lost to each other, craving the touch, the connection, and the love they have been missing the past two weeks.

On the shores of Thetis Lake, the Golden Surge observes boats floating by. Most mortals aboard chuckle at the dragon bound on the shore, surrounded by broken trees, his scales singed with mystic fire. He glowers at them, struggling against the bonds placed upon him, but despite using all his power, they remain unbroken. Shapeshifting is out of the question, as the strands keep him in his dragon form. He growls in frustration at the fact that the Royals are so certain of the bindings that they haven't even bothered to come check on him. "You there. In the boat."

"Who, us?"

"Yes, go get the Queen."

"Sorry, dragon, the castle's in mourning."

"It's been a week."

"Yes, and your punishment is for two." They unravel fishing lines and throw them into the water.

"Look, it's only a matter of time before the dragon hunters find me."

"Haven't you figured it out yet, dragon? There are no hunters. Dragons and mortals are protected. No one's willing to go against the Queen. She deals efficiently with any dragons who don't comply, as you experienced first hand. Also, any mortals who challenge her laws are banished to Hadria. No one is risking their lives over you."

"Sounds like a tyrannical rule to me."

"No, we had a tyrannical king before her. She just has no tolerance for those who harm for fun, put her people in danger, or break the peace pact she made with all the other kingdoms and dragons. It seems us mortals are worth the same as you, dragon. How does it feel?"

The Golden Surge snarls slightly, trying to shift under the bindings. "Then find me another mystic."

"No can do. The only other one in the realm is her son, and he's still a pup. Mystics were essentially extinct until she was born about thirty years ago. Her parents sold her to King Zane when she was nine, and the realm is lucky she didn't cross over under his tutelage. Pretty certain that would have ended the world. Rumor has it, the woman that just died was the one that kept her on the straight and narrow, a mother to her at the castle. Until she met the Phantom, and he stole her from the King. Boy, was the King pissed! Two years later, the pair returned, champions of Raya, and dethroned Zane. Bringing about an era of peace which we love. That was ten years ago, and you're not about to change it. If you had done even a touch of research, you would have known this and been having tea with the Queen instead of being bound by her."

"Wait... The Queen that put me here is only thirty years old?"

"That she is, and she was a mortal before she became that dragon. She is also the first mystic to live past twenty as most burn hot and bright, and then they die, according to history. It makes you wonder what power she will have when she hits the Phantom's age. No wonder he bows to her."

"How is it possible that she was a mortal and now a dragon the size she is?"

"No one really knows, but what we do know is that the Sun Goddess Raya is involved because she burned her symbol on all three of them."

"A thirty-year-old whelp, unbelievable."

"Yes, and that whelp trounced you."

Patchouli

Two weeks later, Pandora moves through the castle, her mind still numb but knowing she needs to move forward. She pads through to the main balcony and steps out into the sunlight. Her eyes survey the city beneath her, watching as they go about their business. She lifts her hands, sending waves of purple magic through the kingdom, as the banners return to their original green coloration and rise to full mast. The castle's black shroud fades as the people in the city cheer in support of their Queen standing on the balcony removing the mourning bans.

The Golden Surge catches the sounds as they carry across the water, lifting his gaze to the shadows of the city on the other side of the lake, feeling his rage grow at being bound for two weeks.

Pandora steps back inside after a few minutes, finding Rendgren standing silently behind her, understanding she put him through hell. She places her arms around him and rests her head on his shoulder. "Thank you, Gren. I am sorry I have been difficult this past month."

He wraps his arms around her and kisses the top of her head. "Love, you may have been a touch difficult, but you have a valid reason and I am not going to hold it against you. Life will not always be easy. We are going to struggle; things can get rough. I know; I have lived for over a thousand years. But we will get through whatever is thrown our way. I want you to understand that I am here for you, no matter what."

Pandora nods, taking comfort in his embrace. "I think I am going to wander around town today."

"Are you certain? You lifted the bans, but that doesn't mean you have to go out there."

"I know, Gren, but I want to."

"Do you want me with you?"

She shakes her head. "No. I am just going to lie in the center of town and listen to the chatter while the kids play. It will distract my mind."

He steps back, lifting her chin to study her eyes, uncertain that she should be doing this, but knowing if she's set her mind to it, there is little he can do to change it. "Take some guards with you."

"I will. Thank you."

He kisses her gently. "Have fun. I will see you when you return."

She smiles, caressing his cheek lightly. "You will see me before I return, because you will be watching from this balcony the whole time."

He chuckles. "You might be right about that."

"I am, Gren. Now, I am going to the city." She squeezes his hand and walks away, making her way down to Kivu to inform him she needs guards. Once they arrive, she strolls through the city, observing people stopping and smiling at her. Some even offer hugs, and she accepts them, feeling the emotions welling within. However, she pushes them aside as she heads towards the city center. Children squeal in delight at her path and race through the city, calling their friends. Once she arrives, she shifts her shape and lies down, hearing the thoughts of those around her and allowing the happiness in the city to fill her. She closes her eyes as the children swarm her, playing with her as her tail swishes around for them while one foot creates a cage to catch them in.

Pandora feels the joy of the children soothe her hurt soul, understanding for her, this is the best medicine as it overrides her pain. A few hours later, she rises and shifts back to her mortal form, laughing as the kids groan in dismay. She hugs a few of them that come forth with their arms out, holding them close for a moment. "I will return next Saturday. Thank you, for all the happiness you have given me, little ones." She gives a slight bow to the parents and heads back to the castle, a slight bounce to her step and a cheerfulness she has not felt this past month. As she approaches the doors, she glances up, feeling her husband stepping back into the shadows to hide the fact that he was indeed watching her. *'Gren, I saw that!'*

'Saw what, my love? I am simply enjoying some fresh air.'

'Sure you were.' She laughs out loud, causing Kivu to look up from his post in shock. "My Queen?"

"It's alright, Kivu." She moves over to hug him. "I am perfectly happy. Thank you for being here." She turns and runs into the castle, leaving a shocked Kivu and four guards staring after her.

The next morning, after breakfast, Rendgren creates a portal across the lake as Pandora steps through it to deal with the rogue dragon waiting there. She narrows her eyes on him, feeling Rendgren step in behind her protectively.

The Golden Surge struggles as she approaches. "Let me out of here! Do you know the risk you have placed me in?"

Pandora remains silent as she approaches and stands before him, studying the dragon carefully. She pulls his thoughts out to play with, flickers of them wrapping around her while she sorts through them.

"What the hell?"

"I would be quiet, Surge; my wife is looking into your thoughts and lifelines to see if it's worth keeping you here or if we are sending you back."

Pandora's eyes glow softly, shifting between the strands of purple filtering from her hands to the images as some of them change, each one showing her different paths as her frown grows.

Rendgren shakes his head. "A frown is not good; it looks like you are going home."

"You don't have the power to send me back."

"No, but we have friends that do."

Pandora continues to focus as twenty minutes pass before the images fade. She turns her back to the dragon and walks to the lake. She picks up a few rocks and tosses them in, watching them skip across the water, deliberating her thoughts.

Rendgren follows, placing a hand on the small of her back. "Talk to me, love."

"He's a risk. He's hot-tempered and has no remorse for what he has done. His only remorse is that he was defeated by a thirty-year-old whelp queen. His rage is uncontrolled and simmers just below the surface, and he still wants you defeated. I don't want him here, Gren."

"Sounds a lot like I used to be, Pandora."

She looks up at him and shakes her head. "Yours was different."

"It wasn't that much different. It only changed after I met you."

"That's where you're wrong Gren; you had rage, yes, but it was controlled.

You were also done with the world and seeking a change, hence being retired. This is deliberately uncontrolled. He wants the fights. He seeks the challenge and the thrill of defeating another dragon."

"So we send him back to his plane."

"His mate is here."

"Damn, really? Are you certain?"

"Yes, I am. I looked at all the threads. I could not rewrite her out."

"Who is it?"

"Patchouli."

"Oh bloody hell; are you serious?"

"Yes, unfortunately. I will need to talk to her before I move forward with this decision."

"That's just what I need. The bloody Paladin Protector, King Ludy, breathing down my neck because I sent him the risk when we should have sent it home. Fantastic." He rolls his eyes in dismay.

"I haven't made my decision yet, Gren; we can still send him home."

"You know Patches is gonna want to meet him."

"Yes... He rejects her in almost all the threads, and I don't want her to go through that. But she needs to know."

Rendgren reaches out to caress her cheek. "I will admit, I felt the same way when I was bonding with a mortal. I was ready to toss you out the door as soon as we dethroned Zane. Perhaps Patches could do the same."

She laughs softly, grabbing his hand and kissing it. "No, you weren't; you were just frustrated with me, Gren. You were never going to kick me out."

He kisses her gently. "Perhaps, but I will never admit to that. I just think we should give Patches a chance."

"Are you advocating for him?"

"No, my dear. I am advocating for love and that love being able to change a dragon from who they were."

"You were ready for change; he is not."

The Golden Surge pushes against the threads, hearing their words carry back to him. "Are you saying I will reject my mate? I would never do such a thing."

Pandora turns to look at the bound gold. "That's exactly what I am saying, and she is a super sweet dragon. I am not putting her through your abuse."

"I would never abuse my mate."

Pandora smiles and walks back to the dragon, calling forth an image of Patchouli, her long wavy blonde hair, her amber eyes, her petite frame, spinning her around slowly in front of him.

"That's my mate. Hot damn!"

Pandora adjusts the image, shifting the human into her dragon form, about a third of the size of Pandora's form, her red scales glittering brightly in the sun.

"What the Hell! She's a bloody Red! There is NO WAY my mate is a red!"

Sadness flickers across Pandora's features. "Exactly. You have made your position very clear. Therefore, you get to reflect some more while I go talk to her."

"You cannot leave me here!"

Pandora snaps at him. "I can leave you here for as long as I bloody well like. Had you respected that the castle was in mourning, you would be free, but you didn't. Now you will suffer the consequences of your actions. Hell, I don't ever have to untie you. I can send you back to your realm bound. How does that sound, Askookattorhenrensurge? Would you be as safe there as you are here? I doubt it. Now, I would suggest you seriously consider where your thoughts go in the next few hours because I WILL ship you back, NEVER to meet your destined mate if they don't change. IS that clear?" Pandora turns to Rendgren, not even waiting for an answer. "Alright, Gren, take us to King Ludy."

Rendgren creates a portal before them, watching his wife step through before glancing back at The Golden Surge, seeing the rage in his eyes. He gives a shake of his head before he follows her through, hearing the dragon's roar as he closes the portal behind him.

Rendgren leads the way up to the castle, standing at the gates as one of the guards narrows his eyes on him.

Pandora frowns in confusion before glancing up at her husband, seeing the wide grin on his face. "Did you do something the last time you were here?"

"I would never, my dear."

"You are lying to me."

Rendgren kisses her cheek. "I am not. It was the first time I was here."

"Gren!"

"I love you."

Pandora rolls her eyes, seeing Runestone approaching the gate. "Greetings, Miss Rune."

"Queen Pandora, what brings you to Hontby? We were not expecting you so soon after lifting your bans."

"Rogue dragon. Patchouli's mate."

"Damn, really? We heard that a dragon attacked the castle in mourning."

"Yes, he's a risk, a fighter, and hates reds. I have sorted his threads, and he rejects her in most of them, but I wanted Patches and Ludy to know if we don't banish him."

"Right then. Let's go to Ludy."

"Thanks, Rune."

"Anytime, my Queen."

"Just Pandora, Rune."

Runestone nods and leads her into the castle, winding her way to a casual room, knocking on the door and opening it, seeing Ludy on the floor with two children crawling all over him. The boy is the taller of the two, blonde hair and dark blue eyes like his father, and the girl, white blonde hair and blue eyes like her mother. "Ludy, Zalgren and Pandora are here to see you."

Ludy shifts his gaze to the pair, attempting to de-tangle himself from the miniatures of himself and Runestone and sit up. "I didn't know you were planning on paying a visit; you should have brought Junior. Trystan and Phen would have loved it."

Pandora smiles. "Next time. This is business."

Ludy sighs. "Alright then." He kisses each of his kids. "I will be back, kids. Go play with your Uncle Myke."

"Sorry, Ludy. I promise next time will be playtime."

"Deal!" He watches his kids race off before rising and leading them to an office. He settles into a chair and looks over at the pair as Runestone moves to sit beside him. "Right, first things first. How are you, Pandora? The world feels your loss."

"Thank you, Ludy. I will always miss her, but I am taking it one day at a time."

"That's good to hear. We are here for you if you need it."

"I know. Thank you."

"Now, what business brings you to my Kingdom?"

"Rogue dragon. Uncontrolled temper with no remorse. A risk I want to send home. He hates reds and apparently one gold now...The whelp Queen, as he calls me, because I trounced him. He also still wants Gren dead."

Rendgren chuckles. "You did more than trounce him, love; he was actually panicking for his life."

"And so he should for what he has done."

Ludy shakes his head. "That bad, huh? So let's send him home."

"If it were only that easy. He is Patchouli's mate."

"Oh damn, are you serious?"

"Yes." She lifts her hands as purple lights flicker in the room, showing the images of the future, of the rejection Patchouli faces, writing the thread with a new rejection. The destruction the dragon in question causes, moving the threads again, with a similar outcome. "She needs to know. I can't just send her mate back."

"So what I am understanding is, if Patches accepts him, you're sending the problem child to my lands? Is this the one that attacked your castle in mourning?"

"The very same, and yes, that's pretty much it. I left him bound on the shores of Thetis for two weeks. He is less than impressed."

Ludy sighs and looks to his wife, Runestone. "What do you think, love?"

Runestone looks between her husband and Pandora. "I think Patches needs to know and perhaps meet him. It's going to be on her whether we ship him back, but we should collect the group just in case."

"Right, let's get her summoned."

Runestone nods and fades from the room.

"Thank you, Ludy. Gren, could you go get Moo and Jeo for us?"

"Of course, love. I will be right back." He creates a portal to the isle of Lochyae, returning five minutes later with both of them.

Pandora greets Jeodina and Kittymoo, hugging them both. "Jeo, Moo. I hope all is well."

"Better than you by the sounds of it. Rogue dragon?"

"Yes, but we haven't decided whether to ship him home because Patches is his mate."

Ten minutes later, Runestone returns with Patchouli, who looks around in confusion at everyone in the room before turning and bowing to her King, uncertainty laced in her voice. "King Ludy. Did I do something wrong?"

Ludy rises and takes her hand. "No Patchouli, but we have an important matter to discuss. Please sit."

Patchouli moves to the seat beside Ludy. "This seems serious."

"Yes, you can say that. Pandora, the floor is yours."

Pandora smiles sadly at Patchouli. She explains the situation about the rogue dragon that attacked the castle, sharing that they returned today after binding him to the shores of the lake for two weeks. She emphasizes that even with time to reflect, he still harbors the desire to kill Rendgren and claim her as a consolation prize, showing no remorse for his actions.

Patchouli shakes her head in confusion. "What does this have to do with me?"

Pandora lifts her hand, calling forth the image of the dragon bound and one of his mortal form beside it. "Because he's your mate. I don't want to see you hurt Patches, but he rejects you in most of the threads I have seen."

Patchouli moves forward to touch the image, feeling the call of the bond even through it. "But not all of them?"

"No, not all of them."

"Which one has he not?"

Pandora glances at Rendgren, shifting her hands and showing the vision in question. "It is time-based Patches, and those are a risk, especially a hundred-year span. It may or may not pan out."

"I am willing to take that risk."

"So be it. Shall we return to Oblait?"

"We shall."

Pandora nods to Ludy. "Thank you, Ludy."

"Anytime. Send Rune home when you are done with her."

"I will."

Rendgren creates a portal to the shores where they left the dragon, watching the five women walk through before following and closing it behind him.

The Golden Surge fights against the bonds as the portal opens before him, his eyes narrowing on the whelp Queen, darkening even further at the sight of Patchouli, supposedly his mate. A Red. Disgust fills him at the thought. His eyes drift to the other three, sensing one is a dragon, and feeling the power of the other two who step to the side. He catches the Red Phantom taking up the rear and closing the portal after them, stepping back away from the five women that approach him. He growls under his breath, narrowing his eyes on him, feeling him weak for letting women do the dirty work around here as he resumes fighting the bindings.

"Patches, this is the Golden Surge, Surge as we have been calling him, but he goes by Henri as human form. Surge, your mate Patchouli."

"I don't have a mate, and she's certainly NOT a Red if I did."

Patchouli turns to Pandora. "May I?"

"Of course, he's bound. If he tries to harm you though, those bindings will cut through him."

She nods and approaches, walking around him, and looks over the dragon before her. His scent wafts over her, taking in a deep breath as she closes her eyes and sways a touch before forcing her attention to the matter at hand. Noticing the melted scales, she reaches out to touch them tenderly, feeling him jump and growl, attempting to get away from her. She runs her fingers lightly over them, shaking her head at his injuries, before moving around to the wing. Fingering the damage, having seen the battle in the vision Pandora showed her. She knows a dragon that can not fly is a dead dragon. Humming softly, she works her fingers along the first tear as she magically mends the rip, fusing and binding them back together.

The Golden Surge fights her every step of the way, calling her names and doing his best to avoid being touched by the filthy red.

Patchouli pays no mind to him, spending the two hours she needs to mend his wing. Once she is done, she turns to Pandora. "Alright, Queen Pandora, mark him and send him back."

The Golden Surge looks up with shock. "Wait... what?"

"And so it will be done." Pandora moves forward, touching a scale on him, burning MFD into it in purple writing.

"What the Hell is that?"

"Marked for Death. Meaning, you come back to this realm again, you will die within twenty-four hours. You have broken the laws of the land and are no longer welcome in this realm. Best of luck, Surge."

"NO WAIT!"

Pandora steps back, watching as Runestone creates a time portal. Moo and Jeo join hands, adjusting the runes around the portal, seeking the timeline that he came from. Once they find it, they nod to Pandora. Pandora looks at the Golden Surge, gives a shake of her head, before magically unbinding him, and using her power to pick him up and toss him through.

"Noooo!" The Golden Surge spins to return, only to have the portal slam shut behind him.

"And so it is done. It will be approximately a hundred years before he returns here."

Tears slide down Patchouli's face. "And when he comes back, you will remove the mark before he dies...right?"

Pandora moves over and hugs her, holding her tight. "Patches, you have the power to remove that mark with your mate bond. You did the right thing."

Patchouli cries against her. "I know. I understand he is not ready. His insults were very clear; it's still very hard."

"Our realm differs from most Patches. In a lot of them, the color of scales matter, and red and gold are natural-born enemies. Even Gren was unhappy when Raya turned me into a gold."

"I was not!"

Pandora lifts his gaze to his. "So you didn't narrow your eyes on my gold body and ask the goddess what she had done in a surly tone."

Rendgren starts to say something before opting to remain silent to the amusement of the others.

"I thought so. What I am saying, Patches, is he will find he will crave your touch again; he will hear your song in his sleep. It will haunt him and call to him, enough so that he will re-evaluate his views on reds and come looking for you. Only then will he be ready to accept you as his mate."

"Thank you, Pandora; I don't think I could handle a true rejection from him."

"I wouldn't let him Patches. That's why I gave you this option. Now, I have shed enough tears this past month for all of us. Let's go spend an afternoon together, shopping in town or something."

Rendgren mutters under his breath. "Right, there goes another one of my dragon hoards."

The others laugh at his comment. "Oooh, that sounds like Rendgren is buying!"

Pandora smiles and moves to Rendgren, caressing his cheek lightly. "I love you, Gren! I will be home later."

Rendgren mumbles good-naturally. "Just don't go over one hoard!"

"Understood." She turns and moves over to the others. "Let's go girls."

Runestone smiles. "Pick a town."

Pandora ponders it for a moment. "Let's go to Rixlen and see what the elves are creating."

"Perfect!"

Rendgren rolls his eyes and portals home while the girl's head to Rixlen.

They wander the Elven market, looking at the wares that are offered, enjoying a casual girls-only shopping trip before Runestone spies a fortune telling shop. "Ooh, Pandora, let's go see!"

The five push the door open and wander in, exploring the variety of items on display. Pandora stops at a semi-revealing outfit, fingering the sheer fabric. Martha's voice filters into her mind, recalling her instructing Habo that she is to remain covered. Moo walks up and places a hand on her shoulder. "Rendgren would love that."

Pandora blushes. "It's a bit see-through, don't you think?"

"That's the point, Pandora."

Runestone chuckles. "You have never dressed in something like this for Zalgren?"

Pandora shakes her head. "No."

"Then I will buy it for you."

"It's fine. I can purchase it."

Just then, an elf dressed in a similar outfit walks out from the back, shaking rattles and a cup full of dice. "Come dearies, come and get a glimpse of your future by Gaelira."

Runestone gently pushes Pandora forward. "Tell us about her future."

Pandora sends a friendly scowl Runestone's way before moving to sit in the chair.

Gaelira rolls the dice on the table and rubs her chin.

Pandora looks at the dice in confusion. "How can those tell the future?"

"Well, it depends on the roll, dearie, and how the numbers come up. Yours are clearly confused. I believe I need to get the crystal ball out."

"Mine are confused? It looks like a 6, 3, and a 1 to me." Pandora catches the muffled laughter behind her.

Gaelira slides the crystal ball over, draping a cloth over it, and murmurs some words before dramatically pulling the cloth off and peering into the ball.

Pandora leans over and peers into it as well. "I see only a glass ball."

"Give it time, dearie, the image needs to form."

"We don't have time, though. The diplomat Dawnelda is going to walk through the door requesting our presence, and I need to buy an outfit."

"I highly doubt that she will, dearie. Now, please be patient and stop distracting me."

Pandora sighs and places her hands in her lap, hearing the bell chime about the door.

Dawnelda gives a nod to the fortune teller, who stares at her in shock before bowing to the others in the shop. "Greetings unto Queen Pandora, Queen Runestone, High Council Kittymoo, Diplomat Jeodina, and your red guest. Queen Diadradey has requested your presence immediately."

Gaelira jumps up in shock, knocking the chair over behind her. "As in *the mystic,* Queen Pandora?"

Patchouli bursts out laughing. "Yes, I would have thought the violet eyes gave that away."

Pandora nods to Gaelira, patting her hand gently. "You will get there, but I really would like to purchase the dress."

Gaelira nods and moves to the outfit, pulling it off the hook and packaging it up. "Of course, Your Majesty. My apologies."

Pandora smiles and hands over some coins. "No need to apologize. It's not like we were branding our presence. Someone else did that for us. We were simply having a girl's day out."

"Thank you for gracing my shop with your presence!"

"You're most welcome; it was entertaining." Pandora nods and follows the diplomat out with the rest of the girls.

Dawnelda leads them through the streets to where the carriage awaits. She gestures for them to enter as she steps up to take the reins.

Runestone cracks up now, laughter escaping as the others chime in. "Oh my Pandora, you really do need to get out more!"

"What's that supposed to mean?"

"It means Zalgren keeps you locked in too much...I see only a glass ball! You know a lot rely on those to foretell the future. They don't just get it in their mind like you do."

Pandora shakes her head. "Really, you can't be serious. They wait for a glass ball or dice to tell them something?"

"Yes, they do."

"That sounds like a lot of work."

"We can't all be mystics Pandora. Some of us work for magic."

"I feel bad for the poor fortune teller when she realized just who was in her shop."

"Oh, don't feel that bad; if she could foresee the future, she would have known. Besides, you bought a dress from her."

"One that your husband will love."

Pandora looks over at the package on her lap. "Do you really think so? It's not like anything I have ever worn."

"I know so."

"You need to become less sheltered, Pandora. Step out in the world, see how the other half plays."

"I don't know what you mean; I leave the castle."

The girls tease her gently. "Oh Pandora, one day you will understand."

Within twenty minutes, the carriage stops in front of an enormous tree trunk with winding stairs leading up. Dawnelda steps out and hands the reins to a waiting elf. She leads the group up, directing them to the queen's social chamber. She bows and steps back as the group of five turn to face the Elven Queen. "So, I have a group of queens shopping in my town, and you didn't invite me?"

Pandora smiles. "We were in hiding. How did you know?"

"I do have a seer myself. Not as good as you, mind you, but she did say you were in town. It wasn't hard to track your movements. Although you have a red with you I do not recognize."

"My Queen, this is Patchouli. We decided amongst ourselves that we needed some girl time to relax."

"Indeed, well then, come and relax."

The five laugh, moving to the lounge pillows as they sit, chat, eat, drink, and just enjoy an afternoon without rules and demands upon them. At the end of the day, Runestone creates a portal for Pandora before taking Patches home as Jeodina teleports back to the Isle with Kittymoo.

Pandora walks in the front doors, giving a nod to the guard, sensing her son sleeping with Spider in his room and Rendgren in theirs. She makes her way through the castle, arriving at the door, and hesitates, glancing down at the package in her hands. She enters the bedroom, eyeing him lounging on the bed reading.

He lifts his gaze, seeing the single package in her hands, arching a brow. "Only one package?"

Pandora looks down at it, fingering it gently. "Yes, just the one."

"Did you buy the other girls more?"

"No, we didn't get far before Queen Diadradey summoned us, and we spent the rest of the day with her."

Rendgren chuckles. "So my dragon hoards are safe for another day."

Pandora nods, feeling suddenly nervous about the dress in her hand. "Yes, they are."

Rendgren places the book down. "Is everything alright, love?"

"Yes, it's been a long day, and I think I just need to freshen up." She moves swiftly to the bathing chamber and shuts the door. Leaning against it, she closes her eyes momentarily before moving to the other side of the room. She senses Rendgren rising from the bed and approaching the other side of the door.

"Are you certain, love?"

"Yes, Gren, I will be out shortly."

Pandora remains against the back wall, turning the package over in her hands, before opening and pulling the dress out. She handles it gently, blushing at the sheerness of the fabric, finding herself wondering if the girls were correct in that her husband would like it. Placing the dress aside, she moves to the washing basin, splashing her face and dabbing the back of her neck. She rubs her temples, knowing that she has faced much worse than wearing a sheer dress for her husband. Pandora takes a few deep breathes and focuses inward, trying calm the nervousness within that she knows she should not be feeling.

Pandora quickly pulls her gown off and moves to the new one, sliding it on and fastening the laces. She turns to the mirror and blushes deeply, pulling at the low-cut neckline, not liking the way it glitters and draws attention to her cleavage. Frowning at her bare midriff, noticing the thin gold fabric covering only what is necessary over her hips, with her legs clearly visible beneath the sheer fabric. She tries to adjust the sheerness, wanting to add another four layers to it, wondering how a woman could prance around in these things. Moving back to the door, she pauses, feeling her husband standing just outside, her hand hesitating on the door handle.

"Pandora, my love. What's up?"

"It's nothing really, Gren, it's just..."

"May I come in, Pandora?"

She backs up a step, panic beginning to set in at what she is doing. "I don't think that's such a good idea."

"I can feel your stress, Pandora." The door opens, and Rendgren pauses, staring at the outfit his wife is wearing.

Pandora blushes deeply and grabs a nearby towel, wrapping it around her as she backs up another step.

His eyes darken immediately with desire. "My dear Seer, what are you wearing?"

She looks down, doing her best to tighten the towel. "Umm, it's a towel."

"What's beneath it, love?" He steps in close, taking her hands gently in his, and watches the towel fall to the floor.

"Well, it is apparently a fortune teller's outfit, but I...."

He pulls her close, kissing her deeply, feeling her sink against him. He pulls back breathlessly as he moves to kiss along her chin to her ear. "I love it."

"You do?"

"Yes, come. Let's go back to the bedroom. I want to explore this fortune teller of mine." He lifts her into his arms and carries her back to the bed, placing her down on her feet beside it. He takes one of her hands in his and spins her slowly, seeing the blush cross her skin as he admires the way the outfit hugs her curves. His fingers trace along the lines of the dress, showing just enough of her and teasing him with what remains covered. His hands caress over her bare midriff, feeling the softness of her skin, hearing her intake of breath at his touch before resting them on her hips as she sways slightly. A grin crosses his lips at what his wife has done, feeling her uncertainty standing there, scantily clad. He trails his fingers up her body to her chin, lifting her gaze to meet his, kissing her lips gently. "Thank you, Pandora. It looks amazing on you."

Pandora blushes again, her eyes meeting him again, feeling his love drawing her in. She forgets for the moment what she is wearing as his emotions overwhelm her, answering with a soft whisper. "You're welcome, Gren."

He pulls her close, his arms tightening around her, kissing the top of her head. "I cannot begin to express the love I feel for you." His hands wander over her as he lifts and places her carefully on the bed, kissing her gently at first before becoming more demanding, seeking more from his wife.

She feels the softness of the bed beneath her and the weight of him as he moves atop her. She closes her eyes with a soft sigh, feeling the fires within that his touch causes and how it commands her, succumbing to his call.

In the morning, he wakes to his wife sleeping peacefully beside him, feeling the wonder within at the surprise and treasure that she is. His eyes drift to the dress lying on the floor nearby, understanding the progress she made in stepping outside her comfort zone and buying it for him. He rises from the bed and collects the dress, folding it up carefully and tucking it away, knowing it is going to be something to add to his treasure pile.

Sixteen

Shifting Dragons

Forty years pass, with Pandora and Rendgren ruling the kingdom in peace and harmony. The Kingdom prospers, and the staff changes as the mortals age, retire, and pass on. They settle into routine visits to the Isle of Lochyae, where Pandora keeps tabs on Pippa's lineage, watching and waiting for the return of Zane's soul. Rendgren observes Pandora shifting her friendships to dragons, elves, and those she will not lose to the passing of time since the loss of Martha and Pippa but wisely remains silent on the fact.

During the week, they balance training in the art of weaponry, tutoring for Junior, which Pandora often sits in on, riding horses through the countryside, or going for an evening flight. New rulers step up in the other kingdoms. Most passed over to their children, those without appointing someone to step in line for ascension. Pandora and Rendgren ensure they keep open communications with their people and the new rulers, keeping the banner of peace across the lands. New dragons move into the realm, adapting to the rules and enjoying the security this realm brings to them. Those that don't are swiftly sent home by the banishment quartet, Jeodina, Kittymoo, Pandora, and Phen, who takes up the mantle of mage, following in her mother Runestone's footsteps.

It is early spring; the sun shines through the balcony doors with a light breeze flowing through the closed curtains. The mixed sounds of birds chirping and the market opening for the day, filter through the patio doors. Pandora wakes and rolls over, draping an arm over Rendgren's chest, resting a head on his shoulder. "Morning, Gren."

His arm tightens around her as he pulls her close. "I love waking up to you in the morning, my dear."

"I do too, Gren. It's going to be a big day today."

Rendgren furrows his brows, trying to think back to something he may have missed but drawing a blank. "It is?"

Pandora lifts herself up, kissing his frowning lips with a smile. "You didn't forget anything. Junior is getting his mortal form today."

He sits up suddenly, looking down at his wife beside him. "What! Really? You're just telling me this now? We have to go to him."

Pandora rolls over onto her back. "He doesn't want us to Gren; he's been trying since his fiftieth birthday. We need to wait until he's shifted to find him, or he won't try today. I made sure a maid accidentally left some children's clothes lying in his room, so at least he won't be running around naked."

"Damn mystics, keeping secrets."

Pandora smiles, taking his hand in hers. "Always, but you love us."

Rendgren studies his wife for a moment, the sheets outlining the body he loves. He shifts and leans down on top of her, kissing her softly, then nibbles lightly on her lips. "You right, I do, every inch of you."

She sighs in delight, feeling the heat of his touch fill her. "He will make us chase him."

"Mmm, I am all for a chase." He kisses along her chin as his fingers seek the skin beneath her sleepers. "He will be easy to find; I will just sense him."

"That won't work unless you know the path into the servant's passage."

He pauses, his gaze meeting hers. "Wait, we have servants' passages?"

Pandora laughs at his quizzical expression. "Oh Gren, you do know that generally servants are not to be seen, right? They have their own hallways."

"I could sense them moving, just never really thought about where they were and why I didn't see them."

"Well, I know where they are. You chase, I will catch."

"Wait, I want to catch him."

Her eyes darken at the challenge, her fingers drifting along his chest. "By all means, my love, try to catch him before I do. I will let you know when the race is on."

"Challenge accepted, my wife." He pulls her close, kissing her deeply as he pushes her sleepers off her.

An hour later, Pandora slips from the bed to the bathing chamber, humming softly as she fills the tub and slips into it. She closes her eyes as the warmth surrounds her, feeling Rendgren enter the room.

"Bathing alone, my dear?"

She sits up; her gaze moving over him slowly. "There is always room."

"Does this mean I am going to smell like berries again?"

Pandora smiles and shifts to allow room for him. "Of course."

Rendgren chuckles and moves to the tub. He steps in behind her and sinks down in the water, pulling her back against him. His fingers twine in her hair, watching as it floats in the water around them as his other hand wraps around her waist. "My love, you make me happier than I could ever imagine."

Pandora leans against him, closing her eyes, listening to his heartbeat beneath her. "I know the feeling, Gren." She lingers in the tub with him, content in his arms, feeling the love they have for each other along their bond. She sighs quietly as the water cools. "We should get out, get dressed and have breakfast. Then the chase will be on."

Rendgren kisses the top of her head. "And may the best dragon win."

Pandora splashes him slightly as she rises. "Yes, me!"

He chuckles, rising as well. "We shall see, my dear."

They dry off, get dressed, and head down to the dining hall to eat. Enjoying light conversation until Pandora catches her child's laughter through the halls. She leans over and kisses Rendgren's cheek. "Good luck, my love." With that, she rises, lifts her skirts in one hand, and runs from the dining chamber.

"Damn, that's not fair." Rendgren mutters under his breath, sensing where his child is and starts in that direction. He reaches out, feeling the path his wife is taking, pausing when he realizes she's moving in the opposite direction. "Hmm, what game are you playing, my wife?" He continues in the direction he can sense his son, rounding a corner and expecting him to be there, only to see a door close, his laughter taunting him. He moves to the door and steps into the room, seeing it empty, sensing him further down the hallway. "Oh, my son, I WILL catch you." He leaves the room and runs down the hallway, opening the door before him, seeing another empty room. "Damn servants passage."... *'Pandora, where are they?'*

'Where are what, Gren?'

'The passages.'

Her thoughts tease him gently. *'I don't know what you are talking about, but*

I do know you went in the wrong direction.'

'I did not, he's here, I can sense him... Or he was here.'

Pandora steps around the corner, watching Junior exit the servant's passage and slide to a stop in front of her. *'No, Gren, He's here; I caught him. West wing.'*

'Bloody hell, I nearly had him.'

'Nearly, but you didn't! The best dragon won, Gren.'

'You played me!?'

'Yes, I might have.'

'Bloody mystics.'

"Mom! How did you find me?"

"You forget, son, I have been a mystic longer than you, and I was once a child in this castle, too. You should have told us you could shift."

"It just happened, and clearly, you already knew."

"Yes, your laughter gave you away. You are adorable."

Junior rolls his eyes. "Really? I am going back to dragon form."

"Your dragon is just as cute, my child." She crouches down to his level to study his chosen form. "You look just like your father."

Child Junior

He mutters under his breath in exasperation. "Well yeeesss, you're a girl! Why would I want to look like you?"

Pandora laughs at his reaction. "Because I gave birth to you, child."

Junior purses his lips and pouts. "Doesn't matter; I don't want to look like a girl."

Pandora picks him up, stands, and sits him on her hip. "Well, at least you still have my eyes."

"Only because I couldn't change them!"

"You are a mystic, Junior; you will always have violet eyes."

"Damn."

"Excuse me? Watch your language."

"Mom, really!? Dad says it all the time, and I'm older than all the staff here, and they use it too."

"Yes, well, your father is old, and that's besides the point. I don't want to hear it from my son. And don't you even think about using the other one, or I will turn you over my knee."

Junior scowls at his mother as he debates her words.

She mockingly makes the same expression. "Just like your father. I have seen that look from him many times."

"Better than the mushy look you always have for him."

"You know your father likes that look."

"Yes, that's because he's tamed; I won't be tamed like he is."

"I am certain your father said the same thing before he met me."

Rendgren arrives, seeing the small boy in his wife's arms, catching the tail end of the conversation. He studies his child, looking very much like him with his mother's eyes. "That's right. And I was certainly NOT going to be tamed by a mortal."

Pandora rolls her eyes. "Gren, you are not helping matters. One day, Junior, someone will come along and tame you."

"Not a chance and never gonna happen, Mom."

"Son, I said that too, and I was old when I stole your mother."

"You still are old, Dad."

"Gren, we've discussed this. You only stole me because I allowed it. I still had to work my way into your heart."

Rendgren smiles, his eyes darkening in desire as he looks over his wife. "I don't just let anyone in, my dear."

Junior squirms from Pandora's grasp. "See, there's that mushy stuff again. Ugh."

Pandora laughs as she places him down. "Alright, Junior, your father and I will behave. Have you at least eaten today?"

"Yes, I had breakfast."

"That's good. Are you going to torment the guards and the poor training dummies?"

"Of course! Now I can learn to use a sword properly!"

"You be careful. Dragon scales are harder than mortal skin. Those swords will cut you now."

He rolls his eyes in exasperation. "I got it, Mom. I'm gonna start with the wooden ones they got there."

"Perfect."

Junior turns and races away as Pandora steps into Rendgren's arms. "He is growing up fast."

"Indeed he is. Come, we should open court; we are already late."

"I suppose." Pandora watches until her son is out of sight before stepping in to walk beside Rendgren to the main hall. She settles in the throne next to her husband as the chamberlain enters the hall, bowing to the pair. "Your Majesties, the people wait."

"Send them in, Tes."

"As you wish, your Majesties."

Pandora and Rendgren go through court, each wishing for it to end today so that they could get back to their son. As the doors close at noon, they rise and head straight to the training barracks. Pandora watches her son swing wildly, bringing a smile to her lips, knowing he is going to be sore later. "Junior, have you been fighting all this time?"

"Of course!"

"Perhaps you might take a rest and care to join us for lunch?"

"If I have to."

"You do."

Rendgren chuckles. "He does take after his father."

Pandora scowls at her husband. "Do not encourage him."

"Sorry, my dear."

"No, you are not; I can see that." She swats at him.

Rendgren dances away and moves towards his son. "Your mother is right. A human form reacts differently than your dragon, Junior. You need to pace yourself, or you will be sore in the morning."

Pandora mutters softly. "More like this afternoon. I know. I have been through it. I will have Joelene prepare Martha's ointment."

Junior rolls his eyes. "I will be fine; I fight every day."

Pandora smiles knowingly. "If you need it, let me know."

The group of them head to the dining room and enjoy lunch together with Junior telling them all about the moves he learned. Pandora smiles, feeling the ache in her memory of when she was sore after swinging a blade for an hour and a half at a training dummy. After lunch, Junior races off back to his room with Spider, bringing a smile to Pandora's lips.

Rendgren catches his wife's smile. "Are you going to be waiting for him, love?"

"I think I will take my afternoon tea in the kitchen at Martha's table."

He laughs and rises, kissing her cheek lightly. "I think I will avoid the kitchen then. Perhaps I might head over to Myrsky's place and enjoy my drink there."

Pandora looks up at him, teasing him gently. "Chicken."

He heads to the door, turning back at her words. "I prefer tactical retreat."

Several hours later, Junior feels an ache all over his shoulders and arms and staggers out of his room. He peaks around the corner at his mom's door and tiptoes past it down to the kitchen. He pushes the door open and sighs, seeing his mom sitting at the table waiting for him, a small jar rolling around in her hands.

"Junior, what brings you to the kitchen?"

He mutters under his breath, scowling her way. "I hurt everywhere."

Pandora laughs at her son's sour expression. "I did the same thing; come, let's go back to your room, and I will put this on."

He nods and turns around, stomping back to his chambers with Pandora following behind him. Once inside the room, he faces his mom. "Is there anything you don't see?"

Pandora moves to sit on the bed, aware of the stiffness in his frame. "Yes, Junior, I tune a lot out, but I know what I went through at thirteen when I learned to sword fight. Now strip."

"When do I get my visions?" He pulls his robe off and tosses it on the bed beside her before turning around to face away from her.

She opens the jar and slathers the cream over his shoulders and down his back. "When do you want them? I can grant them back, but they are overwhelming if you are unaccustomed to them."

Curiosity fills Junior's voice. "How overwhelming?"

Pandora smiles, rubbing it down his arms before turning him around to face her. She touches his forehead, planting a few gentle ones of the staff in his mind but overlapping them with multiple visions.

He clutches the hair at his temples and staggers back a step. "Arrrggg!! What is that?"

"A taste of what they are like, Son, and those are the passive ones."

"I DON'T want them yet."

She grabs his wrist and pulls him in, hugging him tight as the visions fade from his mind. "One day, you will be ready, but not today."

"You know when, then?"

"Yes, Son, I do, and I will filter them in slowly to start until I feel you are ready to face them all."

He smiles as he hugs his mom. "Good. My sister will be very pretty; I will take care of her just like you ask."

Pandora frowns at his words, wondering where he got the idea he is getting a sister. She pulls him back to look him in the eyes. "Junior, your father and I can't have any more children."

"Why not?"

"Because he is red and I am gold. We need to be the same color to have little ones."

"How did you have me then?"

Pandora ponders it for a moment. "Well, in reality, you are special. I shouldn't have been able to have you either, but your father made a deal with the faeries."

"Can we make a deal to get me my sister?"

"I am not certain. I will look into it."

He wraps his arms around his mom, nodding his head. "Thanks, Mom. I can't wait to meet her."

Seventeen

The Sun Burns

Six months later, Pandora sits in her room reading a book to her son, who lies curled up against her. Spider's hackles lift as he rises on the pillow next to her, a low growl escaping. "What's wrong, Spider?" She lowers her book, her skin prickling as her gaze drifts to the balcony, sensing outward but finding no presence on the wall. She reaches out to soothe him as a golden glow fills the room. Pandora turns her gaze to the woman in the center of the glow, dressed in white and gold robes similar to the ones the priestess Gwynevere used to wear.

Her face drains of color, knowing instantly she is here to take Spider home. She nods slightly, tears slipping from her eyes as she draws Spider in close for the last time. She kisses the top of his head. "You be good for the Goddess Raya, Spider. No growling or biting her, alright."

Junior clutches his mom's arm, realizing what is happening. "I don't want Spider to go, Mom."

"Son, Spider has lived a very long time. Much longer than a dog should. He has to go home now."

"Pleeeaase... don't let him go, Mom." Junior's voice cracks as he grabs his best friend and clings to him, hugging him tightly.

"I'm sorry, Junior, I don't have a choice in this."

Raya glides forward to the edge of the bed and looks down at the three sitting there. Her voice is gentle as she speaks, wrapping around them and bringing them solace. "My children, my champions, my followers. Spider was here for you, Junior, but you do not need him anymore. You have grown into a fine young man. He is tired and needs to rest, but I will return his soul when he is needed once again. I promise. Just look for the sun that will mark who he is."

Spider licks Junior's face before he fades away in golden motes of light.

Tears spill from Junior's eyes as he wraps his arms around his mom and sobs against her.

Pandora draws him in tight, wishing she could lessen the pain he is going through, but knowing only time itself can mend a broken heart. Something she had learned when she lost Martha, Pippa and Habo, along with others she had bonded to in this castle.

Raya reaches out to touch Pandora's cheek gently. "Sundancer is also coming home, Pandora. Both were here to guide you and keep you on the path you needed to be on. They have done their job and watched over you. Your family is solid and no longer needs my interference."

"Thank you, Raya, for granting us all that you have."

She smiles and backs away, fading from the room as her voice echoes around them. "I didn't grant it; you worked for it, Pandora. I just assisted when you mis-stepped. Take care of your family. Live, love and be free."

Rendgren feels the power overwhelm the castle, recognizing it from when he called upon her to save his wife. Color drains from his face as panic fills him, missing the fact his staff is dropping to their knees beneath it. He struggles against the shake in his body and searches for his wife with his senses. Staggering beneath the sadness that suddenly overwhelms him, he runs in her direction. He pushes the door open, inhaling sharply at the sight of his wife, curled up with their sobbing son, with silent tears glistening on her cheeks. "Love?"

Pandora lifts her stricken gaze, touching his thoughts instead. *'Raya took Spider and Sundancer home.'*

Rendgren's shoulders sink as he approaches the bed, crawling in with them to hold his family. *'Bloody Hell.'*

'That pretty much sums it up, Gren.' She rests her head on his chest as the three of them mourn the loss of a little dog who was a tried and true companion for fifty-four years.

At Death's Door

Fifty five years into their rule

Pandora opens her eyes, studying the canopy of the bed, feeling her husband shift beside her as his arm wraps around her waist and pulls her in close.

He mutters against her as he breathes deep of her scent. "No visions this early, love."

Pandora laughs softly. "You know they never stop, right Gren?"

"I know, just sometimes they are more apparent in your expression. What's happening today that has your attention this early?"

"Surge is back and will be at the front door by noon."

Rendgren sits up suddenly, staring down at his wife. "And you just casually dropped that?"

Pandora reaches up and pulls him back down. She curls up against him, her fingers lightly tracing his chest. "It's fine, Gren. He actually arrived yesterday but has been delayed getting here."

Rendgren softens beneath her touch. "You're doing, I am assuming?"

"Yes, I want his time to be close. But I will need you to retrieve Patches and invite her for tea."

"She's going to know."

"He's twenty-five years early. She might not."

"It's her mate. Again, I state, she's gonna know."

"You didn't, Gren."

He chuckles. "I was blind and stubborn. Besides, you women, you figure stuff like that out well before us men."

Pandora reaches up to brush his hair aside. "I won't argue with you on that one."

Rendgren pulls her close, kissing her softly. "I didn't think you would."

Hours later, Pandora and Patchouli enjoy tea in the sitting room. She watches Patchouli shift, unable to remain still for longer than a minute. She reaches out to take her hand gently. "Just a little while longer, Patches."

"I know, my Queen. He made it back, though. He came for me!"

"Yes, but did he make it back changed?"

"You know he did, or you wouldn't have invited me for tea today."

Pandora's eyes soften as she smiles at Patchouli. "You are too clever for your own good, Patches. But make him say it. DO NOT rush out to him, no matter what you hear."

"I got it; stay hidden."

Pandora reads the anxiety and anticipation in her, knowing she's not about to stay still. "I will have Gren tackle you if you show yourself too soon."

Rendgren lifts his gaze from where he sits in the corner, reading his book with Junior. "I will not. Don't listen to her, Patches."

"Gren." Pandora shifts her gaze to his, using the tone with him.

"Right. Never mind, apparently, yes, I will."

Patchouli laughs at their antics. "You two are the best. I hope we will be like you."

"It's how you make it, Patches; you are in control. Remember that. If, for some reason, you want him gone, you speak it, and we will make it happen. Hot headed-dragons can be a challenge."

"I know Pandora, and I appreciate that."

Rendgren scowls at his wife. "What are you implying, my dear? I was never hot-headed."

"Never? Let's see. I do recall you storming out of the cave in a rage because I borrowed one of your robes."

"It was mine, and you stole it!"

"And as I said, it wasn't stolen if you knew where it was. Besides, you were welcome to take it off me."

Rendgren growls under his breath, about to reply when a guard comes racing in. "My Queen, there is a MFD at the gates."

"Thank you, Jordan. You may let him pass; I know he's coming." She looks to her son, curled up in his father's lap.

"Well, Junior, let's go put on a show." Pandora waits for her son to crawl out of Rendgren's lap and move to her side. She takes his hand and walks outside, standing in the courtyard, watching the guards escort the dragon in his human form before her, her mark glowing like a beacon for all to see. She studies him carefully as they drop him at her feet, noticing the scars upon him, the defeated posture, and the clear temperament difference. "Henri, you're looking a little rough around the edges. You do know that coming back here means death."

He pulls himself up to kneel before her, bowing at her feet. "Yes, my Queen."

"And yet, here you kneel. I am not withdrawing the mark. Its binding is based on your past behavior."

"I realize that. I am not here to ask for it to be removed."

The air around her chills as her tone grows cold. "Then why are you here?"

"I am here to beg for forgiveness. I know I am only alive because you willed it or made it happen somehow. The only path I knew was to travel back through all the realms where I destroyed a dragon or two. I saw the chaos I left in my wake, and some of that chaos came for me because of what I had done. Families I had destroyed without thinking about it." His eyes travel to the small boy that holds Pandora's hand, thinking if he had gotten his way, another child would be parentless. "Each one that came after me made me suffer and nearly killed me, but each one spared my life with a *Compliments of Pandora*. I don't know how you did it, but I know I owe you my life many times over."

"You don't owe me anything, Henri. You should have just stayed in your realm. There, you could always hold the position you crave, the one where you are the top dragon. That is, of course, until another upstart knocks on your door, seeking to dethrone you simply because they are jealous of the power you hold." A slight edge creeps into Pandora's already cool voice.

"No, I couldn't. I know this mark will kill me within the hour, as I can feel it, but I had to come back. I need to see her."

"See who, Henri? There is no one here that wants to see you."

"My mate."

"You don't have a mate, Henri. You were very clear on that."

"Yes, I do. Her name is Patches, and she has been haunting my dreams ever since you banished me."

"I do believe *she* was the one that said to send you away, so that would be a rejection in my eyes."

"No, she didn't... she couldn't. Not with the way she sang as she touched and mended my wing. There was such a gentleness to it, that I can't believe her sending me away was a rejection. If it was, I need to hear it from her lips, and I would understand. Please take her to me before I die."

"She is a red Henri; that hasn't changed, and you have a blind hatred for reds. I won't do it."

"No, not anymore. I see what you were trying to teach me and I don't care what color she is. I need to hear her song again before I die. She needs to know how sorry I am that I wasted years of our lives when we could have been together. Please, I know I don't have long before this mark takes effect, but I have to see her."

Pandora ponders the man on his knees, letting her son go as she approaches the dragon, lowering herself to his level. She places a hand beneath his chin, lifting his gaze to hers.

Rendgren steps out of the shadows, not trusting the situation his wife just placed herself in.

Pandora meets Henri's blue gaze, pulling on his thoughts, reading them carefully before rising and indicating to Rendgren that all is good. "You can release her."

Rendgren opens the door, and Patchouli races out. She studies the broken dragon at Pandora's feet and approaches cautiously.

Henri lifts his gaze, seeing his mate coming out of the castle, and crawls over to her, wrapping his arms around her legs. "Please forgive me. I know I don't deserve your forgiveness because of what I have done. In my stubbornness, I deprived you of your mate, and you should be happy. I pray you find another mate to bond with, but I had to see you again before I die. You need to see that I regret my actions the last time I was here."

Patches drops to her knees, gingerly taking Henri's face in her hands. "I forgive you, Henri. I have been waiting for you to return because I don't want another mate. I have one."

"You do?"

"Yes, I have you." She pulls him close and kisses him softly on the lips as purple lights surround the pair of them.

Henri wraps his arms around her and pulls her tight. "Oh gawd, I am sorry I am going to die on you."

"You are not, not anymore. You just needed to accept me for who I am."

Henri pulls her back to look over her carefully. "What do you mean?"

Patches caresses his cheek gently. "Pandora marked you for death, yes, and once marked, it cannot be undone. But she puts a clause in all her spells, for she is a mystic and sees everything."

Pandora coughs. "Almost everything."

"Right, almost everything."

"I don't understand."

Patches kisses him again, resting her head on his shoulder as she wraps her arms around him. "A true mate's kiss will overpower her mark of death."

"You mean I just had to kiss you?"

"No. You had to kiss me with a mate bond in place, and you did."

He nods, tightening his hold on her, tears creeping from his eyes. "So I am going to live and have time to get to know you?"

"Yes Henri, you are. But I suspect Pandora will be watching you carefully."

Pandora laughs. "I don't think I will be watching as carefully as your King, Ludy the Second, will be. He's less than impressed that we are sending trouble his way."

Henri shakes his head. "I will not be trouble, I swear!"

"Good. I might have to trounce you again if you are. Perhaps leave you tied up on the shores of a lake for a month this time."

Henri chuckles. "I deserve that. Don't think I don't know I am only alive because of you."

"You are only alive because Patches is such a sweet soul, and I couldn't have her lose her mate because he's a ruffian. Now, make sure you treat her right, or I WILL end you. Is that clear?"

"Very. Thank you, my Queen."

"Good, Gren, please send them home."

Rendgren nods and moves forward, watching as they rise to their feet. "Patches, you know where to find us if you need him dealt with."

Patches nods. "I do, Rendgren. Thank you both for making this happen."

"It had nothing to do with me, Patches; it was all my wife. If I had my way, I would have let him go after the thousand-foot plummet, but my wife had already seen you were his mate and opted not to end him."

Henri's eyes snap to Pandora, who stood with her son once more. "Wait, are you saying she knew before our fight?"

"She knew as soon as she stood on the balcony looking down on you."

"Damn, how do you live with that?"

Rendgren's gaze shifts to his wife. "Well, it's a challenge some days, and you can't get away with anything! Trust me, I've tried. But I love her with all of my heart, even when she scowls at me and taps her foot in dismay at something that I've done that she disapproves of."

Henri laughs. "Better than the... What did you call it, the mother voice and true name? That's unnerving."

"That it is. She sees them all."

"Are you saying she knows Patches' true name?"

"Yes, of all the dragons that cross her path. She sees everything."

Pandora sighs. "Almost everything, Gren."

"Damn. No wonder I lost."

"Yes, well, you didn't stand a chance, but it was fun to watch! And honestly, after two weeks of dealing with her mood swings, it was nice to see her taking them out on another." He creates a ring of fire, opening a portal to just outside Slario. "Best of luck, you two."

Henri takes Rendgren's hand and shakes it. "Thank you." He gives a nod to Pandora. "Thank you for making me see the light."

"You're welcome, Henri. Take care of her."

"I will."

Patchouli leads Henri through the portal, waving as it closes behind them. She turns to Henri, shifts, and leads him to her lair. "Let's go home."

Rendgren moves to Pandora's side, drawing her into his arms. "Is he going to be a problem, love?"

"He will be, but Patches can handle him."

"That's good to hear. I love you, Pandora."

"I love you too, Gren." She looks up into his eyes, studying him for a moment, before resting her head on his shoulder.

"Do you see something I need to know about?"

"Perhaps."

"Are you going to tell me?"

Her arms tighten around him. "How do you feel about moving every fifteen to twenty years?"

"What do you mean by that?"

"It means in about twenty years, we need to consider it."

"Are you saying what I think you are saying?"

"Yes, Zane's soul has returned and will be seeking the throne in about fifteen years, where we will guide Scott on how to rule."

Rendgren kisses the top of her head. "Can we go back to our lair and retire?"

Pandora sighs, her eyes traveling to their son, who is racing around the courtyard. "Alas, no, Junior needs to be raised in this world as the world adapts. One day, I promise, we will retire, but that day is not until Zane finds us."

Rendgren nods, his eyes straying to his son. "I look forward to that day, my love."

Nineteen

Echos of Tomorrow

R endgren and Pandora pack up their belongings into the small moving van, knowing their twenty years are up on Hontby, and they need to move once again to conceal their immortality. He loads the van towing their car onto the ferry, deciding that it is past-time they return to his mansion in Mindriff. A mansion that has not been occupied in hundreds of years, not since he was the merchant Zalgren, a name he went by full time now. It was also a mansion owned by ancestors of his according to the paperwork he had drafted up, along with the inheritance in the bank accounts.

Pandora and Rendgren wander the decks while Junior makes a beeline straight for the arcade. She stops and looks over the water as the breeze plays with her hair, twisting and dancing it around her face, enjoying the wind and salt water spray on her face. Rendgren stands beside his wife, watching her overlook the water, lost in thought, smiling at the fact that she is his, even after all these years. He wraps an arm around her waist and pulls her close, feeling her lean against him as he does. "You know, it would be so much easier to portal or fly. Then I wouldn't hate moving so much."

Pandora smiles, resting her head on his shoulder. "Indeed it would, but this is safer. With all the electronics and trackers out there, I am certain something would find us. We would be those unidentified objects everyone is talking about. Though your portal should be safe enough, it needs to be seen that we arrive, keeping up the image of a new family moving into the neighborhood."

"I know, it's just a long trip ahead of us if we go to Mindriff. Perhaps Ewhela again?"

"It's time to return home, Gren. And we should get back in touch with the Council. Perhaps invite them to dinner every few months. Or go there to visit them. It's only a few hours' drive and a ferry ride now."

"You've seen something?"

"Nothing definite, just what I feel."

He kisses the top of her head as he holds her, following her gaze across the water as his thoughts drift to their lost freedoms. A wry smile crosses his lips, knowing his days of being a wanted legend are done; that the Red Phantom and King Rendgren, along with creatures of an age past, are nothing but written words in myths and stories. All because humans bred and grew rapidly, unlike dragons and elves, where offspring are rare. In their growth, humans began to fear the unexplained as science and technology moved in. And so, those that are long-lived or immortals hide among them, keeping their secrets safe from those that will exploit them. Not that there are many left, and most have moved to the Isle of Lochyae, where the Council has the daunting task of keeping them protected. His arm tightens around her, missing the freedom of flying through the clouds, being forced to remain in his mortal form, hearing her soft thoughts in his mind.

'I know, Gren, I miss it too.'

Rendgren smiles. *'Are you reading my thoughts again, my dear?'*

She laughs softly. *'I am, and feeling them too.'*

'Will we ever get to fly again?'

She turns in his arms, leaning her back against the railing, looking up into his eyes. *'Not likely. I could try warding us, but it is a risk.'*

He nods, sadness filling his eyes as he grows quiet, staring out across the water, seeking her bond as he recalls the past and the times they have lost.

Pandora wraps her arms around him, feeling the loss as well, and murmurs softly. "We should round Junior up; they are going to dock soon."

"In a minute." He stands and takes comfort in holding her, lost in thoughts. A few minutes later, a sigh escapes him as he steps away from her. "Right. Let's go home."

She takes his hand, squeezing it gently. "I look forward to living in your mansion."

Rendgren chuckles, leading her to the arcade. "It's a house. A large one, mind you, but still a house. It is possible it will require renovations. I know the groundskeepers do what they can, but it's been empty for hundreds of years. I doubt there is even proper plumbing."

"It will be another step in our adventures together."

He nudges her gently. "I do recall getting beat up over those steps, my dear."

"I wouldn't know what you are talking about, Gren."

"If only I could show visions as you do, Pandora, you would be in big trouble."

She laughs, rising on her toes to kiss his cheek. "I love you, Gren."

He mutters under his breath as he struggles against the smile on his lips. "Sure you do." His gaze travels to Junior, playing at the pinball machine, a variety of teenagers hanging around cheering him on. "Junior."

"Dad."

"We are going to be docking soon."

"Darn, and I was doing so well."

Rendgren moves over to the game, looking at the numbers and giving a nod of approval. "Impressive Son. Almost the top score."

Junior's hands madly pull levers and punch buttons as a multitude of beeping sounds fill the air. "Yes, I think whoever has the top score is an employee, as there is not enough time on this boat ride to beat it."

Rendgren chuckles. "I suspect you are right."

Junior plays for another minute, placing himself in second, before ending the game. He signs his name in the records and turns to his father with a grin. "Second is good. When we come back, I will be first."

The three of them head back to the vehicle, beginning the week-and-a-half-long journey to Mindriff. At the end of their journey, Rendgren pulls the moving van up the driveway, taking a moment to reminisce about his old mansion. He slips from the van and looks around, seeing the maintained yard, the barn and empty paddocks, before moving around to the other side to open the door for his wife.

Junior hops out of the driver's side and slams the door behind him. "This is your house Dad? How come we have never stayed here before?"

Rendgren chuckles. "Yes, this was my place from before I met your mother. And I don't know, we just haven't."

"Wow! Can I go inside?"

"I am certain it's locked. We need the keys from the groundskeeper."

Rendgren's hands wrap around Pandora's waist and lift her from the van, placing her on the ground beside him. He takes her hand and leads the pair around the side of the mansion to the small cottage at the back. He knocks on the door gently, sensing movement approaching the door.

A tall blonde teenager opens the door, sporting ripped jeans and a hoodie. He narrows his eyes slightly at the intrusion. "This is private property. Can I help you?"

Pandora feels her husband stiffen and tightens her hand on his to soothe him. "Shawn, is your mother home?"

"Yeah, she's home. She's cooking dinner. Wait, how did you know my name?"

"Please tell her that Zalgren is here."

"Fine." He turns in the doorway and yells. "Moooommm!!! Zalgren is here!"

Pandora sighs at the teenager's antics, hearing Junior snicker while feeling her husband is less than impressed. It isn't long before his mother rounds the corner, dropping the towel at her feet. "M'lord Zalgren! You were not due until tomorrow."

"We made good time by hitting all the lights right and no traffic, Carol."

"Clearly. Do come in. I am cooking spaghetti; do you want some?"

"No, we won't intrude. We would like to get unloaded. Are the keys around?"

"Yes, yes, sorry, Sir. Shawn, please fetch the keys for the master of the house."

Shawn's gaze snaps back to the man. "As in *the* owner?"

Rendgren's eyes flash ever so slightly in annoyance. "Yes, as in the one that pays you to look after my mansion."

He bows and nods, racing from the room. "Sorry, Sir; I will be right back."

Pandora nudges her husband gently. "Be nice, Gren, he's a teenager."

He mutters under his breath. "Junior is not like that."

Her thoughts touch his gently. *'Junior is not really a teenager.'*

'Right.'

Carol picks up the towel. "Dinner will be ready in about ten minutes; I will help afterwards if that's alright."

"Where is Ben?"

"He's working late again."

Rendgren nods. "It's fine, Carol, sit and enjoy your dinner. I have Junior and my wife to assist with what little we packed. Later this week, we will need to make a trip into town for what we will need, but for now, we just want to unload and crash. Perhaps order pizza."

Carol nods. "Thank you, Sir. Might I recommend Wood-Fired Pies. It's the best around here."

Shawn runs back into the main foyer with a set of keys in his hand. "I will help you unload until Mom calls me for dinner."

Rendgren accepts the keys with a nod. "Much appreciated."

An hour and a half later, the van is unloaded into the house, with only the key essentials moved to the bedrooms, pizza delivered, and the three of them sit on the couch in the living room talking. At the end of the evening, Rendgren pauses at the room Junior picked, the opposite end of the hallway from theirs, a small balcony and its own private bathing room. "Night Son."

Junior answers absently, focusing on unpacking his stuff. "G'night, Dad, night, Mom."

"Sweet dreams. Don't stay up too late unpacking."

"I won't."

Pandora laughs softly. "I know you better than that, Junior."

Junior turns and smiles at his mother. "I will be quick!"

She shakes her head and heads down the hall to the master bedroom with Rendgren. She sighs in relief as she closes the door, stripping and crawling onto the air mattress they have set up. Rendgren does the same, drawing her close and pulling the cover over them, each drifting off to sleep as exhaustion takes them.

Over the course of the next week, they return the van to the rental place and set about organizing the mansion. Plumbers and electricians come in and modernize the house while keeping the old mansion's feel to it. They make a list of what is missing and make a trip into town, driving past the high school on the way in. Junior peers out the window at the kids milling around while others shoot hoops at the ring, some hanging upside down on monkey bars.

"Mom, I want to go to school."

Pandora snaps her gaze to her son. "You don't need to Junior. Those are teenagers; you are well beyond them."

Junior's eyes remain on the kids as he nods. "I still want to go."

Pandora glances at Rendgren, who shrugs his shoulders. "Alright, we will sign you up tomorrow for next year. I do believe this year ends in a few weeks."

"Thank you."

He turns back to his parents, his brows furrowing as he grows thoughtful.

"Why haven't I gone before?"

Pandora turns slightly in the car and faces her son. "Well, there are a couple of reasons. First, you are not a teenager and have had private tutors, so are well past their learning level. Second, with your visions, we have kept you away from heavily populated areas as I filter them back slowly. A school is full of people, all in a tight space, each with a potential to trigger them, so it could be very overwhelming for you."

"I want to try."

"And you are welcome to; we will stand behind whatever you decide to do."

His eyes drift back the way they came, the school out of sight but still vivid in his thoughts. "I think I want to look like them too."

Pandora glances down to her dress, smoothing the skirts out nervously. She knew this day was coming but finding she isn't ready for it. "We will pick you up some school clothes and visit a hairdresser in the market."

"Thanks, Mom."

Rendgren pulls up into the shopping mall and parks the car in the middle of the lot. They head in, wandering around, looking at all the shops. Pandora turns to Rendgren. "I will take Junior clothes shopping if you want to get the rest of the stuff we need. That way, we cut the time in half."

Rendgren smiles and kisses his wife on the cheek. "You just don't want me to see that you are spending one of my hoards."

Pandora laughs, shaking her head. "Hey! It's not me spending it this time; it's Junior."

Rendgren chuckles. "Right. I knew the day I locked him in the kitchen, the whelp was going to cost me nothing but gold."

"DAAD!!! I am standing right here!"

Rendgren drapes an arm around his son's shoulders. "I am well aware of that, my dear boy. Spend your own hoard."

Junior wraps an arm around his father, rests a head on his shoulder, and looks up adoringly at his father, a smirk crossing his lips. A hint of humor laces his voice as he does his best to keep it serious. "Not a chance, Dad. Mom's buying with yours, apparently. I'm keeping mine safe."

Rendgren shakes his head, muttering under his breath in humor. "Kids!" He turns to Pandora. "When can we kick him out?"

Pandora smiles at the pair. "Not until after he's done school apparently."

"Are you saying I am stuck with him for another year?"

"That's what I am saying."

"Damn Mystics."

Pandora moves over and kisses his cheek, catching Junior's groan at their affection. "But you love us! Come, Junior, let's go spend your father's money." She takes her son's hand and pulls him away, heading to the smaller boutiques, knowing that is likely where the local kids shop.

Rendgren watches them leave, smiling as the love of his life and his son head off, suspecting she is going to give him a run for his money in what she is going to spend on school clothes and supplies. He turns and heads to the furniture store, knowing they need most of the basic stuff in furniture as well as all the appliances now that the place is getting upgrades. He wanders around, looking at the designs, pondering what would suit the mansion best, recalling what it was in its prime and knowing he wanted it back there. Time has aged and taken most of the furniture away from him, and so he disposed of it. He stops in front of a four-poster bed, much like the one in his lair, just as a sales clerk approaches him.

"That is a fine choice, sir, but it requires a large room as it's bigger than it looks. If you have the measurements of your bedroom, I would be happy to tell you if it will fit. It also does come in a queen and a normal king, but the oversized king is the most impressive."

Rendgren turns, looking over the tiny sales clerk before him, a petite brunette with brown eyes sporting a name tag identifying her. "Lauryn, I see. Do you work on commission here?"

"Yes, sir."

"Is there bedding that fits this?"

"Yes, in a variety of colors."

"Right, I will take two, with bedding to go with them. There are other things I will need that I hope you can help me with."

"TWO?" Lauryn gasps in astonishment, her eyes straying to the price tag on it, knowing that in her two years of working here, no one has bought a bed this size.

"Yes, I have the master bedroom to furnish and my son's room. We have been sleeping on air mattresses this past week."

"Yes, sir. Let me get a notepad and write the codes down." Lauryn turns and runs back to the main desk, returning within a minute with a pen and pad of paper, writing the product code down. "What else do you need, sir?"

"Pretty much everything. We moved into the mansion on the hill from a small house." Rendgren goes over what he wants, room by room, including all new appliances and an upholsterer to redo some of the furniture that survived. "It will also need to be delivered; the sooner, the better."

Lauryn writes furiously as Rendgren explains what he needs, beginning to think this customer was pulling her leg. She looks down at her list before glancing up at him. "This is going to be expensive, sir. Are you certain?"

Rendgren chuckles. "Yes, it needs to be done. My wife is currently out there in the mall spending my money as well, so I might as well outspend her."

Lauryn smiles, thinking her commission this month is going to get her the car she wants. "Alright then, let's go shopping, sir." She leads him through the store, going over the furniture, what is good, what isn't, and writing the product codes down as he decides.

Hours later, and thousands of dollars accumulated, Rendgren looks over Lauryn's list, satisfied with the choices. He moves to the counter with her, smiling at the manager's face as she rings the stuff in. He pulls his credit card out and pays for the items, signing his name on the bottom of the slip. "So when can you deliver it?"

Lauryn glances at the manager, who was still staring in shock at the balance on the till. "Azlynn?"

Azlynn turns to Rendgren and nods. "Sorry, two days shipping is standard policy, but if you wish, I will have it arranged for tomorrow."

Rendgren smiles. "Perfect. I will need assistance in getting the furniture to its respective rooms."

She nods. "I will see it done."

"Great, now to find my wife and see what she's spent. Thank you, Lauryn. You are a delight to work with. If I missed anything, I will be back and ask for you personally."

Lauryn blushes. "Thank you, sir."

Rendgren turns and strides from the store, receipt in hand.

Meanwhile, Pandora wanders the mall with her son, looking at the clothing, some of it decent quality, others poorly made for high prices. She steers her son to the well-made stuff, watching as he tries it on in each store, deciding on some that he likes. Jeans, t-shirts, hoodies, some plaid shirts, both pullovers and button-downs, and two pairs of sneakers. Once he choses, she moves forward and pays for his purchases, taking the bags and carrying them as they move to the next store, repeating the process. After a few hours, they head to the hairdresser to see if they can get him in. They stand at the reception as a tall redhead approaches. Her green eyes sparkle as she looks them over, reminding Pandora of her maid Pippa.

"Can I help you?"

Pandora nods. "Yes, my son would like to get his haircut, but we didn't make an appointment. Is it possible there is an opening? If not, that's fine; we will make an appointment for tomorrow."

The redhead looks back at the stylists before looking down at her book, her finger trailing lightly over the paper. "Yes, Madison can do it now if you like."

Junior smiles in delight. "That's great."

"This way, then." She leads him over to a chair that he settles into. She pulls a black salon cape over him and fastens it in the back, gently pulling his hair out from beneath it. "Madison will be right with you."

Within a few minutes, a blonde approaches, with spiked hair on one side that is feathered in layers down the other side, creating an asymmetrical appearance. "Hi, I'm Madison. What style are you looking for?"

Junior shakes his head. "Whatever is in."

Madison moves around, looking over the long black hair with streaks of red. "Do you get it colored? This looks fresh?"

"Nah, that's all natural. It's just like my dad's. But I want it shorter, like the ones I saw at the school earlier."

Madison nods, her eyes drifting to Pandora, seeing her long black hair as well, seeking confirmation that she is cutting all the hair off.

Pandora gives a slight nod as she moves to sit nearby and watch.

Madison nods. "Alright then. Did you want to donate your hair? It's long enough to."

Junior looks up at her. "What do you mean, donate?"

Madison smiles and picks up an elastic. "It's used for creating wigs for those that lose their hair because of medical reasons."

"Yes! Let's do it."

"Sounds good." She measures out his hair, tying an elastic around it, and picks up her scissors, cutting it off just above the elastic.

Pandora gasps softly, sadness filling her within at the loss, her eyes straying to the lock of hair in the hairdresser's hand.

"Mom! It's fine; It will grow back."

"I know, Junior, it's still a shock."

Madison smiles. "Is this the first time you have cut your hair?"

"Yes, I always had it like Dads, but now I want it different."

"Well, we can do that."

A half hour later, Pandora pays for the haircut and turns to Junior, now sporting a shorter, shaggy, layered cut, seeing the difference in his features but finding it accented him well. "Well, I never thought I would see the day, Junior, but it looks good."

Teenager Junior

"Thanks, Mom. I love it!"

"That's good. Let's go find your father and get some lunch."

Rendgren pauses, seeing his wife and son walking towards him, each carrying an armful of bags. He studies his son's new hairstyle, knowing that while he prefers the long locks, this style seemed to suit his son well. "Junior, love, I see you spent all my gold."

Junior laughs, holding his packages up. "We tried Dad."

Rendgren chuckles, his eyes straying to his quiet wife. "Well, at least that's a try and not a success. I trust you are happy with your purchases."

"Yes! Thanks, Dad. I really appreciate that you are letting me try this."

"Well, as your mother said, you are beyond them in both age and learning. Try not to outshine them too much, alright."

"Got it, Dad. Mom said we could grab a burger before we head home."

Rendgren wraps an arm over his wife's shoulders, squeezing her gently. "That sounds good. Your mom and I will put your packages in the car and meet you at the burger joint."

"That's great. Thanks!" He hands his packages off and heads towards the burger joint to find a table for them.

Rendgren walks with his wife back to the car in silence, feeling the range of emotions she is struggling with through their bond. He opens the trunk and places his share of the packages in, watching as she places hers in after him before closing it afterwards. He turns to look over at his wife. "What's up, love?"

She looks up, her eyes bright with un-shed tears. "I am just not ready for him to grow up like this."

Rendgren pulls her in close, his fingers running gently through her hair as the other lingers at her waist. "I understand. We have been lucky. Dragons are self-sufficient at a very young age, and he's chosen to stay with us much longer than others would have. Most are out of the nest by twenty. Besides, it's not like he's leaving us; he just wants to go to school."

"I know Gren, and I know it will be us..."

He places a finger to her lips. "Shhh, we are not talking about what's been seen. Things can change; remember that."

Pandora nods, wrapping her arms around her husband, holding him tightly, her thoughts on the future before stepping away and taking his hand. "Thanks,

Gren." She smiles up at him, her voice teasing him gently. "Shall we go get that burger now and debate who spent more of your gold?"

Rendgren chuckles. "Judging by your packages and how much clothes cost, I bet you did."

She nudges him gently. "They are cheap compared to ours. And I believe the gem is still spinning in the lair. So there are more treasures to be had."

"How many more, my dear?"

"I don't actually know, Gren. As long as the gem spins, there is an unattended hoard somewhere."

He stops and kisses her gently. "Thank you, Pandora, for coming into my life."

She sighs, sinking under his kiss as she steps in close; her voice whispers against his lips as she teases him softly. "You just like the fact that I made you the richest dragon in the realm."

He chuckles. "That too. Come, Junior is waiting."

Pandora and Rendgren return to the mall, seeing Junior sitting at a table, looking around at all the people as he waits, before his eyes lock on his mom. His thoughts touch hers lightly. *I have been focusing on the people's visions around here and working on pushing them aside. I think I can do it, Mom.'*

Pandora smiles, her hand tightening on Rendgren's for a moment. *'I know you can, Junior.'*

Rendgren feels his wife's hand tighten on his, causing him to look down at her before returning his gaze to his son, knowing they are communicating.

Junior smiles, rises, and runs over to his mother, wrapping his arms around her tightly. "Then you need to stop worrying 'cause I can feel it."

Pandora hugs her son tight. "I promise I will do my best, Junior. It's a big step for all of us."

Junior steps back and looks over his mom. "Thanks, Mom. I will only be there during the day; I will still be home after school and in the evenings."

Pandora reaches out to caress his cheek. "You will have football practice after school, so you will arrive in time for dinner, and after dinner, you will either be in the library or your room doing homework. The friends you make will want to hang out on the weekends and some evenings. You are growing up, and I will accept it with time. It's just all so sudden when I am used to having you all to myself other than a tutor here or there."

"Okay, Mom, you are not supposed to be reading my future. Now let's get some food. I am starving." He takes her hand and leads her to the burger joint.

Rendgren chuckles. "You are always starving, Son."

The three of them sit and enjoy their lunch, laughing and bantering with each other, going over who spent more, finding that Rendgren actually won in that department, which only earned him more teasing about overspending well-earned gold. After their day at the mall, they return home to spend family time downstairs, dueling it out with swords and staves.

Twenty

A Fateful Choice

The next day, Pandora takes Junior to the school while Rendgren remains at home for the delivery. She pulls the car up in front and parks it, looking over the building her son is going to be spending a lot of time in. She can see the visions and feel the emotions of the students, even from here, and pushes them aside.

Junior reaches over and pats her hand. "Come on, Mom, let's do it."

Pandora nods and gets out of the car, locking it behind her. She walks beside her son, tuning into his emotions, knowing he is going to need her, but not saying anything to him. She opens the door and watches her son stagger in pain, bracing against a wall as his hands go to his temples. Her thoughts reach out to him, doing her best to calm him. *'Listen to my voice, Junior, focus on it. Hear its softness in the sea of voices. Pinpoint it, draw it in, find it. Once you do, push the other sounds aside and feel only the love I have for you. Surround your mind with that love. This will create a peaceful space and a barrier that you need within to survive this.'*

Junior's hands clench against his head, struggling to do what his mom is asking, reaching for her voice, finding it along with her calm emotions flooding him. After a few minutes, he gives a slight nod, feeling a break in the onslaught of visions as only his mother's voice fills his mind. *'But you will not be here with me.'*

'I know you can do this, Junior, and you will not need me. You have your space that I am in right now, my voice that is soothing you. Replace it with something else. A memory you love, perhaps of Spider, or a song that fills you

with peace or joy. Something that is strong enough to keep the voices out of your space and keep it in your mind always when you are here.'

'*What do you use, Mom?'*

'*Your Father. He is my safe space. He has been since I was twelve, four years before I met him.'*

Junior nods, spending another few minutes within his mind before straightening and actually looking around the school he stands in. "You knew, didn't you? That's why you brought me and not Dad."

Pandora smiles gently at him. "Yes, Junior, I did. Remember, I went through it, but I didn't have a mother to teach me how it worked. I learned the hard way. Now come, let's find the office. If you need another break, we take it."

Junior takes her hand and squeezes it gently. "I think I got it, Mom. Thank you."

Pandora studies him carefully. "Yes, you do." She leads him through the hallways towards the office, keeping her focus on his emotions. She stops at the office door as Junior opens it for her and steps through, looking around at all the people. Some sitting at desks, others moving around with papers in their hands. There are a few students sitting in the chairs against the wall, eyeing them curiously, or rather, Junior. She steps up to the front desk as a clerk approaches her.

"Can I help you?"

"Yes, please; we just moved into the neighborhood, and I would like to register my son Asher for school in the fall."

The clerk nods and pulls a clipboard out, a pen tucked in the top, with a few forms on it. "Please fill these in."

Junior's thoughts reach his moms in shock. '*You are using Asher?'*

Pandora takes the clipboard and moves to the side, answering her son's thought as she fills out the forms. '*Well, I can put Junior, but then the entire school will call you that.'*

Junior smiles at his mom. '*I don't think I have ever heard you use my human name, Mom. I was beginning to wonder if you even knew it.'*

Pandora pauses in her writing, looking her son over briefly, before continuing to fill the form out. '*Of course, I know it, Junior, just like I know your true name, Ashrekibōgrendajunia. You will always be Junior to me, so it was never needed. Now, it is, and I accept it, but it doesn't mean you will ever hear it from my lips again.'*

Junior struggles against the laughter that threatens to overtake him as he answers her thoughts. *'Mom!!'*

Pandora smiles at the paper, completing the form, and handing it to Junior to look over. "Junior, would you like to make sure your mother got it right?"

"Of course, Mom; I mean, you are old, after all." Junior's laughter spills out as he accepts the clipboard, looking over the form before handing it back.

"Bite your tongue, Junior. I am not that old." She accepts the clipboard and moves back to the counter, noticing the students were now paying more attention to her son. She hands it over as the clerk goes over it.

"Asher Red. Age seventeen and going into grade twelve. He will need to come in for a few pre-session exams in August to see where he stands on the learning curve of what the teachers teach here."

Pandora nods. "Of course. But I suspect you will find he will excel at them."

The clerk offers a half smile. "Every parent thinks so. It is still a requirement for new students. Do you have his transfer papers?"

Pandora shakes her head. "No, he has none. He was home-schooled by tutors."

The clerk arches a brow, looking a touch more closely at Pandora and her clothing before looking back down at the forms and what is written. "I don't recognize this address. Where is it?"

"It's the mansion on the hill. We just moved in a week and a half ago from Hontby."

She quickly conceals the shock in her eyes that someone has moved into the place, placing the clipboard down on the counter. She pulls a drawer open and pulls out a few papers, handing one to Pandora and the other to Junior. "Take these. It will give you the basics of what's required for your first day. Date, time, classes, supplies, that sort of thing." She turns to Junior, seeing the much more casual dress than his mother. "It will be quite different from private tutors. You will be in a classroom of sixteen to twenty-five kids, sharing the same teacher, so you will not be the sole focus as you are with a tutor."

Junior nods, looking over his paper. "I got it, thank you."

"Well then. Welcome to Mindriff High. We will see you in August, and school starts the first week in September." She turns to Pandora. "Now, you better make a run for it. Class change is in five minutes, and you don't want to get caught in the hallway with a bunch of teenagers making a dash to their lockers before hitting their next class. It's practically a war zone out there."

Pandora laughs at the clerk's comments. "I have a teenager. It's very much like that at home. You should see his room and we just moved in."

"Mom! It's not that bad!"

The clerk laughs. "Very true. Nice to meet you, Pandora, Asher. See you in the fall."

Pandora smiles before turning to Junior. "Alright, Junior, you are all set. Let's go home and help your father unpack what he bought."

"Yes! I can't wait to get an actual bed again. The air mattress sucks."

She laughs, leading him out of the office and back down the hallway. "I have to agree with you there. At least yours stays inflated; your father and I are more often than not on the floor every morning."

Junior chuckles, "That's cause I took the good one before Dad got to it." He pauses at the sound of a bell ringing and staggers back against a wall in pain. His hands grasp his temples as doors open and visions flood his mind.

Pandora moves to stand in front of him, out of the way of the students, her thoughts reaching for her son immediately. *Find your space, Junior. The one we talked about. Whatever your space is. Seek it, hold it there, push the others out of your mind.'*

'Working on it, Mom, I just wasn't expecting the sudden onslaught when the bells rang.'

A few of the students pause, looking at the pair standing against the wall, one with his hands on his temples, the other looking on with concern, but continue on to their next class. One young man stops before them. "Is he alright, Ma'am? There is a school nurse if he needs it."

Pandora turns to the student, seeing the concern within his brown eyes. She looks him over, noticing a decent build for one so young, with brown hair styled like her son's, his complexion clear but adorned with a light scattering of freckles. She smiles at him, visions flickering in her mind of the boy before her. "Yes, he just has a migraine, and the bells were louder than he expected. He will be fine. Thank you..."

"Kip, Ma'am. Is he coming to Mindriff High?"

"Indeed, Junior is starting grade twelve in September. We just moved into Mindriff a week ago."

"Awesome! Me too! Well, I didn't just move here, but I am going to grade twelve too. Perhaps we'll have some classes together. I better get to my next class! See ya Junior! Get better soon." He turns and dashes off down the hall, disappearing into the crowd.

Pandora remains beside Junior, watching the halls empty, waiting for her son to move.

"I'm good now, Mom. I just need practice." He steps away from the wall and moves to stand beside his mom, taking her hand in his. "Let's go home now."

Pandora smiles as he takes her hand, knowing most teenagers wouldn't dare to do something like that with their mother in a school, and walks out with him. They get into the car and head home in silence, parking it off to the side because of the delivery truck near the door. Junior races out to help, as she follows at a slower rate after him. She looks at the truck, half empty already, before making her way into the house, sensing Rendgren in the bedroom. She heads up the stairs, pausing in the doorway, her eyes taking in her husband with four other men, setting up an oversized four-poster bed, before drifting around the room, seeing the love seat, tables, two wardrobes, and dressers. "You're moving quick, Gren; did you need a hand?"

Rendgren looks up and smiles at his wife framed in the doorway. He moves to her side and kisses her gently. "I got this room, but there are other rooms where they just dropped the furniture; if you want to guide them, that would be great."

"Sounds good, Gren." She shifts to telepathy as her gaze lingers on the bed. *'I can't wait to test that out tonight.'*

Rendgren's eyes darken with desire as he reaches out to caress her cheek. *'Why wait, love? We have all afternoon.'*

'Junior, I will explain later.' She grabs his hand, kissing the back of it, before giving a slight bow and backing out of the room, heading downstairs to where she feels the others working.

Hours later, after all the furniture is in acceptable spots, the three of them curl up together on the couch with Junior in the middle, watching a movie, eating pizza, and drinking soda, grateful to have a home again.

The days of summer seem to fly by, with Junior walking down to the mall daily, working on his mental blocks, knowing that the first few weeks of school are going to be rough. He didn't dare tell his mother about the pain he felt when the bells rang, but he knew by her protective stance and the fact that her voice was in his mind instantly; she already figured it out.

Ben, Carol, and their son move out of the cottage in early August, with Rendgren offering their son the option to continue maintaining the landscape, to which he accepts.

Council arrives, rekindling the friendship they had in the past now that they are closer to this side of the realm. Junior delights in the wrestling matches downstairs with the bears, finally getting close to holding his own against them, all except Treefeared, who still puts him in his place just as quickly as when he was a pup.

In late August, Pandora drops Junior off at the school for his pre-admission exams. She takes a deep breath, struggling to be strong for him, before driving to the main shopping mall and parks the car. Wandering aimlessly, she finds herself in a library, browsing books. She pulls a few out and moves to sit at a table, flipping through them as she absorbs the happiness of the surrounding children. She closes her eyes, recalling the days where she curled up in the city center, letting the children play around her, taking delight in their joy and innocence. A few hours later, she returns to the school and picks up Junior. "So, how did it go?"

"It was easy. I am certain I aced it!"

"Of course you did. Any other kids there?"

"Yes, there were a few noobs like me, but not many really."

"Noobs?"

"Yes, it's slang for newcomers, Mom. I need to get with the times."

"Alright, Junior, just let your father and I know what it means if you intend to use it around us."

Junior laughs. "I think that's the point, Mom; the parents *don't* understand."

Pandora rolls her eyes slightly, giving a side glance at her son as she drives them home. "If you don't want me reading your mind, Junior, you will explain their meaning to me."

"Ouch! Well played, Mom."

On the first day of school in September, Pandora stands in the doorway and watches her son madly pack his supplies into his backpack.

Junior pulls an overcoat over the red t-shirt and blue jeans he is wearing while groaning slightly at the weight of his pack as he shrugs it over his shoulders.

"Are you sure you don't want a ride?"

"Nah, it's good Mom. Parents are not supposed to drive their kids on the first day of school."

"I don't know if I believe that, but..."

"Mom, I know you are worried 'cause I can feel it. I will be fine. I have practiced a lot and I have you in my mind to keep them out."

Pandora sighs, moving forward to hug her son. "I know Junior. I'm sorry. I will try to do better for you."

Junior sighs, hugging her tight. "Mom, I understand. It's been the three of us always. Every time we moved, we stuck to ourselves. We were the quiet, not-seen neighbors, and I get it. I was learning my visions and can feel how overwhelming they are with tons of people around. I know you were protecting me and still are, and you always will. Probably more so than the other kids' parents because we are dragons and mystics, and there is always the risk of exposure. But I want this place to be different. I want to venture out there, in the world, and see what it's really like. It's something that I feel I have to do, and you taught me to listen to those feelings."

Pandora nods, releasing her son and stepping back to look him over, straightening his jacket. "When did you become a parent?"

Rendgren steps into the doorway, having felt his wife's emotions downstairs. "Is your Mother getting mushy on you, Junior?"

"Yes! Dad, she is! She's only supposed to get that way with you."

Pandora smiles between the two of them. "Alright, you two, I will stop being emotional. You better get going, Junior; it's about a twenty-five minute walk to town."

Junior reaches out to squeeze his mom's hand. "I will see you after school, Mom. I will be fine. Dad, take care of her." He passes by his father, giving a nod to him before running down the hall to the stairs and bounding down them three at a time. He lands on the ground floor with a thud and runs out the front door, heading down the driveway.

Pandora feels him move through the house and moves over to the balcony that overlooks the driveway, watching her son skip happily down the driveway.

Junior pauses at the gate and looks up to the balcony, giving a wave to his parents before continuing on to school.

Rendgren's arms wrap around her, pulling her close as he rests his chin on the top of her head. "He'll do fine."

"I know he will, Gren. It's still hard watching him grow up."

Rendgren laughs, kissing her cheek as he whispers in her ear. "My dear wife, he's 340 years old."

"Yes, I know, but he's still my baby."

"You're both babies."

"Well, that's because you're old." Her gaze lingers on the now empty driveway.

"That I am. Now, we have a house to ourselves. Let's go back inside and make the most of it." Rendgren lifts her up gently and carries her back to the bedroom, placing her gently on the bed. He crawls in next to her and pulls her close, just holding her tight, his hand caressing her hair gently as he soothes her. "Love, you know he needs to venture into the world and adapt to it."

"I know Gren, and I knew this day was coming. I just didn't expect it to be so hard, especially as it's the beginning of the end."

He places a finger on her lips, quietening her. "Let's just rest. Then we can romp around the mansion naked because our son is gone for the whole day!"

Pandora laughs, kissing his fingers. "In front of the big bay windows and glass doors downstairs? I think not!"

"Who's gonna see us? We are in a mansion on the hill!"

"Anyone that drives up that driveway, and you belong to me."

Rendgren chuckles. "I do, do I? Getting a wee bit possessive, my dear dragon. And here I thought I owned you. After all, I did steal you fair and square."

She pulls him close, whispering against his lips. "Only because I let you. Now shush and make me forget Junior's in school."

Rendgren's eyes darken in desire as he props himself up and looks down at his wife lying beneath him. "Is that a challenge, my dear?"

Pandora's eyes match his desire, feeling his as well as hers through their bond, her fingers trailing lightly along his jawline. "Are you up for it?"

"Oh hell yes." He pulls her close, kissing her deeply as the two of them swiftly become lost in each other, enjoying a day in each other's arms.

Twenty-One

Navigating Emptiness

A few weeks pass as Junior adapts quickly, making friends easily and fitting into all the cliques that he desires. From the in crowd to the geek squad and everyone in between, each of them seeking to be his friend. He joins the football team after school, as predicted, finding a love of the game and the thrill of the hunt for the pigskin. It isn't long before his human name, Asher, is forgotten, thanks to his newfound friend Kip, who called him Junior upon seeing him on the first day of school. The rest just follow suit, including the teachers, bringing a smile to his lips as he knows this is his mom's doing since she is the one that introduced him to Kip as Junior in the first place. On weekends, Junior hangs out with Kip at his house, but more often than not, they end up at Junior's place, playing video games or tossing the football in the yard.

Pandora watches her son grow and adapt to the mortal world with ease, but in doing so, finds herself at a loss of what to do. Knowing her husband is doing his best to fill the void by keeping her active, from sword fighting and cooking lessons to that which happens in the bedroom. She flips through the book she is reading, her thoughts drifting to the day she dropped Junior off for his pre-exam. Placing the book aside, she glances at Rendgren. "I am going for a walk, Gren."

"Did you want company, love?"

She shakes her head. "No, I just need to think."

Rendgren studies her for a moment, understanding she is taking Junior's step in the world hard, doing what he can to keep her occupied but finding he is running out of options. "If you need me, let me know."

"I will, Gren, thank you." She pads down to the entrance, slips on some shoes, and draws a cloak over her shoulders, tying the ribbons at the front. She steps outside, breathing in the cool air, feeling the sun upon her skin as she wanders down the driveway, heading for the mall. More specifically, the library. Forty minutes later, she is standing at the library window, reading over the volunteer sign carefully before stepping inside to ask about the position. She studies the lady at the desk, helping a young child check out her books, smiling at the happiness she can feel emanating from the girl. Once she is done, Pandora steps up and gives a nod of respect to the librarian.

"Greetings. Might I ask what's involved with volunteering? We just moved here, and with my son in school, I am finding I have time to spare."

The librarian looks Pandora over carefully, the strange clothing and the cloak over her shoulders, looking as if she just stepped out of a fantasy picture book. "Do you have any experience?"

Pandora shakes her head. "No, I don't. Only working with children."

"Well, we are short-handed, so if you are good with children, the rest we can train. The position entails three to four afternoons a week, sorting books and placing them back on the shelves. During that time, the elementary school has after school-programs, so it can get pretty crazy here."

Pandora smiles at the thought of children running around, books in hand. "That would be lovely. Thank you. I really appreciate it."

She returns her smile, offering her hand. "I am Arlyne."

"Pandora." She accepts the hand and shakes it.

"Welcome to the library. Come by tomorrow at two, and we will get you started. I will have forms for you to fill out then."

Pandora's eyes sparkle in happiness as she offers a bow. "Thank you again. I will see you tomorrow." She pushes the door open and wanders through the mall next door, humming softly. Buying some flowers before heading home, her fingers caressing the petals lightly. She smiles at her husband waiting in the doorway for her. "Gren."

"Did you enjoy your walk?"

"Yes, I got a job."

"What? You don't need to work Pandora."

"I understand that, Gren, but I need something to keep my mind from dwelling."

"I have been trying, my love."

She places her bags on the side table and steps into his arms, holding him close. "You have, you really have. And I love you for it. But when I was in the cave, I had Spider. Then, in the castle, I had Junior, Martha, and market day with the kids... And now I have nothing, and I don't want to monopolize all your time."

"You still have Junior, love. He's just in school." He wraps his arms tightly around her. "And I have no complaints about trying to keep you occupied."

"He is. And I know you don't. I respect what you have been trying to do. But I need something for me, so I am going to work with the after-school children's groups at the library."

Rendgren kisses her forehead gently. "Love, you know I will support you in whatever you want to do."

She nods, resting her head on his chest. "I know, Gren. I miss feeling the children's happiness and joy."

He lifts her chin to look at her. "Are you implying I am not happy enough for you?"

Pandora laughs softly. "For a broody dragon, of course you are."

He scowls at her, humor dancing in his eyes. "Broody, am I?"

She rises to her tiptoes, cupping his face in her hands. "Well, not so much anymore, but I love you anyway. It's just that children are different."

Rendgren kisses her gently. "I know Pandora. I remember market days and how you always had a radiance around you afterwards. Your eyes practically glowed in happiness. If this will return that glow, you have my full support."

"Thank you, Gren."

Rendgren pauses as it registers what her hours are. "Wait... After school? Bloody hell, does this mean I am cooking dinner those nights?"

Pandora laughs at his expression, reaching up to caress his cheek lightly. "I did tell you a long time ago that you would learn how to cook in the kitchen."

"Damn Mystics!" He mutters under his breath as he leads her back inside, closing the door behind him.

At the end of September, Junior hands his parents a notice regarding a parent-teacher interview on the following Monday. Pandora looks over the letter carefully, reading that it is to be a general meeting with other parents and students, with private consultations afterwards with each family. She hands it over to her husband. "I will be at the library that day, but I am certain they will let me off early."

Rendgren grins, scanning it quickly. "This is where we find out exactly what kind of handful our son is?"

Junior scowls at his father good-naturedly. "DAD! I am right here, and I am perfect! The teachers love me."

Pandora teases him gently. "Well, you do take after your father, so I find that hard to believe."

"Mom! NO! Us mystics, we gotta stick together. What are you doing?"

Pandora moves over, wrapping her arm around his waist and leaning a head on his shoulder as she studies her husband watching them. "Indeed we do. And I know just how well-behaved you are, for I can see it."

Junior mutters and pushes his mom away, laughter dancing in his voice. "Not fair, and you already sided with Dad. You gotta earn it back, Mom." He turns and runs, laughing through the halls, pausing at the kitchen to grab snacks, before heading to his room.

Pandora's thoughts touch his as he runs away. *'I love you, Junior.'*

'I know you do, Mom. That's besides the point. Bring peace offerings!'

She turns to Rendgren, moving into his arms, "I will meet you there, and you can fill me in on what I miss. Now, I need to go bake a pie apparently. Are you joining me in the kitchen, Gren?"

Rendgren chuckles. "Of course. I shall enjoy watching you bake to get back in our son's good graces."

"Of course you will." Pandora mutters under her breath and heads to the kitchen, feeling the humor radiating off her husband as he follows and settles onto one of the chairs. She places the ingredients on the island and makes the pie she knows will appease her son. An hour later, she pulls it out of the oven and places it on the stove to cool, taking in a deep breath of its scent. She smiles as she sets about slowly cleaning the mess up, feeling her son pacing upstairs, knowing the scent of blueberries and pastry is filling the mansion.

Rendgren chuckles. "You really gonna make him come down?"

She smiles at him innocently. "I don't know what you are talking about, Gren; I am simply cleaning up and letting it cool."

He breaks into laughter as his eyes follow her around the kitchen. "Love. I can see what you are doing. It's not going to work. He's a red!"

She arches her brow. "Do you want to bet on that? Loser cooks dinner tonight?"

"I can agree with that."

"Right, he will be downstairs in less than five minutes."

"He's going to make you bring it upstairs, my love. And no telepathy telling him of our bet."

Pandora smiles, tossing the cloth at her husband as she sits at the island with him. "Use your senses, Gren; he's already on his way down."

"Damn! Really..." He sighs as he tosses the cloth back at his wife. "One day, I will win against the two of you."

"You certainly can try, Gren." She turns as Junior enters the kitchen. "Junior, what brings you down here?"

"I can smell the peace offering, Mom. Besides, my desire to watch Dad cook overrides you siding with him earlier." Humor dances in his eyes as he settles on a chair between them. "Well, Dad, it's getting close to that time; shouldn't you start?"

Rendgren shakes his head, sending a dark look at his son as he rises. "One day, my dear boy, one day."

Junior laughs at his dad's look. "I know Dad, and unlike Mom, I do use my sight against you."

"Clearly." He turns to Pandora. "He is yours!"

Junior rests his head on his mom's shoulder as he wraps an arm around her. "I am both of yours, and you are stuck with me. Now, what are we having for dinner? My vote is for spaghetti; it's the best!"

Rendgren mutters under his breath about living with mystics and moves to the cupboard. He pulls out a plate, thinking of spaghetti as food appears on it, and places it in front of his son.

"DAD! That's cheating. At least Mom baked the pie."

Rendgren smiles his way. "It's not cheating, son; It's utilizing my time wisely. And being a mystic, you should have seen that coming. Now, my dear wife, what do you want for dinner?"

Pandora laughs at their antics. "Well played, Gren. I will have spaghetti as well. Thank you."

Rendgren pulls out two more plates, sliding one over to Pandora as the food appears while he settles on the chair he had just vacated. The three of them banter at the island, enjoying their spaghetti and the blueberry pie afterwards. After the dishes are clean, they curl up on the couch and watch a movie before retiring for the night.

Monday afternoon rolls around, and Rendgren drives to the school, understanding his wife is going to be late because of her volunteer job. He arrives and parks his car, seeing some kids milling around as they wait on their parents. Not seeing Junior, he reaches out and communicates with him telepathically. *'Son?'*

'Dad, football practice ran late, just leaving the locker room; I will meet you in classroom 137.'

'Sounds good, see you there.'

Rendgren walks into the school, ignoring the looks directed his way as he moves along the hallway until he finds the room he is looking for. Inside is a variety of people, including his son, standing and talking with his friend Kip and another two students. Approaching them, he acknowledges those he passes with a nod, his black and red hanfu a vivid contrast against the sea of jeans and t-shirts. His long black hair is elegantly braided on the side, adorned with hairpins holding rubies that match the embellishments along his neckline and sleeves. "Junior, Kip, and I don't believe we have met?"

"Oh Mr. Red! Nice to meet you. I am Oliver; this is Ethan. We play football with Junior."

Several parents subtly adjust their posture as Rendgren strides into the room, each discreetly assessing him as he positions himself beside his son, an undeniable aura of authority surrounding him.

Marcy pushes her blonde hair off her shoulders, fanning herself slightly as her green eyes lock on Rendgren when he enters the classroom. "Who is that, Nikki? He's pretty fine, perfect even. I think I want him. And whatever he is wearing is hot. H.O.T. hot." She watches him join one student, a young man slightly shorter than him, sharing similar features. The only noticeable difference being the student's short black and red hair and his striking violet eyes.

"Oh, that's Junior's dad, Mr. Red. People say they moved from Hontby, and that's the style of dress over there. They bought the mansion on the hill."

"Wait, what? The empty mansion that's been locked up tighter than a drum, for, like ever."

"Yeah, that's the one. He showed up with the deed to it and moved in at the end of the school year."

Marcy's mind wanders to the opulence of the mansion, considering its value and the decades it's remained sealed. In their teenage years, it was a daring challenge to explore its interiors, but the ever-vigilant caretaker swiftly thwarted any attempts they made. A role that passed through generations of a single family, a steadfast guardian of the estate. "He must have money if he bought that place."

"Yes, especially since it's rumored it was the King of Oblait's old mansion. And being the realtor that I am, I wasn't even aware it was for sale."

"A king's mansion... Wow, now I really want him."

"Well, unfortunately for you, Marcy, he's not available. He's happily married, and I mean happily."

"No one is happily married."

"Oh, they certainly are." She sighs wistfully. "To have someone gaze at me the way he looks at his wife... I'd melt, just as she surely does."

"Who is his wife?"

"Pandora, I'm sure she will be here soon. She volunteers at the library."

"Well, I don't care who she is; I aim to have him."

"Good luck, Marcy. They are made for each other. Both of them are perfect."

Marcy laughs at her friend's comment. "Never underestimate the power of my mind and body, Nikki."

Nikki shakes her head. "I think you might have found your match on this one."

"We'll see. I think I might just wander his way." Standing up from her chair, she navigates through the room, engaging in brief conversations as she makes her way closer to Rendgren. Despite her efforts to maintain a cordial smile, she feels a hint of irritation as multiple people intercept her, delaying her progress to her destination.

Twenty minutes later, Pandora enters, clad in a purple and green hanfu, a cloak over her shoulders as she pauses at the doorway. Her violet eyes sweep over the assembled parents, briefly pausing on Marcy before locating her husband across the room, offering him a warm smile.

Rendgren feels her immediately, his eyes darkening with desire as they lock onto his wife. Crossing the room towards her, he misses the fact that Marcy steps deliberately into his path. He gives an imperceptible nod, "Excuse me," and maneuvers around her to his wife. He pulls Pandora into his arms and kisses her cheek. "Love, you are earlier than I expected."

Pandora nods, her eyes finding Marcy's again, before returning her attention back to her husband. "Yes, Arlyne said I could leave early as there were no kids at the library. Did I miss anything?"

Rendgren shakes his head, taking her hand in his and leading her back the way he came. "Not yet; I think people are still gathering. Come, let's get back to Junior."

Marcy's gaze shifts sharply to Pandora, a surge of jealousy and resentment rising within her at Pandora's striking beauty; her long black hair, violet eyes, fair complexion, and impeccable figure, dressed similarly to her husband. She observes them returning to their son's side, not even sparing a glance in her direction.

Nikki walks over and smiles, her voice low and quiet. "Strike one, Marcy; he didn't even notice you were there."

Marcy scowls darkly at her friend Nikki. "He will. I will have him. Mark my words. It's just a matter of driving a wedge between them."

"They seem pretty solid, Marcy. I don't think that you'll be able to do it."

"We will see. If I can't drive a wedge into him, I will drive a wedge into her."

Shortly after, the teachers begin by reviewing the students' progress and outlining their ongoing educational objectives. They respond to inquiries, addressing concerns parents have regarding large class sizes, teaching methods, and grades, aiming to alleviate the worries of the majority in the room. Once the general discussions conclude, the teachers lead individual parents and their child to separate rooms for private sessions. The remaining parents engage in casual conversation, mingling with one another as they await their turn for the private meetings.

Rendgren and Pandora accompany Junior when one of his teachers calls his name, being guided to an empty classroom down the hall. The teacher smiles and shakes their hands. "Welcome, I'm Mr. Fowler. I suppose we are here to discuss your son, though I am uncertain about what there is to address, to be honest. He's getting straight A's, exemplary behavior, and is a pro at football. Everyone seems to love your boy. Even Mrs. Spoons is advocating for him, and she is '*difficult to please*' according to any student you ask." Mr. Fowler hands over the reports, providing a detailed overview of Junior's progress during the first month at school for Rendgren and Pandora to review. "If he keeps doing this well, he will get scholarships and invites to any university he wants."

Junior nudges his father. "See Dad! I told you so. They love me."

Rendgren chuckles, ruffling the hair on his son's head. "I wasn't concerned."

"Uggg, you and Mom both. Don't touch the hair!" Junior bats his hand away and moves to stand next to his mother.

Pandora side-steps away from him, teasing him lightly. "Hey, you included me in that statement of yours, Junior; find yourself another savior."

"Mom! It's you and me! Remember?"

"Oh, I remember. Next time, omit me, or I will side with your father."

Junior wraps his arms around his mom, hugging her tightly. "I love you, Mom!"

Pandora taps her foot gently on the floor in amusement. "You love me when you want me on your side. Otherwise, you love your father."

"Mom, enough facts. I love you right now. That's what matters."

Mr. Fowler laughs at the family's antics. "Now I see why he's so lovable. You three have a wonderful family dynamic. Keep up the good work. I wish all parents were as comfortable with their kids as you are. Now, I need to go round up another set of parents and speak with them. Thank you for attending, and we will see you at the next one." He shakes their hands again and leaves the room.

Pandora smiles at Junior, taking his hand in hers for a moment. "Well, Junior, I am proud of you. Let's hit the ice cream parlor on the way home and celebrate with a movie of your choice."

"Deal! I call shotgun!"

Rendgren frowns slightly as he looks at his son. "Shotgun?"

Pandora pats Rendgren's shoulder. "You are so behind the times, my dear husband. He can have the front seat today; he's earned it."

"How is shotgun equivalent to the front seat?"

"Dad! Just chillax!"

"Junior, your father's not up on your slang. Stop confusing him."

Junior laughs and leads them out of the room, calling across the hallway. "I will see you tomorrow, Kip!"

"Fo'shizzle Junior!"

Rendgren looks at Pandora, who shrugs her shoulders, her thoughts reaching to his gently. *I will explain later; just go with it.*

The group pile into the car, hitting the local ice cream parlor for burgers, fries, and ice cream, heading home with their dinner. Junior races in to put the movie on as Pandora and Rendgren follow at a respectable rate, converging in the living room and enjoying their evening together.

After the movie, Pandora and Rendgren retire to the bedroom, each stripping out of their robes and crawling under the covers. Pandora rolls over and faces Rendgren, her eyes studying him carefully.

He sighs softly. "I know that look, love. What's up?"

"There was a lady at the meeting. Marcy is her name. She has her sights set on taming you."

"You know she doesn't have a hope in hell of succeeding."

"I know that, Gren, but she's going to get very determined to split us apart, including trying to shame us and divide us. Whatever it takes to get you, so we need to be careful."

Rendgren pulls his wife close, caressing her cheek lightly. "I love you, Pandora. We are bound and bonded as one, forever, with Raya's blessing and an oath to her. She can try, but she will fail."

She smiles, cupping her hand against his, feeling his touch within her. "I just needed you to know. She was rather pissed when you walked right past her to get to me tonight."

"Wait, I walked past her?"

Pandora laughs softly. "Yes, she stepped right into your path. Blonde, green eyes, slender build, about my height."

"Can't say I noticed. My wife is the only one that draws my attention in a room... Besides Junior, of course, but that's different. Wait, how is it you noticed this? Your focus was on me; I could feel it."

"Oh, the rage emanating from her was not hard to miss. Even if I hadn't seen it, I could feel it the second you turned your attention on me, only intensifying when you ignored her."

Rendgren tightens his hold on his wife as he kisses along her neck, feeling her body responding to his touch. "We will deal with her if we need to. Now, I think we should continue this conversation later."

Pandora nods, closing her eyes and losing herself to her husband's touch, succumbing to the passion that he creates within her.

A week and a half later, Junior and Kip engage in light-hearted banter in the locker room after football practice, joining others as they strip out of their gear, shower, and exit the school. Several parents linger, anticipating the end of after-school activities to pick up their children. The inseparable pair stroll toward Kip's mom, Shels, who patiently waits by the car.

"Are you walking home, Junior? Or do you want a ride?"

"I'll walk; It's not that far."

Kip glances around as the rest of the team filters out behind them. "So I know the others have been dying to ask, so I will. You have a sun tattoo already? I thought you had to be twenty-one to get those."

Junior reaches up to his chest, where Raya's mark is burned upon him. "Yes, I think twenty-one is the age. My parents gave it to me when I was young."

"That's not cool, man."

"It's not so bad."

"They should have your consent before giving you a tattoo; I mean, what if you don't like it?"

Junior laughs, shoulder-checking his friend. "It doesn't matter whether I do it or not. It's there permanently, and I am not arguing with my parents about this. I have seen them fight. I don't stand a chance against them."

Kip looks at him in surprise. "Your parents fight?"

"Yes, all the time; One day, you will see it."

Marcy leans against her car, watching Junior walk by with Kip, overhearing their conversation. A smile crosses her lips as she ponders what it means; that apparently, they didn't have the perfect relationship everyone seems to think they do. Her eyes land on her daughter as she devises a plan to use this insight of information on how to split them up.

"Kaspina dear, I want you to make friends with Junior."

"Mom, he's the most popular kid in the school. Everyone wants to. I'm sure he won't want to hang with me."

"Well, find a way. Perhaps flirt a little and work towards being his girlfriend."

She laughs, packing her instrument into the trunk. "Doubtful, Mom. He doesn't even like girls."

"You mean Kip and him are an item?"

Kaspina rolls her eyes at her mother as she closes the trunk, her eyes drifting to Junior and Kip. "No, Mom, that's not it at all. They are BFFs. What I am saying is he doesn't want one. He growls in disgust at people kissing in the hall... Like actually seems to growl."

"Then be his best friend."

"Kip got that position, Mom. No one's taking it, and everyone's jealous of him." She moves around to the side of the car and hops in.

Marcy moves to the driver's side and gets in with her. "Find a way, Kaspina."

"Why, Mom? Why are you so interested in him?"

"No reason; I just think it would do you good to be in his circle of friends. That boy is going places, according to your father."

"Yah yah. I know. He excels at everything he sets his mind to. I hear it from Dad as well. I will think about it, but don't get your hopes up. We are in different leagues."

Twenty-Two

Behind the Grandeur

Early October, Pandora receives a notice from the school stating there is a scheduled meeting with the parents regarding the Yule dance and fair. She sighs as she looks it over, grateful at least this one is in the evening, and she can go alone. She moves to the kitchen with the letter, placing it on the counter as she sets about starting dinner while pondering how she could help. She slices the carrots and potatoes to go with the pot roast, knowing she isn't exactly the crafty type, but could bake a few pies for it.

Rendgren meanders into the kitchen, and sees the letter on the counter. He picks it up and frowns as he reads it. "Does this school do nothing without the parents?"

Pandora laughs as she puts the roast in the oven and sets a timer. "It's their annual Yule festival. You do not need to go to this meeting, Gren. I can manage it alone."

Rendgren moves over to kiss his wife's cheek. "Great! I will leave it to you then."

She shakes her head, wrapping her arm around him, and rests her head on his chest. "It's probably best. I would love to say, out of sight, out of mind, but she's plotting even as we speak."

"She won't succeed, love."

"I know, Gren. She's just going to test our patience, and I don't like that."

He hugs her tight. "Pandora. You and Junior are who I love. That's never going to change."

She closes her eyes, feeling his love on their bond, as she remains in his arms.

"Thank you, Gren."

A few days later, Pandora sits in the school classroom, reading over the requirements and requests for the event, doing her best to tune out the anger she could feel emanating from the corner.

Marcy mutters to her friends, Nikki, and Lucy as she sits in the corner with them, her eyes sending daggers at Pandora, who appears to actually be reading the handouts. "Gawd, these chairs are so uncomfortable. I don't know how our kids manage it all day. Perhaps we should have these meetings at someone's house, especially if we have one every week or two until December." A unanimous agreement echoes within the room at Marcy's comments as they all shift in the chairs simultaneously. Marcy's gaze zeros in on Pandora, knowing this is a way to get into the mansion and closer to Zalgren. "I think we should vote. I vote for Pandora's house."

Pandora snaps her gaze up, looking carefully at Marcy as the others all agree instantly. She shakes her head. "I don't think it's such..."

"Yes! I think most of us have always wanted to see what the mansion is like, but it's been locked until you moved into it."

"Please, Pandora?"

Pandora's gaze shifts to Raven and Joela, both sincere, as she feels the ball of rage approach her.

Marcy places a hand on Pandora's shoulder, her grip tighter than it needs to be. "Of course, it's fine; we can make it on a Saturday perhaps, when everyone is off work."

Pandora pulls Marcy's hand off her shoulder and pats it gently, understanding her implications. "I will ask Gren."

"I am certain Zalgren won't mind."

"Oh, I am positive he will. He doesn't like people in his home. Perhaps he can take Junior to the movies or something."

"Oh no, he needs to be there... I mean, our husbands will be. Who will they talk to?"

She arches a brow as she places the papers aside. "Indeed, who?" She scans the room, observing the genuine hope in most of the parents, evident in their desire to see her home compared to the stark contrast of the calculated shrewdness and ambition in Marcy and her companions, Nikki and Lucy. "Fine, the next meeting will be at our house." She sighs inwardly as conversation fills the room about what they might encounter inside the mansion.

Pandora rises, gives them a nod, and leaves. Knowing Rendgren will be less than impressed about her bringing people into their domain in two weeks. She walks home, lost in her thoughts as she steps up to the house, feeling Rendgren upstairs in the library with Junior. Padding silently to the kitchen, she pulls out one of their special mugs as tea fills it. She sets it on the island as she sits down to ponder how to handle Marcy and sort through threads.

Rendgren feels his wife enter; his eyes drift to the hallway but senses her enter the kitchen. He rises and pats Junior on the head, earning an exasperated *Dad!* "I will be right back. I think something is bothering your mother."

Junior's focus remains on his laptop, typing away madly at his homework. "Alright, Dad."

He moves down to the kitchen and looks over his wife, studying her expression as she stares at the cup of tea before her. "Love, is something wrong?"

She looks up and shakes her head. "Nothing out of the ordinary. Marcy and her gang wish to hold the next meeting here."

"What!?"

"Only three of them have something planned; the others honestly wish to see the mansion."

"We already know what Marcy wants. It's me, but she's not getting it."

"I know that, Gren; It's hard because Junior wants to be a part of the school and its communities where I really just want to tell her to stuff it. Actually, I want to tear her to shreds and not play political bullshit with her."

Rendgren chuckles. "You've been a dragon too long, Pandora; it's rubbing off on you. I feel that anytime anyone even looks at you."

"How do you do it? How do you not tear them to shreds?"

"I remember who you love and who you come home to."

She rises to her feet and wraps her arms around him. "Thanks, Gren."

He places a hand under her chin and looks into her eyes. "I will always love you, Seer. You are my mate. For eternity. No one is splitting us up, let alone a petty vindictive mortal that's unhappy in her own marriage."

"I love you too, Gren."

"Come, Juniors talking about watching a movie. Let's forget about this and watch it with him."

"Thank you for making me feel better."

"Always, I am your husband. I am here for you." He nudges her playfully. "And I've been a dragon WAY longer than you have, so I can control the dragon's fire better...clearly."

She laughs, pushing him away, her eyes darkening with desire. "You think so. How about instead of the movie, we go up to the bedroom?"

"Oh, you are evil, Seer. No, just for that, I am going to show you just how much control I have." He steps in and kisses her deeply, his hands roaming over her gently, feeling her sink against him as she surrenders to him. He steps away, struggling against himself, and kisses her cheek lightly. "Ok, you're right, I have no control." He picks her up, throws her over his shoulder, and drags her upstairs to the bedroom, kicking the door closed behind them.

Two weeks later, Pandora moves about the house, knowing that the crew of parents are arriving within the half hour. She pauses in the living room, drawing on her powers to shroud the dragon painting, suspecting that anyone that knows their history will recognize it and put it together.

Rendgren arches a brow at the blank wall. "It looks too blank. Perhaps a painting of something else?"

She nods, weaving her magic into a painting of a purple dragon perched on the side of a castle.

"Purple? Not red?"

Pandora laughs. "Purple's my color, Gren, and reds up there every other day of the year."

"Yes, but you love red." He draws her in, kissing her gently.

"I do." She sighs against him as she wraps her arms around him, resting her head on his shoulder.

"It will be fine, love."

"I know. I just wish Marcy would back off."

"She won't; she's jealous of what we have and wants it. On that note, I think I will go lock some doors."

"Probably a good idea, as she is going to wander."

"So downstairs, the bedroom, the den... anything else?"

"Perhaps Junior's room, though I suspect he will hide in there. Might actually do her good to come face to face with an angry teenager."

Rendgren chuckles. "Alright, I will let Junior know."

Pandora watches him head down the hallway as she turns to the kitchen and sets about getting the snacks ready, plating crackers and cheeses, along with a variety of meats. She pours the chips into bowls, shaking them to settle them before placing them next to the platters. She fills the cooler with ice and places sodas and water on top. Rendgren returns to the kitchen, looking at the trays ready to go out into the dining room. "Veggies and dip?"

"Right." She moves to the fridge and pulls out the veggies, setting about slicing them and placing them on a platter, while Rendgren moves the filled trays out to the dining room. Pandora retrieves the dip out of the fridge and pours it into a bowl, setting it in the center of the veggies. She then gathers the paper plates and carries both into the dining room, where he is arranging them on the table.

"It looks like we are all set."

"Thank you, Gren."

Rendgren turns to Pandora, caressing her cheek lightly. "I will support you in everything, even if I have to allow that wretched Marcy in my house."

"I know Gren, and if it wasn't for the others, I would have shut her down."

"I know you would have. We will handle this just like everything else."

Junior rounds the corner, scowling at his parents. "Ugg, you guys! Guests are coming, and you're getting mushy! Pllleeease."

Pandora leans on Rendgren. "Junior, I am surprised to see you out of your room."

"I want food before I get invaded."

"Well, not this food. Get it out of the kitchen."

"Seriously? Mom!"

"Yes, this is for the guests. You want it; you come out while the guests are here."

"Not likely!"

"Then the kitchen is your choice."

"Fine!" Junior makes his way to the kitchen. He pulls out one of the magical plates, and locks the cupboard afterwards. He scowls at his mom as he walks past her, his plate filling with food.

Pandora mutters under her breath. "He is yours!"

Rendgren chuckles at his wife. "He is ours."

"Yes, I suppose he is." Pandora lifts her gaze, sensing the steps that approach the house. "Of course, it would be Marcy's gang that shows up early."

"You had to know it. I will let you get the door while I hide in the den until others arrive." Rendgren kisses her softly and makes a swift exit.

Pandora shakes her head and moves to the door at the knock. She opens it and smiles at the trio. "Welcome, please come in." She leads them into the living room, catching Marcy's gaze narrow on their family portrait in the main foyer. "Please find yourself a place to settle."

"I don't see Zalgren around."

"Oh, he's in the den doing some last-minute stuff. He will be out shortly." Immediately noticing they neglect to mention why their husbands are missing.

"That's too bad; we came early, hoping for a private tour."

Pandora smiles. "Well, I am afraid you're going to have to wait until the others get here. Really, it's just a house with a lot of rooms."

"Yes, but look at this room; it's magnificent. I am certain all the rooms are like this."

"Actually, most of them are empty."

"Really, empty?"

"Yes, we don't need them. We only furnished the rooms we use."

"Wow, it must be nice to have that much extra space."

"I suppose I never really thought about it. Excuse me, I heard another knock. There are snacks on the table; help yourself."

She turns and heads back to the front door, catching Marcy's whisper about trying to find Zalgren. She smiles at the next group. "Come on in. Marcy, Nikki, and Lucy are already in the living room." They nod and follow Pandora in, settling themselves into chairs. After about fifteen minutes, the rest of the Yule council arrives with their husbands.

Ground Floor

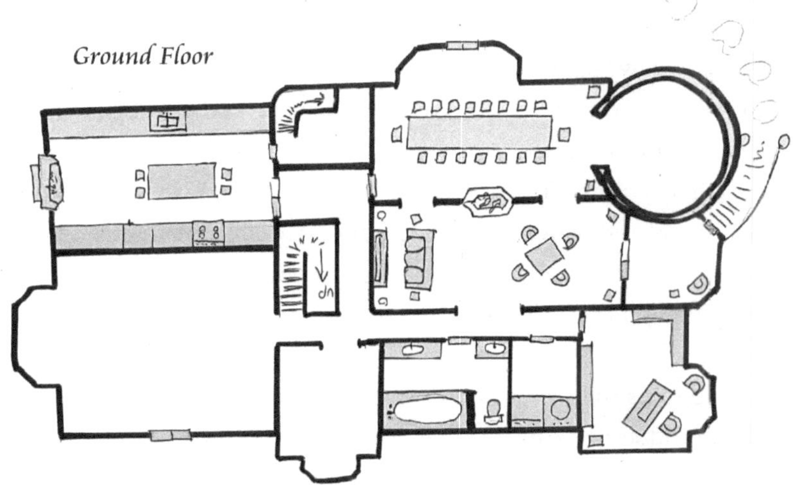

Zalgren's Mansion

Upper Floor

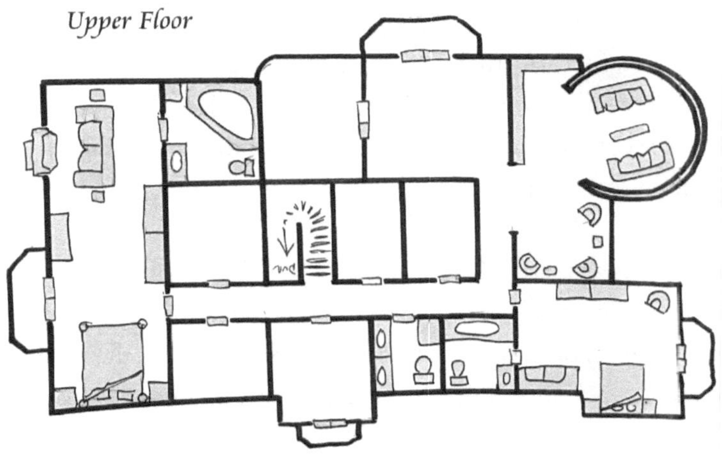

Pandora smiles at the group. "Now that we are all here, I can show you around the place, though we do only use a small amount of the rooms, so a lot sit empty. This is our living room and dining area." She watches as the group looks over the rooms, a blend of timber and stone walls, the couches and chairs in black velvet with red satin overtones. The notable feature of the room is a large painting of a purple dragon placed above the TV. The dining room contains a long table in a rich red wood with matching chairs, the seats a deep red velvet. A large tapestry of a castle hangs on the wall behind the dining room table next to the glassed-in balcony.

Pandora catches the whispers on the sixteen-person table and the feasts that could be had and smiles, knowing they rarely use it. "If you follow me, I can show you the kitchen." She leads them out of the dining hall and through double doors into a kitchen nearly as large as the room they just left, hearing the gasps from the woman as they enter. The cupboards are a light oak that line the kitchen on two sides. The countertops are heavy granite, matching the island in the center of the room, with four bar stools set against the backside. On the far wall, a brick oven takes center stage, while a modern oven and fridge adorn the wall to their left. White lace curtains flutter in the breeze from the open window above the kitchen sink on their right.

"WOW! This kitchen is amazing, Pandora."

Pandora smiles at Joela. "Thank you. We spend a lot of time here or in the library. More so than the living room because Junior dominates it with his video games. The other door in here leads to the storage and the cellar that we don't use." She watches as they wander the kitchen before guiding them back out and down a hallway, hanging a right into the ballroom. Marble floors sparkle in the sunlight streaming through the glass doors on two sides of the room. The stone walls are bare, but a few benches sit against them in various places.

"You have a dance hall? Seriously?"

"Yes, apparently."

"Have you had balls in here?"

"Not us, we just moved in here at the end of last school season, but I would imagine in the past, there have been."

Marcy's eyes glint at the thought of a darkened night, dancing with Zalgren here on this floor. "You should throw a ball! Could you imagine?"

Pandora smiles at Marcy coolly. "That's probably not going to happen. Come, I will take you upstairs." She leaves the ballroom and heads up the stairs to her left.

"Where does downstairs go?"

"Oh, it's just a large room down there."

She leads them through the passage upstairs. "These doors are all the bedrooms, but most of them are empty. She steps into an open room where three overstuffed chairs in red velvet sit with small tables in between. Bookshelves run along two of the walls opposite a circular wall. Inside the circular room are two soft black leather couches flanking a coffee table. "This is our library." She steps through into another open room. "And this is a room we were intending to furnish because of the breathtaking views from the balcony, but never have, obviously. Our room also features a balcony, although the view does not compare to this one." She pushes the balcony doors open, pausing at the view of the town below them before stepping aside and letting all the others look.

Raven steps out and gasps softly. "You can see the entire city from here."

"Yes, just about. When we decide what we want to do with this, we will furnish it, but for now, it's just another empty room." Pandora waits until they finish admiring the view before turning and leading them back downstairs to the main floor. She turns left at the bottom of the stairs, reaching the arch of the living room. "This is the main bathing chamber, and next to it is the laundry room." She opens the door on her right, letting them peek in, seeing the super-sized claw-foot tub in the center of the room.

"Oh man! I would love to soak in that tub!" The others murmur in agreement.

Pandora laughs softly. "I will admit, it does have advantages. We have one in the master suite as well." She continues down the short hall to the door at the end, knocking lightly before stepping in. "This is Gren's office, or man-cave as some call it." The den is dark wood, much like the living room, dominated by a large oak desk, dragons carved into its sides. A computer buzzes quietly on top of it with a stained glass reading lamp, also picturing dragons illuminating the desk area. Mostly empty bookshelves line three walls, with one overstuffed chair sitting in the alcove and another occupied by Rendgren.

Marcy immediately steps in, eyeing Zalgren at the computer. "Enough work,

Zal. You should come out and plan with us."

Rendgren arches a brow at Marcy, his gaze drifting to his wife. "I will shortly."

Pandora smiles at the group. "That's about it for the tour. These are the rooms that we use. Let's return to the living room."

Marcy pouts slightly, debating moving forward to see the screen of his computer. "What's he working on?"

"Business stuff."

"What sort of business stuff?"

"None of my business stuff. I don't ask, and neither should you."

Marcy's eyes lift in shock at Pandora's comment and look. She wisely turns and follows the others back to the living room.

Rendgren ducks his head, doing his best to hide the laughter that threatens to escape. *'Nice one, love; wouldn't want her to know I am playing solitaire back here.'*

'No, we wouldn't.' Pandora winks his way before closing the door after her, settling them all back in the living room. She moves to sit on one of the dining room chairs that she has spread around the room to accommodate extra guests.

The group chatters about the mansion for about fifteen minutes before they set about discussing what they were planning for the Yule festival. They split into groups, as each goes over what ideas they have.

Pandora feels Marcy slip out of the dining area, following her path along the hallway to the stairs. Her thoughts touch Rendgren's. *'Marcy is on the move.'*

'I sense her.'

'Nikki is also on the move, but towards the kitchen. We hid the plates, right?'

'Yes, and that cupboard is locked.'

Rendgren walks out of the office, seeing Marcy slip up the stairs. He follows her up, catching her hand on their door handle. "Can I help you, Marcy?"

"Oh, I was looking for a bathroom."

"Upstairs?"

"Well, yes, the downstairs one is occupied."

"I am sure it is. Right this way." He leads her down the hall and opens the main bathroom upstairs.

Marcy nods and steps in, closing the door after her. She moves about the room, peeking in the cupboards, finding it all empty except for two hand towels and toilet paper. She washes her hand and steps out, seeing Rendgren standing there, and makes her way back downstairs.

Rendgren follows her and moves to stand with Pandora's group, resting his hands on her shoulders, massaging them gently, feeling Marcy's gaze bore into him. *'I think I upset the poor dear.'*

Pandora briefly scans the room, seeing the three huddled in the corner as the others work on plans. *'Yes, she will try again.'*

'I am certain she will.'

An hour and a half later, most of the discussions finish and people mill about chatting. Pandora stands at the door, thanking and bidding goodbye to those that need to leave. Marcy takes advantage of the chaos and disappears again, determined to see the master bedroom.

Rendgren shakes his head, kissing Pandora's cheek lightly, before moving to follow. Once all the goodbyes are done, Pandora drifts over to the dining table, grabbing a small plate of food, and sits in the chair near Joela, Raven, and their husbands, Ian and Victor. She glances over, seeing Nikki and Lucy on the couch talking between themselves. Marcy pads quietly up the stairs, pausing at the top, remembering Pandora mentioning a balcony and recalling one as they entered. She moves down the corridor, suspecting it is attached to the room at the end of the hall. She opens the door, her eyes widening in surprise as they land on Junior sitting in a chair reading.

"What the hell?!" He picks up the football nearby and throws it at Marcy's head. "GET OUT OF MY ROOM! MOOOOOMM!!"

Marcy dodges it, only to hear it caught behind her. She turns to see Zalgren looking down at her, a football in his hand, and a displeased expression upon his face.

"Did you get lost again, Marcy? I do believe the bathroom is vacant downstairs."

She bats her lashes, trying to wrap her arms around him. "I just wanted to see your room, Zalgren."

He sidesteps her embrace, narrowing his eyes darkly at her. "That is not happening, Marcy. Please return to the living room. I find you wandering upstairs again. I will wander your ass out the front door. Is that clear?"

"Very." She frowns in dismay at his look. She slips past him and all but stomps back to the stairway.

Rendgren turns to Junior, tossing the football back at him, watching as he expertly catches it. He waits until he feels Marcy at the bottom of the stairs before speaking quietly to his son. "You would think, being a pro football player, you wouldn't miss."

Junior chuckles. "She moved quicker than I expected."

"Clearly, I had to catch the ball. Next time, don't miss."

"Next time, I am just tackling that damn woman."

Rendgren laughs. "I doubt your mother would approve."

Junior chucks the ball at his father. "Like she's going to approve of this conversation? You better get back down there."

He catches it again, rolling it in his hands. "Yes, I might need to furnish one of the extra rooms or crash in here tonight."

"NOT a chance, Dad!"

"Good to know you are in your mother's court." He tosses it back with a grin.

Junior catches it, smiling widely at his father. "Always, Dad. Us mystics, we gotta stick together."

Rendgren laughs and closes the door. He heads back downstairs to his wife and moves to sit at the table with her.

Pandora studies him a moment, giving a shake of her head at his innocent look. "Gren?"

"It's nothing, love. Your son is on your side."

Pandora smiles. "You are just figuring that out now?"

"Clearly."

Marcy drags one of the dining room chairs over and sits at the table with the others as Nikki and Lucy follow suit. "So Pandora, tell us how you met."

"We met in Oblait."

"Really, where abouts?"

"Well, it was in the market in Teshem, actually." Her eyes lift to Rendgren's, recalling the first day their eyes connected. "I was out on my Saturday morning walk from the castle when we ran into each other."

"Wait, castle?"

"Yes, my parents brought me to work there when I was nine. I guess they figured it was better than the farm life they had."

"Did you get to see the King?"

"Yes, fairly often, but I spent a lot of my time in the kitchen or in my room."

"Wow, so what happened after you and Zalgren met?"

Pandora smiles. "Well, he returned a week later and practically stole me from the King. Didn't really give him a choice in the matter, and I've been with Gren ever since."

"So was it like love at first sight?"

Pandora laughs. "No, not quite. It was rocky to start, but we worked through it, and now we couldn't be happier."

Rendgren chuckles. "Rocky? Good to know that's how you are labeling the first year of our relationship."

Pandora arches a brow. "And what would you call it, my dear?"

He scowls slightly. "There were a few bumps to sort out."

"That's right, a few bumps, so rocky."

Marcy looks between them. "So let me get this straight. You were a farm girl that got a job in a castle and now are married to Zalgren and live in this mansion?"

"Yes, I suppose so, though the mansion is Gren's really. It's been in his family for generations; I'm just along as his wife."

Rendgren reaches out to take her hand. "You are more than *just along*, love. You are everything to me."

Marcy's eyes darken with jealousy. "So the family has money."

"Well, Gren's does."

"How much are we talking about?"

"I wouldn't know, Marcy, that's his department." Pandora lifts her eyes to Rendgren, the corners of her lips tipping slightly at the thought of all the dragon treasures she granted him.

Rendgren scowls ever so slightly at Marcy's prodding. "It's enough that we don't have to worry about finances, and that's all you need to know."

Marcy nods, her eyes finding Lucy's, knowing she intended to find out. "So, do your parents still own the farm, Pandora?"

"No, they passed away. I believe the neighbors absorbed our farm."

"You don't know? Shouldn't you go back to the farm and check, perhaps take it over again?"

Pandora smiles, understanding her implications; send the wife back to the farm and get her out of the way. "It's not my life, and my parents and I didn't see eye to eye. I was sad when they passed, yes, but my life is here with Gren and Junior."

"Of course. I would still be curious if my parents died and left a farm behind."

"I guess that's the difference between us, Marcy. I have Gren; he's my world now. Not the farm. Besides, if my parents wanted me to have the farm, they would have willed it to me, and they didn't."

"I suppose that's true." Marcy turns to Zalgren. "So Gren, what drew you to Pandora?"

Rendgren narrows his eyes, his tone growing cold. "It's Zal or Zalgren to you, Marcy. Only my wife calls me Gren."

"Right, sorry, Zal. I am just so used to her calling you Gren, I misspoke."

Rendgren smiles coldly. "Of course. Just make sure it doesn't happen again. Now, as to what drew me to her, it was her eyes and the way they stared at me in the street. I knew at that moment I was coming back for her."

"Why didn't you take her right there then?"

"She was protected by the King's guards."

Marcy snaps her gaze to Pandora. "You mean, you were established enough in the castle that the King sent guards with you in town. What were you doing? Sleeping with the man?"

Rendgren chuckles, his eyes darkening with desire as his eyes roam over his wife. "Oh no, I was the first and only man to be with her. That I guarantee."

Pandora blushes at the sudden turn in the conversation, shifting her gaze towards the table. "I think I would rather not discuss this."

Joela reaches out and squeezes Pandora's hand. "It's alright to be old-fashioned. I praise the fact you kept yourself pure for your husband. A lot can't do or say they have. Can they... Marcy?" She sends a pointed look her way. "It takes a significant amount of strength to stick to your guns like that."

"Thank you, Joela. I appreciate it."

Marcy scowls at Joela before turning to Pandora again. "So how did you deserve such an escort?"

"Oh, it wasn't just me. It was when any of the women left the castle. He was very protective and didn't want us harmed."

Rendgren's thoughts touch hers, teasing her gently. *'Liar.'*

Pandora glances his way. *'You placed me in this position, Gren. Now get me out of it.'*

He chuckles. "Yes, the King was generous that way. He took care of those in his castle."

"Yes, generous. That's right." Pandora coughs slightly. *'NOT any better, love.'*

"Wow, it must have been amazing working for the King."

"Well, yes, I suppose. I never really thought about it."

"I have never even met the Royals, and here you are, a farm girl, working for the King in his castle, seeing him daily. Man, I would be all over that."

"Marcy, I was nine when I started there. Those are not thoughts a nine-year-old has, and as I grew up, he was just a person in the castle to me. I never really thought of him as King, other than we had to bow and address him as your Majesty or Sire."

'My Dear Wife. I did not realize just how good you are at lying.'

'You are going to pay for this later, Gren.'

'You're the one that brought them into the house, love.'

'Oh, so you're making me suffer.'

'That's right.'

'You do know you never want a mystic mad at you, right?'

'Or a woman, and you are both. But I am willing to risk this!'

"So how often did you see the King exactly? What does he lock like? Is he good-looking? Could you have gone for him if Zal hadn't stolen you away?"

Pandora returns her attention to those at the table. "Marcy, he was twice my age, and then some. Far too old for me to even consider, and I grew up with him. I guess he could be considered good-looking, with deep green eyes and long blonde hair, but I never saw him in that light because he was more like a father figure to me."

Rendgren starts to cough and choke, moving away from the table to get a soda from the cooler.

Pandora smiles slightly. *'Having issues Gren?'*

'No love, not at all.'

'It seems like you were.'

'Father figure, really? And too OLD for you?'

'What? Am I supposed to say he was evil and kept me locked in my room? Or that you are old? Like really old.'

"Sounds like a dream."

"For some, I suppose, but not for me. It was simply work. I found my dream in the market and hoped that he would come back for me."

Rendgren takes a sip, watching his love. "Was there ever any doubt?"

"Yes, Gren, there was."

"Well, I knew I was coming back for you. I just needed a week to make it happen."

Raven smiles. "Aww, that's sooo sweet! You guys have an epic love story."

Pandora smiles. "Thank you. Now enough about us."

"But this is getting good. What did the King do when Zal took you away?"

"Well, he wasn't happy about it, but there was nothing he could do. It's not like he owned me."

Rendgren chuckles, moving over to place a hand on Pandora's shoulders, kissing her cheek lightly. "He just didn't want to hire new staff, but I forced him to anyway."

"Yes, he was definitely resistant to change."

Marcy narrows her eyes on Zalgren's hand resting on Pandora. "So, a farm girl, and now look at you."

"There is nothing wrong with being a farm girl, Marcy."

"Uggg, digging in the dirt, please. Shoot me now."

Pandora rolls her eyes slightly. "You do realize that the food in the grocery store comes from farms, and that position demands a measure of respect."

"Only a farm girl would say that."

Rendgren turns his gaze sharply on Marcy. "Actually, that's not true. If there were no farms in the world, we would starve to death. Meat, dairy, and vegetables all come from farms. It takes a person with a powerful strength of will to work on a farm and do it well. They deserve respect. My wife has that strength, and it's one of the things I love about her."

Marcy nods, realizing she is battling both of them, and backs down. "Right, I never really thought of it that way. So what do you do, Zal?"

"I work."

"But at what?"

"It's not important."

Marcy nods, opting to change tactics at his look. "What are you guys doing for Halloween? It's a week away. Do you have your costumes?"

Pandora shakes her head. "Probably just be a night in. We will have candy here if kids decide to trek up to the mansion."

"Wait, you're not dressing up or going to Halloween parties?"

"It's not something I really thought about, to be honest. I don't tend to dress up in costumes."

Rendgren's eyes darken in desire. "I remember one outfit that you dressed up in, my dear. It hugged your curves perfectly."

Pandora blushes. "Yes, well, it was..."

"Amazing. You looked fantastic in it."

Marcy catches the blush. "Exactly what kind of costume is it?"

"It was a fortune teller outfit I bought in Rixlen with some girlfriends."

"Oh, do you still have it? Can we see it?"

"No. Now that I think about it, I haven't seen it since the night I wore it."

Rendgren kisses her cheek. "I still have it."

Pandora snaps her gaze to his. "You still have it?"

"Yes, it was the first time I saw you in costume. Why wouldn't I?"

Raven claps her hands together. "See, epic romance. I am certain my husband can't even remember my first Halloween costume with him."

"Of course I do, Raven."

She turns to her husband. "Alright, Ian, what was it?"

"Ah... it was a cat costume."

"No, it wasn't. I was the chick from the space show with buns in her hair."

Ian shifts uncomfortably. "Are you sure? I only remember the cat."

Raven shakes her head. "That's because it was more revealing." She turns to Pandora. "The less you wear, the more they remember it."

Marcy looks at Raven and Ian momentarily, turning her attention back to Pandora and Zalgren. "Go get it Zalgren, let's see it?"

"No can do; it's locked away in a chest."

Pandora mutters under her breath. "No wonder I haven't seen it."

Rendgren squeezes her shoulders lightly. "It's safe, along with our wedding outfits. Both were very special days for me."

Pandora returns her gaze to him. "Wait, you kept our wedding outfits too?"

"Of course."

"But it was purple."

"Yes, and I married you in it, so I kept it."

Marcy looks between them. "You got married in purple, Zal?"

Rendgren chuckles. "Indeed I did. Matching outfits, actually, thanks to my wife's adoptive mother and her sewing skills. Had I known, I would have pre-bought us outfits in black and red."

Pandora laughs. "I can see that. You were less than impressed by the color choice."

Rendgren mutters good naturedly. "Well, we all know who Martha favored!"

"Clearly me, but there was red in it, too."

"Not enough, my dear. Not nearly enough... and there was no black."

Marcy frowns slightly at the pair. "So why would you get married in purple if you didn't want to?"

Rendgren shakes his head. "Because it was Martha, and you didn't cross her. If you did, you were likely to end up over her knee with your butt in the air and a wooden spoon in her hand before you even finished the word, *No*."

Pandora chokes in laughter at the image, knowing he is very much right. "Gren is right. Martha was all that and more."

"Wow... I would have thought you would have stood your ground if you didn't want something to happen."

Rendgren's eyes darken at Marcy's insult. "Oh, I do, Marcy, but there are two women that I wouldn't risk crossing in my life. One is my wife, and the other was Martha."

Marcy frowns, not liking his statement, or that he is so attached to his wife, suspecting she is going to need to step up her game if she is going to land him. "Well, I suppose we have taken enough of your time. Nik, Luce, Let's go."

Raven nods. "Yes, I suppose we should too. Thank you, Pandora, Zalgren. Your house is lovely."

Pandora rises as the others do. "Thank you. I will see you at the next meeting."

Joela stands and looks around. "We never really decided. I guess I will host it next time."

"Sounds good."

Pandora escorts them all out of the house and locks the door behind them, doing a scan of the living and dining room with a sigh. She moves to the stairs and yells upstairs. "Junior, it's safe to come out of your room now." She returns to the table, gathering a few of the plates while telepathically reaching out to them both. *'Say nothing that will indicate we are not who we are. Nikki's phone is recording us in the kitchen.'*

Junior growls in disgust as he leaves his room. *'Wow, they are that petty that they record us now?'*

'Yes, they want something to tear us apart and are hoping they will find it.'

'Some people. I wish we could just eat them.'

'So do I, my dear child.'

Rendgren chuckles. *'You two are so bad!'*

'Well, I learned from the best, Gren.' Pandora smiles and carries the platters into the kitchen, setting them on the counter, watching Junior enter behind them. "What are we going to do with all this extra food? It's going to go bad before we can eat it."

"I could call Kip. He lives near a farm; their animals might like it."

"Good idea."

"Alright, Mom, I'm gonna go grab my cell. I will be right back."

Rendgren moves over to Pandora's side, drawing her into his arms, his hands lingering on her waist. "Well, love, you survived. I'm proud of you."

"Thank you, Gren."

"What do you say we leave Junior to deal with the food and make our way to the bedroom?" He leans in and plants sloppy, noisy kisses on her neck.

Pandora bites back her laughter, closing her eyes as she feels his touch within. "Hmmm, I think Junior might hate us for doing this to him."

"Junior will kick us out as soon as he sees us."

Just then, Junior walks in. "Ewww. Get a room!"

Rendgren chuckles. "See, what did I tell you? Junior, I think we might just do that." He lifts Pandora into his arms. "Have fun cleaning up."

"Wait! Are you seriously leaving this all to me while you go get it on?"

"That we are, Son." He carries her out of the kitchen.

Junior mutters under his breath as he calls up his friend Kip. "Hey ya, Kip, how would you like to help a friend in need... Yes, my parents left me in charge of cleaning up, but there is an excess of food here, so we thought perhaps the farm next door might want it. Really? Great! I will see you shortly."

A few minutes later, there is a knock on the door, and Junior runs to the front door, swinging it open. "Kip? Ooh, it's you."

"I'm sorry. I seem to have left my purse here."

"I haven't seen it; do you remember where you set it down?"

"I think in the kitchen."

"Right, come this way."

"Where are your parents?"

"Oh, they are in the bedroom doing things I don't want to know about."

"Really. Do they do that to you a lot?"

"All the time. Worse than rabbits."

"Oh my!" Nikki blushes as she picks the purse up. "Here it is. Thank you."

"You're welcome."

Junior leads her outside, seeing Marcy in the car waiting before closing it and locking it, muttering under his breath at the nerve of the woman. He enters the kitchen and does a mental scan for any more listening devices and finds nothing. He sighs in relief as he moves to the window, watching the car back down the driveway. "Daaddd! They're gone!"

Rendgren laughs as he leads Pandora back into the kitchen.

"You almost had me there, Dad! I should have sent the purse into the bedroom with you and Mom."

Rendgren chuckles. "We didn't make it there, Son."

"I know; I could sense you were hiding in the ballroom. Besides, you never do that extra noisy smooching like the kids at school. You have far more class, but I bet it angered her knowing you were taking Mom to the bedroom."

"I suspect you are right, Son. But really. Worse than rabbits?"

"Hey. It made her blush and might shut her up for a bit."

"I suspect it will definitely make her think twice about listening in."

"Good, the woman has some nerve."

Pandora moves to assist with packaging up the meat. "She will get what's coming for her soon enough Junior."

"I want to slap her for thinking she can split you and Dad up."

"Well, she may have succeeded in the past, but she will not with us."

"I know, Mom, but I still want to slap her."

"I understand, Junior, I do too, but we need to play this right."

Junior ponders it a moment and nods, a slow smile crossing his lips.

Pandora studies him for a moment, seeking flickers of images flash before her eyes. "Be careful, Junior, in whatever you are planning."

"I will, Mom. Thanks." He kisses her cheek and goes back to packaging the food up.

Monday rolls around, and Junior sets a plan in motion, walking with Kip in the hallways during break. "I will see you later, Kip. I need to find Kaspina in the band room."

"Really, Junior, a girl?"

"It's not what you think. I just need to talk to her."

"Mind if I come along?"

"If you want."

"Well, she's cute!"

Junior shrugs his shoulders. "I suppose. Her mother is annoying. I would not want to get involved with that."

Kip laughs, pushing his friend away. "I am not getting involved with her mother."

"You would if you hooked up with Kaspina."

"Who says that's gonna happen?"

"I do."

Kip stops and looks at Junior. "How can you know?"

"Cause you have the same look in your eyes as my dad when he looks at my mom."

"I do not!"

Junior laughs. "Alright, perhaps not yet, but it's close. Come on, let's go." He heads to the band room, finding Kaspina, and moves to sit next to her, catching the subtle stiffening and scent of nervousness upon her. He smiles patiently. "We need to talk. Somewhere private."

She places her instrument down and looks around briefly, seeing her fellow bandmates wondering what is happening. "Sure. There is a side room we can go to."

Junior rises. "Great, let's go."

The three of them head into the small office, closing the door after them. Junior feels the band class shift closer to the door as he guides them to the far side of the room and keeps his voice low. "Alright, here's the deal. I know your mom wants you to get close to me so that she can land my father. That's not happening."

Kaspina pales, shaking her head. "I told her I wasn't playing her games, Junior. I prom..."

Junior holds up his hand to quiet her. "I am not blaming or accusing you. I am stating facts. Now, I imagine she is pestering you nightly?"

Kaspina nods silently.

"Good, Kip and I will hang with you to keep her quiet. In exchange, I need a favor from you."

She looks between the two hesitantly. "It depends on the favor."

"I want your bandmates to make me a song for the Yule ball. I will hum or sing it, and you will learn and record it."

"If you have the sheet music, we can practice it."

"There isn't any that I know of. That is why I am seeking your help."

"We can try, but there are no guarantees."

"Perfect, it's a deal. Tomorrow, and from this day forward, you hang with us while at school. Kip, you cool with this?"

"Of course."

"Great. Thank you, Kaspina. I look forward to working together." He turns and leaves the office, smiling at the others who suddenly jump away from the door. He leaves the band room with Kip, their chatter fading as they head to their next class.

Twenty-Three

Gems of Intrigue

One day in early November, Pandora leaves the library and wanders the mall while she waits for Rendgren to pick her up. She looks at her cell, thinking they are later than usual, but knows that Junior has been spending extra time at school. Pausing at a clothing store, she stops to look at some styles on the rack when she feels the ball of angst approaching her. She sighs inwardly, turning to see Marcy and her two friends advancing, knowing by their thoughts they have no intention of playing nice.

Marcy spots Pandora and whispers to her friends. "Let's have some fun, girls. I want to see how the farm girl does without her husband protecting her." She walks towards her, narrowing her eyes on Pandora's black and violet dress. "Oh look, it's the farm girl Pandora, who weaseled her way into money."

Pandora stiffens slightly and gives a nod to the trio. "Ladies."

"What brings you here, Pandora?"

"Oh, I'm just browsing while I wait for Gren and Junior."

"In that dress?"

Pandora looks down at it, smoothing out her skirts. "Obviously. I am wearing it."

"Don't you think it's tacky and pathetic to be still wearing something with cheap crystals from another country? I mean, even your son has changed his clothing."

Pandora smiles calmly despite the dragon fires rising within. "I love this dress. It's my style, and my husband loves them as well. I would also hazard a guess that this dress is worth more than you make in a year, Marcy."

Marcy moves to touch it, then backs off as if it was the plague. "Ugg, doubtful."

"It doesn't really matter what you think. You have your style, and I have mine." She offers a slight bow before she turns her back to them and walks away.

Marcy frowns at being dismissed in front of her friends, steps forward, and grabs her wrist to stop her. "Fine, let's prove it, shall we?"

Pandora's eyes snap to Marcy's hand grabbing her, her gaze darkening as the dragon fights for its freedom to flatten the woman. She reaches over and pries her grasp off her wrist before leveling a glare her way. "Of course, Marcy. Where do you propose we do that?"

Marcy steps back, feeling the air shift around her, but pushes it aside, determined not to be outdone by a farm girl. "There is a jeweler in the mall. Kip's father Ryker, actually. Let's go talk to him. If anyone knows, he will."

"So be it." Pandora follows Marcy through the mall to the jewelers. As she enters the lavish store, she's greeted by display cases forming a horseshoe layout. Each adorned with an array of gems, necklaces, bracelets, and rings, all shimmering under specifically designed lights to accentuate them. Her gaze lands on a taller man, slightly shorter than her husband, with dark brown hair, deep brown eyes, dressed in black pants, a pale blue button-down shirt, and a dark blue tie.

He briefly acknowledges their presence, to signal that he's spotted them, while finishing up with a customer at the counter. He bids them goodbye and watches them leave as he turns and approaches the foursome. "Can I help you?"

Marcy sends a dark look at Pandora. "Yes, this woman is saying her dress is worth more than my yearly salary. I wish you to inspect it and tell her it is simply not true."

Ryker looks over at Pandora, noting the unique outfit she is wearing. He could see the sparkle of gems in the sleeves and neckline, as well as layered down the skirt, all of which match the hairpins that adorn her hair. "Are you certain?"

Pandora shrugs her shoulders and places her hand on the glass counter. "If that is what she wishes, by all means, inspect the gems."

He nods, raising the lid of a small box by the register, and retrieves a tiny magnifying glass. Gently, he takes hold of Pandora's sleeve, lifting it to inspect the gems closely. He moves through several along the sleeve in silence, studying each one carefully before meeting her gaze. "Are they all like this?"

"Of course. My husband is not cheap despite the fact that my gems cost less than his because they are amethysts. Though the diamonds tend to be more costly, and I have some of those in the neckline."

"May I?"

"No, you may not. Know that they are just as real as the ones in my sleeves."

He nods in understanding and turns to Marcy. "Having *not* looked at them all, I estimate there is about fifty thousand dollars' worth of gems in the sleeves of the dress alone."

Marcy gasps, her gaze returning to Pandora once more, a flare of anger evident in her eyes at the sight of the woman adorned in such an expensive dress.

Rendgren enters the mall, feeling the irritation of his wife as he searches for her mentally. He finds her and heads in her direction swiftly, noticing they are in the jewelry store, and walks in casually. He studies the group before him, the sales clerk, his hand still holding the sleeve of his wife's dress. Marcy glaring with rage in her eyes while the other two stare in shock at Pandora.

Ryker eyes Rendgren as he enters. "Do I know you? You look familiar."

"Not I, good sir. I have not been to your store before. Just here to pick up my wife." He moves to Pandora's side and places an arm over her shoulders. "What are you doing here, love? We buy our gems in Ewhela."

Pandora pulls her hand back from the jeweler and wraps her arm around his waist, leaning a head on his shoulder. "Oh nothing. Marcy was criticizing my dress and thought perhaps the gems were nothing but glass baubles."

"I love those dresses on you." He leans in to kiss her cheek, pulling her tighter. "And the fact they come off easily." He turns to Marcy, studying her clothing and the jewelry, rolling his eyes at her appearance, indignation laced within his voice. "Marcy, my dear, perhaps your husband cuts corners on your jewels, but I do not. My wife deserves and receives only the finest. To imagine I would consider clothing her in anything less is beyond me."

Pandora smiles knowingly at Marcy. "I know that, Gren, and she just learned that."

"Right then, are you done?"

"Yes."

"Good, Juniors in the car with the pizza."

Pandora gives a nod to the group. "Always a pleasure Marcy... Nikki, Lucy." She turns and walks out of the store with her husband, hand in hand, heading back to the car where Junior waits.

Ryker watches them go, studying his hanfu, and the gems sewn within it, matching hers. He waits until they leave the store before he turns to Marcy and her friends. "Well, Marcy, those two clearly have wealth. She is correct in that amethysts are not as expensive as rubies or emeralds. If they are as real as hers, which by the way they glinted and the color of them, I suspect they are... His is worth far more than hers. Sight unseen in that I can't confirm, but I estimate the worth of both gowns at over a hundred and fifty thousand dollars."

"WHAT!? Are you saying their pathetic style of outfits are worth about the same as my house?"

"Yes, that's exactly what I am saying."

"And they are flaunting them like that in public?"

"Well, I wouldn't say flaunting. It looks to me like they are just wearing them. You are the one that dragged her in here to confirm there authenticity."

Marcy glares at Ryker before turning to her friends. "Nik, Luce, Let's go." They nod and follow her out of the shop, heading back to the food court. "How is it possible for anyone to have that kind of money? I have seen them both in several different outfits."

Nikki shakes her head, uncertain how to soothe her friend's temper. "Well, it's family money. Clearly, he inherited it and is spending it fast. Look at the bright side; he might be penniless soon."

Marcy frowns as she ponders her options. "No, if I get him, I want his money too. Perhaps I can imply his wife is a money sink, especially as she clearly favors those expensive dresses. I need to ponder this further."

Later that week, Marcy approaches Lucy at the bank. "How much is in his account, Luce?"

"I cannot tell you, Marcy. I could lose my job."

"Just a hint, inquiring minds would like to know."

"Marcy, just leave it be."

"I can't. I want him, and I want to know."

"You shouldn't interfere."

"She's just a farm girl; what is she going to do?"

"It's not her I would be worried about; it's him; he seems very possessive of her."

"Yes, well, that will change. Give me a number, approximate it even."

Lucy sighs and types in a series of codes into her computer, searching for Zalgren's account, her eyes widening slightly at the balance.

Marcy's eyes flash in delight. "That good, huh?"

"Let's just say he will never have to worry about finances even if he goes on a massive spending spree and buys several mansions like the one he owns. In all my years of being a teller, I have never seen a balance so high."

"So how did a farm girl land a tycoon like him?"

"Perhaps because he loves her."

"Nah, that's not it. She said they were rocky at the start; I can make them rocky again; I just need to figure out how."

"Marcy, I think you need to give up on him."

"Not a chance."

Twenty-Four

History Lesson

Several weeks pass, with Marcy frequently visiting the jewelry store, questioning Ryker on the cost of each gem in the outfits, and inquiring about the process of selling such gems. Especially as she has counted at least another four outfits on Pandora, not to mention the ones her husband is wearing whenever she gets the chance to see him picking her or his son up. While spending time at the store, she notices a severe lack of customers, realizing rather suddenly that she can use this to her benefit. An evil glint fills her eyes as she turns to Ryker. "Ryker, you seem to have no customers. Are you doing alright financially?"

Ryker scowls at Marcy. "It's none of your business."

"But it could be. We could sneak into their mansion and take a dress. Cut the gems out, and you could sell them. No one would even know."

"People can't afford those gems in Mindriff. That's why they go to Ewhela."

"So you go on a road trip to Ewhela pretending to buy but sell instead."

"Marcy, that's stealing. I don't want any part of it."

"It's not like she's gonna know. She's got at least ten of those dresses."

"Please leave."

"Think about it, Ryker. I've been to their mansion. We could be in and out before they even know it."

A few days later, Marcy overhears Rendgren and Pandora talking about taking Junior to a football game on the following Saturday as a surprise to him. Delight fills her, knowing it would give them more than enough time to be in and out before anyone even notices. She makes her way to Ryker, smiling as she enters, ignoring the distaste in his expression. "Ryker, have you paid your rent to avoid the eviction notice yet?"

"No, Marcy, I haven't, but you know that, don't you?"

"Why yes, I do believe I do. I also know that certain people will be out of their mansion next Saturday afternoon at a football game as a surprise to their son."

"Fine, just this once, Marcy, and only to get me out of debt."

"Deal!"

Saturday afternoon, Marcy waits outside the mall, watching Ryker leave and head towards his car. She steps in beside him, an oversized bag on her shoulder in which to hide the dress. They get in the car and drive up to the mansion, pulling around and parking out of sight of the main road. They exit and look around, seeing the area deserted as they head up to the main door.

Ryker approaches the door, retrieving an assortment of tiny picks from his pocket. As he reaches for the handle and twists, he's surprised to discover the door unlocked and swings open effortlessly before him. "Why would they not lock this?"

"I'm not sure. Perhaps they don't expect anyone to break in. Either way, this makes it really easy for us."

"I am not comfortable with this, Marcy; something doesn't feel right."

Marcy smiles in delight and steps through the doorway, heading directly into the living room. "It's fine. You worry too much. It's not like they will notice a gown missing. And their door was unlocked. It could be anyone that broke in."

Shaking his head, Ryker enters the main foyer, casting a glance over the furniture before his gaze settles on the family portrait. There's a faint sense of recognition as he studies it briefly, yet chooses to push past the feeling, trailing after Marcy deeper into the house. He stops in the living room to stare at the portrait of the three dragons, each bearing a sun symbol on their scales, with a tiny pup baring his teeth at their feet.

Sudden dread fills him as he recalls just where he recognizes the family picture from. "Marcy. Did you say their son has a tattoo?"

"Yes, of the sun. His parents gave it to him when he was young."

His body shakes in fear, looking around at the mansion, seeing Marcy stepping into the hallway. "We need to go, NOW!"

"But we haven't gotten the dresses yet."

"NOW, Marcy!" He lunges forward, seizing her hand, and pulls her swiftly out of the house, firmly shutting the door behind him as he pushes her towards the waiting car. He opens the door and urges her in quickly before running around to the other side. He fumbles with the keys as he starts the car and backs it up, speeding out of the driveway and back down the road. "Oh my god, what have we done? How could I be so stupid?"

"We haven't done anything, Ryker; we didn't even get the dress you promised."

"It's not going to matter, Marcy. We are as good as dead." His whole body shakes in fear as he struggles with the reality that they just broke into the Red Phantom's house, that he still exists and is living in Mindriff. He shakes his head, mentally berating himself for not figuring it out. The old style of clothes and wealth. The very fact that they moved into the mansion that's been shut down for three hundred years. His mansion. He pulls up to Marcy's house, hitting his brakes, and turns to her, catching her glare his way. "Get out!"

"Fine. But I don't see what the big deal is." She slides out and slams the car door after her, watching as he speeds away.

He drives home, fear guiding his every movement as he parks the car and sprints into the house, calling out for his wife. "Shels!"

"In here, Ryker. You're home early."

Ryker runs into the kitchen, his panicked eyes landing on his wife. "Where are my college books, Shels? We kept them, right?"

She looks at her husband in surprise, noticing the visible shake in her husband's body, his unusually pale complexion and the terror in his eyes. "Yes, they are downstairs. You look freaked out; is everything ok?"

"Yes, I need those papers." He turns and runs down to the cellar, madly sorting through all the bins.

Meanwhile, Rendgren feels the intrusion into their domain and leans over to his wife. "There is someone in the house. I will return to pick you up."

"Play nice, Gren. Marcy's just jealous of what we have."

He kisses her gently, hearing Junior's growl on the other side of her. "I always play nice."

She blushes softly at where his thoughts were going. "That's not what I was talking about."

"But that's what you are thinking. I can see the blush staining your cheeks."

She pushes him away playfully. "Go!"

Rendgren laughs, rises from his seat, and makes his way out of the stadium. His thoughts touch his wife's gently as he strides to the car. *'Later, my love, just you wait.'* He drives back to the mansion, annoyance flaring within that Marcy would dare to break into their house. Parking the car and getting out, he notices the stench of her perfume immediately mingling with another he couldn't quite place. Heading in the front door to the living room, he picks up the enchanted pearl his wife created. He focuses on it as an illusion appears before him, confirming that Marcy was in the mansion but also showing the jeweler as well. He frowns as he watches them, seeing the look of panic on his face as he stares at the painting of them above the TV. "Bloody hell." Rendgren places the pearl down and returns to his car. He drives to Ryker's house, having picked his son up there many times, and parks on the road out front. He walks casually up to the door and knocks lightly on it.

Shels hears the knock and moves to open the door. "Can I h... Oh wait, you must be Junior's dad. He's not here."

"Yes, I am here to see your husband, actually. May I come in?"

"Of course, he's downstairs looking for some college thing; this way, please." Shels leads him into the kitchen, just as her husband hits the top of the stairs, his eyes looking down at a binder in his hand. "Ryker, Junior's father is here to see you."

Ryker's expression drains of what color he had left in his face as his gaze meets the Red Phantoms. The book slips from his rigid grasp and falls to the ground in front of him. He sinks to his knees, bowing in reverence before Rendgren, his entire frame quivering with fear. "Please don't kill me. I didn't know, I swear. I didn't mean to. I won't say anything, I promise."

The aura of fear radiating off the jeweler kneeling before him fills the room. Rendgren bends down and retrieves the report, flipping through it with a casual air that masks his careful scrutiny of the contents. "What gave us away?"

"Nothing. You just struck me as familiar when I saw you in the store, but it didn't quite click until I laid eyes on the painting in the living room."

He frowns, his fingers tapping lightly on the report. "There are inaccuracies in this that I will not clarify. Now, here's the deal. I should kill you right now for breaking into my territory, but my wife wouldn't like that. And being that she's a mystic and all, she would see it. She would make me sleep on the couch for at least a year, and you are simply not worth it to me. Since we only got to

Mindriff within this past year, I don't really want to pack up and leave again because there is a dragon hunt at our door. As I am clearly in a generous mood, you will say nothing about who we are to anyone. Is that understood?"

"Yes, Sir." Ryker nods, remaining on his knees, head bowed.

"Did you tell Marcy?"

"No, Sir."

"Good, Don't." Rendgren looks around the house and over at Ryker's wife, who stands in shock and confusion while her husband bows to this man like he is royalty. "Now, clearly, you are in debt as you tried to steal a robe. Likely planning to cut the gems out as the hanfu's are quite identifiable as ours. How much do you owe?"

Ryker dares to risk a glance at his wife before bowing his head again.

Rendgren arches a brow. "Oh, the wife doesn't know."

"No, Sir. No one has the money to buy jewelry, especially with the cheap knockoffs coming out."

Rendgren studies the man kneeling and still shaking before him, an exasperated sigh escaping him. "Fine, I will pay your debts off in exchange for your silence. If *anyone* finds out who we are, I will place *all* the blame on your feet, and you will cease to exist. Is that understood?"

"Yes, Sir."

"Good. Now, to make my wife happy and to prove I can play nice, if you bring in rubies, emeralds, diamonds, and amethysts, I will consider buying some of them off you. We buy in Ewhela as they know us there, and we have been buying from them for hundreds of years."

Shels looks over at the man in her kitchen. "Wait, hundreds?"

Rendgren turns to her. "Yes, hundreds."

Shels shifts her gaze between the two of them, knowing she is missing something. "What is going on?"

Rendgren ignores her question and continues to address Ryker. "You are to keep your wife silent on this matter, as well as your son, who currently has his ear pressed to the bedroom door."

"Yes, Sir."

Shels feels her temper flare at having her question ignored by both men in the room and stamps her foot. "Silent on what exactly?"

Rendgren hands the report over to her, giving her time to flip through it. She stops at the picture in the report; her face paling as she compares it to the man in her kitchen. "This can't be possible. This was three hundred years ago."

"Give or take when he based the report on, yes. We ruled Oblait for just over a hundred years and have been moving around to keep our identities safe, not staying longer than twenty years in one place."

"Are you really saying that you are the dragons in this report?"

Rendgren's eyes shift to dragons as flames enter them, fires forming on the tips of his fingers before he extinguishes them. "Yes, and NO one is to find out. Is that understood?"

She pales as she backs up a step, nodding in fear. "Won't hear it from me."

"Me either."

He turns to Ryker, still kneeling on the floor. "Good. Now, my wife needs someone she can talk to besides myself and Junior. So, to keep you honest, the three of you will come for dinner every Sunday evening. Is that understood?"

They both nod, not daring to object to the dragon standing in their kitchen. "Perfect. I will see you tomorrow night at five sharp, at which point you can bring your expense reports, and we will go over them while the ladies chat. Now, I need to return to the football game where I left my wife and child. Have a pleasant night." He gives them both a nod and strides from the kitchen. He returns to the car and drives back to the game, slipping into the seat next to his wife, watching the last hour of the game with his family.

After the game, Junior dominates the conversation about the exceptional plays and how he needs to try them in practice as Rendgren drives them home. The conversation remains lively as they enter the mansion. Junior turns to his parents and gives them each a tight hug. "Thank you. You are the best. I loved that game. It was amazing."

Pandora hugs her son back. "You are most welcome. I am glad you enjoyed it."

"I can't wait to show Kip Monday at practice."

Rendgren chuckles. "You can show them tomorrow. I invited him and his family over for dinner."

Junior turns to him in shock. "Wait, Really?"

"Yes, really. I thought perhaps with you out in the world, we should advance out as well."

"That's even better, Dad! Thank you."

Pandora turns to Rendgren, studying him a moment before nodding slightly. "Before you get too excited, Junior, I do believe your father needs to speak with us."

"What do you mean, Mom?"

"Your mother is right, Junior; let's go to the kitchen and have a chat."

Junior frowns, feeling some of his excitement diminish as he looks over his parents, before heading to the kitchen with a sigh. "Something's up. I can feel it."

Rendgren nods and follows them, waiting until they sit before sitting himself. "Alright, Junior. You are aware I left the game today."

"Yes, I saw. I figured you had something to do."

"I did. Apparently, someone broke into our house today."

Junior narrows his eyes. "By that Marcy woman. I thought I smelled her wretched scent."

"Yes, by her and Kip's father."

Junior rises suddenly, the bar stool crashing to the ground as he shakes his head, feeling crushed. "No, he wouldn't."

Pandora nods. "He did, Junior. Please just listen to your father."

Junior picks up the stool and sits on it, slumping down on his elbows. "Why Dad?"

Rendgren places a hand on his shoulder. "Because he's in a lot of debt, Son, with no way out. Marcy offered one with the gems in your mother's dresses."

Junior looks at his mom. "Did she get one?"

Pandora shakes her head as Rendgren continues. "No. They did not. They did not make it past the living room. Apparently, Ryker, Kip's father, did his college thesis on us. He recognized the painting in the living room. At that point, he dragged Marcy out of the house and drove her home."

Junior pales, feeling crestfallen at the thought of moving again. "So he knows we are dragons then. Does that mean we have to move?"

"We should, but we are not. I went to their house and had a talk... Well I talked, they listened. Kip was in the bedroom with his ear to the door, so I am not certain exactly what he heard, but both his parents know who we are. I suspect they have filled Kip in. Now, I have agreed to pay off their debts in exchange for their silence. All of their silence. It is possible that Kip may react differently around you when he finds out, and I hope, for your sake, he does not, because

I know you value him as a friend. This is why I invited them for Sunday night dinners. Both to keep them honest and to have us step out into the world you have."

Junior looks up with hope in his eyes. "Really?"

"Yes, it's time we trusted the human race again, and you are the reason we are taking this step."

Junior rises and hugs his father tight. "Thank you Dad!"

Rendgren returns the hug. "You're welcome, Son."

Junior steps back. "Wait. Does Kaz's mom know?"

He shakes his head. "No, Ryker did not tell Marcy, and I would prefer it if you did not tell her daughter. I made it very clear that if anyone else were to find out, they'd bear the full brunt of the blame."

Junior nods in agreement. "I understand, Dad. I know this is my fault."

Rendgren reaches out to place a hand on his shoulder. "This is NOT your fault. It is simply circumstance."

"But if I hadn't wanted to go to school, you wouldn't be out there, and Marcy would not want you or Mom's dresses..."

Pandora smiles at Junior. "Junior, your father is right. It is not your fault and could have happened simply when I went to the market. Marcy is unhappy in her own marriage and jealous of others with happiness in theirs. Do not blame yourself. We don't."

Junior nods, feeling his mom's calmness within, moving to hug her as well. "Thanks Mom."

"You're welcome, Junior. Now, you better go write those plays out before you forget them."

"Yes, awesome plan, Mom! Have a good night." His grin returns as he spins and bounds from the kitchen, heading up the stairs to his room and slamming the door closed after him.

Pandora smiles at Rendgren. "Thanks for playing nice, Gren."

Rendgren chuckles, moving to draw her into his arms. "You're welcome, but you owe me another dragon hoard."

She smiles, resting her head on his chest. "Deal."

The next night, Kip's family pulls up the driveway and parks. Junior paces on the balcony above, a nervous energy within that he is unaccustomed to, wondering how his friend is going to react. He watches them exit the car and move to the front door. He senses his mom answering it and hears her voice in his thoughts as they settle in the living room.

'Junior, get your butt down here.'

'Be right there, Mom.'

Pandora turns to the group. "Junior will be down in a minute. May I offer you tea, coffee, soda?"

Ryker and Shels shake their heads in silence as they sit on the couch nervously. Kip remains standing, his eyes shifting to the painting above the TV, one he has seen many times. "Is it true, Mrs. Red? Are you really those dragons?"

Pandora smiles at him. "Yes, Kip, it's true."

Kip glances momentarily at Junior as he steps into the living room. "Junior too?"

"Yes, Junior too."

"That little one is him?"

Pandora laughs. "Yes, but he is not so small anymore. That was when he was about thirty years old."

Kips snaps his gaze to Junior. "Wait, so how old are you really?"

Junior sighs. "Three hundred and forty years old, give or take a few months."

"WHAT!! But you are a teenager like me."

Pandora interjects gently. "Kip, dragons age differently as we are immortal. It's complicated, but even at three hundred and forty, Junior is pretty much a teenager, perhaps closer to early twenties. Partly because of the way we age and partly because we kept him sheltered so as not to expose ourselves."

Kip grows thoughtful, his eyes moving around the three of them, glancing to his parents before looking at Pandora. "Well, I know my parents are nervous wrecks, going over the protocols of how to behave in the presence of a Royal family cause apparently you are a King, Queen, and Prince. But to me, you are Mr. and Mrs. Red, and Junior, my BFF. That's not changing, even if you add dragons to that."

Ryker and Shels gasp slightly. "Christopher Joseph Moore!"

"Wait, your real name is Christopher?"

"Yes, and don't you dare tell anyone that, Junior. In fact, I think I should get your real name as I am pretty certain Junior is not it."

Junior laughs and moves over to hug his friend. "I wouldn't dare Kip! My human name is Asher, but my Mom hates it."

"I don't hate it, Junior."

"Right, that's why you have only ever said it once in my entire life, and that was when you were registering me for school. Not that it matters 'cause I am pretty damn certain you knew Kip was going to be my BFF and deliberately called me Junior to him."

"I don't know what you are talking about. I just prefer Junior over your other name."

"Exactly Mom! Proving my point with that statement."

Kip laughs at the pair. "It's okay, Mrs. Red. I hate my name too; that's why I go by Kip."

Junior mutters under his breath. "I don't hate my name though. Come, let's go upstairs till dinner. Mom and Dad took me to a pro football game, and I wrote the moves down."

"Not fair! You got to go to a pro game?"

"Yes, and if you talk nicely to my Mom, she can show you bits of it."

"Junior!"

"What?! You said that they already knew who we are, so they are gonna know that you and I are mystics. Might as well get it all out there if we are welcoming them into our family."

Pandora sighs. "Fine, after dinner."

"That sounds great." The two run upstairs, leaving the four to sort things out downstairs.

Pandora looks over at Kip's parents, feeling the fear radiating off them. "Alright, I can feel your emotions and read your thoughts. Ryker, why don't you join Gren in the den and go over your deal? Shels, you can join me in the kitchen and help with dinner while we talk."

Kip's parents look at each other nervously at the thought of splitting, reluctantly following Pandora's suggestion. Several hours later, the six of them are laughing as they sit in the living room, bantering as if they had been friends for years. Pandora shows Kip a few images of the game, hearing the shocked gasps from his parents at her powers before discussing the basics of what a mystic is capable of compared to a dragon. At the end of the evening, they enjoy group hugs with a promise to stay in touch during the week and that they would bring the food next week.

Pandora closes the door after them, her eyes straying to their son, knowing his desire to attend school started all of this. "Thank you, Junior, Gren; it was a lot of fun."

Junior hugs his mom. "Yah, Mom, it was. I can't wait till next week. Now, I need to study a bit before school tomorrow. Sweet dreams."

Rendgren and Pandora watch him go before locking the door and retiring to the bedroom themselves.

Twenty-Five

Fight Club

End of November

The next couple of weeks, Kip and Junior bond even tighter than before, taking him downstairs to show him the training room and watch his parents fight. Junior even dares to show Kip his Draconic form down there. Later in the week, they sit on the couch talking about it as Kip's eyes move to the portrait. "Well, you are definitely larger than you were. How big are you now compared to your parents in the painting?"

Junior lifts his gaze before returning to the video game. "About half their size in the painting, I guess. They don't fit downstairs, even lying down. They can only shift in Dad's lair, but their claws alone would probably be larger than the average car."

"Damn! No wonder my parents were freaked."

"And you weren't?"

"Nah, I figured you were still my friend, even if you were this prince or dragon." He chuckles. "I can't believe you are a prince, though. No wonder everyone flocks to you."

"Of course, you would focus on the prince over the dragon."

Kip nudges his friend. "Well yah, princes are real, dragons are make-belief, don't you know? I'm not going to be labeled as crazy in my old age when I lose my mind and start talking about you being a dragon."

Junior laughs. "Pretty certain we will be three cities away by then, so you are safe."

Kip shakes his head, watching his character die again on the screen. "Do you really have to move every twenty years?"

"Yes, but we can stay in touch now. People get suspicious because we don't age like you do." Junior pauses, his draconic senses picking up someone nearing the manor, along with the stench of perfume. "Oh bloody hell, what is she doing here?"

Kip looks towards the door. "Who?"

"Marcy."

"How do you know she's here?"

"I can smell her, and we can sense people approaching us." Junior rises and moves to the door, opening it before Marcy gets to knock. "What do you want?"

"I need to speak to your Mom about a few things."

"She's downstairs fighting with Dad."

"Fighting?"

"Yes. Dad usually wins, but Mom is determined that one day she will beat him."

"Really? I thought they were happy together."

"They are." Junior narrows his eyes. "But they like fighting, so why shouldn't they do something they like?"

"How can you like fighting? I would like to see your Mom, please, to make sure she's alright."

He glances at Kip, and rolls his eyes, reaching out telepathically to his mom, *'Mom, that annoying Marcy is here, wanting to see you.'*

'It's fine, Junior, bring her down.'

He mutters under his breath about the unannounced guest as he faces Marcy again. "Follow me." He turns to his friend. "Come on, Kip." Junior leads her and Kip downstairs to a larger cavern beneath the mansion. Walls rise sixty feet in the air, with a set of stone doors inset along the back wall. A four-inch padded floor fills up most of the room. Swords, staves, and axes hang in racks nearby, and a small washing station sits to the left of the entrance.

The sound of wood striking draws Marcy's attention to Pandora and Zalgren fighting in the center of the room with pole-arms, immediately noticing the skill that both of them have.

Rendgren draws on strength and slowly drives Pandora back until he pins her to a wall, a staff across her throat. He smiles in delight. "I think I have won, my dear. You should concede defeat."

She narrows her eyes on him as she tries to push him away from her, only to feel his resistance. "I will never concede defeat while I am still standing." She tips and slides her pole-arm down to sweep it at his feet, causing him to jump back out of her strike. She presses the advantage, forcing him back into the center of the room.

His eyes darken in desire. "Is that so? Challenge accepted." He renews his attacks on Pandora, each hit adding a touch more strength behind it.

Junior mutters under his breath to Kip. "Oh boy, Mom's done for now."

Kip shakes his head. "Yep, she is."

Marcy turns her gaze to the pair. "What do you mean?"

Junior looks over at Marcy. "Mom issued a challenge to Dad, and Dad loves his challenges."

The three turn back to watch the pair striking at each other, the clacking of the staves as each of them blocks the other's strike, circling around the floor.

Junior watches the fight, a scattering of images flickering through his mind, and mutters under his breath. "Oh bloody hell." He runs forward, grabs a staff, and jumps into the ring, landing near his mom. He drives his staff down to the floor and blocks his father's strike from taking his mom off her feet.

"Junior?"

"Dad."

He shifts his red eyes to his son, delight flashing in them as he arches a brow. "You know the consequences of interfering?"

"I do."

"And yet, here you are. Are you siding with your mother then?"

"I am."

"So be it." He backs up, giving them time to adjust, before stepping in and driving them both back with ease. He plays with them for about ten minutes, watching as they tire beneath his attacks, then decides to claim his first prize. With a quick flip of the staff, he takes Pandora off her feet and stands over top of her, placing a foot gently on her chest.

Junior growls under his breath. "Way to go, Mom! Now I am gonna get trounced."

Pandora sighs and remains still beneath Rendgren's feet. "Sorry, Junior. You weren't supposed to interfere."

Rendgren smiles at his son, his eyes darkening slightly at owning his wife.

"You know I don't give up my claims, Son. Forfeit now, and you won't end up like her."

"Can't do that, Dad. You know I have to rescue her."

"Go ahead and try."

Kip shakes his head, standing next to Marcy. "Oh boy, I can't look."

Marcy turns to Kip. "Why ever not?"

"Mr. Red has taken control of Mrs. Red. That means Junior needs to defeat him to get her back, and I have yet to see that happen; he always gets destroyed."

"Why doesn't Pandora get up and fight him? Her staff is still in her hands."

"That's not part of the game. Once down, you are out. His standing on her means he claimed her in this battle."

"You know about this fighting then?"

"Oh yes, Junior and I have sparred down here, and he destroys me. Seeing his father fight is a whole other level. I would never want to get on his bad side, cause right now, he's just playing with his wife and son. I can't imagine what he would be like if he ever meant business."

Junior moves around his father, seeing the visions filter through his mind, trying to sort them out before he ends up flat on his back like his mother.

Rendgren recognizes the look and steps forward, leaving his prize long enough to force Junior to move, circling around Pandora and keeping his son away from her.

Marcy glances at Kip. "He's not standing on her anymore; she could stand now."

Kip shakes his head. "Junior needs to get to her. Until he does, she's still considered captured."

Another few minutes pass before Rendgren makes his move; his staff sweeps the feet out from beneath his son as he swings it around and places it on his chest, touching him enough to know he captured him as well.

"Damn." He rolls his eyes back as he lays there.

"Next time you debate stepping in to save your mother, Junior, you might want to think twice."

"Never!"

Rendgren chuckles, grabbing his hand and pulling him up. "I want pizza, my dear boy, made from scratch." His eyes darken with desire at his wife lying on the floor before pulling her up too, kissing her gently. "My love."

"Really, Dad? From scratch?"

"Yes."

Junior growls under his breath and leaves the battleground. He drops his staff in the holder. "Come'on, Kip. We gotta make pizza."

"Wait! I wasn't fighting; how am I part of this consequence?"

Junior laughs and pulls him from the room. "Cause you feel the desire to help your best friend out."

Pandora hands her staff to Rendgren as she moves to the side and washes her hands before turning to face Marcy. "What can I help you with, Marcy?"

"I came to talk about the ball, but then your son said you were fighting. I was concerned."

"I am sure you were. As you can see, I am fine."

"You do this all the time?" Her eyes stray to Zalgren, who is organizing the room.

"Yes, several times a week at least."

"Zalgren should teach a class. I know the kids at school would love it."

Rendgren coughs slightly as he heads over to stand behind his wife, wrapping an arm around her waist. "Sorry, Marcy, I only like fighting with my family. It means I get out of cooking dinner." He kisses his wife's cheek. "Which I do believe, my love, that Junior is up there alone, and he shouldn't be."

Pandora laughs. "He has Kip helping him, but fine, I will see you upstairs. Come, Marcy, we can talk on the way back to the kitchen. Apparently, I need to help my son make pizza."

"Just order out."

Pandora shakes her head, leading her back up the stairs and away from her husband. "That's not the deal. The winner chooses dinner and how it's made. Pizza from scratch is what he requested." She reaches upstairs, guiding her to the front door. "So what are you after Marcy?"

"I came to discuss the decorations for the ball."

"I didn't think you were on the decorating team."

"I'm not, but I had ideas."

"Then you should present them with the team leader."

"Right, I forgot Paige was the team lead for decorating. I will go talk to her."

Pandora reaches the door and stands beside it. "Alright then, have a good night, Marcy." She closes the door after her, clicking the lock into place. She turns back and heads to the kitchen where her son is making dough. "Junior."

"Bout time you got here, Mom. It's your fault I have to make dinner."

Pandora laughs, moves to the fridge, and pulls the cheese and meats out, setting them before her to grate and slice. "My fault? You're the one that stepped in."

"Yes, well, I saw Dad sweeping your feet out. How could I not stop him?"

"I appreciate it, Junior, but you do know I can defeat your father any time I want, right?"

Rendgren leans on the door frame. "Is that so, my dear? Rematch then?"

Pandora turns, eyeing her husband with a smile, her voice light and teasing. "It's true, and you know it. Besides, I am obligated to cook you dinner now."

A wicked grin crosses his lips. "Just like you let yourself get stolen."

"Yes, that about covers it."

He chuckles and moves to sit at the counter with her, kissing her gently.

Junior grumbles under his breath. "If you are gonna get *mushy mushy*, go find another room. Trying to cook dinner here."

Rendgren laughs. "One day, Junior, someone will wrap you around their finger like your mother did with me." He reaches out and pulls the meat over to slice it as the four of them banter in the kitchen.

"Highly doubtful, Dad!"

Pandora rises and moves to the cupboard, sorting through the cans. "Lovely. We are out of pineapple."

Kip reaches into his pocket for his phone. "I think we have some Mrs. Red. I will call my parents."

Rendgren smiles. "Invite them for dinner, Kip."

"Fo'shizzle Mr. Red. Thank you."

Marcy watches from the outside, jealousy burning within at the unity they have and the fact that, somehow, Kip made his way into that circle.

A week later, Junior spars with his father downstairs, moving with perfection, blocking his father's strikes while landing a few of his own. He sidesteps his father's sweep, dropping his staff between them, and pushes forward, using his dad's staff as a brace and forcing his father off his feet.

"Yes! It actually worked! I gotta tell Mom!"

Rendgren lies on his back in shock that his son defeated him. He pushes himself to sit up, feeling his son's delight at the win.

Junior turns to his dad, a wide grin on his face. "I want spaghetti and meatballs... Dad!" He spins and races from the room, calling out. "Mom! Your move worked! Dad's cooking tonight!"

Rendgren smiles and rises to his feet, sensing his wife in their bedroom, and makes his way there. He stops in the doorway, eyeing his wife in the loveseat reading, noticing immediately that she didn't lift her eyes to him. "Love."

"Gren."

"Junior learned a new move today."

"I heard."

"I have to wonder where he learned it from."

"He has been reading a lot of books on how to fight with staves."

Rendgren glides gracefully across the room. "I get the impression it was another that taught him the move."

Pandora's eyes lift, following his body up to meet his gaze, giving the best innocent look she can. "I wonder who that could be."

Rendgren lifts the book out of her hands and places it open on the table nearby. "Oh, let's see. I do believe he said as he was leaving. *I have to tell Mom her move worked.*"

Pandora follows her book to the table. "I was reading that, Gren."

Rendgren takes her hand and pulls her up to stand before her, wrapping an arm around her waist and dragging her close, kissing her neck lightly. "No, you were guiding our son on how to defeat me."

She closes her eyes, feeling her body weakening to his touch. "I wouldn't know what you are talking about."

He lifts her into his arms and carries her over to the bed, dropping her on it. "Really? Why don't I believe you?"

She smiles, her violet eyes darkening as she meets his gaze. "Perhaps because you owe our son spaghetti and meatballs."

He crawls into the bed on top of her, studying her features, the desire mixed with humor in her eyes. "You really can beat me in the fighting ring."

"You knew that already, Gren; you've known it ever since the day you researched mystics in Krine."

He kisses her softly. "So why let me win?"

She blushes softly, reaching up to touch his forehead as she transfers over a vision of her emotions. "Because I love the look you give me when you win. The desire that darkens your eyes to the perfect shade of red and the rush of feelings within knowing you want me and have me because you won."

Rendgren growls softly, his hold tightening on her as he buries his face in her neck, feeling her emotions wash over him. "Oh gawd, you know I love you, whether you use your powers of foresight to win or not."

"I know, Gren, but there is just that edge of something when you do win and after sparring with you. I desire that edge. If I am going to win, I want to win because of me and not my powers."

"If I didn't have to make dinner, I would give you that edge."

She caresses his cheek lightly, passing on another round of emotions, no less intense. "No, you wouldn't. You would love me, but you only have that edge when you win."

He groans against her, feeling her emotions flood him again, noticing the subtle differences in both, not willing to let her go as he takes in who she is. "How did I get so lucky?"

Pandora wraps her arms around him, feeling the security he offered her in his arms. "Well, it took a bit of convincing, and I did have to die to get you to accept it."

He chuckles, meeting her gaze, before kissing her deeply. "I love you, Pandora, and that doesn't even cover the depth of what I feel for you."

"I know, Gren, I feel the exact same for you."

He closes his eyes and holds her tight, breathing in her scent, feeling the love he has for her washing over him. After about ten minutes, he growls under his breath as he kisses her cheek and sits up. "Thanks to you, I should get up and make dinner. Though I do think you should be obligated to help me with what you have done."

Pandora laughs, caressing his cheek lightly. "Yes, you should, and I was simply reading my book Gren."

"Really?" Rendgren rises and moves to the book, picking it up, scanning the page it is open to. "Alright, my love, what was the last thing you read?"

Pandora mutters under her breath as she slides out of bed. "I believe it was about faeries."

Rendgren arches a brow. "And what does this page say about faeries?"

She sighs and rolls her eyes. "Something about rolling meatballs while a dragon makes spaghetti sauce."

Rendgren grins as he places the book down and takes her hand, leading her down to the kitchen, where they set about making dinner. He moves to the fridge, pulling out tomatoes, onions, eggs, and other sauce materials, as well as the brick of cheese, placing spices, eggs and breadcrumbs on the island where Pandora was working.

Pandora opens the freezer and pulls two packages of hamburger out, moving her hand over them as purple lights thaw the meat out. She hands one over to Rendgren and opens the other, dumping it in a bowl, and setting it on the island. She sits on the bar stool and sets about mixing the ingredients, taking small handfuls of meat and rolling them into balls, placing them on a nearby plate.

Junior enters the kitchen. "Mom! Why are you helping Dad?"

Pandora laughs. "Well, because your father was smart enough to figure out what I had done, Junior."

Junior slumps into the chair next to her, pulling the cheese forward to grate it. "Damn!"

Rendgren moves over to pat his shoulder. "You did well, Son. Very few can fight and take a mental direction, let alone be successful enough to take me off my feet. One day, you will surpass me naturally."

Junior mutters under his breath. "I didn't, Dad. Mom created an illusion of your moves for that fight, and I have been practicing with it all week."

Rendgren snaps his eyes to Pandora. "She did what?"

Pandora shakes her head, scowling at her son as humor danced in her eyes. "Thanks for throwing me under the bus, Junior."

Junior shrugs innocently. "Sorry, Mom. You were already in trouble, and he probably knew anyway."

Rendgren growls as he moves to stir the sauce. "I should turn you both over my knee for plotting against me."

Junior laughs. "Good luck with that, Dad. I will just make sure Mom gets caught first, then I know I am safe."

Rendgren looks at his son in shock before drifting to his wife, his eyes darkening in desire. "Yes, you might be right in that department, Junior."

"I know I am."

Pandora shakes her head. "Junior!"

"Mom! I am not blind! I know who runs this house, and as much as Dad likes to think he does, he doesn't. You do." He laughs, rises, and races from the kitchen as both his parents watch him.

Rendgren turns to scowl at Pandora. "He's yours!"

Pandora shakes his head, scowling back. "Oh, he might be mine, but he takes after his father!"

Twenty-Six

The Unspoken Past

In December, the day they have all been planning for arrives, the Yule market and ball. Pandora dresses that morning in red and black, choosing her husband's colors for the day. She arrives with ten pies, placing them on the donation table, before setting out to help with odd jobs during the day. She does her best to avoid Marcy, but feels her angry gaze more often than not. Rendgren arrives an hour before the ball with food for his wife as they sit in a quiet corner, spending time together before the dance.

A silver disco ball spins in the center of the gym, with colored lights reflecting off it and bouncing along the floors and walls. Pine wreaths with red bows adorn the walls, some of them sprayed with white snow. A raised stage with a DJ and his equipment sits along one wall. The front of it boasts large red and green bows with strands of popcorn strings between them.

The parents wander the sidelines, chaperoning as the students frolic and dance. Pandora's thoughts drift back to her ball and the day Rendgren took her to the faeries, thinking how very different this style of dance is. She understands dance has many forms, but the students' form of jumping around and waving their arms around madly is beyond her. An hour later, at Junior's request, she follows him out to the dance floor, stumbling through the new-fangled steps he is teaching her.

Seeing Zalgren is now alone, Marcy shifts along the wall and stands next to him. "Zalgren, let's go dance."

"No, Marcy, I am chaperoning."

"So is your wife, and she's out there dancing."

"Yes, with our son, because he asked her to. And when that's done, she will return to chaperoning. Go dance with your husband."

"He doesn't dance."

"Neither do I, Marcy. That is why my son is dancing with my wife."

Marcy steps in closer, moving to wrap her arm around him. "It's just one dance. I could teach you."

Rendgren sidesteps her embrace, his eyes darkening dangerously on her. "I said NO... Now, your husband is over there watching your disgrace. Please be respectful of both parties and return to his side."

Marcy narrows her eyes at his insult, turns, and stomps off towards the opposite side of the gym.

At the end of the dance, Junior takes his mom's hand and squeezes it. "Stay here Mom; don't you move." Junior grabs Kip and Kaspina and goes up to the stage. He speaks quietly to DJ Joe, a classmate of his, who hands the microphone over to him. Junior smiles as he looks out over his schoolmates. "Mindriff High! Welcome to Yule. I just want to make a few announcements and interrupt the dance if I may."

The crowd cheers in approval as the four of them stand on stage.

"Great! Now, Yule is a time for celebrating and appreciating all that you have. As some of you know, or suspected, my family has wealth, and I have always had private tutoring. That is, until we moved here and I asked to attend high school. My parents were hesitant, but agreed and supported me with this decision. Everyone at the school has made the experience amazing by welcoming the new kid into your circles." He turns to Kip and Kaspina. "Especially Kip and his girlfriend, Kaspina." He smiles as his friends blush, looking at each other in shock. He takes each of their hands and places them together. "Ah, admit it, you two adore each other. Might as well make it official."

Kip scowls at his friend but pulls Kaspina closer as the school cheers again.

Junior turns back to the students, the teachers, and the parents around the outside chaperoning. "Now, I know a lot of you didn't like the fact that our parents are here chaperoning, but we all need to be thankful that they are here, supporting us. They are the ones who are always in our court, even when sometimes it feels like they are not. As you all know, and I am not afraid to admit it. I love my parents. They are the ones that raised me, shaped me, and made me who I am today."

He turns to Kaspina and pulls her out of Kip's arms. "Now, Kaz here, and her friends have helped me to create something special for my parents. I think it tested everyone's patience with me over the past six weeks." He pauses as Kaspina nods in agreement, his eyes sweeping over to the other band members, also nodding. "But we did it, and I am super proud of the work they have given me." He pulls a disc out of his pocket and hands it to Joe. "If you want a copy of this, please see Mr Brasswell on Monday, and he can burn you one."

He watches Joe slip the CD in and set it up on his computer, giving a nod to Junior that he is ready. "Alright then. This is a dedication to my parents. I would not be standing on this stage if not for them, cause, well, they created me... And because of this song. Mom, Dad. This one's for you. Dad, get out there and dance with Mom."

Rendgren frowns slightly at being forced to dance in front of the school but steps away from the wall and approaches his wife, who remains standing in the center of the floor. He takes her hand in his, kisses the back of it gently, and bows to her. "My love. Apparently, our son is forcing us to dance together. You wouldn't happen to know anything about this?"

Pandora shakes her head as she drops into a curtsy, stepping into his arms. "No, Gren, I don't."

The students shift away from the pair, giving them space to dance and watching the interactions between them, especially with how highly Junior spoke of his parents.

Junior, seeing his father with his mom, gives a nod and turns to Kaspina and Kip. "Go dance this with them. You deserve it." He waits until they join his parents on the floor. "Alright, DJ Joe, hit it."

The song filters over the gymnasium, bringing a gasp to Pandora's lips as Rendgren groans and pulls her tight. As the music envelops them once again, memories resurface, each one reliving the day they first heard the song in the faerie realm. The dance is slow and sweet. Tears slip from Pandora's eyes at what Junior has done, having never expected to hear the song again. Rendgren struggles to control his emotions and not create a portal back to their bedroom, right here in the middle of the dance. The feelings they have for each other emanate from them, in the way they hold each other, the way they move, and the way they look at each other. It fills the gymnasium as the other students watch the dance with awe and amazement at the love displayed between the pair.

Meanwhile, Junior makes his way off the stage, and works his way through the crowds, delight filling him as he feels the emotions of his parents and his classmates seeing their love on display. Flickers of anger edge in as he steps up to Marcy, smiling coldly at her expression of disgust as she watches them. "You're looking a little green, Marcy. Perhaps you should reconsider trying to steal my father away from my mother. Especially now that they have the song that bound them together in the first place. Their love is eternal, and you are not getting between that."

Marcy turns to glare at Junior, her eyes dark with fury at the arrogance of this child. "You have no idea who you are dealing with."

"I can say the same thing regarding us, Marcy. Do enjoy the rest of the dance." Junior offers her a slight bow before turning and disappearing into the crowd.

Marcy continues to glare at the couple before stalking out of the dance hall and back to her car in frustration, not understanding what he sees in that woman.

At the end of the song, Rendgren steps back and gently places a hand under Pandora's chin, lifting her gaze to his as he did in the realm of the fey. He studies her eyes, feeling their bond within, the love they share, forgetting at that moment that they are in a school full of teenagers. He gently brushes a few of the tears aside with his thumb as his thoughts touch hers. *'Those better be tears of happiness, my love.'*

'They are, Gren.'

He steps in. His arm wraps around her waist to support her, and kisses her deeply, feeling her body succumb to his touch before pulling back breathless, hearing the surrounding cheers. He touches her flushed cheeks. "I love you, Pandora, with all my heart and soul."

She steps into his arms and wraps hers around him, tears still falling from her cheeks. "I love you, Gren."

Junior slips through the students, seeing his parents hugging, and moves in, wrapping his arms around them.

Pandora pulls an arm off Rendgren and wraps it around Junior, kissing his cheek. "Thank you, Junior; you have no idea what this means to us. I never expected to hear that song again."

Junior smiles, snuggling into his parents' arms. "Yes, I do. I love you guys so much! I needed you to know that."

DJ Joe watches the group hug, smiling at the sight of it. He picks up the mic and taps it, attempting to draw attention back to him. "Alright, everyone. Let it be known for the record that Junior's growls at people kissing in the hallways is clearly for show. As we can all see, he is capable of being mushy. Good luck girls; he's still single! Now, group hug and let's get this party back on track." The students swarm the threesome as a giant group hug forms with them and their parents, all surrounding the love in the center.

The DJ starts the music, picking an upbeat song, watching as they separate and start to dance again. Junior leads his parents off the dance floor, finding a corner that is vacant, and turns to them. He pulls out a CD and hands it to his mom. "Here. I had a copy burned just for you."

Pandora takes the disc and turns it over in her shaking hand before handing it over to her husband. She wraps her arms around Junior and holds him tight, feeling immense love for her son. "Thank you, Junior. How did you do it?"

Junior buries his face in his mom's neck, whispering into her ear so no one else could hear. "I went back into the past Mom, through the life threads, and I saw things I probably shouldn't have, but I wanted to do this for you. Once I found the faeries and their songs, I watched you and Dad dance. I saw the love and felt the power of you two connecting. I knew it was that song that I needed to recreate for you, and so I played it over and over in my mind till I learned it. Then I hummed it to the band and picked at their tones, and added the bells and sounds until it sounded perfect. I think they all wanted to kill me by the end of it."

Pandora laughs and brushes her tears aside, stepping back to look at her son, "Oh, Junior, I am certain they did not want to kill you."

Kaspina and Kip step up, hand in hand, smiling at the group of them as Kaspina answers her. "Oh, they did, Mrs. Red, but we could see how important it was to Junior. And now that we have seen the two of you dance to it, we understand completely why he was so picky. It's like one of those faerie tale romances, and the song suits you perfectly. I am sorry my mom is being such a nuisance."

Pandora watches Junior hug his father as she turns her attention over to Kaspina. "It's alright, Kaspina. We know what your mother is up to, and she won't succeed. Nor do we blame you or your father for her actions."

Kaspina nods, stepping in to hug Pandora. "Thank you, Mrs. Red."

Pandora hugs her gently, stepping back to take her shoulders. "Now, you kids have spent too much time with us adults. Get out there and dance!"

The three of them nod, laughing as they skip back to the dance floor. Pandora moves to Rendgren's side, taking his hand and leads him back to the wall to stand, feeling an overwhelming happiness within as they chaperone the rest of the dance. At the end of the evening, Junior runs up to his parents. "We are going to an after-party, Mom, Dad. I am gonna crash there for the night."

Pandora nods. "Have fun, Junior. I will see you tomorrow afternoon. Don't drink too much. Hangovers are painful."

"Wait, you know about hangovers?"

"Yes, the day after my sixteenth birthday, my one and only."

Junior laughs at the thought. "I wish I could have seen that."

"No, Junior, you don't." She switches to his thoughts. *'And don't go looking for it either, for there are things in my past with the King you do not want to see.'*

'I know, Mom, I have already seen it. It only makes you a stronger person in my eyes.' Junior hugs his mom, answering in her thoughts. "Alright. Let's go."

Pandora smiles, watching them race across the room before turning to Rendgren. "Well, it looks like we have the house to ourselves. Shall we go home and play some music?"

Rendgren growls slightly, his eyes darkening in desire as he pulls her close and nuzzles her neck. "If only we didn't have to drive." He sweeps her up into his arms and carries her out to the car at a swift rate, missing the shock, amazement and gasps from others at his actions. He places her down and opens the door for her, assisting her in and closing it afterwards before circling around and hopping in the driver's door. Within minutes, they are on the road, heading home for a night to themselves.

Junior watches from the shadows before turning to his two best friends. "Success! Kip, I am staying the night at your place. Perhaps one day, I will get my sister."

Twenty-Seven

Bullets of Fate

Kips' parents increase their visits over the holidays to more than once a week as the families unite and bond, enough so that Pandora and Rendgren invite them to meet the Council and their diplomats on New Year's Eve. The group enjoys fine conversation and laughter as they watch Junior and Kip fail miserably in trying to defeat Treefeared. Afterwards, they head upstairs to the comfort of the couches, where they ring in the New Year together with exquisite food and drinks. The evening passes with peace and happiness as they all spend the night in the mansion, departing the next morning with hugs and well wishes.

A few days later, Pandora pulls her cloak on at the end of her library shift, giving a nod to Arlyne. "I will see you tomorrow."

"Sounds good, Pandora. We have three classes tomorrow. It will be crazy."

"It will be, but I love it." Pandora laughs as she heads out the door, knowing she needs to stop at the market for Rendgren. She crosses the street and enters the mall, glancing around as a shiver runs through her body. Her gaze sweeps the surrounding area and sees nothing unusual. She frowns slightly, reaching out to Rendgren in her mind. *'Gren, is everything alright at the mansion?'*

'Of course, Junior's doing homework, and I am preparing dinner. Did you need a ride?'

'No, it's fine.'

'What's up, love?'

'I don't know Gren, but something is not right.'

'You be careful, Pandora.'

'I will, Gren.'

Pandora enters the grocery store, picking up the needed items, and leaves the shop, heading to the main doors when she pauses. She staggers beneath the flood of grief striking her and turns around, her eyes landing on a small child staring at her. Pale blue eyes, white blonde hair tied in a messy ponytail. An oversized hoodie pulled over what looks like pajama bottoms. A brief vision crosses her mind of her parents dropping her off at the mall before the sound of screeching metal fills takes over, feeling the death within it. Pandora puts a hand to her temples, feeling the pain from the child once more, seconds before she feels her arms wrap around her legs.

"Mummy said you would help me. Uncle Tom killed her cause I saw him with a bad lady."

Pandora kneels before her and draws her into her arms. "How do you know that, child?"

"Cause I saw it. Just like I saw the jar of lights that Uncle Tom has, and he didn't like that. He's mad cause I told Mummy, but Mummy didn't believe me till this morning when she saw it too."

Pandora frowns slightly, struggling to get a read of the child through her emotions, feeling a block around her. "What's your name, little one?"

"Lily. Are you going to be my new Mummy?"

"Well, I can't say. First, we need to call your mom and dad; then contact the police if they don't answer."

Her eyes well with tears, a few of them slipping down her cheeks. "They won't. The car crunched them 'cause they couldn't stop."

"Shh, we will figure it out, sweetie." Pandora brushes the tears aside while her mind reaches for Rendgren. *I am going to be late, Gren; eat without me.*

'Pandora, what's going on?'

'I will explain when I get home.'

'As long as you come home. I can feel your stress and fear.'

'I will Gren…' She shuts the link off and returns her attention back to the child, feeling Rendgren pushing to get back into her thoughts. Pandora moves to a nearby bench and sits the child down. She pulls out her cell phone and hands it to the child. "Alright, first, we need to call your parents."

Lily shakes her head and pulls her own out. She swipes it open and brings up her parent's number, places the call, and hands the phone to Pandora. "They won't answer. Uncle Tom will 'cause he stole Mummy's phone."

Pandora places the phone to her ear, listening to it ring. "Lily, is that you? Where are you?" She hears a man pick up, feeling an instant darkness within. She reaches out to steady herself as her eyes look down at the child, overwhelmed by a whole lot of emotion between the pair.

"Lily? Is that the owner of this phone I found in the market?"

"Yes, is she not with it?"

"Doesn't seem to be. I will turn the phone in at the lost and found for her mother to find." Pandora doesn't wait for a response and disconnects the call. Her fingers glide across the screen, suspecting and finding the tracking monitor on it. Powering off the phone, she picks the child up. "Come on, Lily, we need to get out of here quick." She strides to the lost and found, dropping it off with a minimal explanation. Pulling the hoodie up over the child's head, she wraps her cloak around her. Pandora leaves the mall at a brisk pace, feeling the darkness descending upon it, and heads further into town to the police station, knowing the accident and the child need to be reported. Fifteen minutes later, she breathes an audible sigh of relief as she steps inside the warm station and moves to the front desk.

A clerk approaches her. "Can I help you?"

"Yes, I found a child in the mall, and we can't get a hold of her parents. When we called her mom's cell, a man answered, who she confirmed is not her father."

"Right, come this way. I will have Officer Nathan help you."

"Thank you." Pandora follows the clerk to a small room. She settles on the chair and places Lily on her lap, holding her close as she waits, doing her best to bypass the barrier she seems to have surrounding her. Within a minute, a medium-height man walks into the room, brown hair, a neatly trimmed goatee, dressed in a uniform. She can see the green eyes doing a sweep of them as she smiles. "Greetings Officer Nathan."

"Greetings, Miss?"

"Mrs. Red, Pandora."

"I understand you found a child?"

"Well, yes, she found me, actually." Pandora explains the situation at the mall and how it wound up with her here.

"How about we try calling your mom from here?" Nathan's eyes shift to the child fearfully clinging to Pandora. His voice is gentle as he dials the number she gives him, hearing it ring twice before a man picks up.

"Yes?"

"Hi, this is Officer Nathan with the Mindriff City Police. I am looking to speak with Penelope Winters, please." He can hear the muffled sound of movement before a slight whisper. *'She took her to the bloody police... Hang up the phone, you idiot.'* A distinctive click sounds as the line goes dead. He furrows his brow as a frown crosses his face, staring at the phone before placing it back on its receiver. "Looks like you are right, Mrs. Red. Something's going on. We will need to fill in a report and place the child in foster for the night."

"No. I feel that whoever is seeking her, still wants her. I will foster her as it's not fair to the others if someone comes looking for her."

"Fair enough." He pulls papers out of the desk, taking all the information that he can get from the pair. "Would you like a ride home, Mrs. Red?"

"That would be lovely. It's a long walk to the mansion from here."

"This way, then." He gives a nod and rises, leading through the back of the police station.

Pandora hesitates at one desk, her eyes sweeping from the nameplate of Officer Leomund to the shroud of darkness surrounding him. Realizing that Officer Nathan is gaining distance, she tightens her hold on Lily and picks up her pace. She doesn't need to glance back to know the officer is heading into the room they just vacated. Within a few minutes, they are in the back of a police car, tinted windows embedded with bars surrounding them. Officer Nathan chats about nonsequential stuff as he drives them home, parking in front of their mansion about fifteen minutes later.

Pandora whispers to the child as she lifts her into her arms in the back seat. "When I tell you to run, you run straight for the door and inside. Do not knock. I will protect you until then." She waits until he opens her door, sliding from the car and facing him. "Thank you, Officer Nathan. I appreciate the ride."

"You're welcome, Mrs. Red. I will be in touch."

Images cross Pandora's mind as she turns suddenly and steps to the left, feeling the burning pain in her shoulder as she drops to the ground. "RUN Lily. Run now!" Pandora weaves an invisible shield around her, watching the child scramble to her feet and run for the door. She closes her eyes as she tracks the child's progress, touching Rendgren's. *'Gren, get her to Junior; she needs protecting.'* Pandora heard and felt several more shots strike her magic, grimacing slightly in pain as she struggles to stay alert.

Officer Nathan draws his gun and steps against the car to use it as a shield. He faces the woods that surround the mansion nervously. "Stay down, Mrs. Red."

Rendgren hears the gunfire and feels the pain of his wife. He runs downstairs and sees the small child running into the house, tears streaming from her eyes. "They shot her! And they killed Mummy and Daddy." He picks her up quickly and runs to the living room, dropping her on Junior's lap. "Your mother's been shot. Get her downstairs."

Junior scrambles to catch the child, looking at his father in shock before lifting her up and running for the cave below the house and barricading themselves in.

Lily sniffles, looking up at Junior. "You're my new brother. I'm Lily."

Junior places her on the mat, looking the tear-stained child over, recognizing her from his vision of having a younger sister. "Yes, it appears that I am. I'm Junior."

Lily nods, repeating his name quietly. "Junior... You're a dragon."

Junior does his best to conceal his surprise at her statement, his thoughts immediately reaching for his father. *'Ah, Dad, we have a problem. This girl knows I am a dragon somehow.'*

'WHAT? Deny it!'

Junior moves to kneel before the child. "No, Lily, I am not."

"Yes, you are. Just like your Mummy, but she's a different color."

'Dad! She knows Mom's one too, and that we are different colors. Something's off with her. I can't read her at all.'

'Just keep her safe. I will ask your mother.'

'Got it.' He returns his attention to Lily. "We will discuss this later. Alright."

She nods and wraps her arms around him, holding him tight.

Pandora closes her eyes, trying to focus the pain away, feeling Junior and Lily downstairs in the manor, knowing the child is safe.

"Pandora!"

Officer Nathan keeps his eyes trained on the woods, his gun resting on the roof of his car. "Stay there, sir; someone has a gun aimed at the car and house."

Rendgren growls, his focus drifting outwards, feeling the shooter running away through the woods and continues to his wife. He drops to his knees beside her and draws her into his arms. "Pandora, stay with me."

She squeezes his hands, opening her eyes briefly, drawing in a jagged breath. "It hurts, Gren."

"Shhh, I know love." He lifts her carefully into his arms and moves to the back of the police car, sliding in the open door. "She needs to get to the hospital fast. Get in and Drive. NOW."

Nathan nods, closes the door behind him, and slides into the driver's seat. His hands shake as he picks up his radio, calling it into the station; the inflection in the speed at which he talks indicates the nervous adrenaline within. "Sshhots fired at 1786 Mindriff Way. The mansion on the hill. Transporting one casualty. Adult female, barely conscious. Gunshot wound to shoulder. On route to the hospital. Shooter unaccounted for." He flips his lights and sirens on, turns the car around, and speeds back to town.

Rendgren pulls his wife close, trying to stem the bleeding from her shoulder as he reaches out to her telepathically. *'What the hell, wife? Our mortal form is not invincible.'*

'I know Gren. They intended to kill the child, but I couldn't let her die. She's Junior's mate.'

'What?'

'There is more going on here, Gren. I can see that her parents left her, knowing they were going to be killed, and wanted her to be safe. Both her and her mother are seers, not very strong though. The child clearly recognized me in the mall, but there is a block on some of her threads, and I haven't had time to sort through why yet.'

'Damn, Junior's mate is a seer. Bloody well outnumbered with three of you in the house. Now I understand why you took the bullet.'

'Junior won't know until she's twenty, and that's when their bond will click, so until then, she will be his little sister. Our daughter.' Her thoughts fade as she slips into unconsciousness.

'Understood.'

Officer Nathan looks in his mirror at Rendgren, sitting in silence as he looks down at his wife, red and blue lights dancing off his face, and steps on the gas. He weaves through traffic, doing his best not to jar his passengers, occasionally laying on the horn when a car wouldn't move, getting to the hospital in no time. He jumps out and opens the back door, watching as Rendgren slips out and places her onto a gurney that is waiting. Officer Nathan moves up beside him as they wheel her into the hospital. "I am certain she will be fine."

Rendgren narrows his eyes before turning his darkened gaze on Nathan, watching him back up a step in fear. "You better find out who did this to my wife before I do."

Officer Nathan pales drastically at the threat, knowing he meant it by the tone of his voice. "Yyyes, sir. There are officers on the way to your house as we speak to search the woods."

"Good." Rendgren turns and strides into the hospital, moving to the waiting area as they perform surgery to remove the bullet. He paces back and forth before the nurses politely ask him to stop. Sighing, he moves to sit in the nearby chair, tapping his foot as he watches the clock hands tick by slowly. Trying to distract himself, he pulls his cell out and calls his friend. "Shels."

"Zal. What's up?"

"I am at the hospital. Pandora's been shot."

Shels' voice rises a few notches. "WHAT do you mean she's been shot? Is she going to be okay?"

"I hope so, Shels. She's been in surgery for about forty minutes now."

"I will get Ryker to close shop. We will be there as soon as we can. Where's Junior?"

"He's at home. The police are swarming the forest around our house."

"Do you need us to check on him?"

"No, he's safe downstairs. I will call him shortly. Thank you."

Marcy sits nearby at the table with Lucy and Nikki, smiling in delight at hearing the one-sided conversation. She rises and looks at her friends. "It appears I need to go."

"Right now? We just got here."

"Yes, it seems someone might need consoling, and I am just the person to do it."

"I still think you should leave them be, Marcy. He clearly is not interested."

Marcy levels a look at Nikki. "He will be, very soon." She pulls her car keys out and heads to her car.

Twenty minutes later, Rendgren sits in the recovery room with his wife, watching her sleep. His gaze moves to all the tubes and wires they have her hooked up to, not liking the fact that she needs to stay here for a week. He lifts his gaze, frowning slightly when he catches the cloying scent of Marcy, wondering what the hell she is doing here. He watches her sashay into the room wearing a low-cut blouse and a short skirt, barely covering her ass. "What are you doing here, Marcy?"

"I heard someone shot your wife. I am here to offer you support."

"I am not interested. Go away."

"I am just here to help with whatever need or desire you have." Her fingers trace down to the hem of her skirt, lifting it slightly.

Rendgren's temper flares at her blatant attempt at seduction, his stomach turning in disgust. "No, you are not. You are here to divide us, but our love is stronger than that."

"How can you be sure? You haven't even tried me." She runs a hand over his shoulder seductively.

He jerks out from beneath her touch and rises swiftly, placing space between them as he turns to glare at her. "I don't need to, Marcy, and I will prove it. Caress my wife."

"What?"

"Do it. Touch her like you love her."

Marcy frowns and moves forward. She reaches out to caress Pandora's cheek lightly, receiving no response.

Rendgren moves to the opposite side of the bed. He smiles coldly at Marcy and caresses Pandora's other cheek, hearing her soft murmur of his name as she shifts her face closer to him. "Do you see that, Marcy? We are bonded. And by touching her here, I can make her gasp." He watches her gasp lightly in her sleep. "Or here will draw a sharp intake of breath. She knows my touch because I have complete control over her body, and she responds to my touch because she trusts me completely. I know every inch of her and how she reacts to me because she surrenders willingly. Something I am betting you do not, because you are all about controlling the entire relationship."

Marcy narrows her eyes on Pandora and her reaction to his touch. "Control is not love."

"No, it's not, but it is a part of *our* relationship. She is the one that tamed me from my wild days. She calms my fire and my rage and, because of this, controls me during the day, and I trust her to put myself in her hands. It's all about balance to make our love work, and we have it. Our love has spanned countless difficulties, and your meddling will not break it. If not for her, you would simply go missing, or, at the very least, be in jail for breaking into my house. The only reason you are free right now is because of her control over me.

Do you understand Marcy?"

Marcy backs up a step with a barely perceptible nod.

"Yes. I can see that you do. We share control over each other. She controls me by day; I control her by night. And you will never get in between that. Now get out of my room and STOP interfering in our relationship."

Marcy turns and books it from the room, catching Shels race past her towards the room she just vacated. She glances back as a wave of jealousy floods her when Shels wraps her arms around Zalgren.

Rendgren breathes a sigh of relief as Marcy leaves, seeing Shels run in right after, catching her as she launches herself in for a hug. "Shels."

Shels tightens her hold on him. "How are you holding out Zal?"

"It's been a very long hour."

"I would imagine. Ryker's on his way; he's parking the car." She looks around, ensuring no one is around and whispers. "I thought you were immortal."

"We are, but we are not invincible. Things can still kill us, and our human forms are not much stronger than yours against metal and bullets. If I could get her home, we could mend her, but because they shot her in front of an officer, we have to do this naturally. She's stuck here for a week, and I will admit, I hate it."

"She'll be fine. She's strong, Zal. We will be here to help watch over her."

"Thanks, I could really use a coffee."

"Did you want me to get it?"

"No, I need to stretch. They haven't found the shooter yet, but once she wakes up, I WILL." His eyes flash with fire as rage fills him swiftly.

Shels backs up a step, understanding why you never wanted to piss off a dragon. She places a hand on his arm, attempting to calm him. "Alright Zal. Calm the fires... others will see it. Go get your coffee."

He looks down at the petite woman, another that had edged her way into his life. "Yes, you are right. Thank you." Rendgren leaves the room and heads to the cafeteria. Seeing Marcy at the door, he scowls and steps around her as he approaches the counter, asking for a coffee. He pulls out some cash and places it down, sensing her moving towards him. He sidesteps her arm snaking around his waist and snatches it firmly. "Try that again, and I WILL break your arm. Is that understood? I thought it was very clear that I LOVE my wife, and you are NOT getting in between that."

The cashier gasps and places the coffee down, then backs away.

"I just wanted to offer a hug like Shels did."

"I DON'T want your hugs, Marcy. Go find someone else to torment. Hell, I don't even like you in the same room as me, let alone standing right next to me." He snatches his coffee off the counter and strides away, feeling her angry gaze boring into his back. He stalks back to the room, the rage at the woman growing with each step.

Ryker and Shels look at each other. "Everything alright, Zal?"

"It's that bloody Marcy. If it was not for my wife, I would show her what it's like to piss off a dragon."

Pandora whispers softly. "Gren, don't let her get under your skin. That's how she works."

"Pandora, you're awake." He quickly hands his coffee to Ryker and moves to her side, taking her hand in his.

"Apparently."

"DON'T you ever do this to me again! I already had you die on me once; that was enough."

She smiles, squinting to clear the fuzziness in her gaze from the drugs, feeling a heaviness within her as she tries to focus. "I wasn't going to die, Gren... I moved so...."

Rendgren squeezes her hand. "That's good. I don't think I could survive if I lost you."

"You would..."

"Wait, have you seen something?"

"The threads always shift, Gren... But at the moment, you are kind of stuck with me..."

"Good."

Shels looks at the pair. "Wait... she died?"

"Yes, when she had Junior. She was mortal like you at one time, but a mortal cannot survive the birth of a dragon."

Pandora closes her eyes, trying to focus her thoughts and speech. "Then he messed with my grand designs. He called upon the Goddess Raya and turned me into a dragon."

"And I would do it again!" He frowns slightly, recalling the day. "It's extremely rare that a human can even get pregnant with a dragon. You never did explain that, my dear."

"It's called a mystic and faerie food... and well, what happened for three days afterwards."

Rendgren blushes slightly, giving a side glance to their friends. "Yes, well, I didn't really think about it, I suppose."

"Well. I wasn't certain either, to be honest; I just knew our child would end me."

He caresses her cheek. "Out of your hands."

"Yes, it was."

Shels laughs. "You guys are so cute."

Rendgren mutters under his breath. "Cute! I can't say that the Phantom has ever been called that."

Shels pats him on the back. "He has now!"

Rendgren growls playfully. "Can I eat them?"

Pandora rolls her eyes, laughter in her voice. "No Gren! You can't."

"Damn, I am sure they would taste great."

Ryker shakes his head, placing his hands in the air as he mockingly backs up a step. "Hey, you're the one that invited us into your lives."

"Don't remind me, I should have just eaten you back then for breaking into our house, but I didn't want to sleep on the couch for a year."

"A year, Gren? You think it was just going to be a year?"

He kisses her cheek. "Yes, well, I would have found my way back into your bed... Somehow."

Pandora blushes softly at his thoughts. "Yes, you would have. I have no willpower when it comes to you."

Rendgren's eyes darken as they roam over his wife. "Yes, it's one of the things I love about you."

Shels shakes her head. "Alright. Enough bedroom talk, you two. Pandora, you should rest."

Rendgren growls at his friends but nods and leans in to kiss her forehead. "She's right. Sleep, my love. One of us will be here watching over you."

Pandora nods, feeling the drowsiness of the drugs kicking in, and drifts off to sleep.

The week passes, with the four of them taking turns, either staying at the hospital to watch over Pandora, or to keep Lily safe in the mansion while maintaining their normal lives. Rendgren returns to Lauryn and orders furniture for Lily's room, as well as personal effects and toys, despite keeping her downstairs for now with Junior. He checks in with Officer Nathan daily, wanting to know what they are doing to find the shooter, as well as taking up a patrol of his property, reaching out with his senses but finding no one skulking about.

At the end of the week, the hospital releases Pandora into Rendgren's care, with strict instructions that she is to keep to light activities for the next few months. Upon returning home, Junior and Lily wait in the hallway, out of sight of any windows. Junior moves up to hug her. "Mom, don't do that again. Okay?"

She draws him into her arms as best as she can with her arm in a sling. "I won't, Junior."

"Good."

Her eyes drift to Lily, feeling her mixed emotions. "How are you, Lily? I know it's probably been very hard on you."

Lily nods. "Yes, but the dragons have kept me safe."

Junior sighs. "About that. I DIDN'T tell her."

Pandora arches a brow. "Did you deny it?"

"Of course I did!"

Pandora laughs, tightening her arm around her son. "Junior, Lily is a seer. It's like a mystic, but not as strong."

"Seriously? This has been stressing me all week!"

"Your father knew."

Junior turns to scowl at his father. "Oohhh no, he didn't."

"He did; I told him the child was a seer on the way to the hospital."

"DAD!!!!"

Rendgren shrugs. "It slipped my mind. Sorry, Son."

"Ooh, I can't believe you did that to me!"

Lily smiles at Pandora, moving to wrap her arms around her. "I like my new brother. He's funny."

Pandora smiles, holding her close. "I am certain there will be some days you won't. Now, if you are to blend in with this family, we need to change your look. Gren, you bought two combs, right?"

"Yes, they are on her dresser. She chose the room with the balcony, which I don't approve of."

"It will be fine, Gren." Pandora leads Lily to her room and sits her down, picking up a comb. She entwines purple lights into the comb, watching it absorb the magic before running it through Lily's hair. With each stroke, her blond hair shifts to jet black. "Now, your eye color; violet or red?"

Lily smiles up at her. "Violet like yours."

Pandora catches Rendgren sigh as her hand glows a soft purple, running it gently over Lily's closed eyes. "This magic will hold until you are around twenty; at that point, your eyes will slowly shift back to blue. Now place this comb someplace secure. When you want to go blond again, use it to undo that which I have done." Pandora moves to the balcony and weaves purple lights around the frame; a wall of purple forms momentarily before fading to nothing, mimicking the same effect in her windows. She remains in front of the door as she works her way around the house, magically shielding it from any stray bullets. "Alright, the house is safe. You are to stay inside for now, Lily, until we find out who did this. Do not answer the door if anyone knocks."

Lily stares at herself in the mirror, not even recognizing herself. She looks down at the comb in her hand and moves to tuck it in the jewelry box on her dresser. "I understand."

"Good, now I need to rest. I am feeling tired. But if you need us, just knock on our door."

"I will."

Rendgren shifts over to her, muttering under his breath about light duties and magic not being part of that. Lifting her into his arms, he carries her to their room and kicks the door closed behind him. Moving over to the bed, he places her down gently and crawls in next to her. He pulls her tight into his arms and breathes deep of her scent. "I missed you."

Pandora curls up into his arms, feeling his love encompass her, yawning slightly as sleep calls to her. "I missed you too, Gren; I love you."

"I love you too, Pandora." Rendgren feels her body relax, allowing himself to doze with her.

Lily looks over to Junior, smiling at her brother standing in the doorway. "Do you want to play with Barbies?"

Junior laughs at her hopeful expression, knowing this sister thing is going to be an unfamiliar experience for him. "Of course."

Twenty-Eight

The Abducted Gambit

Three weeks pass as the family adapts to having a daughter, Junior learning more about dressing dolls than he expects but loving his new little sister. Rendgren and Pandora learn her likes and dislikes, as well as bringing in a tutor to keep her schooling up. All of them comfort her when she feels the loss of her parents or her identity, with Pandora and Rendgren finding her in their bed at night, more often than not, as she cries herself to sleep. Pandora heals faster than the doctors expect, giving her clearance to return to work with light duties when she feels up to it. Which brings up many discussions between Rendgren and Pandora about her wish to return to work at the library. Rendgren wisely backs down, knowing when Pandora makes her mind up, he is not changing it but does convince her to wait till early February to start.

On her third day back to work, Pandora's thoughts reach out and touch Rendgren's. '*My love, those that are after Lily are coming for me.*'

Rendgren stops sparring with Junior, feeling Junior's staff strike him. '*What do you mean, Pandora? You better not let them take you.*'

"Dad?"

"Shh, your mom is talking…"

'*Gren, we need to know why they want Lily. They are going to offer to exchange me for Lily. They will not harm me, and nor will I let them.*'

'*They already shot you, Pandora.*'

'*Gren, I was shot because I took Lily's bullet, and an officer was there, so I couldn't fight back. I have value to them.*'

'*Yes, and you have value to me.*'

'Gren, trust me. When I don't show up at the house, contact the police. Give them a chance first. If they haven't found me by midnight, I give you full permission to rescue me. By then, I should have sorted back through their past to determine where this is going.'

'I don't like it, Pandora, but when that clock strikes twelve, everyone involved is dead.'

'Yes, they will be. We cannot have them coming for Lily.'

Rendgren's eyes travel to his son, who stood watching, before moving to Lily. Catching her features pale suddenly, fear clearly written in her expression. "Lily, it's alright."

"They are taking her. I can see it."

Rendgren hands his staff to Junior and moves to Lily's side, kneeling before her. "Pandora will be fine. My wife is stronger than she appears."

Junior moves up next to them. "What's going on, Dad?"

Lily blinks her tears away. "They want me. They took her because of me."

"Yes, I imagine they are taking her as we speak, as she has foreseen it as well. But they will not get you, Lily. I promise." He draws her into his arms, feeling the shake in the child's body. He turns to Junior. "We are to call the police in thirty minutes when your mother doesn't return and give them a chance to find her first."

Junior shakes his head. "You are connected. We can just find her and destroy those that took her."

"No, Son. She needs time to sort through their threads to determine what exactly is going on."

"I don't like it, Dad. She was shot by them already."

"I don't either, but your mother is alone and can handle herself. I have seen her power. Now that she doesn't have to protect anyone, they won't hurt her. I guarantee it."

Lily sniffles, rubbing at the tears in her eyes. "I don't want to cause you problems."

"You aren't Lily. We need to find out why they want you dead. It's clearly something they think you have foreseen, or you helped them with. Pandora can't see it on you, which is a concern, and there is only one other person that has been able to block her power. Lavinia."

"Who's Lavinia, Dad?"

"She's a witch, Son. One who has a vendetta against your mother because your mother stole something of value from her. She sent assassins after her when she was thirteen and was almost successful in killing her."

"What if she succeeds now?"

"I am certain your mother would have informed me if she had made it back to this realm. If she has, we need to be prepared because that won't be the only problem returning. It means the King will as well. If it is her, somehow the witch has connected with those that want Lily dead. That is why we need to wait before we raze the house. It will also be dark, so it will make it just that much easier."

"I don't like it."

"I don't either, but I know your mother. She has powers that even we have not seen. She told me when we first met that she wasn't playing all her cards, and I suspect she never has."

"What do you mean?"

"It means that your mother is stronger than even we know, for she keeps a lot of her powers close to her heart."

"Why would she do that? Are you saying she doesn't trust us?"

Rendgren reaches out to touch his son's cheek. "No, Son. She trusts us with her life. But this is something she learned at nine years old and a hard habit to break. And if something came up that required her to show us her power, she would without question. It also means that if someone were to capture us and use magic to divulge information, we cannot give them the full extent of what your mother is truly capable of."

"I don't understand."

"It means that your mother will be fine."

Pandora hears the van speeding up the road and senses five individuals inside, images flickering in her mind as to how it's going to play out. Turning, she observes the vehicle come to a stop as masked men quickly jump out and surround her, forcing her into the vehicle. Before the doors even close, the van takes off as the men bind her hands and feet together, following with a blindfold. After an hour of travel, the van stops, and they carry her into a house, placing her on a chair and lashing her to it. Once there, they remove the blindfold, scowling at her in dismay.

Pandora narrows her eyes on her captors. "What do you want?"

"The girl that you stole from us. Since you have been extra diligent about always having someone in the house with her, we have done the next best thing. Her for you."

"You are making a mistake. Leave her be, and you will survive."

"She knows too much. She's gonna die."

"Knows too much about what?"

"We are not telling you, lady. Then we would have to kill you."

Pandora rolls her eyes as she studies each of them carefully, sensing more moving upstairs. "I've watched enough TV to know you intend to anyway, because you let me see your faces. To add to that, one of you already tried."

"Yes, somehow you got in the way."

Pandora smiles coldly. "So are you even certain the child knows what you think she knows or that she will even talk? She hasn't yet."

"Yes, she's a special child."

"All children are special."

"She's really special."

"How so?"

"We can't tell you."

"Can't or won't? Either way, my husband is not trading her, so this plan of yours will fail."

"Lady, I get the impression that you are pretty damn important to him."

"I am, but that doesn't mean he will trade me for an innocent child. Greater good and all."

The man smiles coldly. "I think he will. I have heard the stories around town about how he has eyes only for you, and no one can get between that. Pretty certain that a child you just met doesn't have that skill when an expert at breaking relationships is struggling with it."

"So Marcy is somehow involved with this." Pandora sighs in dismay, seeing the man pale before her. She smiles as she studies him, sorting through his lifelines back into the past. "Oh... You don't think we don't know what she's doing? Trust me. My husband will only tolerate her interference for so long before he gives her what she wants, and I can guarantee she won't like it, nor can she handle it."

"What are you saying?"

"I'm saying my husband has a temper, and I'm the one that controls him during the day. Left unchecked, who knows where that temper will take him, but I do know this; he will find me. You better hope the police find you first because my husband is going to be pissed, and you really don't want to see him mad. He has destroyed entire towns on whims; you will be nothing to him."

He laughs hysterically. "Destroyed towns, whatever. We are not concerned with a man who wears a skirt. You should be more worried about your own safety."

She smiles patiently at them. "Worried? Why? Because you think you are a threat to me? You would not have captured me if I had not let you."

"Oh really? And yet you are here, tied to that chair over there."

"True, but I need to determine why you want the child and who is really behind this endeavor. I am certain you are not smart enough to plan this on your own. I don't think Marcy even knows about the child. She's more interested in stealing Gren from me, so I suspect you just overheard her complaining to Nikki and Lucy, which means you frequent the market where I found the child. There has only been one strong enough to block my power, and that was hundreds of years ago... And she's not here yet, so there is something else. I will figure out why you want the girl dead and what she has on you." Her eyes glow ever so softly as she studies the man before her, watching as he backs up a step.

"What the hell are you talking about, Lady?"

"The fact that the child you want dead is not the only one with magic at their disposal."

The man pales, a slight hesitation entering his voice as he glances at his companions. "I don't know what you are talking about."

"Let me go and forget about the child. Live your lives. Continue on this path, and you will die when my husband arrives."

"He won't find you, Lady; we made sure there was no trace of us."

"He will, and he will kill you." Hours pass as she methodically sorts through everyone's timelines, doing her best to work her way around the blocks that are in place. Her eyes move to the obsidian necklace around their throats, recalling that Lily wears one, suspecting she just found her nemesis. Her eyes glow softly at the one dozing, twisting her hands slightly in the ropes as the clasp opens and the necklace slides down to the carpet. She glances around before returning her attention to him. She smiles, sifting through his threads at a rapid rate, knowing her time is running out, frowning as she finds the exact moment Lavinia contacts them. Her thoughts touch Rendgren's lightly, knowing he was closing in on the house. *'Damn, Lavinia's involved.'*

'Is she there?'

'Not that I can see, Gren.'

'Good, I will be there soon.'

Pandora looks up at the one pacing, her eyes traveling to the hallway, knowing there is one watching the door. "My husband is on his way. Surrender now and live."

"You're delusional, Lady."

She bites back a smile as they all hear a knock on the door.

"Who the hell is that?"

"My pissed-off husband."

"That's highly unlikely."

She shrugs her shoulders. "Don't say I didn't warn you."

The man at the door opens it and stares in surprise at Rendgren before fumbling for the gun at his hip.

"I do believe you have my wife." Rendgren smiles coldly at the man that opens it, his eyes flashing with fire as they slit to dragons. Rendgren reacts swiftly as the man reaches for a gun and rips it out of his hands, tossing it to the side. His fingers elongate into claws, raking the man across the chest, flames burning the open wounds as the man cries in agony. "And I am here to take her back!"

The man screams in terror as he turns to run, only to have Rendgren shred him, dropping him on the ground at his feet. The rest of the bandits shift nervously at the scream, some turning to look towards Pandora. Purple lights surround her as a vision of her husband shredding their friend appears between them.

They back away in fear. "What the hell is that?"

Pandora smiles coolly. "My husband. I warned you he has a temper, and when you kidnap a mystic, you best be ready to play with both fire and magic." Her eyes glow softly as the ropes fade from her hands and wrap around another as he looks down in shock. She rises as Rendgren steps into the room, his eyes blazing in anger, narrowing on the remaining five backing away from his wife. Pandora smiles at her husband. "Gren."

"Love? I trust they did not harm you?"

"They didn't."

"Did you get the information you needed?"

"I did."

"Can I end them?"

"You can. I am not even gonna tell you to play nice."

"Good."

The bandits recover as Pandora and Rendgren talk. Each of them pulls out their gun. "Don't even think about moving."

"Bad boys. Did you not listen?" Pandora weaves purple lights around the weapons, fading them from their hands to the table behind her. "See, the child is ours now and will remain that way. You should have just left well enough alone. I imagine you sold or traded your souls to Lavinia, so please say hi to her when you return to her." Pandora creates a mist of purple lights, closing and sealing all the doors and windows in the house. She lifts her hands, drawing a rope of magic to the one she bound. "I need this one, Gren; you may play with the rest. Have fun. I will be in the basement."

Rendgren watches them scatter, two heading upstairs and one for the basement. "Love, did you want that one?"

"I got him, Gren; you get the others. No one is leaving this house alive."

His eyes darken dangerously. "Understood."

Pandora follows the man downstairs and draws on her magic, creating a shimmering shield around her, feeling the bullets bounce off it as she steps through the curtains. She faces her palm forward, her shield spitting off magical darts that strike the man, causing him to jerk back in pain with each hit before collapsing to the ground in a heap.

"Whhaatt are you?"

Pandora glares at the man in tow, reaching out to pull his necklace off, fingering it as she studies it. "Well, Uncle Tom, I am a mystic. A much stronger version of your niece. But there is something blocking my magic on her, perhaps this necklace as it looks like one she is wearing, or it's tied to the deal you made with a soul witch." Her eyes do a sweep of the room, moving to the wardrobe that stands out of place. She opens it carefully, noting the black cloth, the candles, and the pile of smeared entrails, all laid out within runes, alongside a book with writing. Sitting in the center is a jar, a dark green glow within it, as small sparks of light bounce off its edges. "Activate it."

He shakes his head. "I can't."

She frowns, her eyes slitting into dragons, searching through his threads now that the barrier is gone. She feels his fear at his realization that the woman they kidnapped is not what she seems. "Hmmm, you are right, you need four other gems and their hands." Her thoughts touch her husbands, flashing images of the four men. *'Gren, I need their left hands and the necklaces around their throats.'*

'Attached?'

'No, just their hands are fine.'

'Understood.'

Rendgren narrows his eyes on the man quivering before him, bleeding from several rake wounds. "Apparently, my wife needs this." His claws hook around the necklace, ripping it from his neck as he finishes the man off. He summons his blade and removes the hand before turning to the one cowering in the corner. Lifting his hand as a ball of flame appears, he hurls it the man's way, hearing his scream of pain as fire engulfs him. Rendgren returns back along his path of carnage, removing the hands and necklaces needed and bringing them down to his wife.

"Love, here is what you requested."

Tom blanches and staggers back a step, only to be jerked forward by Pandora. "Are there any more alive?"

"No, the last one is burning as we speak."

"So the house will go up in flames."

"Yes."

"Well, I don't want it to yet." She lifts a hand and pauses the flame, leaving the man suspended in death. She turns to Tom, her eyes glowing dangerously on him. "Activate this altar, and you might survive."

"No."

"I don't think you understand. I am not giving you a choice." Pandora guides him magically towards the altar, drawing on his thoughts and pulling them forth on how to work it. She places the hands on the panels they need to be before fitting the gems into the runes. Scowling as she turns back to Uncle Tom. "Now, you either place your hand there willingly, or Gren cuts it off, and I do it. The choice is yours."

Tom pales, glancing between her and her husband, and places his hand on the remaining trigger. The mirror flashes suddenly as an image appears, looking back at them.

The witch narrows her eyes on Pandora. "You! What are you doing?"

"Clearly interfering... Again. Why these men, Lavinia?" Pandora studies the witch in the illusion before her, glimpsing the realm that she and Zane rule; the potent power they wield. Her eyes narrow on the amulet around Lavinia's neck. She reaches through the liquid mirror with strands of purple magic and seizes the necklace, tearing it off. She hears Lavinia wail and feels the witch's claws rake against her shield. Images filter into her mind, seeing where her intent is. "Really, Lavinia, replacing another soul on a child of Royalty. Do you not have any creativity? Ooh, wait... You are intending to replace all the Royal souls, starting with this one. But why tie in the child?" Pandora studies her carefully, sensing Lavinia's rage through the portal. "The child saw it, and Uncle Tom overheard her telling her mother. He came to you, and that's why you want the child dead. You do know I can foresee the future as well?"

"You were supposed to be dead."

"Did you forget that dragons are immortal?"

"But not invincible. I had hoped someone would have killed you by now."

"Let us be Lavinia. You succeeded in the realm you rule with Zane. Be happy there. You men are dead. I am breaking your tie to these mortals and stopping your plans to destroy this world."

"You can't do that!"

"Too late; Gren killed all your men but this one. I have the amulets and their hands. In order to end your connection here, I just need to destroy the altar and the amulets tied to it. Goodbye, Lavinia." Pandora channels her magic into Lavinia's gem, her eyes glowing a bright purple as the room hums and pulses around them. She weaves several runes along its edges, hearing Lavinia's curse as the gem shatters, followed by the rest, ending the connection with her realm. Reaching over to the mirror and touching it gently, Pandora channels her mystic fires into it, watching it melt beneath her touch, the scent of scorched wood and glass burning their nostrils. The jar that is feeding off the other realm cries in agony as it shatters, the motes of green fade away into the nether. She turns to Uncle Tom, seeing him drop to the floor unconscious, knowing that with breaking the stone tied to him, his life is ending. Pandora calls forth a parchment, writing upon it a letter of confession, in the death of the Winter family for reasons unknown, and the inside connection with Officer Leomund to make it seem like an accident. She drops the parchment on the body and releases the fires in the house above.

"Let's go home, Gren."

"How are we going to explain this Pandora? The Police know someone kidnapped you."

She smiles at her husband. "They won't remember once they read the letter. In fact, they will forget that Lily even survived. They will report that she died with her family in the car crash."

Rendgren nods, creating a portal back to the mansion, arriving in the cave below, seeing Junior and Lily waiting.

Junior studies his parents carefully. "Is it done?"

"Yes, Son. We stopped Uncle Tom and his crew. Lily belongs to us now. No one will come looking for her."

"Yes, I finally got my sister."

Pandora turns to Lily, who remains quietly watching them. "I hope that is acceptable, Lily. If not, we can find you another family."

Junior frowns, moving to Lily's side. "No, Mom, she's part of us now."

"It's Lily's choice, Son. It's not ours."

Lily's expression wavers between hope and fear. "Mummy said I would have a new family, but what if it doesn't work out? I am not a dragon like you all are. I am different."

Pandora moves over to Lily and picks her up into her arms. She holds her close and kisses her cheek lightly. "We don't care that you are not a dragon Lily. You will still be our daughter, and we will love you as we love Junior."

She hugs Pandora back, nodding against her. "Then you are my new Mummy, Daddy and Brother."

Rendgren beckons to Junior as they both wrap their arms around Pandora and Lily for a group hug. "Welcome to the family, Lily."

After a few minutes of the group hug, they head down to the kitchen for ice cream. Pandora keeps her arm around Lily, understanding this is a significant step, recalling her own experience at nine years of age when she moved to the castle. After finishing their ice cream, she carries Lily upstairs and tucks her into bed, kissing her forehead. "Sleep in peace, Lils; the bad guys are all gone."

Pandora leaves the room and kisses her son goodnight. She takes Rendgren's arm, and they head to their own rooms to retire for the night. In their bedroom, Pandora goes to her dresser immediately, with Rendgren watching. She pulls out a small satchel, opens it, and dumps two gems into her hands. She fingers them carefully before placing one in Rendgren's hand. "Carry one at all times on you."

"Your masking gems? Only two?"

"Yes, one for each of us. They don't know Junior or Lily well enough to scry on them."

"Did you know?"

"Yes, I knew when Rune gave me the stones that I needed six stones. One each for the four I helped escape and two for us."

"You foresaw three hundred years into the future?"

Pandora smiles, caressing his cheek lightly. "It's not any different from seeing three hundred years into the past, my dear Phantom."

He nods, tucking the stone on him before drawing her in and holding her close. "It's not going to end well, is it?"

Pandora shakes her head, wrapping her arms around him. "It's too early to tell."

He nods, remaining silent and holding his wife tight.

The month passes in peace, with Lily adapting into the family as if she has always been there, pestering Junior to play with her when he's around. Kip and him end up caving, finding their time split between Barbies, football, and video games, though neither is willing to admit they play with dolls outside the mansion.

Twenty-Nine

Book One – Future

Pandora wanders into the living room from the balcony, loving that spring came early this year. She smiles at Junior, who's sitting on the couch playing video games with his friend Kip. "Junior, I am going to the market. Did you need anything?"

"It's a shopping mall Mom; you're going to the mall. You are so far behind the times. And I'm good, thanks."

"Right, mall. You know it will always be the market for me."

"That's because you're old."

"Watch your tongue, Junior. I am only nineteen years older than you."

He turns to look at his mother, dressed in her violet and green hanfu. Chains dangle around her waist and across her chest, amethysts inset along the neckline and sleeves of her hanfu. "Are you wearing that? In public?"

"Yes, I am."

"Mom! It's sooo old-fashioned! You need to adapt to the modern times."

"There is nothing wrong with this. Now, don't be too loud; your father is sleeping."

"He's always sleeping, Mom."

"Well, that's because he's old!"

Junior laughs. "Don't let Dad hear you say that."

She moves over and pats his head. "He's sleeping, he won't. I will be back in a few hours. Lil's is upstairs reading."

"Aww, Mom, don't do that." He swats her hand away.

She laughs softly. "Alright, Junior." Her eyes drift to the painting in the room above the TV, a family portrait they had done before dragons had to go into hiding. The three of them in their dragon form, with their tiny dog Spider baring his teeth, commissioned by the renowned artist and his wife, Stephyn and Glynda Stefflyrs. She drifts back, recalling the day they posed for it when they ruled a kingdom and brought peace to the realm before retiring, watching as cities grew up around them. "I will be back in a few hours."

"Alright, Mom, see you when you get back."

Pandora walks down to the town, having always hated those big metal boxes everyone rides in, even if her husband loves them. She wanders through the shopping center, picking up a few things and tucking them in her bag before stopping at the puppies in the pet store window. She watches them for a moment, recalling Spider, feeling a sadness within her when they lost him to old age. Pandora crouches down to their level, watching as one comes forward to the glass, licking at her fingertips, while the others back away, sensing more than what appears before them. "Well, you are a brave one, aren't you? You are sure to find a home quickly." She rises and turns away but stops as she hears a howl; her violet eyes shift back to the puppy, whose tail immediately starts wagging. "Oh, little one, you are going to get me into so much trouble." Entering the pet store, she looks around, her gaze landing on the teller. "How much for the puppy in the window?"

"Which one, miss?"

"The black one, with the white sun mark on her chest."

"Fifty dollars."

"Right. I will take her."

The man nods, moves to the pen, and picks up the pup, returning with her and placing her into Pandora's arms. "Do you need supplies?"

"No, I am certain we have some." She hands over the money.

"Alright then, have a good day, miss."

"You too." Pandora smiles, feeling the puppy squirm in her arms and lick her face, bringing a laugh to her lips. "Well, Gren is going to have my hide for this, but first, we need to give you a name so he can't kick us both out." She ponders it as they walk home. She pushes the gate open and closes it behind her, placing the puppy on the ground, and watches as she bounds after the bugs in the grass. "Alright, Bug, you need to behave around him, though I am certain Junior and Lil's will love you."

She turns and heads for the house, crossing through the main entrance as the puppy follows behind her. She heads her son's way, hearing the video games still playing. "Did your father wake up, Junior?"

"No, Mom, he...Wait, YOU bought a dog? Spider?"

"Yes, I did, and her name is Bug."

Junior drops the controller and runs to the pup, dropping to his hands and knees and holding a hand out, watching her tail wag as she jumps into his lap. "Dad's gonna kill you!"

"He can try." She places her packages on the table and sorts through them, pulling out several bunches of flowers, knowing they need tending to first.

"Flowers? Are Auntie Sol and the others coming for dinner?"

"Yes, dear, on Saturday. Along with the Council."

"Awesome! I can't wait! Fight club with the Guardians!"

She lifts her gaze, feeling her husband moving through the mansion, hearing his voice well before she saw him. "Why do I feel a rodent in the house, my love?"

"I don't know what you're talking about, Gren."

He rounds the corner, eyeing his wife up and down, desire flaring in his eyes, even after hundreds of years together. His gaze travels down to Junior, who sits on the floor with a dog in his lap before shifting over to Junior's friend, who is sitting on the couch and watching the entire exchange silently, game controller hanging in his hand. "YOU bought a Mutt!?"

"Yes, Gren, I did. Her name is Bug. You will adapt, just like you did with Spider." She arranges the flowers in the vase.

"I will never admit to that."

"You don't have to. I saw the truth."

Rendgren's eyes narrow slightly, shifting to the movement of the flowers she is arranging. "OH no, Bloody Hell. You didn't invite Honors Light for dinner."

"Yes, dear, I did. And the Council."

"Some days, my dear, Some days."

She turns and smiles his way. "Every day, Gren, and you love it."

He moves over to her side, pulling her in close, running a hand lightly over her forehead, brushing her hair aside as he kisses her gently. "I love you, not it. There is a difference."

Junior picks up the pup. "Ewwww. Get a room!"

"We have a room, Junior. Get out!"

"Dad!!!! Come on, Kip, let's go outside and play ball."

Kips looks at the pair, turning to his friend. "Are you gonna let your dad talk to you like that?"

"Oh, hell ya. Do you know how old he is? My dad is like the second most powerful person in this world. He can easily kick my ass."

Kip follows along behind. "Wait, second? So who's the first?"

"My Mother."

Rendgren watches his son vacate the house, his eyes landing on his wife. "So, my love, you want to tell me why they are coming for dinner when they were just here?"

"We are going to need them."

"Damn, he finally made it back?"

"Yes, and he's coming right for us."

"When?"

"In a few months. Perhaps mid to late July. His witch is currently in Oblait searching for us."

"So that means we are not staying here. Damn, it finally felt like home. Are we returning to the lair?"

"We are. Junior and Lily will not be."

Rendgren nods, pulling her close and holding her tight. "They are not going to be happy."

Pandora shakes her head. "No, they are not. I am certain Junior has an idea, but won't say anything until it happens. He will be sorting to find a way around it like I am."

Rendgren kisses the top of her. "There is no way around it, is there?"

"No, Gren, there is not."

Thirty

Plans in Motion

Days later, Pandora absorbs the children's delight as she sorts through the March issues of the magazines, tagging them with their library codes and placing them on the shelves. She looks up, feeling anxiety interrupting her calm happiness like a brick slamming her upside the head before it walks in the door. Her eyes land on Brian, frowning slightly, having not seen him in the library before. He approaches her and stands nearby, watching her work. "Can we talk?"

She studies him a moment and turns to Arlyne. "May I have ten minutes?"

"Of course."

"Thank you." Pandora gestures to a table in the back corner, well away from the rampaging kids. She walks along beside him, sorting through his thoughts, watching him sit and play with his tie nervously. She settles at the table with him. "What's up, Brian?"

"I would like to apologize for my wife's actions. I know about her affairs and that she's been trying for your husband for some time. It pains me greatly, but I suffer for Kaspina's sake. I have tried everything to return to where we were before we lost our son, but it's like there is a bridge between us that's broken, and no matter what I use or do, I can't repair it."

"Brian, you don't need to apologize. It's not your fault; it's hers, and she won't succeed with my husband." Pandora takes his hand gently in hers, feeling the loss of the child within him. "What if I can mend that bridge for you? Would you take it? It is a risk, and it could injure you in the process... Enough so that you will end up in the hospital for a week or two."

"What do you mean?"

She sighs softly. "I cannot say exactly, but I can say my past is returning soon. It's a past that you don't want to cross, but I did and pissed it off. So now it's hunting for my death."

Brian looks at her in confusion. "I don't understand. How does that fix Marcy and I?"

"There will be a fight between us. People are going to get injured. You could be one of them. It will make her realize just what you mean to her when your life is at risk, when she doesn't know whether you will live or die."

"Is it going to be that much of a risk?"

"Yes, and no. I will stop most of the attack, but it will hurt you. Broken ribs, perhaps?"

"How will you stop an attack? And what attack?"

Pandora smiles patiently. "I can't really explain more until it happens. Just know you want to be standing at the front. Closest to me and my past."

"How will I know?"

"You will know. Everyone is going to know very soon. I will message you to be at the mall the day he finds me."

Brian looks her over intently, feeling a hope in this woman he has not felt in a long time. "Then I will do it because I cannot live like this anymore."

Pandora rises, offering him a hug, feeling the pain that he carries within. She whispers quietly to him. "You will be Ok, I promise. It's gonna hurt like hell, though."

He nods against her before stepping back. "Thank you." He turns and strides from the library, glancing back as he reaches the door before stepping outside.

Pandora spends the next few months sorting threads, practicing her swordplay with Junior and Rendgren; teaching Lily to defend herself as well as how to work her visions. Lily continues to adapt to the family, but still has nights where she crawls into bed with Pandora crying. Junior relinquishes Bug, placing her on Lily's bed one night, watching as she curls up against her, quieting the tears, recalling how much he relied on Spider in his growing years. Meetings increase with the Council, Honors, and Kip's family while they discuss plans and what's going to happen at the mall. Pandora does her best to give them all of the possible outcomes.

In late June, Ryker, Shels, and Kip assist with packing the mansion's belongings into the lair. This includes clothes, jewelry, magical dishes, paintings, couches, and a few recliners. They furnish the bare space in the main room and kitchen, transforming it into a more livable environment. Rendgren creates two additional rooms off his lair, one serving as a bedroom for Lily and the other for Junior. They move their bedroom furniture into the lair, consolidating the living spaces. Rendgren stares at his prized dragon desk, feeling Pandora walk up behind him. "Bring it with us."

"Where would we put the computer? We can't take any electronics."

"True, but replace the desk with the table from the lair."

"Good plan. Kip, Junior, please fetch the kitchen table from the lair."

"Got it Dad."

Junior and Kip replace the computer on the table while Ryker and Rendgren carry the desk through the portal, placing it in a nook. Pandora follows, carrying the dragon lamp she bought him many years ago. Shels and Lily each carry an armful of books while Kip and Junior grab the loveseat. Shels pauses at a yellow parchment, with flowing script pressed within two panes of glass, surrounded with a wood carved frame, dragons etched into its sides. "What is this?"

Rendgren lifts his gaze to the frame before drifting to his wife. "It says my wife officially belongs to me forever."

Pandora laughs. "That's our marriage certificate, and it doesn't say that, but Gren likes to think it does."

Rendgren draws her into his arms. "Yes, it does, and there are thirteen witnesses that will side with me on the matter."

Pandora rolls her eyes, resting her head on his chest. "Alright Gren. But I think they will side with me on this one." She turns to whisper to Shels. "Don't listen to him."

Junior shakes his head, placing his end of the loveseat down in the room, watching as Kip mimics him on the other side. "Mom's right, if anyone owns anyone, she owns Dad."

Rendgren tightens his hold on Pandora, sending a dark look his son's way. "Junior, I can still turn you over my knee."

"But you won't, Dad, cause Mom won't let you." Junior stretches brazenly, a mischievous grin crossing his face as he turns to his parents. "Are you sure we have to do this?"

"Unfortunately, yes. Mindriff is no longer an option for us to live. By the end of the week, magic is going to be exposed, and we will need to be in hiding."

"Damn, other than that annoying Marcy, I liked it here." He stomps back through the portal into the mansion to get another box as Kip and Lily follow him.

Ryker watches his son step back through the portal as if it was nothing more than a door. "Will you come back?"

Rendgren shakes his head. "Not for a while and not likely in your lifetime, I'm afraid. We choose our form as we grow, and while we can temporarily disguise ourselves, it's only for a matter of hours. The magic to keep a disguise up is not worth the risk."

Pandora mutters quietly. "Right, speaking of temporary. Your shields on this place need mending."

Rendgren looks down at his wife. "My shields have kept this place safe for fourteen hundred years or so, love."

Pandora glances towards the mansion, keeping her voice low so the kids will not hear. "Not while we sleep."

Rendgren nods. "Right, I will go help the kids."

Pandora walks out to the entrance with Shels beside her. "It's really over for you, living in the mortal world."

She nods sadly. "It is for now. We will return. I just don't know when."

"What happens if Zane wins?"

"Then I suggest you pack your things and head to the Isle of Lochyae. There are druids that will protect you."

"The King is that evil?"

Pandora turns, taking Shels' hands in hers. "It is not the King I am worried about."

"What do you mean?"

"It means, if I die, the Red Phantom will return with a vengeance, starting with King Zane. And my son will follow suit with ALL his powers that I have been filtering back slowly. Lily will be lost in the chaos, and so I need you to take her with you."

"Oh damn, I read those stories. The world is not prepared! If it comes down to that, I promise I will take Lily, but you need to win."

"I will do my best, Shels, but the risk is there. I won't know until we battle out what threads he's going to play. He has power now, more so than when I was his slave."

Shels nods, studying her friend, not entirely comprehending how their magic worked but understanding the gravity of the situation. She whispers softly. "You will win."

Pandora smiles and turns to the entrance, weaving her hands as purple strands of light flowed from them, twisting and snaking upwards, as well as back through the passages. She follows the strands with her mind, encompassing the cavern with her magic, placing a shield up over them, blocking them from the real world and all that it entails. Within a minute, she turns back to Shels. "Come, we should return before they come looking. There is still a fair amount to move in here."

Shels pulls her into a tight hug. "I will miss you. I am glad that Zalgren invited us into your lives."

Pandora hugs her back. "I am too, Shels. It is nice to have friends again. It's been us for so long, I forgot what it's like. Thank you."

Once they move all the desired furniture, they look around at the cave, knowing this is going to be their home for the near future. Pandora leans on her husband, her thoughts touching his. *'Give them the mansion, Gren. You know we aren't returning, and it deserves to have someone love it.'*

Rendgren nods, kissing the top of his wife's head. "Ryker, Shels, Kip. Please come with me." He leads everyone downstairs, hearing their gasp at the underground lake, continuing on till he reaches the hoard. Ryker stops and stares at the gold while Shels exclaims in shock. "Is that real?"

"Yes, it's real. A lot of it is from Pandora. It was a deal she made when I first kidnapped her. Her dog's life for dragon treasure. I added over one hundred hoards because of her."

Shels moves in with him, glancing back at her husband standing there. "How much is here?"

Rendgren picks up a couple of coins and hands them to Shels. "I don't rightly know, but I know each of those coins you hold is about one hundred grand on the market right now."

She stares at them in shock before looking around at the piles that doubled her height and went back as far as she could see, with no ends in sight. "I think I am going to faint."

Rendgren chuckles. "Go ahead, just make sure you roll around in it first."

"Seriously?"

Rendgren arches a brow, gesturing to the gold. "I need to retrieve something from the back. Roll away."

Shels laughs and moves to a pile, laying on it and laughing, with Ryker finally breaking free from his shock to join her.

Kip turns to Junior. "Wow, Junior, I knew you had wealth, but this is unreal."

Junior shakes his head. "This is Dad's wealth. I have my own hoard, but it's not even close to this big."

"Can I see it?"

"Sure." He leads Kip back up the passage to a smaller room with enough gold to fill a couple of bedrooms in the mansion. He picks up a couple of coins and hands them to Kip. "Here, take this for your college and to get you started in a house of your own. You are my bestest friend ever, Kip, and I will miss you."

Kip hugs his friend close. "Ditto Junior. I am gonna miss you."

Rendgren returns a few minutes later, an old parchment in his hand, seeing Lily and Pandora standing together, watching their friends' enjoyment. "Alright, you two. You may each take a few coins back with you."

"What? Wait, it's your hoard."

"It is; I am giving you enough to set you for life. As well as the coins, Pandora and I have agreed that you shall have the deed to the mansion. She's yours now. She needs someone to love her."

"You don't need to do that, Zal."

"I do. She's been empty for three hundred years. I will admit that in all the places we have lived, this one was home, and not because it was mine, but because Junior stepped out into the world. Because we invited you in. Your family added with our family and made it a home. The others were just places we lived. Because of that, I want you to keep it a home."

Tears fill Shels eyes as she rises and hugs Rendgren tightly. "Gawd, I am gonna miss you guys. Thank you."

Rendgren hugs her tightly back, his eyes finding Pandora's and Lily's, before drifting back to Junior re-entering the lair. "I will miss you too, Shels. I really will." He steps back and hands the deed over to them. "Take care of her and keep her in the family. When we return to the world, we will look them up. I promise."

"We will, Zal; we promise."

"Good, now let's go spend the last few days in the mansion, sleeping on air mattresses."

"Arg, really. Can't we sleep here?"

Rendgren laughs. "No, Son, we can't. And I took the good one this time."

"Fine, I'm sleeping on one of the couches we left behind."

"Lily gets that."

"Seriously?... Aarrgg sisters!"

Lily giggles at her brother's antics. "He can have the couch, Dad."

Rendgren moves to Lily and ruffles her black hair. "No, you get the couch. Perhaps I will make Junior sleep on a bedroll like your mother made me do for a year."

Junior huffs and rolls his eyes. "Fine, air mattress it is."

The two families return to the mansion, with Rendgren closing the portal after them. They head to the kitchen, enjoying the rest of the day in light banter, knowing within the week their lives will be changing.

A few days later, Pandora reaches into Brian's thoughts, telling him to head to the mall, feeling the shock within his mind at her telepathy. *'Brian, today is the day; remember, no matter what you see, be out front. I will protect you. It will be scary, but it is the only way to mend that bridge.'* She looks at Rendgren and Junior. "Go to the mall; Shels will be here shortly to watch over Lily. I will meet you there."

"Got it, Mom; I will meet you in the food court."

Rendgren nods. "I will meet you outside, love. We can do this."

"We can." She watches them leave, waiting until Shels arrives to look after Lily. "Remember, do not fight him. Agree and go willingly." Once she is certain they are secure, she heads to the mall to await the battle, finding Junior in the food mart where they agreed to meet.

Rendgren leaves the bookstore with a book in hand, seeing Marcy is waiting for him. He narrows his eyes as she sashays over and rests a hand on his arm. Growling slightly, he grabs her wrist and backs her against the wall forcefully. He slides a knee in between her legs to pin her down as the book drops to the ground beside him. He can smell the fear emanating off her as he restrains her. Rendgren leans in and whispers as his hand tightens on her wrist. "What's the matter, Marcy; this is what you wanted, isn't it? To see what it's like to have my attention."

His hand shifts to claws as he caresses it along her cheek, revealing through the transformation the truth of his non-human nature. His eyes slit as the dragon from within emerges, his breath hot against her skin. "Do you really think that you can handle me? To tame me, the Red Phantom. In the 1500 years I have been alive, there is only one person that has been able to tame me, Marcy. Want to take a wild guess as to who that is? Let me give you a hint. It's my wife!"

Fires dance in his eyes and around his claws as she struggles to free herself, but he just tightens his hold. He growls, a deep growl, against her neck, his voice dangerous as he whispers in her ear. "Why are you struggling, my dear? You've been pushing this on me for almost a year. Do you not like playing with fire? Perhaps you should learn just who you are getting involved with, for meddling in the affairs of dragons is just going to get you burned." A devilish smile plays upon his lips at finally confronting her as she sags against the wall to her knees, shaking in fear.

Rendgren magically calls the book up from the ground and slaps it into her hands. "Read it. I want you to know just how lucky you are to be alive, Marcy. In fact, the only reason you're alive is because of my wife and the control she has over me. A wife I have loved for over three hundred years. Someone you didn't *ever* have a chance of stealing me from. She is my heart, my love, and my soulmate. A simple-minded mortal like you, has no chance in hell of splitting us up." He creates a ring of fire in the mall, earning some screams of panic from passer-byers and steps through the portal. "And if you EVER make a move on me again, it will be your last. Is that clear?"

Marcy nods.

"Good." He closes the portal after him.

Thirty-One

The Battle for Survival

Pandora sits in the mall having coffee with Junior when she feels his presence. She takes her son's hand gently in hers. "Stay here, Junior. Play it right. Remember to shield yourself. Do NOT think that you can take it."

"I got it Mom. Is Dad ready?"

"I believe he'll be here soon. He is teaching Marcy a lesson."

"Good. That woman is unbelievable. I am glad Dad is finally doing something about it."

"Junior, your father restrained himself because I asked him to. One day, you will understand."

"Doubtful. I mean, who does that? Who tries to split up marriages?"

Pandora pats his head, earning an exasperated sigh. "She is unhappy in her own marriage, my boy, and doesn't understand how people like us can be happy. She wants it and sees her only way to have it is to get part of the one that has it. One day, you will have a mate that someone will want, and you will need to control your fires as well."

Junior rolls his eyes and laughs. "Me? With a mate? Doing that kissy stuff? NO way!"

Pandora smiles and rises. "I will remember this and bring it up when that time happens. Now, I need to face Zane; you know when to appear."

"Yes, Mom, I do, and through the side door."

People gather outside as Zane calls for the seer. Each of them wondering who the tall blonde is, wearing a gold crown, embedded with emeralds, dark green velvet robes, and looking like he just stepped out of a medieval history book.

"King's seer! I know you are in there. GET OUT here and face me!"

Pandora moves gracefully through the mall towards the main door. She pauses at a very pale Marcy and stops to stare at her. Pandora smiles at the fear in her eyes, knowing she had her run-in with her husband. "What's the matter, Marcy? Did the dragon bite your tongue?" She steps in close, her eyes slitting to dragon eyes as flames build around her. "I am sure he warned you, but I am done playing nice. He's not the only dragon around here with a temper. I just take the slower route to destroy people, but I DO destroy them. Now, I do believe I hear my name being called. It seems the King my parents sold me too for a thousand gold has finally found me. One that beat and whipped me regularly and kept me locked in my room. That was something I left out of my story when you asked what it was like to live with him. The very one that Rendgren, the Red Phantom, stole me from three hundred years ago, give or take. I guess that might have pissed him off. Though it could have been removing him from the throne, stripping him of his kingship and trying to light him on fire. Or perhaps it was the fact that I called a war upon him, and he's come to finish it." She smiles coldly. "I guess I am about to find out."

Marcy gasps in surprise. "As in King Rendgren and Queen Pandora?"

"The very one's Marcy. You really did not stand a chance of stealing him away." She turns and heads to the main doors, pausing to look back. "Now, I would say, if you ever set eyes on my husband again, I will lay waste to you. But if I survive this, Gren and I will be leaving Mindriff, so you will never get the chance to." With that, she turns, feeling Marcy's stare upon her back, and steps through the main door with others, wanting to know who the strange man was screaming for the King's seer.

"There you are, King's seer." Zane smiles in delight as he sees the seer step outside, surrounded by mortals.

Pandora moves forward gracefully and stops thirty feet from him, giving him a bow. "Welcome back, Zane. I see you found us. That's rather unfortunate, but it's not like we were hiding. We did, after all, return to Zalgren's mansion. Or would you prefer I call him Rendgren, the Red Phantom?" She could hear the whispers behind her of the people, each wondering who this man was and why he was addressing her as King's seer. Her heart sinks as she knows the world is not ready for magic to return, but this confrontation is going to change all that. That the world is going to spiral in a different direction, where science takes a backseat to the unknown.

"Yes, it took some time to track you, as you kept your power hidden well, King's seer, or is it Pandora now?"

"Yes, well, I didn't really ever want to see you again, but here we are. As for my name, it was always Pandora, Zane. You just never cared to ask." The distaste is evident within her voice as she recalls her past.

"So who's going to win, King's seer?"

"Do you really want to know Zane? Go back. Forget about us."

"I can't do that, seer. You destroyed my life and my plans."

"Did I though? You rule a whole other realm happily. What is this one to you? Times have changed. Go back, final warning."

"Ah, so you have seen the battle play out."

"Yes, with several endings."

"Do I win, Seer? Is that why you want me to return?"

"No, Zane, you do not. You don't have the power to defeat me. I just don't want this world turned upside down because magic here is now a myth, and they are not ready for it to return."

"Well, that's too bad, isn't it? SHIFT!" He lifts his hands, the palm glowing red as he sends a bolt of fire her way.

The people behind shuffle and move around, some screaming in terror, others gasping in shock at the magic displayed.

"NO, I will not." She weaves her fingers and conjures a shimmering purple shield, feeling the force of his strike as she deftly steps to the side. Small motes of purple lights lift from her fingertips and streak towards Zane, staggering him back. Turning to her left, she creates a ring of purple lights beside her and steps into it. Reappearing ten feet to the side of Zane. A crackling green beam from behind her streaks through the space she just vacated. "Ah, there's the witch Lavinia. I knew you had to be lurking somewhere. I see you've upgraded your puppet."

Zane growls and charges Pandora. "I am not a puppet!"

Pandora laughs, sweeping her hand in an arc as a wave of purple energy explodes from her. It knocks him away and slams him into the side of a car as she shifts her position again. "But you are. The witch controls you. She convinced you to come back and defeat me. GO HOME, Zane. Don't make me do this."

He circles around her, studying her carefully, the confidence that she exuded, but knowing between the pair of them, she was no match for them.

Pandora moves with him, watching both their movements and the bystanders that hugged the shopping mall. She catches the slight movement in their hands as they both send bolts towards her. Deflecting one as the other strikes her, causing her to stagger her back a step, to Zane's delight. She straightens and returns the favor, twisting her hands slightly and forming a rune in the air. She slams her palm forward into the rune, sending a stream of purple at the witch, impacting and flinging her off her feet. Her eyes glow softly as they return to Zane while backing up another step and shifting to the left.

Zane growls and turns to the car beside him. He lifts it up and tosses it at the seer with ease.

Pandora draws on her shield once more, feeling its weight in her arms as it strikes her barrier. She quickly places her palm up with her left hand, expending some power, and slides the car over her. Metal screeches and crunches as it slams into the cars behind her.

"Mom!"

She turns as she hears her son's voice coming from the side of the mall, seeing a green bolt spring from the witch into her son. "JUNIOR!" She feels a brief measure of panic as he drops in a heap to the ground and takes a deep breath, returning her focus to the fight.

Zane watches in delight as the boy drops, seeing the fear in Pandora's expression. He laughs as he sends a wave of fire her way. "So you have children of your own. I guess NOT anymore, King's seer."

Pandora's eyes narrow dangerously as she lifts her hands, purple fires meeting his, curving his fire around her to the car behind her. She can feel the heat against her skin, the smell of the paint burning her nostrils, as the metal curls and twists under the power. Visions flicker in her mind as she creates a ring of purple stars and steps through the portal, placing her fifteen feet further away. Her eyes drift to the car crashing into the melted one, catching the rage in Zane's eyes when he realizes he missed.

She smiles coldly at him as she turns her palms up before her and blows on them as if she had dust in her hands. Tiny motes of purple light dances around her, glittering like the amethysts she wears in her clothing, exposing the cages beside her as they flicker into reality. "I still do, Zane. I have a son and a daughter, but you know that. That's why you wanted me to shift and strike you. So that

I would kill the two innocents you have caged, my daughter Lily and my good friend Shels."

Her eyes move to Lavinia, watching as she debates who to go for. Pandora draws within as runes dance around her. She reaches up to one, caressing it lightly with her fingers, and sends another wave of energy into the witch, watching her slide backwards into the mall. "But you forget Zane, I AM a Mystic. I SEE the threads and can rewrite them to my benefit, and have done so. But I will give you the dragon you seek, for now it is needed." She shifts then, motes of purple and gold blending, growing in size as she transforms into her dragon form, towering over the people and the mall. The gold of her scales glitter brightly in the daylight, but pale in comparison to Raya's mark upon her chest. She growls slightly as smoke billows around her, flames licking at her claws. She can hear the screams from the people, more running in terror now, others running back for the doors, only to find them blocked by those inside already.

Pandora reaches out to both cages, and draws them into her claws, beating her wings and lifting herself into the air at Zane's roar. She turns her body to shield the cages, feeling his beam strike her side, hissing slightly in pain at the demonic energy within. Her violet eyes search the mountain range behind her, knowing Rendgren is up there, catching the movement of red and barrel rolls with the cages in her claws.

Rendgren glides past her and plucks the cages from her claws, the screams of the people intensifying as a second dragon comes into play. Pandora alters her flight, knowing the witch is going to her son next. She tucks her wings and dives, her body slamming into the mall wall as she lands with her four feet surrounding her son. She uses her wing to shield him as the wall crumbles at impact, narrowing her eyes dangerously on the witch. "Evil witch. Mama dragons get very angry when someone attacks their wyrmling."

Some people scatter at how close she is, running along the wall to get away from the dragon, whose claws alone were the same size as vehicles around them. Others drop and cower in the corner at the power billowing off her, praying they remain unseen in this battle.

Pandora feels the witch's magic strike her, growling in pain as she sidles to the left. She brings her tail around and slams into the witch, lifting her into the air. Pandora inhales and breathes deep, before exhaling and releasing her mystic fires on Lavinia. Lavinia's scream of agony blends with the people's screams of fear. The stench of burning flesh fills the air while ash floats all around them. She turns her gaze to the running people, her roar of anger shaking the very foundation of the building next to them. Pandora pivots her gaze over to Marcy, cowering in fear, resisting the urge to breathe on her as she returns her attention back to Zane. Seeing the shock in his expression that she killed his witch so easily, she takes that moment to shift back to her mortal form. Her fingers caress her son's cheek lightly, catching his wink as he lay there. "Bad Son, you scared your mother. I WILL be turning you over my knee when we get home."

"I shielded, as you said, Mom!"

She pats his head and rises, her eyes drifting to Rendgren as he lands on the mall, parts of the building crumbling under his size. She returns her attention to Zane. "Alright, Zane. Here's the deal, your witch is dead. It's three of us against you, but I am willing to play fair. You and me. Mystic against Demon. No others, No Gren, No Junior, No innocents. You go for anyone else in this area, and I WILL end you immediately. This way, you might actually win. Can you do it, Demon? Can you face me one on one, in a fair fight?"

Zane narrows his eyes. "It's a deal, King's seer. I want your word that the other dragons will submit to me if I win."

"I cannot give that to you, Zane. I can say if you do succeed in defeating me, they will not interfere and leave you be, but they will destroy you if you try to stop them from retrieving my body."

Zane grins evilly. "So you have seen a thread where I defeat you."

"Yes, Zane. I have seen many endings. I win, you win, and we both die. It just depends on what threads you choose and which ones I manipulate."

"So be it. The war was called when you left my castle. We finish it here and now. May the best one win."

Zane calls forth a blade, flames dancing on its edges. Pandora does the same, but twin blades, shorter than his, trailing purple streams as she moves them. Zane charges first, his blade crashing into hers as she staggers back a foot under the power. She narrows her eyes and spins, her blades gliding through the air as she strikes his midsection, ducking under the swing of his blade as she dances back. They parry back and forth, the seer expertly blocking Zane's attacks, feeling the strength behind his hit, forcing her into a more defensive fight.

"So the Seer can still sword fight? I wondered why you were so determined to learn."

"Getting stabbed by assassins will do that, but yes, I foresaw this fight, and Gren ensured I knew how to defend myself."

"I will kill that dragon after I kill you." Zane steps in, driving power into his strike, forcing her blades down as he lifts a free hand to strike her across the face, taking her off her feet.

Pandora drops under the strike, hearing the growl from her husband and her son's cry, along with the gasps from the people watching. She rolls over quickly at the flash of fire descending upon her, and lifts her blade, deflecting it to the side as her other blade slashes the underside of his arm.

Zane howls in rage as he jumps back from her attack and narrows his eyes on the seer.

Pandora rises back to her feet, spitting the blood out of her mouth as she glares at him. "So we are going to play that game, huh, Zane? So be it." She moves forward, drawing on her mystic powers to shield her, feeling his sword bounce off it as she rolls with his swing. She plunges her primary sword into his shoulder while dropping her second blade. Placing her hand in the center of his back, she releases a burst of power. "You should have just stuck to sword fighting, Zane." She watches him fly across the parking lot and slam into a car and recalls her second blade back to her hand.

Zane growls and straightens to face the seer, his grip tightening on his blade as he stalks back towards her.

Pandora watches him carefully, her eyes glowing softly as she sorts through the threads as they play out, madly reweaving those with endings she didn't like. She spins suddenly, lifting her hands as a wave of flame comes her way. Purple motes of light shift most of it, but she feels a sting in her skin as some filters through. She narrows her eyes, knowing a demon would not play fair, and drops her weapons, shifting to full magic now.

The pair battle it out, striking each other and shielding some of the magic, including Zane picking up nearby cars and tossing them at the seer. The people watch the display in fear and awe, like something out of a fantasy movie right here in the parking lot of the mall.

Pandora keeps her bubble of protection up against Zane's magic and redirects the flying cars to crash into others in the lot. She can feel her body weakening at the amount of magic she is using to defend herself and sort through threads at the same time.

Zane grows frustrated that the seer is holding her own and not using fire against him as he expected, which would have given him the advantage. He sends a double bolt at her, taking her off her feet with the second hit as she slides back along the pavement.

Rendgren snarls as he watches his wife drop again, his claws tightening on the stone wall as the bricks crumble beneath him. "Get up, Pandora."

Junior sits up, seeing his mom lying still on the ground. "MOM! You gotta win!"

Pandora lies still for a moment, hearing both her husband and Junior telling her to get up. She can feel the pain, along with the drain upon her, and closes her eyes for a moment. Knowing they don't quite understand just how much energy it is to rewrite threads as they happen, let alone defend yourself against the power he is throwing out. She weaves her hands in the air. Purple runes of light appear instantly before an inky blackness shrouds her. Lights dance around her and absorb the intended drain. She rolls over and struggles to her feet, her eyes finding Rendgren's, before glancing at the mortals that remain watching their battle. "You've learned new abilities, Zane. But so have I."

Zane stalks over to her, seeing her stagger as she rises and grabs her throat, lifting her off the ground. "King's seer, you called a war you cannot win. First, I escape you at the castle, and now I have you at my mercy."

Rendgren growls on the mall roof, causing people to shift away from him. "Pandora, Defeat him already!"

Pandora reaches up to the hands at her throat, her eyes tiredly meeting Zane's, the corners of her lips tipping upwards slightly. "It's not over until one of us is dead, Zane." Her body morphs as she shifts to pure cosmic energy momentarily, and channels it into him, exploding outward. She feels the force wave slam him back, sending her in the opposite direction as she hits the wall behind her and slides down it with a groan.

Zane bellows in pain, slamming into a car and rolling over it, landing on the pavement behind it. He lifts the car in his rage and flings it aside, his eyes narrowing on the seer against the wall.

Pandora uses the wall to support herself as she rises quickly and sends another wave of chaos magic at him, followed by a second and third.

He staggers back, fury filling him as he sheds his human skin. He straightens his new form, standing over ten feet tall. Deep red skin with black scarring, glowing orange eyes, horns protruding from his skull with wreathes of flame around his body.

Pandora smiles coldly, her eyes glowing a vibrant purple as she shifts away from the people nearby. "Now there's the demon I begged my parents not to sell me to. The one I lived with for nine years of my childhood and could not tame. The demon that whipped and tortured me to get the gold dragon that would kill him. One he foolishly came back for..."

Zane roars, his flames escalating around him as he pulls them into a wave and sends it forward into the seer.

Pandora draws on her shield, watching the flames surround it, feeling the heat of it even within her defenses. She turns as the people scream, seeing the bricks behind her melting under the demon's power, and growls quietly. She pulls one hand off her shield and weaves a rune, sending it out to create a wall, stopping the molten brick from reaching the people.

Zane pulls his fires off her and narrows his eyes on the seer as he watches her protect the mortals that remain nearby. His rage grows, suspecting she clearly cared more for them than she was letting on. He turns, sending a bolt at the man standing in front. He spots the purple shimmer, arriving seconds too late, grinning at the man as he slides backwards across the pavement to lie still, feeling delight in his heart at the sight.

Marcy screams and runs forward. "Brian!" She collapses at his side and draws him into her arms as the other townsfolk drop to their knees in terror, expecting to be the next one to drop.

Pandora smiles tiredly as she sways slightly, giving a nod to the city folk, a dome forming over them to protect them from further attacks. She stumbles forward to Zane, sending out a line of purple light, wrapping around his wrist as she draws his attention back to her. "Right then, I knew you couldn't do it, Zane." She turns her hand palm up, sending a purple ball of light into the air that explodes like a firework.

Rendgren growls and jumps to the ground, cars crunching beneath his weight as his tail swings around, sending a few flying to clear the playing field. His red eyes turn on Marcy, flashing with fire as they narrow upon her before shifting back to human form. The corners of his lips twitch as he sees the color drain from her face, turning his attention back to his wife. Junior rises and hurries to his mother's side, slipping under her arm to stabilize her.

Ryker moves forward in the crowd, clutching a football in his hands. "Pandora Catch!" He hands it to his son Kip, who hurls it over to her like a pro.

Pandora sends her magic at the pigskin, melting it as five crystals separate, landing in a circle surrounding Zane. Purple magic springs up around him, penning him in place. "I know you have magic against my bindings now, but not against my cages. Now, this war will end in your death." Portals open around them; Jeodina and Vynloren step out, followed by Solilque and the five guardians of Lochyae in bear form. Rendgren steps forward to aid Junior in supporting Pandora, positioning her beside Vynloren before stepping into their respective places. The bears make a circle and call forth a dome of magic over the group of them as sirens fill the air.

Pandora's eyes meet Zane's, feeling the rage within him as he glares at her. "The thing is, Zane. Dragons are immortal. Demons are not. You have a lifespan, a long one, but still a life span. I cannot kill you with fire, as it enhances your power, and right now, we are evenly matched despite feeling my powers waning. That is why it could have gone either way. You stood a chance if you had just fought me, but you didn't."

Police cars surround the group, and the officers step out and survey the surrounding destruction. Using the doors as protection, they train their guns on the thirteen of them. "YYyyou there, stand down now!"

Zane roars, his eyes filling with flame as he bursts his fires outward, seeking to melt the cage with his power, but the cage resists, which further infuriates him.

Several officers react to the demon, firing their guns at the creature, only to witness their bullets drop as they strike Council's shield.

Pandora turns to the officers. "Police of Mindriff. Your bullets cannot kill him, nor can they get through the magic that protects us. Magic that you are not ready to accept and understand. My husband and I will surrender and come willingly after we complete what we need to do, and that's to end this demon so he can no longer bring pain to the realm."

Zane growls as his claws rake at the shields, tearing at the fabric of her magic but finding it secure. "You don't have the power, Seer, and you can't keep me caged in her forever."

Pandora smiles his way, one that doesn't reach her tired eyes. "You are correct, Zane, I don't, but Vyn does. I have the power to create and destroy, which will enhance his power. The rest are here simply for support should something go wrong." She turns to Vynloren and channels her magic into him. "Alright, Vyn, I need your chrono-mancer power. Fast forward him till the end of his life." As purple lights envelop them, the others falter under the overwhelming power the duo is unleashing. Her gaze locks onto Zane's. "Goodbye, Zane. This time, I truly mean it."

Time shifts in the globe for the demon as he ages under the pair's magic. Pandora feels the drain on her as she focuses, hearing Zane's scream as he fades into oblivion five minutes later.

Vynloren catches Pandora as she sinks to the ground, his eyes finding Rendgren's as he passes her over to him. "It's done; the demon is gone, and we should leave too. We have exposed ourselves, and there will be consequences for it."

Pandora nods, her voice barely a whisper as she rests in her husband's arms. "Take Junior, Lily, and Bug. Raise them right, Vyn."

Junior rushes forward. "No, Mom, I am not leaving you and Dad."

"You have to, Junior; this is not our world. It's yours. Your father and I have talked about this, and we will be returning to his lair to retire."

"No, you are going to hibernate. I can see it! I'm a mystic too, remember. You can't lie to me."

"Junior." She reaches out to touch her son's cheek lightly, a few tears slipping down her cheeks. "Your father is old. I am not so old, but that fight drained me more than I care to admit. It was a genuine possibility that Zane would have defeated me, but I was banking on his demonic side to attack an innocent. I need to rest, and this is the way to do it. I love you, Junior. I WILL always love you. You take care of Lily; she's your family now. When she reaches of age, if she desires it, talk to Vyn, and he will time-stop her, making her immortal like you. Remember. Move every twenty to thirty years, and I will see you when I wake up."

"Mom, please! Don't. I am not ready to be without you and Dad."

"You can; we raised you right. We raised you to survive. Please, Junior. Find your place in this world and make it work for you. Live, love, and be free as your father and I have."

Junior hugs them both tightly. "Gawd, I love you both sooo much!"

Pandora hugs him back as tightly as she can in Rendgren's arms. "Jeo will take you back with the council. Stay with them for a while until this calms down. Now, get to the mansion before the police. Lily, Bug, and Shels are there. They should find only Shels in it, and she knows what to do and say."

Two portals open, one that the bears and Vynloren proceed through and the other that Jeodina and Junior do, each giving one last look as the portals close. Rendgren assists Pandora down as she sinks to her knees, lifting her hands above her head as he follows suit. Within a few minutes, the shields drop around them.

Seeing the guns aimed at his friends, knowing they will not understand, Ryker runs in with his hands up. "Please don't shoot them! They will not hurt you. They protect the innocent."

The police move forward and cautiously cuff the pair as they rise. Pandora stumbles slightly as the police guide them into the back of a police car. Once the doors are closed and they are on the road, Rendgren removes his cuffs magically and draws his wife into his arms, feeling her doze against him. The officers' eyes widen at the hands free in the mirror, immediately radioing that one of them is free in the back seat as their car gets surrounded. "Just take us to the station; we said we would surrender, and we have. I am simply holding my wife."

The officer looks warily in his mirror as he drives to the stations and parks the car. He gets out and opens the door, backing away and training his gun on him as the others surround the pair.

Rendgren slips out and pulls Pandora into his arms. "Right then, lead the way." Rendgren turns as more cars pull up, seeing Shels escorted out as well. "The mansion is deserted. We found her in the kitchen with three cell phones beside her. It doesn't look as if anyone lives there other than some furniture is covered with white sheets and a locked computer and laptop sit on a table in a den of sorts."

Rendgren smiles at his friend. "Shels."

"Zal."

"I trust you are alright."

"Yes. Thanks to you and your wife."

"Good. Take care of Ryker and Kip; you are good people."

"I will Zal. I will say this, I do like flying."

"I wish we could have taken you for an actual flight, but there is too much tracking out there."

"I understand, Zal, I will treasure the fact that you both took me for a fly.

Ryker is gonna be jealous as he's the one that idolized you in college."

Rendgren chuckles. "It will be something you can hold over him."

"Oh I will! Count on it."

"Enjoy the mansion. It deserves a family living in it after being vacant for so long."

"We will Zal. Thank you."

He gives her one last look as the police split them up, with Rendgren and Pandora led to one room and Shels into another. Rendgren places Pandora in the chair next to him, studying her carefully before shifting his chair so that she can lean up against him. The officers come and go, interrogating the families about what happened at the mall and what exactly the demon was. They are clearly unhappy about not receiving satisfactory explanations but uncertain about how to articulate what they saw. It isn't long before cell phone videos swarm the internet and news, which only verifies what is being said. Ryker even shows them his college thesis, explaining who and what they are. After a few hours of receiving the same story from everyone, they guide the couple to a holding cell and lock them in.

Rendgren looks over at Pandora, feeling hibernation sinking into her. "Alright, love, let's go home." He creates a portal behind him and lifts her into his arms. He gives a nod to the officer staring in shock at both the portal of fire, and fields of gold behind him. Rendgren steps through and magically tosses five coins at the guards. "To pay for the damages the fight cost." He closes the portal behind him as alarms go off in the building. Rendgren carries his wife to the bedroom and places her gently in the bed, slipping in beside her and pulling her close. He kisses her softly before allowing himself to drift into hibernation with her.

Ryker sits in the room with his wife, waiting for the officers to release them as they hear the alarms sounding. Ten minutes later, an officer storms into the room. "Where did they go?"

"Who go?"

"Zalgren... Rendgren and Pandora. Where would they go that would have a lot of gold?" He places the coins on the table. "Coins like this."

"Ooh, that would be his lair. It's written in history that he had the largest dragon treasure alive and that the mystic only helped him grow it, adding nearly a hundred dragon treasures to his own hoard. Each one of those coins is worth about a hundred grand."

"How do you know that?"

"Because he gave us some for helping him load the mansion's belongings into it. The gold in that place could easily fill several malls, three times over at least, and we didn't even see the back of the cavern. I will say, it was a sight to behold, and even better, he even let us roll on it like it was ours. Billions of dollars beneath us. That will be a day to remember."

"Where is it?"

"That's the thing. No one knows. No one has ever been there non-magically except Zalgren, Pandora, and their son. The rest have been portaled in, and well, magic, undefined and all. You can't tell where you are. Oh, and if you are thinking of tracking us, they made us leave all electronics at the mansion. He's a clever dragon, that one. I guess that's why it's never been found in the fifteen hundred years, give or take, that the Red Phantom has been alive. I doubt anyone ever will, especially now that they have returned there to retire."

"So what you are saying is that they are gone, and we are not going to find them."

"Correct, that's what I am saying, and if they do re-emerge from that cave, it certainly will not be in our lifetime. They are dragons, they are immortal, they come and go when they please, and none of us will be any wiser."

Thirty-Two

Darkness Returns

Junior stands in his parents' room, watching them sleep a moment, before moving to the vase beside the bed. He pulls the old flowers out and replaces them with fresh ones. As he stands arranging them on the night table, he feels a shifting in the bed beside him. He turns to see his mother open her eyes and look around groggily. "MOM! Welcome back!"

"Junior? What are you doing here?"

"Refreshing your weekly flowers. Lily! Moms awake!"

"Weekly flowers?"

Lily runs into the room, having stopped her age about twenty-four, striking blue eyes and pale white blond hair. "It's so good to see you awake Mom; Is Dad awake?"

Rendgren mumbles, burying his face in his wife's neck. "Yes, he's awake and what the hell are you doing in our room?"

"Yes Mom, weekly. I figured either way, it was a win-win situation. They wake you up, cause you love them or Dad cause he hates them. I mean, you've been hibernating for sixty-seven years, twenty-two weeks and three days."

Rendgren pulls his wife closer. "Kids! You tell them to move out and they keep coming home. Can't you just magically lock them out?"

Junior laughs as he jumps on the bed followed by Lily. "I love you too, Dad!"

Rendgren mutters good naturedly as he wraps his arms around his kids. "Gawd, the bed's not big enough for us all. At least there is no mutt here to take all the free space."

"Oh, he's around somewhere. His name is Ant."

Rendgren sighs in exasperation. "You know, AT ONE point in my life, I WAS retired, alone, in this cave."

Pandora smiles at him. "But it was boring. That's why you came looking for me."

He sighs, kissing her softly. "Don't think I don't know that you MADE me come looking for you." He shifts his eyes to his son. "What, no grumble or growl of disgust? Shouldn't you be scrambling out of my bed and leaving your mother and I alone?"

Junior hugs his family tighter. "Not today Dad. Today you are stuck with us."

"Great. That's just great. When exactly did that change?"

Junior looks at Lily and smiles. "About fifty-seven years ago when I fell for Lily. Hard."

Pandora smiles, and reaches up to Junior, her fingers tracing over the scar that lines his face.

Junior cups her hand gently. "The world needs you, Mom. Dragons and monsters are back. Ever since your battle in Mindriff, they have been searching for you. Because of that, someone found a way to open a portal they cannot close. Henri and Patches protect Hontby's people. Myr and Violet, along with the elves, are protecting Lamadow. Two newer dragons, Drake and Amber, are helping with the dwarves in Ewhela. Vyn, Jeo, Honors and Council are struggling to protect Lochyea but that's where everything is converging. I have been helping out there as much as I can 'cause Spokane and Sibath are unprotected. It's bad enough that I moved Lily and Ant into the cave to keep them safe about ten years ago. The new creatures are attacking anything they can and we are running out of people that can stop them. Cantara is in trouble Mom... Deep trouble."

People

Kingdom of Oblait

King Rendgren (Tall, black hair with red streaks, often pinned up with a crown of sorts, red eyes)

Rendgren, the Red Phantom (31 meters in height and 35 long)

Merchant name - Zalgren Red

True name - Zalgrenzarendaguran (Zal-gren-zah-Ren-Da-guur-anne)

Disclaimer - Rendgren the Red in this book, is based on the same dragon in my Chahaya Durmada series - The Five Swords of Power. (Upcoming) I, as the writer, fell in love with the dragon and felt he deserved another storyline not tied to Chahaya so this tale occurs in another time, place, and realm.

Queen Pandora Concordia Boxxe (Black hair, violet eyes, mystic)

Dragon form (Gold - 29 meters in height and 30 long)

Junior (Red dragon with violet eyes, mystic blood)

Human name - Asher Red

True name - Ashrekibōgrendajunia (Ash-re-Kibō-gren-Da-Junia)(Kibō - Hope Japanese: Junia - Junior Japanese)

Spider - Chihuahua

Castle Staff

Head housekeeper - Martha (Blue eyes, brown hair, mixed with light gray)

Chamberlain - Kivu (Human male - blonde hair, gray eyes)

Guards - Benson, Iyan, William

Guard - Kenworth - banished
Kitchen maids - Elo
General staff - Kelsey, Wilma
Main cooks - Fil, Ray
Stable hand - Sandor
Gardener - Lisette
Teshem Townsfolk
Healer - Irma
Healer - Roger
Tailor - Habo
Apprentice Tailor - Son - Alex
Male Blue Dragon - Myrsky
Female Purple Dragon - Violetarion
Dragon rider - Kyle
Gnome with Black Bull - Somassen
50 years later
Chamberlain - Tes
Headkeeper - Joelene
100 years later
Captain of the Guard - Jordan

Kingdom of Hontby

King Ludy - Paladin Protector (Human, blonde hair, blue eyes.)
Queen Runestone - Mage (Human, ice blue eyes, white hair.)
Prince - Trystan
Princess - Phen
Offspring - Ludy the 2nd
Mage - Antimagic (Myke) (Human, green eyes, bald with salt/pepper goatee)
Healer - Gronkus (Human, brown eyes, light brown hair, mustache and beard)
Red Dragon - Patchouli aka Patches
True Name - Patchoulianrubraflammae (Patch-ou-li-ian-Rub-ra-Flamm-ae)
Rogue Dragon - Henri - Golden Surge.

True Name - Askookattorhenrensurge (Ask-oo-Kattor-henren-Surge)

Kingdom of Lamadow

Queen Diadradey and King Robertts (Elves)
Diplomats - Dawnelda and Nelowyna (Elves)
Fortune teller in Rixlen - Gaelira

Kingdom of Sibath

Painters - Glynda and Stephyn Stefflyrs

Kingdom of Ewhela

Black Dragon - Drake
Brown Dragon - Amber

The Isle of Lochyae

No King, run by a Council
Council - Auggie, Keandre, Kittymoo, Treefeared, and Yuui (Elven guardians - bears)
Diplomat - Copper dragon - Jeodina
True name - Jeodoragonadina. (Jee-o-Dor-agon-a-Dina)
Diplomat - Bronze dragon - Vynloren
True name - Vyndrakoloreth (Vyn-Dra-kol-o-reth)
Seers old Maid - Pippa
Zane's Captain of the guard - Dunivan
-Twin girls and a boy
Great great great grandson - Scott
Seers old Guard - Xyl

Wife of Xyl - Melissa

Honors Light

-Gwynevere - Human priestess of the Goddess Raya (Blue eyes, blonde hair)

-Ridgestalker - Dwarf hunter (Blue eyes, bald, white beard)

-Solilque - Elven Guardian (Blue eyes, purple hair, bear)

-Myrlani - Elven of sorts Shaman (Blue eyes, white hair)

-Cecil - Gnome Mage (Blue eyes, black hair)

-Aleandi - Human rogue (Blue eyes, red hair)

300 or so years in the future

Sibath - Mindriff

Pandora and Zalgren Red.

Son - Junior - Asher Red

Daughter - Lily (child seer)

Caretakers of mansion - Ben, Carol and son Shawn

Mindriff Mall

Sales clerk furniture store - Lauryn

Manager furniture store - Azlynn

Hairdresser - Madison

Librarian - Arlyne

Teachers at Mindriff High

Mr Fowler - Science

Miss Spoons - English

Mr Brasswell - Band

Mr Brian Walkins - P.E.

Parents

Nikki Morrison - Realtor

Lucy Milne - Bank teller

Marcy Walkins - Administration

-Daughter - Kaspina

Raven Millar

-Husband - Ian

-Son - Oliver

Joela O'Neil

-Husband - Victor

-Son - DJ Joe

Ryker Moore - Jeweler

-Wife - Shels

-Son - Christopher Joseph (aka - Kip)

Paige Wright

-Son - Ethan

Penelope Winters

-Daughter - Lily

Bandits ring leader - Uncle Tom

Mindriff Police

-Officer John Leomund

-Officer Nathan Crowell

Another Realm

Witch - Lavinia

King Zane Evilian (Human, green eyes, blonde hair)

Mother of Zane - Rimorhia

Father of Zane - Wallace

Age Chart	Start	Ball	Stolen	Pup	Return	10yr	20yr	25yr	30yr	40yr	50yr
Seer	9	16	18	19	20	30	40	45	50	60	70
Gren	1193	1200	1202	1203	1204	1214	1224	1229	1234	1244	1254
Junior					0.6	10.6	20.6	25.6	30.6	40.6	50.6
Spider			2	3	4	14	24	29	34	44	54
Zane	25	32	34	35	36						
Martha	45	52	54	55	56	66					
Pippa	20	27	29	30	31	41	51	56	61		
Dunivan	24	31	33	34	35	45	55	60	65		
Twins					1	11	21	26	31	41	51
Boy						9	19	24	29	39	49
Grandson								2	7	17	27
GG-son											4
GGG-Scott											
Xyl	23	30	32	33	34	44	54	59	64		
Kivu-Ch	28	35	37	38	39	49	59	64	69		
Tes-Ch							14	19	24	34	44
Jolene						18	28	33	38	48	58
Richard-Ch											5
Jordan -Gu											8
Ludy	19	26	28	29	30	40	50	55	60	70	
Runestone	17	24	26	27	28	38	48	53	58	68	
Trystan-son		0.3	2.3	3.3	4.3	14.3	24.3	29.3	34.3	44.3	54.3
Phen-dau			1	2	3	13	23	28	33	43	53
Ludy the 2nd								3	8	18	28
GG-son											5
Surge					A694						
Patchouli	301	308	310	311	312	322	332	337	342	352	362
Myrsky	540	547	549	550	551	561	571	576	581	591	601
Violetarion	455	462	464	465	466	476	486	491	496	506	516
Jeodina	570	577	579	580	581	591	601	606	611	621	631
Vynloren	314	321	323	324	325	335	345	350	355	365	375
Treefeared	380	387	389	390	391	401	411	416	421	431	441
Kittymoo	274	281	283	284	285	295	305	310	315	325	335
Keandre	310	317	319	320	321	331	341	346	351	361	371
Yuui	260	267	269	270	271	281	291	296	301	311	321
Auggie	307	314	316	317	318	328	338	343	348	358	368

Age Chart	60yr	75yr	85yr	100yr retire	110yr	125yr	150yr	175yr	200yr	300yr	340yr
Seer	80	95	105	120	130	155	170	195	220	320	360
Gren	1264	1279	1289	1304	1314	1339	1354	1379	1404	1504	1544
Junior	60.6	75.6	85.6	100.6	110.6	135.6	150.6	175.6	200.6	300.3	340.6
Spider	Goddess Raya enhanced										
Zane											
Martha											
Pippa											
Dunivan											
Twins	61	65									
Boy	59	64									
Grandson	37	52	62								
GG-son	14	29	39	54	64						
GGG-Scott		3	13	28	38	63					
Xyl											
Kivu-Ch											
Tes-Ch	54	69									
Jolene	68										
Richard-Ch	15	30	40	55	65	67					
Jordan -Gu	18	33	43	58	68						
Ludy											
Runestone											
Trystan-son	64.3										
Phen-dau	63										
Ludy the 2nd	38	53	63								
GG-son	15	30	40	55	65						
Surge		A769									
Patchouli	372	387	397	412	422	447	462	487	512	612	652
Myrsky	611	626	636	651	661	686	701	726	751	851	891
Violetarion	526	541	551	566	576	601	616	641	666	766	806
Jeodina	641	656	666	681	691	716	731	756	781	881	921
Vynloren	385	400	410	425	435	460	475	500	525	625	665
Treefeared	451	466	476	491	501	526	541	566	591	691	731
Kittymoo	345	360	370	385	395	420	435	460	485	585	625
Keandre	381	396	406	421	431	456	471	496	521	621	661
Yuui	331	346	356	371	381	406	421	446	471	571	611
Auggie	378	393	403	418	428	453	468	493	518	618	658

Contributors

Cover Design - R Dey.

Portraits - Digitally created and edited.

Beta readers - M Verronneau, W Harrison, N Doyle, E McMonnies.

Arc reader - T Street.

Editor - T Street, N Doyle.

Editing Software - Free version of ProWritingAid, Google Docs with Grammarly, Impact, Atticus.

Assists - Officer N Brown for his help with my police questions so google didn't flag me as a person of interest.

Author Portrait - G Woodward.

Additional Information

Thank you for taking the time to read my stories and I hope that you enjoyed them. If you have, below is a list of my other books. Please feel free to follow me, or add me via Goodreads or Facebook. Also, reviews are important to self published authors, so please take the time to leave one. Thank you.

Social media

www.facebook.com/AuthorRandiAnneDey
www.facebook.com/groups/randiswriting
www.goodreads.com/author/show/45347028.Randi_Anne_Dey

Published Books

The King's Mystic: Oct 2023
The Dragon's Mystic: May 2024
Cantara's Mystic: Apr 2025
Madison's Web: Mar 2024
Dragonscales Divide: Nov 2024
Chahaya Durmada: Five Swords of Power: Eta 2026
Fae Guardians Poppy: May 2025
You Stole my Shroom: Jul 2025
Dance, Little Dove: Nov 2025
Dating the Damned: Oct 2025
Leather and Legacy: Jan 2026
Royal Deception: Tails Scales and Tiaras Anthology June 2024
The Emperor's Violet: Cabs and Crime Anthology Sept 2025
Salt Water Secrets: A Whale of a Tale

About the Author

Randi lives in Victoria, BC. Canada. She is a dog groomer by day and a writer/gamer/reader by night. She partook in the SCA and taught medieval dance for fifteen years. From 2004 until 2022, she attended the Faerie festival annually, keeping fantasy alive in her heart. With multiple books published, she hopes they will draw you away from the modern world and into a land of intrigue and fantasy, where magic, dragons, shifters, fae, vampires and kings roam the lands.

www.ingramcontent.com/pod-product-compliance
Lightning Source LLC
Chambersburg PA
CBHW060649190726
48289CB00002B/334